QUEST OF THE DRAGON TAMER

BY COLE PAIN

BOOK 1 OF THE ORACLE SERIES

Map completed by Sherry Kitts. Thank you for believing.

CHARACTERS REFFERENCE

The Lands

Newlan Kingdoms
Zier*
Wyrick Razon – King
Renee Razon – Queen
Ren Razon – Crown Prince
Quinton –Ren's Captain
Neki – Swordsmand
Galvin – Swordsman
Bentzen – Swordsman
Markum – Librarian and Seer
Lazo, Jasta, and Justin – Triplet
Advisors

Oldan Kingdoms
Yor*
Ramie Augustus – King
Javi Augustus – Queen
Reese Augustus – Crown Prince
Ravi Augustus – Princess
Fraul – Ramie's Captain
Tec – Swordsman
Nigel – Ramie's Brother
Meg – Ramie's Sister
Sherri – Nigel's Love

Crape
Valor Kahn – King
Chris Kahn – Crown Prince
Manda Kahn – Princess
Ista – Collective Leader/Sorceress
Vos and Yov – Twin Advisors
Bor – Captain of Valor's Guard

Fest
Lorlier – King
Davis – Crown Prince
Marianne – Princess
Alise – Princess
Gregory – Lorlier's Captain
Korin – Swordsman
Brice – Stablehand

Ketes
Bostic – King (Renee's cousin)
Paul – Crown Prince
Sass – Princess
Raymond – Head of Castle Guard

Quar
Alezza – Princess
Bort –Alezza's Captain

Other Characters
Michael Razon – Ren's Uncle
Eli – Stardom's Priest
Grauss – Sage (Neki's Grandfather)
Presario – Recluse, Man of Most
Knowledge
The Black Knight – Nigel
The Avenger – Aaron
Zorc – The One (Wizard from
Alcazar)

Druids
Marinus – Drek (Druid Leader)
Feher – High Priest
Avalon – Marinus's son
Welch
Morrus

*Controlling Kingdom

Chapter 1

The dragon's roar shook the stones of the castle. Ren rolled, dodging the poisonous flames by a hair's width. The dragon watched him rise and back away, its golden eyes gleaming with unprecedented rage. Deprived of all sustenance, the smell of Ren's sweat and blood tantalized its senses. Long chains dragged the ground as it shuffled forward, still weary from days of drug-induced sleep.

Soldiers considered it sport to beat the dragon chosen for a dragon match with whips, flails, and other terrifying instruments. Ren hadn't witnessed this dragon's humiliation, but he saw the results. Blood marred its golden hide and a patch at its neck had been struck so many times two scales had fallen. Fresh blood still seeped from the wound, coating the creature's underside and transforming its golden beauty into a hideous monstrosity.

Ren donned his faith like armor, but the light in his mind flickered incessantly, allowing doubts to infiltrate his confidence. His plans were crumbling like dry leaves in his fingers. The Maker had placed him on trial and declared him guilty. Ren had looked to the Maker's laws all his life, but now even those laws had lost their power. When they had chained him, they hadn't chained his body – they had chained his soul.

He had no sword, no shield, and no protection, but he wouldn't harm the dragon even if he had the option. Dragons were beautiful, majestic creatures. Not many of them still existed. Destroying it would destroy a part of him.

The dragon stepped closer, releasing another mind-numbing roar. Ren judged the distance. Another step and he would take the one chance both he and the dragon had at life. It was a desperate attempt, for it would reveal an ability he had kept hidden since he was a child. Years before, the people coveted those who possessed the Druid power of calling. Now, it was never discussed, and those with it were shunned.

On the balcony, Valor of Crape, the new supreme ruler of Newlan, observed the match with devious eyes, a safe distance from the dragon's rage. His flaming-red hair matched the fire of conviction in his gaze. Vos and Yov, the king's twin advisors, stood behind him, gray advisor robes blurring their duality to one. Ista, Valor's chancellor, rolled a red crystal around in her palm, piercing green eyes watching Ren's every move. A circular pendant, marking the order of the Collective, hung around her neck. At first glance the delicate swirls of the metal appeared beautiful, but upon closer examination those delicate swirls became snakes, looped head to tail in deceptive grace.

The Collective's supporters had multiplied in recent years. A religion that glorified physical pleasure and secular cravings, its hypnotic call had lured many into believing its future promise of magic. The Collective alleged a powerful prophet would soon arise who would bring magic back from the grave and bestow it to those loyal to the Collective's call. Ren could do little as the apostate religion spread throughout the Lands, but when the Collective started persecuting the priests, his reaction had aroused the Collective's fury.

People from all over the Lands surrounded the courtyard, deathly silent as the dragon inched closer. They had come for a ball. Instead, they had witnessed an insurrection. Most didn't care whether Ren lived or died. He was just a name to them. Ren caught Ramie's eye. Although the king of the Old Lands didn't betray his thoughts, Ren could only hope his recent visit to Yor had won Ramie's trust. If so, what he was about to do might spur Ramie to action.

Ren's supporters stood apart from the rest. As Ren feared, Manda and Chris weren't among them. Ren's stomach twisted into knots. They had tried to warn him, but they had been too late. Ren didn't know what Valor would do to them, but he feared for his friends. He sought the triplet advisors, trying to convey his concern, but if they understood his look Lazo, Jasta, and Justin gave no indication. They stood as still as death, emotionless faces pale and fatigued. Ren's cousins, Paul and Sass of Ketes, stood beside the advisors, Sass's golden locks a stark contrast to her brother's dark complexion. Ren's heart went out to her. His capture had left her questioning her fundamental beliefs. He wished he could reassure her he had no intention of dying that day, but Valor had allowed him no visitors. Quinton stood at the front of the throng, hand on the hilt of his sword, ready and willing to come to his aid. Ren shook his head, warning his captain to keep back.

Valor's soldiers lingered across the clearing. Ren quickly found Valor's captain. Bor was a burly man with a short growth of beard. The keys to the dragon's shackles hung interwoven through his belt. His hand tapped them every few heartbeats, a crooked grin playing on his lips.

The dragon took another step forward. Ren tensed, ready. Just as the poisonous flames licked the air, Ren dropped to the ground, lifted his hand, and called to the power he had kept secret for over ten years. The keys at Bor's belt swayed in response. Ren could feel their weight and shape. He could taste their cold metal and rusted ends. Before a breath had past, Bor's belt lifted and broke. The keys took to the air, following Ren's silent call.

Shock riveted across the crowd as the keys landed in Ren's open palm. Ren regained his footing and dove beside the dragon's right talon just as flames licked by him. Luckily, the dragon's chains were heavy. The dragon couldn't lift its poisonous talons or Ren would already be dead.

Ren rolled to his side and jammed the first key into the dragon's shackles. The dragon heaved a gut-wrenching roar as the shackle imbedded deeper into already broken flesh, but the lock remained closed. Ren muttered an apology as he tried the second key. The lock twisted and snapped open. Ren rolled under the dragon's belly, tearing the shackle free.

The air screamed as the dragon's spiked tail whirred past him and crashed to the ground. Clumps of soil erupted from the earth and rained on the stunned crowd as Ren quickly crawled to the second talon. Before he could insert the first key, the shrill whistle came again. Ren melted to the ground as the spikes sailed through empty air just above his head. Careful to stay low, Ren quickly continued his search. When the final key turned the lock, he jerked on the chain and darted to the dragon's hindquarters.

The dragon wailed a victory cry when it realized its front talons were free. As Ren began probing the third lock, he felt the air move in his direction. Risking a glance, Ren found the spiked tail poised beside him, black spikes gleaming wickedly in the morning sun. The dragon's golden eyes watched him and the heat from its breath brushed past him, but no flames followed. Dragon's weren't dumb creatures. It knew what Ren had just done. But it remained leery. Its tail jerked with each twist of the key.

Over the roar of the crowd, Valor yelled for the dragonhunters to subdue the beast. Ren spun just in time to see a group of hunters rush forward and cock their tainted arrows, but the dragon had seen them as well. It heaved a blast of poisonous flames and coated the men with fire. Ren turned away as the men's death cries stilled the crowd to silence.

Ren worked furiously. He only had heartbeats until Valor would send more troops. When the third shackle fell free, Ren darted to the last of the dragon's restraints. Just as the key slipped into place, a powerful blow fell on his shoulder, knocking him paces away.

At first Ren thought the dragon's spikes had caught him, but when he regained his footing he turned to look into Bor's sienna eyes. Sword in hand, Valor's captain grinned, but before Ren could react, Bor jerked forward, four black spikes protruding from his chest. Blood oozed from his open mouth. The dragon flicked its tail, tearing the wound open further, and tossed Bor's lifeless body to the ground.

Ren quickly diverted his eyes and knelt beside the final chain. When the shackle snapped free the dragon rose to its full height, muscles quivering with effort, and unfurled its wings.

The crowd took a step back, ignoring Valor's demands to subdue the beast and overtake the prisoner. The dragon bellowed in the dawn. Its call was immediately answered by another roar.

It didn't take long for Ren to find the second dragon in the sky, slicing the sun's rays into rivers of golden light. It was an older sire, where age had mellowed its golden scales to a grayish hue.

Screams echoed in the dawn as people scurried in all directions, desperate to flee the dragon's wrath. Ren stood transfixed, watching the old sire dive closer, bellowing a warning to those who had captured one of its own, but before the flames could come, the golden dragon answered the sire's call and took to the air.

The two dragons quickly rose higher, silhouetted by the rising sun. The courtyard, a heartbeat ago in melee, was now filled with silence. As the dragons broke into clear sky, Ren watched speechlessly as the old sire's grayish coat glistened against the blue backdrop like stars at midnight.

Ren blinked in shock. He wasn't looking at an old sire at all. He was looking at a silver dragon, a creature that had disappeared during the rains of the Dark Ages, over nine hundred years before.

A shiver crept up his spine as an old childhood legend came rushing back, and when the silver cast its gaze to the ground, its biting blue eyes validated Ren's deepest fears.

Magic.

Ren turned to the balcony. The crowd cowered against the keep, staring over the ramparts at the dragons' flight, save one. Ista stood where he had last seen her, rolling the red ball over and over in her palm.

"Dragon Tamer," she whispered as she met his gaze and smiled.

- - -

Markum stopped to wipe the sweat from his brow. It had been very dry of late, and his footfalls hurled dusty clouds skyward, making it impossible to draw a pure breath. Squinting into the sun, his sharp hazel eyes found his destination: the Eye of the Dragon, named for a gap in the mountain's face that looked similar to a dragon's eye.

The formation had inspired *The Legend of the Silver Dragon*, a popular children's tale dating back to the Dark Ages. The story claimed the Eye of the Dragon was a gateway to another world, and when a silver dragon entered the Eye in search of a better life, it granted all people the gift of magic. But as the years passed, and people abused their newfound power, the silver dragon decided to return to its own kind in order to abolish magic and rid the world of evil.

The legend alleged the silver dragon would return one day in the hopes of finding the people willing to regard magic with respect and fear. Written over nine centuries ago, when all trace of silver dragons abruptly vanished, the legend hadn't gained much popularity until after the Wizard War, when the wizards of the Alcazar destroyed all trace of the Quy.

No one knew how the wizards had accomplished the feat, but everyone understood the rationale behind it. Barracus, a powerful mage, had betrayed the Code of the Alcazar by creating an army of horrifying creatures to conquer mankind. The wizards of the Alcazar tried everything to stop the beasts, but nothing harmed them, much less killed them. The only solution was magic's destruction. When the wizards destroyed the Quy, all with magic died, not only Barracus and his creatures but also every living creature possessing the Maker's gift of the Quy.

Magic's annihilation had occurred almost four centuries ago and ever since *The Legend of the Silver Dragon* had gained in popularity. Although the story was a fable, children continued to look for the infamous blue-eyed, silver dragon in the tale.

Markum drew a long breath as he studied the Eye. The hollow peered down at him with chilling intellect. The stones surrounding the Eye appeared to form the rest of the dragon's head, only accentuating the illusion. Markum almost expected hot breath to begin seeping out of the stone nostrils. A breeze whipped through the gaping hole and cooled the sweat on his brow, sending a chill over him even though it was a hot day. After a few breaths the beauty of the Eye became frightful, like the stone dragon was analyzing his worthiness. His heart drummed a steady rhythm as he wiped his brow and tried to regain his senses. It was a beautiful day, and it would be a beautiful view. Besides, the story was just a legend, and the dragon was just a rock.

Markum forced his legs to start the final ascent, but before he had taken two steps a deafening roar exploded around him. Markum glanced up just in time to see a silver dragon soar through the Eye, bellowing to the dawn. If the dragon's skin wasn't shock enough, Markum found himself staring into poignant blue eyes. With a vehement curse, Markum stumbled down the rocky path just as spray of dragon's fire exploded before him.

Dragon's fire wasn't only searing heat and scorching pain, it was poison. Because the poison was attracted to heat, if not treated with deft speed the poison would spread through the bloodstream, heat the body and quickly explode the heart. Ironically, the only cure was to place a scalding cloth over the wound, forcing the heat, or the poison, to seep into the hotter conduit instead of the body.

But there was no one around to help, no blanket to scald and no water to heat. He was at the dragon's mercy.

Markum dug in his heels and tensed for the inevitable. When nothing happened, he turned.

The dragon sat below the Eye, staring at him with wild blue eyes. Although smoke still seeped from its nostrils and its mouth was parted to inhale a quick breath, it made no move to attack.

Then the dragon's eyes began to change – first to a muted silver, then to a sickening red. Markum feared the dragon's red eyes more than the threat of attack. They were corrupt, evil. He could almost feel hate oozing from their core.

With a rising sense of panic Markum bolted down the path, sure the deafening blast would soon follow. But instead of fire, the dragon released a dense black fog.

Sudden blackness surrounded him, and as it seeped inside his veins he felt himself begin to change. Markum tried to fight it, but the black fog was too strong. Madness crept into his heart and mind. Hate spilled into his veins.

Markum screamed.

And woke up.

It was just another dream.

Swallowing back his panic, Markum sat up and glanced at the sundial in his window – midmorning. By now his prince would be dead.

Markum had already cried his fill. He had nothing left but emptiness. Ren had been accused of his father's murder, and several reliable witnesses had confirmed the ludicrous charge. The triplet advisors were fighting day and night to discover the truth in order to refute Valor's lies, but they had uncovered nothing.

Yet the dreams were still coming. This one was even more vivid than most. Markum shook his head and stood, the hollow ache in his chest deepening as he thought of Ren's execution. Valor's sense of justice was ironic. The masses christened all Razon kings Dragon Lords due to Zier's golden dragons, but Ren never participated in the annual dragon hunts. Ren was the first true Dragon Lord because he had fought since birth to eradicate the hunts, much to the chagrin of his father. Ren wouldn't harm a dragon; everyone in Zier knew it. Yet Valor had placed Ren against something he would never fight.

Valor had been hungering for the Zier throne for years. Somehow he had killed Wyrick himself, but the advisors couldn't put the pieces together. Everyone knew Ren and his father had their differences. Ever since Ren had met his uncle, Michel, Wyrick had been unbearable to the prince. Other kingdoms knew the rumors, but they didn't know Ren. Ren loved his father, despite Wyrick's rejection. Ren would never harm Wyrick, and he would die before he harmed the Zier people.

Markum had adamantly refused the triplet advisors requests to stand with them during the dragon match. He just couldn't bear to see Ren's death. The advisors had tried to give him hope, telling him anything was possible, but Markum knew Ren couldn't escape.

Markum rose and threw on his cloak. He needed to find the advisors. Even though Valor would deny Ren a proper burial, Markum had vowed to visit Ren's grave before leaving Stardom. Markum didn't know where he would go or what he would do, but he couldn't stay here, not without Ren.

After combing his hands through his unruly brown hair, Markum opened his bedroom door and strode into the black marble hallway. Although the reflection of golden chandeliers and candlesticks still wavered in its polished surface, Valor hadn't wasted any time transforming the hall. Where before rich tapestries lined the walls, filled with Zier's history and lineage, now the walls were bare. Where before powerful statues of Zier's great kings towered over entrants, now the hall was empty. It was a stark reminder of recent events.

Markum was so engrossed in his own sorrow he didn't see Quinton until Ren's captain was right before him, grabbing his shoulders. Quinton's soft gray eyes danced with renewed hope.

"Ren's alive, Markum! Praise the Maker, we have another chance to save him!"

Markum stood, stunned, as Quinton described the events in detail. The golden dragon of Zier, stitched in the center of Quinton's black uniform, danced with his words.

"Go to the library. The advisors are waiting." Quinton slapped him on the shoulder and hurried past.

"Quinton?"

Quinton turned, brown hair tousled from worry.

"Did you say a silver dragon?"

"Yes. What of it?"

"Did you see its eyes?"

Quinton frowned. "For the love of the Maker, Markum, didn't you hear me? Ren's alive. To the Abyss with the silver dragon!"

Quinton uttered a curse before hurrying down the hall.

Markum stood silently as something nagged his consciousness. It was something Quinton had said – a side note to the miracle, a title given to a miracle worker.

Dragon Tamer.

"May the Maker have mercy," Markum said, recalling an ancient verse. Markum clenched his fists. He had to find that verse. He had to tell the others . . .

Dragon Tamer.

"May the Maker have mercy," Markum said again. Ren's trouble had only just begun.

- - -

When Michel sat down, clouds of dust floated into the air. He groaned, every limb aching, and reached for his water skin. The new colt would be the death of him. It was as spirited as Renee had been when she first arrived at Stardom. Michel smiled, but the memory brought more pain than joy. His loss hurt as if it were yesterday. It would only lessen when his brother died.

Michel winced, ashamed of his thoughts, and quietly whispered for the Maker's forgiveness. He had no right to condemn his brother. They had both fallen in love with the same woman, but Wyrick was first born. He had first rights.

Michel lifted the leather skin to his lips, almost laughing when he remembered the golden mug he used to hold at Stardom. It was ironic. He didn't miss the castle, the servants, or the wealth. He only missed one thing, and that was something he could never have.

Closing his eyes, Michel let his tired muscles relax. He had seen the earth more than he cared for that day. The colt had bucked him off at every turn. His entire body felt bruised, but it was his pride more than anything else that was raw and tender. He was getting old. Breeding the king's finest stallions would one day be transferred to another, and he would quietly pass out of thought as if he had never been born. His horses were all that kept his name on the lips of the people.

As the sun's rays warmed his worn limbs, Michel gave himself over to well-earned rest. The horses circled the training ring outside, their pounding hooves creating a rhythmic music. Their song floated in his dreams, taking him back in time.

The day had been bright and a bird's song echoed on the wind as he rode bareback through the fields at full gallop. The wind burned his eyes, bringing the tears he couldn't cry on his own.

When he reached the stream, Renee was already there. They didn't speak. Each heartbeat was precious and each look revealed their feelings. As the sun rose higher, they sank into each other's arms. Although they dozed, Michel was fully aware of the sounds around him: the sensual trickle of water, the soft movement of the grazing horses, the grass dancing in the breeze.

A soft groan caused him to roll over and reach for Renee. She wasn't there. Michel stirred, a sudden pain in his chest.

The sound came again. Michel opened his eyes with a start, the dream dissipating as quickly as it had come, and came to full attention. The worn board on his front landing groaned under stealthy weight. Someone was outside, someone who didn't want to be heard.

Michel reached for his sword just as shadow of a man passed across the floor. Michel spun, catching a brief glimpse of the soldier's bald head before a flaming torch was hurled through the window.

Michel ran to the door as shouts echoed on the wind. Broken glass exploded to his right as more torches were thrown inside. Michel yanked on the door but something was blocking it from the outside. He tried to cut it down, but his sword was dull from years without use. Michel turned, choking as the smoke ensnared him and the heat began to build.

The men were already boarding up the windows, trapping him inside.

He had let down his guard. After all these years, he thought he and Wyrick had come to a silent peace. When he had first left Stardom he had been expecting an attack, even waited for one, but now he felt betrayed. He had never asked Wyrick for anything in over twenty years.

Then a thought struck him: Wyrick must know about Ren. Michel's eyes burned with shame. There was no fight left in him. His brother wanted him dead. Now, he would never be able to ask for Wyrick's forgiveness. And Ren . . .

The horses screamed. A crash indicated they had broken free of their pen. A soldier shouted orders for the horses to be gathered for the Crape crown.

Michel heaved for air. The Crape crown?

Fear's cold grip clutched Michel's soul as the flames rose around him. Wyrick would never allow his lands to be taken, not with any breath in his body. And if Zier had been overthrown . . .

Michel fell to his knees, resolve deepening in the pit of his stomach. He had to survive. He may be Ren's only chance.

Michel crawled on his hands and knees, searching for the board he had never nailed down. After all these years he didn't know if the escape tunnel would still be passable. When had he last been inside, five years ago? Ten? But it was his only chance.

With frantic fingers Michel searched each board, choking as the smoke grew thick. Finally, one board lifted under his touch. Michel dove into the hollow head first, pushing himself through the narrow gap in the earth.

- - -

Ista didn't turn when the door opened, and she didn't transform into the beauty she had once been. Her true image reminded Valor of her power. She ruled Newlan. Although he could have the title in name and bearing, she ruled him.

Valor's children sat opposite her, bound and gagged. Chris sagged against Manda, too weak to sit up on his own. His shaggy blond hair was matted with fever, and every so often his eyelids fluttered wildly. He hadn't responded well to the sleeping herb given him, but then Ista knew he wouldn't. Chris Kahn would soon give up the fight.

Ista offered Manda a sympathetic smile. The redhead's face flared with rage as she muttered something incomprehensible through her gag. Ista chuckled. Manda's biting green glare amused her. It was a pity Manda didn't have the gift. Her spunk would have given her great power. Chris, on the other hand, was one of the gifted Ista had decided to sacrifice. Valor needed to prove his loyalty.

As Ista rose from her chair, she dipped her hand in a silver water basin and doused her brow. Valor's gluttonous eyes followed her approach, but he didn't speak. He knew better.

She ran her deformed fingers down Valor's cheek. "What news have you brought me, my king?"

"The soldiers have returned. Michel Razon won't be a problem."

Ista smiled her satisfaction. "And the silver dragon?"

"The dragon hunters left at high sun," Valor said. "They'll find it soon."

Ista closed her eyes, reviewing the prophecy. Soon she would understand how the dragon could help bring the darkness. Soon now, she would understand everything.

She almost grinned. The prince's love for dragons would suit her plans nicely. Ren would never fulfill his princely duty and kill the beast.

Still, she needed to be sure. When the dragon hunters captured the dragon, Ren would witness the dragon's fate. The prince's last hope would be dashed, and her rule would be secure.

Ista studied Valor, wondering whether she still needed him. Not really, but then a slip in the hall too soon could mean other rulers would try to unseat her. Her pawns were ready, but she felt it wasn't the time. She would let Valor live, for now.

"And the woman?" she asked.

Valor shook his head. "The soldiers flogged her unmercifully. She still wouldn't yield."

"A true martyr," Ista said. "She will ensure my victory."

"A Maritium woman?" Valor said with a hint of disgust.

Ista smiled at Valor's confused look. Valor thought he knew everything; he knew nothing. "The prince knows she's the last of the Maker's chosen. He'll do anything to save her pain."

Ista turned back to the water basin. It was too hot in Zier. Ista immersed her hand in the cool water and dotted her forehead, shuddering as the memories came rushing back: her skin melting from the heat, her hair burning with the surrounding flames. She had the wizards to thank for her suffering. But she had survived. Oh yes, she had survived. For almost four hundred years she had planned her revenge. Magic's destruction had no effect on her powers and the time weave had given her life. Soon now she could reveal herself to the people. Soon now she would have her revenge.

"Throw the woman in the cell with the prince. And when the dragon arrives, bring them both to the courtyard."

Valor's eyes narrowed. "But Ren - "

"He's the one, Valor."

Valor stiffened. "You don't mean . . ."

"Yes, he passed the test. He's the Dragon Tamer. After he fulfills the prophecy, I'll make him mine." She had waited years for Ren Razon's birth – the Chosen, the Dragon Tamer. Only he could fulfill her desires. It was almost time.

Ista picked up a thin needle and held it between them. Behind her, Manda released a low moan.

"I've always wanted Ren Razon to bow to me," Valor said.

A slow smile enveloped Ista's deformed lips.

Chapter 2

Before Ren opened his eyes he knew he was back in his cell. The cold stone beneath him and the chill in the air was all too familiar. Ren rolled to his side, head throbbing and body aching from the beating he had endured.

The silver dragon's haunting blue eyes had plagued his dreams. The legend was a fable, a child's tale, yet Ren found himself almost believing the impossible. With the Collective's promise of magic's return, the blue-eyed dragon would substantiate the Collective's authority to many. The legend was too engrained in the hearts of the people.

Ren heaved a heavy sigh. He didn't want to think about the silver dragon. He had enough trouble already.

He searched the darkness, studying the walls of his confinement. He had probed each stone, desperately searching for a way of escape, all the while knowing his search was futile. There were hidden passageways throughout the Stardom castle. His uncle Michel had been entrusted with the tunnels' secret in order to protect his brother, the king. If escape was needed, the tunnels would be revealed; if not, the secret would be passed to the next heir. It was a Razon legacy Ren had taken to heart. He had memorized each passage years ago. None of them came to the isolation cell. His prison was secure.

Ren closed his eyes, praying to the Maker for guidance, but no reply followed. He had grown used to the silence over the years, and had kept his faith strong despite it, but now he felt his faith failing. In all his prayers he had never asked for long life or riches; he had only asked for direction. He didn't understand the Maker's indifference.

Had he angered the Maker with some past deed? Had he missed his divine path? Ren heaved a weary sigh. Eli, Stardom's priest, had always told him everything in this life was a test, a choice to do either good or bad. He knew he had failed the Maritium. If he had chosen another way, would the Maritium still be alive?

At one time the Maritium were held in higher esteem than the bravest warriors, for they were warriors of the true God. Kings relied on their guidance and battles were won and lost depending on the blessing of the Maritium. After the Dark Ages, where wizards battled for control of the Lands, the Maritium were called on as liaisons between the Lands and the Alcazar. The Lands refused to receive wizards without a trusted member of the Maritium at their side. No one knew the exact relationship between the Maritium and the wizards, but the Lands welcomed it, and in time the Maritium helped rebuild trust in magic.

Years later when Barracus betrayed the Alcazar and created horrors far worse than the Dark Ages, magic became frightful once again. After magic's destruction the Maritium were shunned because of their close association with the Alcazar.

Marked by their violet eyes, the Maritium shrank form society. Although most didn't see a member of the Maritium during their lifetime, those who felt the Maker's call to teach journeyed to the Maritium for instruction. Eli, Stardom's priest, was one of those.

The Collective began to form about the time Ren was born. Many seeking direction flocked to their secular call. A few years ago the great persecution began. The Collective hunted down the Maritium and used them for human sacrifices. They justified their actions by taunting the Maker, calling on his intervention if the Maritium were the true prophets. Because of the Maker's silence the Collective proved their sanctity to many. The Collective won supporters and preached the Lands needed to abolish the Maritium before magic could rise from the grave.

When word of the Collective's abominations reached Zier, Ren immediately went in search of the Maritium. After coming across a small troop of the Maker's chosen, Ren's men guarded them day and night, traveling quickly back to Zier. One woman immediately caught his attention. The Maritium surrounded her, never letting her venture too far ahead or behind. She never looked directly at Ren, and no words were spoken, but he instinctively knew she was their leader. She was the Collective's primary target.

On the third night, members of the Collective attacked. Their bald heads, recently shaved for ritualistic sacrifice, shimmered with newly applied oil. Although Ren remembered very little of the attack, he did remember the Collective's eyes. They were like branding irons, red hot with the desire to kill and smoldering with an inner fire that could only come from the guardian of the Abyss. Each had the same look, the same dementia. It was hideous to witness. They looked neither to the right nor the left. They plowed straight ahead, focusing on the Maritium leader, not the swords that were slicing them down. It wasn't until then that Ren truly understood the sacrilege of the Collective's doctrine. They didn't worship a god at all, but they lauded the destruction of anything godly. And their doctrine, saturated with physical pleasure, truly strove for the annihilation of faith in the Maker.

Ren and his men were greatly outnumbered. The Maritium had no weapons, only their faith. Serving as a human shield to the lady at their center, they died quick, painless deaths. When Ren realized the Collective's intent, he abandoned the fight and spurred his mount to the true target, but he was too late. Ten of the Collective surrounded the woman. One man held a dagger to her throat. A thin stream of blood oozed from the tip to stain her white blouse.

She looked straight at him, ordering him with her eyes to keep back, but the shock of seeing her face, more so than her look, brought Ren to a sudden halt. Her face was tan, and her auburn hair, streaked with sun-made gold, had fallen from its clasp to define the delicate lines of her face. Her eyes, more violet than the winter dawn, danced in the moonlight with a power he could only regard with wonder. There was a calmness to her features and a serenity in her stance that startled him. Standing there, surrounded by her enemies, she seemed in complete control, yet she didn't fight when they dragged her away, nor did she make a move to escape when they forced her onto the back of a horse. She just watched him with vivid, violet eyes, commanding him to yield.

Ren didn't understand her silent plea, but he felt himself opening to her call, giving himself to the air between them. When he felt a movement inside him, he didn't question. He surrendered to the warmth spreading through his limbs, filling him with a peace so vast he was sure his entire body had risen from the earth. But as her silent whisper filled him, the shock of her words brought him to his knees.

Time and space do not exist for you and me. As of this breath, I am yours.

Ren didn't know what those words meant, but he felt their effect in every fiber of his being. She was inside him, everywhere. He understood her thoughts as if she were standing right beside him, whispering in his ear. She yearned to take this burden from him, but she could not. Her compassion humbled him and mystified him at the same time. How could she think of him at that time? He wanted to cry out, do something, but there was nothing he could do. The Collective had her. They would kill her if he acted. He could see it in their eyes.

Then she was gone. That reality sent him to the brink of madness. The beauty of her feelings covered him with a blanket of protection, but also plunged him into horror – for he could sense when they tortured her.

A gripping fear clutched his chest during her torment, but it was his own fear he sensed, not her own. She still carried the same serenity he had seen in her eyes. Her only true anguish came when they tied her to the ground before the pole of the Collective, forcing her eyes on the emblem of the perfect circle of snakes.

He had followed the Collective's trail, but it disappeared in the middle of a muddy field. Only a bottle remained, uncorked and discarded beside the last hoof print. They had vanished into thin air.

A rage built inside him during his search. It was a rage so vast it almost consumed him. He would not stop until he found her. He had ridden back to his father's lands, where Wyrick was hosting his annual ball. Most kings would be in attendance.

Ren decided to speak to every king about the Collective and plead for support in his cause. Although his father had laughed at his attempts to save the Maker's chosen, other kings would take his cause more seriously. He hadn't known about Valor's involvement until it was too late.

He had made a fatal mistake. Ren leaned his head back against the cold stone. He had underestimated the power of the Collective. And the Maritium woman? He hadn't sensed her in days. Ren shivered as darkness seeped inside his soul at his failed attempt to save her.

A soft moan startled him. Ren rolled to his feet, suddenly acutely aware of another's presence. A slight form lay at the far side of the cell, white shirt illuminated by the scant light coming through the narrow slits at the top of the cell door. As Ren approached, a woman's shape came into focus.

Her soiled shirt hung in shreds. Numerous welts streaked across her back and deep gouges from a lead-tipped whip oozed blood. Muttering a curse, Ren took off his boot and shook out the yellow jim blossoms he had managed to pick on his way to the dragon match. If mixed with water, the petals would form a soothing paste. He had planned on using the petals for his own cuts, but the girl's wounds required immediate attention. Taking his uneaten bowl of gruel, he quickly scooped out its contents and crushed the petals in its hollow. Pouring in a slight bit of water from the washbasin, Ren began beating the mixture into a healing salve.

He spread the salve over the woman's wounds, careful not to waste one drop. After he had covered half her back, she stirred.

"Hold still," he whispered. "I'm a friend."

The woman stiffened but didn't move away. When the bowl was empty, Ren set it aside. "Finished," he said. "You should feel better soon."

The woman pushed herself up. Although her face was bathed in shadow, he could sense her smile.

"My prince," she said, inclining her head. "Thank you." Her voice was soothing, almost peaceful, surprising Ren after the beating she had endured.

"Please, call me Ren."

When she didn't respond, Ren motioned to the cell walls. "This place commands no titles."

"But a prince you are," she said, her smile bringing life to her words. "These stones cannot take that from you. It's in here." She leaned forward and placed her hand on his chest.

A slight tingle shivered through him at her touch. Ren strained to see her features, but the shadows lingered around her. She seemed very familiar, although Ren couldn't imagine how he knew her.

"Do I know you?" he finally asked.

"I'm Aidan."

Her name wasn't familiar. Ren searched the darkness, desperate for her to speak. He knew that voice. Ren swept his gaze down the outline of her shape, daring to hope for the impossible.

"Aidan, are you . . . "

In response, Aidan touched his check. Inside, something stirred in response.

"Yes."

Ren yearned to see her eyes, prove to himself she was truly who she claimed, but Aidan stayed where she was, bathed in shadow.

"You told me something when they captured you," Ren said. "What was it?"

Aidan didn't reply for a few heartbeats, but when she did her words were laced with conviction. "Time and space do not exist for you and me. As of this breath, I am yours."

Ren drew a shallow breath as she spoke the words he could never forget. "I am yours," Ren said, searching the darkness. "What did you mean by that?"

"You would have sacrificed your life to save me that day," Aidan said. "In exchange, I gave my life to you. The Maker granted my request."

"I'm sorry," Ren said. "I'm not sure what you mean."

"I'm connected to you, my prince. We call it the 'unica' or 'union' in the modern tongue. When your emotions are high I can feel them, just as you can feel mine. At a certain intensity of feeling there's a type of bridge between us. My thoughts can flow over on this bridge as if I were speaking directly to you. In time you'll be able to send thoughts to me as well."

"The Maritium can pair with a mind," Ren said. "That's why the wizards valued your companionship. Your link proved to the people the wizards just intentions."

"Yes and no," she said. "When the Dark Ages passed, not only were the Lands fearful, but the wizards as well. Because the people trusted us, the wizards asked if we would be willing to help rebuild trust in the Alcazar."

Ren suddenly understood. "The wizards gave you the link."

"Yes." Aidan motioned to her eyes. "The mark of the wizards' gift. After the Dark Ages the wizards recognized a need for constant testing. They thought of the Druids and the way they could link with a mind. The wizards knew it was the only way to regain the trust of the people, but as you well know the wizards didn't trust the Druids. By establishing the link in us, we could judge each wizard's intentions. We established annual tests. If we discovered a wizard with evil propensities he was given to the Druids."

Ren sat back, wondering why he hadn't put the pieces together before. It was amazing how two religious races could have such contrasting values. The Druids were the antithesis of the Maritium. Although zealously religious, the Druids deemed it their religious right to control mankind. The Druids could also link with a mind, but instead of reading it, they destroyed it.

Aidan sensed his next questions and answered before he asked. "Barracus tricked us. He passed our tests, but he had split his mind. He painted us a picture of goodness and light when he was just the opposite. Most wizards chose a Maritium guide to prove their goodness. Barracus didn't request one. We should have suspected something, but in those days we could barely meet demand. Our race rarely married, so our population was on the decline."

"Some Maritium linked to just one wizard?"

"Yes, like the link between us," Aidan said. "If Barracus had requested a guide he couldn't have hidden his true desires. A one-to-one link is intimate and final. If you link to one, you can never link with another. Think of the unica as a marriage. If a righteous woman marries a man she would never defile herself with another. She immerses herself with him and only him. But if she isn't joined to one she can accept many suitors, judging them superficially but never intimately. It's the same with the link. Those who choose to guide many can be fooled. Those who choose to guide one cannot. At the height of emotions a person's true nature is revealed."

Ren didn't know how to respond. When she had linked with him, had she read his every thought? Color rose to his cheeks. He quickly changed the subject.

"You said the Maritium rarely marry. Is that due to the link?"

Aidan nodded. "In a way, the link is a marriage, but it's rational, not zealous. The unica is intimate, but it can never be passionate. Yet because of it I can never marry. Our link is too strong to allow my feelings to drift to another. With a one-to-one link marriage isn't only forbidden, it's unpalatable."

Her words left him slightly shaken. He remembered the jolt he had felt when she first touched him. Its intensity had left him slightly off balance. Ren clenched his fists, forcing back the thoughts she had negated. Taking his silence for acceptance, Aidan lifted her hand and cradled his cheek.

"You feel this?"

Ren nodded, unable to find the words as his feelings rose to the surface. They were like the waves of the sea, blown and tossed by the wind. They overwhelmed and comforted at the same time. Ren closed his eyes, shivering as the sensations grew hot.

Aidan took her hand away. Ren could hear her shallow breath in the silence of the cell. He wondered if she had felt his reaction, but remained silent.

"That's the bond," Aidan said simply, as if proving her point.

Ren nodded and turned away, unsure if he wanted the bond or not. If the bond was as confining as Aidan described, why would he?

"Aidan, I can't – "

"Ask me to sacrifice a normal life? You've just given me one. My people were born to link, to help guide those chosen. I've been waiting for you for a long time, my prince. I regret nothing."

Ren leaned back against the cold stone, unsure whether to feel elation or horror. She had yielded out of duty, but he had yielded out of something far greater. In the days to come how would that affect him? And if she ever discovered the truth, how would she respond?

"Would you like to denounce me?"

Ren turned, surprised. "I can do that?"

"Yes."

"Would that set you free?"

"No," Aidan said. "I would be free of you but never free to join another. I would be alone."

"Then of course not," Ren said, unsure if he was relieved or disappointed. "I would never denounce you, Aidan, I promise you that. You've become part of my life. I'm honored you chose me, but I hurt for you as well."

"Why?" Aidan asked.

"If the bond is as confining as you say, you'll never know the beauty of love."

Aidan leaned forward until the torchlight from the corridor cast her face in a gentle glow. All Ren's apprehension melted away. He knew without a doubt who she would become to him. Whether or not she could or would he refused to consider or question.

She arched her eyebrows, drawing attention to her violet eyes. They drew the torchlight like jewels, so vibrant and pure they shook him like the sea at sunset.

As the corners of her mouth lifted into a smile, Ren found himself grinning back.

"The union is beauty enough," she said. "Now, I give you my vow."

Aidan lifted his hand. "We join in faith, blind faith. It's this faith that bridges the way between us, even if we cannot see. Everywhere you go, there I'll be. Have faith in that, and have faith in me, as I will have faith in you – blind faith."

"Aidan," Ren said, bowing his head, "it's a pleasure to finally meet you."

Aidan's smile widened, lighting the dark corners of the cell. "The pleasure is all mine."

- - -

Lazo looked up when the library door opened, unsurprised to find Ramie Augustus and his captain, Fraul Joste, silhouetted against the light of the great hall. Lazo had been expecting the king of the Old Lands since that morning.

Bentzen and Galvin, two of the castle guard, and Quinton, Ren's captain, rose from their seats. Quinton flashed Lazo a look of caution, but Lazo quickly dismissed it. Quinton didn't trust outsiders, but Lazo had a feeling Ramie would be needed in the weeks to come. Valor was now the recognized leader of Zier, hence the supreme ruler of Newlan. The only man who could possibly unseat him would be Ramie, the supreme ruler of the Old Lands.

Lazo leaned back in his chair and glanced at his siblings, Jasta and Justin. The twins' pale blue eyes barely moved in Ramie's direction. Both were chattering with their inner voice, reviewing laws and treaties in search of one that could free Ren. To anyone else it would sound like nonsense, but to Lazo it was order in chaos. Jasta and Justin were trying to solve many mysteries at once.

At times Lazo found himself wishing he wasn't part of the trio. Although he had been honored his entire life for his intellect, trained at the Advisor Convent where all twins went to train, he was a triplet, separate from the twins yet isolated from the rest of society.

Twins could hear each other's thoughts. While one studied mathematics, the other could read the histories, but both learned at the same rate. A triplet learned even more rapidly, yet was excluded from the twins in subtle ways. Although he could hear the twins' thoughts just as they could hear his, he was a separate entity, yet forever joined to the twins by a curse called the Mar. The Mar meant sure death. No twin had ever survived it; no triplet had ever tried.

Jasta and Justin ceased their incessant chatter when they realized another had walked into the room.

Lazo didn't have to motion for Ramie to enter. The king of the Old Lands quickly made his way to the table. Lazo had yet to meet a man shorter than the Augustus leader, but when Ramie entered the room everyone seemed to shrink by comparison. Ramie had a commanding presence that demanded total submission, if not fear.

"How long?" the king of Yor demanded.

Lazo didn't have to think on the question's context. There was only one subject dear to Ramie's heart – his brother, Nigel Augustus.

Although Ramie seemed furious, underneath his strong exterior Lazo could sense his unease. Only seventeen when he took the throne, Ramie had earned Oldan's respect and reverence. Two years before Jarek Augustus' death the Druids had claimed Nigel, Ramie's older brother and true heir to the Yor throne. Although everyone knew Ramie was the stronger leader, Nigel's death had devastated the Lands.

Lazo frowned. He and the twins had met Nigel the year prior to his death, when Nigel had first discovered he had the Druid power of calling. It had been revealed in front of many, and word had spread like the ten winds.

After the Wizard War, people feared anything akin to magic, and the Druids loathed others obtaining a power they saw as their own. Druids had a unique sense of body and spirit, giving them special abilities. Druids could call objects to themselves with a mere thought. At times that ability was born in the masses, challenging Druid superiority. That's when the Druids used their second power, a power only Druids possessed – the power of closing.

Lazo had seen a few Druids in his day and he never cared to see another. They were hard men with hard eyes, the type of men who would kill without reason. Religious zealots, the Druids preached their superiority and never missed an opportunity to try to claim it. Fifteen years ago they had almost succeeded.

The Druid closing power could not only change a man, it could destroy him. When Druids entered a mind, they would force what they could from that mind and lock it away forever. In times past they could even lock away magic. They claimed to open an internal mental door, force the vice or memory behind that door, and lock it away. Once the trait was locked away it could never be retrieved. And if the Druids locked away the calling power, an innate ability and not a learned trait, some died, some went insane, but all changed – drastically.

Seventeen years ago the Druid leader, Kasim, decided it was the Druids' religious right to rid the world of corruption and began closing people from anything he considered vile, including the calling power birthed in those non-Druid. Soon their cleansings grew to unfathomable levels. People were locked away from wanting drink, craving sex, or any number of things. Mass panic claimed the Lands. Many didn't even leave their houses.

Then the Black Knight rode, driving every last Druid back to the island of Dresden.

How the Black Knight evaded the Druid power still remained a mystery, but he did. If the Druids refused to leave the Lands, he killed them. It was that simple. No one knew the Black Knight's identity, and no one cared. He was a hero to everyone but the Druids.

Nigel's calling ability came before the ride of the Black Knight. When the Druids came for Nigel, he was killed, along with his sister and future bride.

Lazo studied the king of Yor. Ramie had loved his brother fiercely and Nigel's death had devastated him. Many believed Ramie had hired the Knight, but no proof existed. To this day the Black Knight remained anonymous, but Lazo had his suspicions.

"Ren discovered he possessed the calling ability when he was twelve, my king," Lazo replied. "He kept it hidden, knowing, as you do, the people would fear the Druids' return."

Ramie's dark eyes flashed with something Lazo had hoped to see - fierce protection. Ramie had currently substituted Ren for Nigel. In Ramie's eyes, Ren was his brother, and this time Ren was a brother Ramie could save.

"Tell me what you know, Lazo. I want to help."

Lazo motioned to a chair. Ramie shook his head, indicating he would stand. Fraul took it instead and propped his boots on the table. Although a casual act, Fraul's gray eyes were intense. Fraul's lanky appearance surprised many soldiers, but Lazo had never seen another best the man. Despite his thin, gray ponytail and well-weathered skin, Fraul had the brawn of a soldier half his age. Fraul gave an imperceptible nod as his eyes drifted to the library door.

"I've called Bentzen and Galvin to recount that night," Lazo said, glancing at the two motionless men beside Quinton.

Ramie turned to face the trio he had failed to acknowledge before. After a brief inspection, he inclined his head. "Quinton," he said in greeting before he focused his hawk-like gaze on Bentzen. "You confirmed Ren's presence in Wyrick's chambers?"

Lazo winced at Ramie's chosen words. Bentzen blamed himself for Ren's capture. The look on Bentzen's face wavered between dismay and horror. It was the first emotion Lazo ever recalled seeing on the soldier. Bentzen was a harsh man, as tall as a mountain and as hard of heart. No one could befriend the guard, and few knew his name. But in all of Lazo's years he had never seen greater loyalty. After fulfilling his duties, Bentzen voluntarily stationed himself at Ren's door every evening: a silent, trustful companion. Ren had tried on numerous occasions to lure Bentzen away, but Bentzen merely met his eyes and shook his head. Ren had finally given up, and over the years an unbreakable bond had formed between the prince and the guard.

"Yes," Bentzen said, intense blue eyes filled with self-loathing. "Valor asked us who entered Wyrick's chambers before we knew of the murder. We would have never – "

"We know, Bentzen," Lazo said in reassurance. "No one questions your loyalty."

Bentzen nodded but his face flared with shame. Galvin fared no better. His deep brown eyes were bloodshot and weary and his long blond hair was tousled from turbulent sleep. If Bentzen was the mountain, Galvin was the stream. When you looked in Galvin's eyes you felt cleansed in some profound way. His eyes held his heart and his heart belonged to his prince. Both would die before betraying Ren.

Lazo turned back to Ramie, trying to keep the regret from his voice. "When the guards entered Wyrick's chambers they found him dead and immediately reported it to me. Valor was conveniently with me at the time and came along to question Galvin and Bentzen. When Ren was implicated, Valor immediately took command as ranking king."

"And Valor has the right?" Ramie asked.

Lazo gave a grim nod. "Valor has every right. The only Razon heir has been accused of treason, and Ren's closest relatives, Paul and Sass of Ketes, are related to the queen, not Wyrick. Ren is the last of his line. With Wyrick dead and Ren sentenced to die, Valor's kingdom reigns supreme."

"But didn't Wyrick have a brother?"

Justin nodded. "Michel Razon lives at the base of the Sierra Mountains. He left Stardom over twenty years ago, but he still breeds stallions for the crown. I fear for him," Justin said, pale blue eyes filling with memories, "but Valor refuses to let anyone leave the grounds. We tried three times to send a messenger to warn Michel of the danger. It's been days now."

Although Jasta murmured internal reassurances to her twin, she said, "We fear Michel is already dead."

"Not yet."

Lazo blinked in stunned confusion as Michel emerged from the far side of the library, strides away from the door. Fraul rose to his feat, sword in hand, poised to strike on Lazo's word.

Michel was filthy, covered from head to toe in dirt. Blood seeped from a wound on his shoulder, and his hands were raw and bleeding.

"Fates, Michel," Lazo said. "How did you get through the guards?"

In reply, Michel stepped aside and motioned to a section of the library wall. It was hollow.

"There are false walls all over Stardom," Michel said in explanation. "Their secret was given to me and only me. They saved my life when Wyrick . . . " Michel let his voice trail off as he glanced at Ramie. "When Wyrick and I had our disagreement."

Ramie didn't seem to notice Michel's hesitation. He walked over to the open wall and peered inside. Turning to Lazo, he pointed. "If Valor discovered the tunnels he could have killed Wyrick himself without anyone's awareness."

"No," Michel said. "I skirted every passageway. No trail leads to Wyrick's chambers, but one leads to Ren's."

Lazo rose from his seat. "From where?"

"The third room in the guest suites. Do you know who was staying there?"

A blinding fear clutched Lazo's chest. "Manda and Chris."

"Have you seen them since Ren's capture?"

Lazo shook his head. "No."

Michel's voice lowered. "I overheard Valor talking to his chancellor. They're sending two people away from the castle tonight. It didn't sound favorable."

"May the Maker have mercy," Lazo whispered. "Valor's own children tried to warn Ren."

Quinton pushed back his chair, jaw clenched in worry. "I'll send a troop after them."

"How?" Ramie asked. "Valor isn't letting anyone leave the grounds."

Michel tapped the wood above the hollow. "They can leave through here. This passage moves underground, through an old, abandoned silver mine, and ends beside the orchard outside the city walls. I fettered some of my horses there. I can show them the way."

- - -

The night was overcast and shadows lingered around every corner. Manda glanced back at Stardom, a knot of horror in her stomach. She would never see Ren again. May the Maker have mercy. She was riding to her death.

Vos rode before her, a rope linking her saddle to his. The moonlight danced on his pasty skin as if caressing a lover. His limp, black hair fluttered in the slight breeze, drawing attention to his gaunt neck. Manda shuddered. The twins' had always unnerved her. Now she understood her aversion. They belonged to the Collective. They defied goodness and light.

Manda twisted her hands, trying to undo the ropes that bound her, but it was futile. There was little feeling in her limbs.

Beside her, Chris lay tied to his mount. He had yet to open his eyes.

The gates of the castle loomed before them, but the grounds were eerily quiet. Everyone from the highest-ranking official to the lowliest stable hand was attending a banquet honoring the new king of Zier. Even if she could scream through her gag, no one would hear her.

When they reached the gates, Manda's hopes flared. Evann, one of Crape's most trusted soldiers, was standing guard. She had known Evann for years, long before Ista and the twins had entered her father's service. Surely Evann hadn't been swayed to the order of the Collective.

Evann quietly talked with a Fest soldier who stood outside the gates. Manda had always envied Evann's sun-bleached locks, but the

28

Fest soldier's white-gold hair was a beacon in the moonlight, damning the darkness surrounding him.

"I have a message for Lorlier," the Fest soldier said as he pushed a rolled papyrus through the iron bars. His eyes drifted to the twins, then Manda. There was absolution in his gaze, and for a brief heartbeat Manda thought the Maker had sent her an angel.

Evann took the message and inspected the seal. He began raising the portcullis before he detected the twins' slight movement behind him.

Evann lifted his hand to halt their approach, but when his eyes caught Manda, bound and gagged, his face became steel. He reached for his sword.

"Hold your weapon," the twins said in unison. "We have orders from Valor."

Evann drew his sword anyway. Within a heartbeat he had it pointed at Vos's throat. Manda held her breath as Vos lifted a parchment from the folds of his robe. Her father's seal glimmered in the torchlight. Evann took it but didn't back away.

"You," Evann said, holding it out to the Fest soldier, "read this."

The soldier ducked under the half-raised portcullis and took the note. Although his face was hard, his eyes betrayed his unease. He unwrapped the parchment and skimmed it before he read, "'I, Valor of Crape, the Supreme ruler of Newlan, do hereby order my children back to Crape. For their own protection they should be restrained at all times. Let no man speak of this for my children's reputation. Let no man interfere with these orders lest his life become forfeit.'"

Evann's eyes strayed to Manda. "I don't understand," he said. Manda tried to speak but only a muffled moan came out.

Yov shifted in his saddle. "They were found in Ren's chambers at the time of his arrest. Valor fears his children could be implicated in the murder of the former king of Newlan. Valor ordered his children home for their own safety."

Evann lifted an eyebrow. "Bound and gagged?"

"Manda loves Ren," Vos said. "She's already implicated herself to save him. And Chris would do anything for his sister."

Manda turned away as Evann searched her face. She had never been good at masking the truth, and she wouldn't try to do so now.

The Fest guard stepped next to Manda. Vos's pallid gaze followed his movement, but the man didn't seem to notice. He looked up at her, midnight eyes hardening in accusation.

"She should be tried for the crime if she confessed."

"Indeed she will be, Korin, but not here." The twins watched the Fest soldier with obvious distaste. They clearly knew each other. Manda studied Korin again. There was something about him she immediately trusted despite his incriminating stare. A sudden jerk of his hand caught her attention. Tucked behind his back, hidden from the twins' sight, his hand motioned her down. At first Manda didn't catch his meaning. Then she realized he wanted her to fall off her mount.

"She looks like a feisty one," Korin said. "Watch yourself."

Manda screamed through her gag and twisted her body, feigning an attack. Her feet, tied to the stirrups, acted as a counterweight as she flung her body toward the soldier. She felt the saddle spin out of control as she fell, unprotected, to the ground. Korin caught her. She immediately felt the ropes binding her hands behind her loosen.

"Fight," Korin whispered in her ear.

Manda wrenched back and forth as her mount bucked. Vos leapt out of the saddle, shouting for Evann's help. Manda felt another rope loosen as Korin worked at her restraints and slipped something between her palms.

"I'm sorry," Korin whispered. "This is all I can do."

Then her world went black.

- - -

Aidan sat beside Ren, careful not to touch her tender back to the cold stone. The torchlight framed her face in a slight glow. Whenever she looked at him, his heart gave a slight jump.

"Aidan, why haven't the Maritium come out of hiding before this?" Ren finally asked. "Magic has been dead for almost four centuries. The people would have accepted you back long ago."

Aidan grinned. "We never went into hiding. Everyone knew we lived on the coast of the Black Ocean." Aidan's eyes sparkled with mystery and her grin widened at his confusion. "My prince, the wizards told us to live alone before they destroyed magic. Although magic is dead, everything with magic did not die.

"Only living things, wizards, Barracus' creatures, magical creatures, all of whom had the thread of the power, died when magic died."

Ren frowned. The thread of the power connected someone's mind and soul to the Quy. If you had the thread, you could use magic. If you didn't, magic was forever lost to you. "Grauss the Sage has written about the thread. He claims that when the wizards destroyed magic they merely destroyed the thread, not magic itself."

"Grauss is right," Aidan said. "If everything magical died, my ancestors would have died because of the magical gift given to us. Although the wizards created the link with magic, the link itself isn't magical. It's much like the Druid ability to enter minds. It's become part of us. We don't have the thread of the power. We don't have the ability to invent magic. And just like us, there are other things, mostly non-living things, that are magical without using magic.

"We were the guardians of such things, things the wizards wanted to hide from society. Even though magic was destroyed, those objects were still dangerous."

"Such as?"

"Have you seen the crystal, the one Valor's aide carries?"

Ren nodded, recalling the red crystal Ista always twirled in her palm.

"It's the most dangerous object ever created. It's connected to the Plains of Desolation. It commands the dead."

Ren shivered at Aidan's words. The Desolation Plain was the realm between the life plain and the Abyss. The Mynher, the Watcher's minion, lives there and is charged to catch spirits before they plunge to the Abyss. Most of the time dying souls descend too quickly to be caught, but at other times souls have a prolonged death and sink more slowly. If the Mynher succeeds in catching them before they fall, they are doomed to the desolate plain for eternity. The Mynher forever searches for a way to release them into the world to bring destruction to the living. Some in the Lands bow to the Mynher in the hopes he will ensnare them on their way to the Abyss so they might have another chance at life.

"What can it do?"

Aidan shook her head. "I don't know. Our ancestors thought the less we knew of the magical items we possessed the safer we would be in the future. I disagree. I know just enough to be dangerous." Aidan paused, creasing her brows in thought. "It's made of silver dragon's fire."

Ren started. Although he had seen the silver dragon and looked into its blue eyes he didn't want to admit what he had seen. Magic was an enigma, a mystery better left alone. As Aidan held his gaze, he felt their connection sharpen with his panic. The peace he always sensed with her touch flooded through him. He relaxed, focusing on her words and not the implications.

"How do you know?"

Aidan lifted her brows, drawing emphasis to her violet eyes. "When you're sleeping by the campfire, how do you know the fire is there when your eyes are closed?"

"By the heat."

"That's exactly how I can sense fire in the crystal," Aidan said.

Ren thought he understood. "But a silver dragon's?"

Aidan drew a slow breath, thinking over his question. "The crystal's fire is alive. It moves and breathes. A campfire, a forest fire, does not breathe. It heats, it spreads, but it doesn't move and breathe. Dragon's fire does. It's poison moves, taking over whatever lies in its path.

"And there's another quality I cannot put to words. I didn't know what it was until I saw the silver dragon. The silver dragon has the same property, the same heat, the same movement, and the same breath."

Ren closed his eyes. Wizards of old claimed silver dragons were the most powerful creatures in existence. Their skin, their talons, the poison of their flames, all were used to invoke powerful magic.

Although silver dragons didn't use magic directly, in a sense, they *were* magic.

"Ista knows I can tell her the secret to unlock the crystal's power."

"I thought you said the crystal's secret had been lost long ago."

Aidan smiled again. "Magic is a gift from the Maker. Therefore, I understand magic. To me, its rules and laws are as simple as right and wrong. This world is governed by the threat of light versus darkness. The Maker fights for this world to be light while the Watcher fights for this world to be darkness. Each thing has the possibility of becoming good or evil. The silver dragon isn't exempt from this universal truth. Its return heralds magic's rebirth. Magic's return can bring ceaseless beauty and allow light to rule, but it also brings the threat of total destruction, through the darkness."

"Dragon's fire," Ren said, suddenly realizing what Aidan was trying to tell him. An ancient magical maxim claimed if you commanded the source of an object, you commanded the object itself. If the crystal was created by silver dragon's fire then silver dragon's fire could awaken its power.

"The dragonhunters are bringing in the silver dragon." Aidan kneaded her hands, a look of cold apprehension in her eyes.

"She knows then."

"I don't think so," Aidan said, "or she wouldn't need me. But she knows something. I just don't know what."

Ren leaned his head back against the cold stone, trying to determine Ista's plan. Ista had called him Dragon Tamer. What did she mean by that? And what, if anything, did that have to do with Aidan?

He studied Aidan's profile in the dim light, searching for answers, but none were forthcoming. Once again he felt helpless to save her. Aidan would die to keep the crystal's secret secure.

But now he knew the secret as well. Ren rose to his feet. "Why did you tell me this?"

Aidan lifted her gaze to his own. The scant light from the torch in the hallway lit her eyes with amethyst flame. He could feel their connection sharpen with her heightening emotions.

"You know the peace within me," she said. "Nothing they do can hurt me. They can take nothing from me." Her eyes bore into him, commanding him to understand. "After me, she will look to you, but you cannot yield, no matter what they do to me. Promise me, Ren, promise me you will hold fast to the light."

"Aidan, I won't let you die."

Aidan studied him. "What will be will be."

Anger welled within him. "Aidan, if you're so convinced you're going to die why tell me the secret when it could have died with you?"

"That's exactly why," Aidan said, face softening as she closed her eyes and smoothed her brow. "My ancestors were wrong. They should have handed down every ounce of knowledge they possessed. I won't make the same mistake. To fight the darkness you have to know the darkness."

"I myself would like to know less of it."

Aidan leaned forward, a sad smile on her face. "Do you remember when I said the wizards didn't destroy magic, they merely destroyed the connection?"

Ren nodded. "They severed the thread."

"Yes, but the thread still exists. Humans differed from other magical creatures. Only some of us had the thread. We're still breeding magic, my prince, but instead of being alive and thriving the thread lies broken, dormant. It's only a matter of time before someone powerful, someone with great need, uses the emotions of love, hate, and pain to reunite the thread and rebirth magic. The wizards of old have sent the silver dragon as a warning to the very man who will rebirth the power."

"That's impossible," Ren said. "Magic's destruction happened four centuries ago. Surely in all that time if we still had the thread someone would have already reunited it."

Aidan lifted an eyebrow. "Some Maritium have linked to those who have the broken thread." Her penetrating gaze caused him to shift in discomfort. "I'm one of those."

Ren stiffened in warning, every muscle on alert.

"You think your confinement is punishment for some deed you committed?" Aidan said, searching his face. "This," she motioned to the walls, "is recompense for your wrongs? No. The Maker has plans for you, my prince. You just have to listen."

- - -

Korin's heart beat so rapidly he thought he might not live. Pressing his back against the tree, he inched around its trunk and took another look at the guard pacing in the shadows. His build was the same. His hair was the same. Everything was the same.

Korin was looking at his own reflection.

He felt his mind clearing, the presence slowly melting away. His resolve to escape deepened in the pit of his stomach until it claimed him like a disease. All he wanted was a chance to live a life of his own, a chance to be free of the pain.

The guard stopped to look up at the sky. The small golden dragon stitched to the front of his black tunic glimmered in the moonlight. Korin could hear the guard's frantic thoughts as if they were his own. He too worried about the prince.

When the guard turned, Korin quickly concealed himself. He had no weapon, only a small shovel. It wasn't his intention to harm anyone, the guard especially, but he had no reason for being there, and if he was found there would be questions. The mere thought of divulging his knowledge sent revulsion to every fiber of his being. He didn't want to reveal the things he had done. If spoken, the acts would become real, a part of his life he would have to face.

The leaves rustled as the guard moved closer. Korin pressed his body against the tree, sweat and tears raining down his face as the presence continued to dissipate. He relished it, craved it, and as the presence continued to diminish, another sensation took its place: peace, profound peace.

It had been years since he felt the peace as intensely as he felt it now, but it had always existed. It was a small ray of light in his mind that he escaped to when he was the target, or the instrument, of pain. The light had been easy to find when he was young. The older he became the more he had to fight the presence and swim through the madness to find the light. But if he found it and clutched it, no matter its size or intensity, he was able to grasp the hope of freedom and deny the presence complete control of his mind.

The guard released a sigh. Korin tensed, heartbeat pounding in his ears. The presence was now only a small pinprick. Was it because of the guard? Korin held his breath. On the way to Zier, the pressure had lessened, or at least became easier to fight. He had never been like the other Collective. They hungered for the pain, fought for survival with madness in their eyes, and were loyal to the one who commanded them. When he was given a suspicious look he became an actor, and his act had fooled everyone for over twenty years.

He closed his eyes and let the peace penetrate him. He clung to it, breathed it as if it were air. A moan escaped his lips. For the first time in his life the presence was gone.

Korin knew he needed to meet the man behind him. The man may very well be his salvation. Korin gathered his strength, relaxed his muscles, and stepped from the tree.

Only the empty night greeted him.

The guard was hurrying back to the castle. Korin drew in a breath to call out, but the breeze snatched his voice and his words faded into the evening. The peace quickly dissipated and the presence once again tightened its grip. Fear shook him as he leaned into the tree and slowly slid to the ground. Wrapping his arms around his knees, his body shook with sobs.

"You fool. Did you think you were through fighting?" he said to the night. Looking down at the small shovel at his belt, his reason for being there came back in a rush. With the residuum of peace inside, his conviction deepened. Let Ista find out. Let her call him while he was trying to discover a way to end it. If she did, so be it. He would die fighting. Was death worse than life? He shivered. Death had always terrified him. Death would put him with the Watcher forever.

He shook those thoughts off and recalled the perfect peace he had felt only a breath ago. He would have to find the guard again, but for now he had a task to complete, the first he had actually assigned himself. He looked out into the night, letting a small hope rise inside him. Maybe tonight he would escape the pain.

He darted to the next tree, then the next. Soon he was in the graveyard, walking among the dead. Careful to keep in the shadows, he made his way down the rows of mounds until he came to a freshly dug grave. Korin dropped to the ground and began to dig.

- - -

Ramie looked up when the library door opened. A small, mousy boy entered, keen hazel eyes surveying the room with incredible wariness. His mop of unruly brown hair caught the torchlight and cast shadows on his face, making him appear much older than his years.

Lazo rose from the chair and motioned the boy forward. "Come, Markum. The king of Oldan has joined our cause."

Markum barely glanced at Ramie as he placed a book on the table. Ramie started when he saw the silver dragon on the cover. With trepidation he noticed the dragon had blue eyes. He had been avoiding the topic. A silver dragon was concern in itself, but a silver dragon without silver eyes? Ramie shuddered.

He had heard people whispering about the Collective's promise of magic. Many were pointing to the silver dragon as a sign of the Collective's power. Soon, they said, magic would be bestowed on the faithful. Ramie repressed a sudden chill.

Lazo folded his hands beneath his chin and waited for Markum to speak. Ramie was surprised to see respect in Lazo's gaze. Behind the third advisor, the twins' faces held the same reverence. Ramie studied the boy more closely. Although he was slight of stature, and young, Markum did have an aura about him, a certain bewitchment.

Markum slid the book to Lazo. "Ren's in trouble."

Ramie almost laughed. Ren was in the dungeon, scheduled for execution, and Markum thought he was in trouble? But when Lazo leaned forward, contrasting eyes, one blue, the other green, intensely focused, Ramie held his tongue.

Markum tapped the book. "The dragon was a test. Ren passed. He's the Dragon Tamer."

"And what does that mean, Markum?"

"You saw the silver dragon's eyes?"

Lazo rubbed his pointy beard. "They were blue."

"The legend is true, Lazo. When the dragon hunters bring in the silver dragon magic will be reborn."

Fraul's gray eyebrows furrowed with worry. "But how is that possible?"

Markum motioned to the book. "The love of the Dragon Tamer."

Chapter 3

Markum ran through the forest, not bothering to dodge the branches that slapped his skin. The snarl of the huge two-headed wolf behind him spurred him faster. He had no weapon, only the lone book he clutched in his hand. He knew it held the secret he needed to defeat the beast, if only he could stop to read it.

Wolven were one of the most feared magical creatures of all time. Swords were useless against them, for with every cut the wolven became stronger. And if you severed one, two more would form. Not that Markum knew how to use a sword anyway. He was a librarian, not a soldier.

He broke through the surrounding trees and surveyed the clearing with a quick glance. A lake sat directly before him, to the left jagged cliffs dropped to a chasm below, and to the right large boulders obstructed any kind of escape.

Markum jumped into the chilly water, the beast right at his heels. He plunged deeper, arms flailing, praying he could find more strength, but he knew he couldn't swim fast enough. He swallowed water. His lungs burned. Fire whipped through him as he gasped for air. He clutched his throat, waiting for the inevitable.

His lungs filled with water, but instead of choking he relaxed. Shocked, he realized he was breathing water as if it were air. Markum turned to see a man floating beside him, long black hair reaching to the surface like a plant hungry for sun. His eyes held the knowledge of centuries. They peered into Markum's soul, analyzing his abilities with a mere glance. Markum didn't know which to fear more, the two-headed wolf or the man. The man seized Markum's arm and held him fast as the wolf swam closer. Markum tried to pull away but the man's grip was too strong. Closing his eyes, he screamed.

And jerked awake.

The torches surrounding the library were almost burnt through. The advisors sat across from him, absorbed in the prophecy Markum had discovered. Lazo looked up from the eerie words, concern in his contrasting eyes. Michel cocked his head to one side, listening as the silence in the castle deepened.

A dragon's roar sounded in the dawn. Markum and Lazo exchanged troubled glances

Michel spun toward the door. "It's happening," he said. The advisors rose without a word. Markum remained in his seat, panic stricken.

They had talked all night about the prophecy and what to do when the time came, but they were far from analyzing every contingency. Quinton had been alerted, along with others loyal to Ren, but no one knew what their role would be, or how they should react. They hadn't realized the dragon would be captured so soon.

The Chosen's love will shatter, igniting an inner raging storm, when the dragon will rip open his mind and the power will be born.

Markum finally found his footing and followed the others. Michel darted down the stairs as the advisors hurried to the soldier's quarters. Markum wanted to help his prince, but he didn't know how to fight. His cowardice shamed him. Markum stopped in mid-stride, vision blurring. He was terrified, but he couldn't run and hide. Ren needed to escape. With rising conviction, Markum turned and followed Michel down the stairs.

People streamed through the arched entranceway of Stardom, crying in terror. Someone knocked him back a step. Markum stumbled to the wall and hugged it for support. When he finally made it to the landing the crowd was too thick to pass. Markum scrambled over the railing and fell on a blacksmith's bench, tipping it over and spilling the abandoned tools.

The silver dragon stood on a pulley, dragon hunters surrounding it. The dragon curved its neck to the sky and bellowed a gut-wrenching wail through its muzzle. Chains surrounded the creature but none were holding it in place. The dragon was free.

The dragon thrashed its tail, knocking wagons cubits into the air, as the dragon hunters threw down their gear in a desperate attempt to find more drug-laden arrows to shoot into the beast. The crowd that had gathered to see the creature now scurried in all directions, shouting fervent prayers to the Maker to save them.

Looking skyward, the dragon wailed another cry, breaking its muzzle with little effort. One of the hunters picked up a nearby lance and aimed it for the dragon's chest. The dragon shrieked as it reared back to spew fire over the man, instinctively protecting its chest with its wing.

Ren stood between two shocked guards on the far side of the pulley, face twisting in worry. Markum followed Ren's gaze to a few Crape soldiers standing near the edge of the melee, holding an auburn haired girl between them. Ren twisted, breaking from his captors' hold, and broke into a run.

The dragon hunter released a cry as he brought the lance behind him. The dragon's neck coiled like a cord, mouth opening. Hot fog drifted out, then a hint of fire. But before the lance could fly or the fire could begin, Ren toppled the hunter.

A Crape soldier darted in front of Markum and picked up a dragon hunter's discarded bow. Bending to his knees, he nocked an arrow and aimed it at Ren. The tainted tip dripped with the sleeping potion. For a dragon the drug could bring sudden cataplexy, but for a man it could mean death.

Markum spun to the blacksmith's bench and surveyed the scattered tools. A large iron ax lay propped against one leg. Markum quickly gripped the heavy tool and flung it at the soldier. The force of his throw knocked the soldier to the ground and caused Markum to stumble backwards. When Markum regained his footing, he gasped. The ax had impaled the man's head, killing him instantly. The soldier's eyes stared blankly ahead and his cracked skull sent tremors down Markum's spine. Markum fell to his knees, begging the Maker for forgiveness. He hadn't meant for it to be a fatal blow.

Something in the man's cerebrum caught the light. Markum's stomach twisted as he leaned closer. It was a needle, so thin it was barely visible. Markum slid it out only to find two more needles beside it.

For a thorn will go unnoticed by those who reap destruction on the masses and permeate the Lands.

A shadow fell over him. Markum froze, needle in hand, realizing he may never see his prince to show him what he had found. This was the end of the line. He had been discovered.

But when he turned it wasn't a Crape soldier who greeted him; it was Ramie and Fraul.

Ramie stared at the man's split skull before his eyes drifted to the needle in Markum's hand.

- - -

It was a known fact dragons had an inner mode of communication, but as Ren held the dragon hunter down he grew nervous. Had the golden dragon he had helped before spread his scent to the silver? Although his instincts were usually correct, this time his life hung in the balance.

As the silver drew a deep breath, for a split second Ren thought his instincts had failed him; but when he heard the deafening blast he knew the fiery wrath had missed him.

Ren turned to find the dragon watching him with a twinge of annoyance. Its tail lashed back and forth, knocking pieces of the pulley in the air. Ren slowly rose to his feet, the dragon hunter with him. When the man reached for the lance Ren blocked him. The man hesitated before backing away.

People too terrified to move had cowered under wagons and taken cover in the trees. The dragon hunters had retreated, but many were nocking their arrows.

Ren's eyes sought Aidan. She crouched between the hunters and the dragon, back once again bleeding from her morning torment. Ren took a quick appraisal, seeing again what he already knew in his heart. Aidan was trapped. The dragon blocked all paths of her escape, and if it breathed its fiery wrath at the hunters Aidan would be charred.

The bows were nocked and ready but the dragon had already seen them. Now it was a race against time. The dragon reared back. The dragon hunters took aim.

A sword lay discarded a short distance away. Ren lunged for it just before the dragon spewed fire and landed between the dragon and Aidan. The silver beast bellowed a warning.

Ren grabbed the nearest hunter's bow, hampering his aim. A few stray arrows shot past, well out of range. One of the dragon hunters shoved past Ren and fell to his knees, arrow aimed at the dragon's chest. Aidan stumbled forward to stop the soldier but one of the hunters circled his whip around her throat, dragging her back.

Dragon's fire enveloped the kneeling hunter but the man had already let the tainted arrow fly. It embedded deep in the dragon's chest. The dragon screamed to the dawn.

Aidan fell to her knees, trying to pull the whip from her throat. Ren brought his sword down, severing the whip and some of her captor's fingers.

"Are you all right?" Ren asked, kneeling beside her.

She nodded in his shoulder. Her eyes found his. "Hurry."

Ren spun, desperate to reach the arrow. It only took one arrow to weaken a golden dragon. The silver was much larger, so it would take two or three, but Ren couldn't delay. The silver needed to escape. Even if Ista knew nothing about the dragon's ability to awaken the red crystal, Ren wanted the sire far away from Stardom. As he took a few steps forward and lifted his hand to call to the arrow, the dragon turned and focused its uncanny blue eyes on Ren.

Ren thought he saw an understanding flicker in the silver's gaze, a human understanding. Before he could decipher the change, a shrill scream shattered the air. It was a cry so piercing not even the wails of the dead could compare.

Aidan careened to the ground. No soldier touched her, no wound was on her, but death was in her eyes. Then everything became still. Not even the dragon moved. The air became thicker. Ren dropped to his knees and lifted Aidan's body in his arms. Her eyes fluttered open. "Something hurts."

"Aidan? What is it? Tell me what is happening."

Aidan shook her head. "Ren, please . . . " She brought her hand to his face and brushed his lips. "Please." A fiery desperation lit her eyes, matching the one churning deep in his soul. For a heartbeat he doubted his instincts, doubted the spark in her eyes, but when she whispered his name again he closed the distance and met her lips.

"Blind faith," she whispered just before her hand rolled limply to the ground.

Ren screamed her name, but Aidan didn't respond. Her head rolled to the side and her arms went slack. A dusty light hovered above her. It trembled before it slowly began to move. When it touched him a warmth shivered through him. It felt like her smile, the way he felt when he looked into her eyes.

Somehow the light was linked to her. The light was stripping her spirit, taking her from him. He prayed for it to change direction. The dragon roared in pain as the light brushed its silver skin.

Ren suddenly understood. Someone was transferring Aidan's spirit inside the dragon. Someone was using magic.

He remembered Aidan's words. He had the broken thread.

He closed his eyes and felt it inside him, churning with anticipation. It was a strength he had drawn from since he was a child yet something he had never fully known. It was a heat, a light, a fire of conviction, and for the first time in his life he held nothing back. He breathed it in, welcoming it to unleash the fury of his emotions. He felt the Quy flood inside him.

The earth rocked beneath his feet. People screamed in terror, but he didn't hear them. His mind was focused, sure. Finding the dusty light, he commanded it return. Aidan's spirit drifted toward him, but as soon it moved her silent scream tore through the air. He felt her pain. She was already merging with the dragon. If he forced her back she would be torn apart.

His hopes crumbled. The dragon bellowed as more of Aidan's spirit seeped through its skin. Ren whispered for her forgiveness. Her spirit would be lost inside the dragon, engulfed in the dragon's essence. Although her spirit would live she wouldn't remember.

Without her body she would become the dragon. The dragon would be too strong for her to resist.

But if her body went with her . . .

Ren looked down at Aidan's limp form. Her hair spilled over his arms in an auburn waterfall. Her eyes were shut as if in sleep. He brought his emotions to the surface and cultivated them to flame. His pain came first, burning hot, blazing through him with angry precision. Then came hate, black as night, incessant and demanding. Then came love, rising through him like a tidal wave: fast, sure, furious.

The emotions roared inside him, swelling with force.

He focused on the light in his mind. He breathed it in, letting it fill him to the point of pain, and slowly began weaving her body in the air, memorizing her shape, her essence. Within a few breaths he had created almost a blanket of her form. It moved above him like a specter before it began seeping inside the silver creature, joining with her spirit, keeping her whole.

As the last of her essence left him Ren fell to the ground. Who had done this? The ground shook with violent pulses, but he rose without pause. Onlookers screamed and stumbled away, but the dragon had yet to move. It watched him with an inexplicable perception. Its eyes were slightly clouded, as if the dragon were a twin listening to its other half.

Everything around Ren was vivid, clear, but the screams behind him were far away. His mind throbbed as the Quy's thread pulsed with his heartbeat and tingled through his body with a vibrant intensity. Where before he felt determination and love, now he felt rage – intense rage. It burned to be released. Someone near him emanated the residue of the power. He saw it in the air: a fine trail of conjuring particles, vibrating more violently than the surrounding atmosphere. The trail led to a downstairs window.

Nothing existed but his target and his rage. He held onto the rage, stroked it, and intensified it. The window shattered at his command. Valor and a deformed woman stood in front of the broken shards of glass. The woman's hideous features were reforming into a guise she had worn since she arrived at Stardom.

"Release her."

Ista smiled. "Never."

Ren gripped his sword and started for the window. Valor shouted for his guards. As Ren broke through the remaining glass he shoved Valor aside and pushed Ista against the wall.

"Tell me how to release her," he said.

"Tell me the secret of the crystal."

Ren pressed the sword to her throat, drawing a thin stream of blood. The shouts of soldiers echoed down the hall.

Valor regained his footing and drew his dagger.

Ista smiled. "Join me, Ren. I can clear your name."

"Never."

"Pity," Ista said. "Aidan will never again be whole."

Two of Valor's guards grabbed Ren from behind. One guard hit him in the stomach as another beat his hand against the wall, trying to force him to release the sword. Ren kicked the man in the groin, knocking him backward. The man let go, but the other was already there.

"Take him!" Valor demanded.

The dragon roared in fury.

Ren grabbed the thread of light in his mind as his rage built. A sharp crack sounded as he released the Quy with whip-like ferocity. The guards holding him flew backward through the air. Out of the corner of his eye Ren saw a Crape soldier beating Quinton to the ground and another hauling Michel to his feet.

Guards from all over the Lands ran toward the window with bloodied swords, intent on his capture. Without warning, dragon's fire enveloped them. The dragon bellowed a final warning and took to the air.

Ren stumbled toward the window, desperate to reach Aidan, but she was already gone. The peace of their connection immediately scattered. In its place was a hollow void. The shock of it almost brought him to his knees.

Shouts were all around him: cries from men who fought to protect him, screams from guards to capture him. When Ren finally turned to face Valor, the new king of Newlan had victory in his eyes.

Ista stepped forward, crystal in hand. The sunlight caressed it, igniting it in crimson flame. Ista picked up a small glass bottle and hurled it to the floor. A hissing red smoke oozed out and reached for Ren.

Ren did the only thing he could do – he ran.

Screams came from behind. Whatever evil the bottle contained was affecting Ista's men.

Ren quickly turned down a hall that concealed an entrance to a hidden passageway in a side closet. He didn't see any guards, but he could hear them approaching. He stumbled to the door. Just as his hand touched the knob, his cousin, Paul of Ketes, rounded the corner.

Paul's fierce dark eyes found Ren and motioned him inside. Ren nodded his thanks and dove through the door, fumbling for the gnarled wood in the back. He heard Paul scream as steel hit steel.

Ren whispered a silent thanks to his cousin as his fingers twisted the gnarled knot of wood. Heartbeats later he was in the dark bowels of the tunnels, turning corners by memory, making his way to the lower depths of the castle – to the dungeon.

Chapter 4

Fraul grabbed Ramie's arm and silently ordered him to stand back, but Ramie remained rooted to the earth. The girl in Ren's arms looked dead, but she had been fine heartbeats ago. Just as Ramie was about to voice his concern a riveting pain seared his mind.

A scream tore from his lips. It was a foreign sound, something he hadn't heard since he was a child, but it was quickly swept away and lost among hundreds of other cries. As his knees buckled, Fraul grabbed him and hauled him to his feet.

"Stay up! Don't let them know you have it! Be strong!"

Ramie found his footing, but his mind seemed to be incinerating inside him. He dug his fingernails into his fists and thought of his brother. Nothing could hurt him more than his brother. The emotional scar immediately swept to the surface and he sensed the difference between the two afflictions. One was so painful he thought he might die, the other so painful he did not want to live. But they neutralized each other, and soon the pain subsided into something he could bear.

When Ramie regained his composure he opened his eyes to total confusion. Multitudes were on their knees, clasping their heads with anguished faces. Others ran to the gates, desperate for a quick escape. Guards from all over the lands hurried toward the castle, others fought the throng, and others, many of whom were Ren's guard, were sprawled in their own blood.

Trumpets blared as Valor walked out on the stone balcony above the courtyard. A few murmurs started. Fraul pushed Ramie back until they were at the outskirts of the crowd. Fraul's grip tightened on Ramie's arm as Valor's gaze swept the assemblage.

"Lords and Ladies," Valor said. "What you have just felt was magic being reborn. As some of you know, I'm of the order of the Collective. We knew this day would come. Today we have been proven right. Each of you now has a choice. You may join us or to join the one who opposes us - Ren Razon."

Valor turned and held out his hand to the open balcony doors. A wrinkled hand caught hold of Valor's and a horribly deformed woman emerged from the shadows.

She was rail-thin, with long black patches of hair reaching her waist. Her piercing green eyes had almost sunk to her nose, or what was left of her nose. Two small fissures formed it, and no bridge or bone remained.

Breaths caught and a few women shrieked in terror. The deformed lady seemed to grow even more hideous as her smile withered. Heartbeats later the air around her wavered. As the magic worked she became a beautiful woman with straight jet-black hair and green eyes that scanned the crowd with both sorrow and authority. Multiple gasps filtered through the throng.

"I'm sorry to frighten you, my children," Ista said, her voice a sweet titillation, "but I wanted you to see me for who I truly am instead of who I once was. My name is Ista Deus and I'm a sorceress from the Alcazar." She paused as a wave of excited exclamations filtered through the throng. She took another step forward and placed long slender hands on the marble railing, stilling the crowd to silence.

"When magic was destroyed I thought I would die with the rest, but miraculously my life was spared. As a young girl a fall cracked my skull, and the healer had to insert a metal plate to aid in reconstruction. Although the plate blocked the deadly effects of wizard's destruction, enough of it caught me to melt the plate and change my form. The fire that destroyed the Alcazar did the rest."

She paused and bowed her head. A few in the crowd murmured about the horror of her story. Ramie felt ill. When Ista looked back up there were tears on her cheeks.

"I formed the Collective in the hopes of preparing you for this day. Prophecy warned me I would have to emerge to fight an evil in the Lands. Ren Razon is that evil. Everyone here knows Ren has battled the Collective's influence, shunned our prophecies of magic and rebelled against the voice of the people. He cherishes the old religion that glorifies prostrating ourselves before an unknowable Maker, one who cares little about our dreams or ambitions. Ren opposes change and progress, and abhors everyone who has answered the Collective's call.

"Wyrick worried about Ren's unyielding attitude and planned to renounce him as heir. That is the very reason Ren took Wyrick's life. But now, my children, we have the power to stop the evil one. When I saw Ren might escape I called upon the power in you all to fight him. I rebirthed the Quy."

A few surprised exclamations echoed across the courtyard, and this time there was an underlying current of excitement. Fraul muttered under his breath as Ramie uttered a curse. Only they knew Ren had unleashed the power, but they couldn't prove it. Everyone had seen the battle, and they had seen Ren flee.

Ista scanned the crowd again. "There's more grave news, I'm afraid. Valor's children, Manda and Chris Kahn, were the first to suspect Ren. They disappeared days ago. We fear the worst."

Ramie drew in a breath and glanced at Fraul. His captain was red-faced and visibly fuming.

"Ren would kill himself before he would harm Manda and Chris," Fraul mumbled.

Ramie knew Fraul spoke the truth. Ren and the Kahn siblings were fast friends, despite Valor's influence. Ramie had always suspected Ren would one day ask for Manda's hand in marriage. Now it may be too late.

"Unfortunately, when I rebirthed the Quy, Ren attained the power as well. He's strong and prophecy has warned me he will use his power to try to regain the throne, stifle the order of the Collective, and deny your rights to use magic.

"I've come to believe the fates spared me for a purpose, but I hadn't known that purpose until today. My children, fate has selected me to be your guide. We must join together to stop the crown prince of Zier, and we must work together so the Lands can discover the wondrous gift of magic.

"Children of the Lands, will you head my voice? Will you allow me to teach you how wonderful magic can be?"

People shouted their assent. Ramie scanned the crowd. None were in Zier's black and gold.

Valor stepped forward, taking Ista's hand. "We will welcome her, won't we, Newlan!" There were more cheers. Ramie gritted his teeth. If Ista had conquered Zier herself many would question her motives. But she hadn't; Valor had. Ista offered her services, nothing more. That alone would prove her innocence to many.

"How did you survive all these years?" someone yelled below the balcony.

Ista looked down at him and smiled like a patient mother. Her long hair fluttered sensuously in the breeze. "Sorceresses don't give their secrets, my child."

A ripple of laughter careened through the crowd. Ramie turned to Fraul and raised an eyebrow. Fraul scowled.

"I urge those who felt the Quy reconnecting inside them to stay and begin training. Those who did not, go home and spread the word that a New Alcazar will be built in Zier for all to learn."

"What about the Druids?" someone shouted. "They could close us from the power."

"Yes, they could, my friends," Ista replied, face twisting with severity, "but they won't. If they do they will have to answer to me." There were whispers of approval and thanks. Ramie was stunned. These people were trusting Ista to save them from the Druids?

"There's something you should know about the Druids," Ista continued, voice softening. "The Druids were warned of this day by one with the sight years ago. When they closed people from the calling power they were trying to stop this destruction. The Druids aren't evil. Although they were too zealous in their closings, they did so out of fear."

Ramie's face darkened. Nothing about the Druids was good.

"Now that the power has been reborn the Druids will be fearful. We must make them unafraid. I'll send a messenger to them. If we are to defeat Ren, the Druids may be needed. But I assure you the Druids won't harm us. I'll see to that."

Ramie thought about his brother's fate. He could see the same happening to Ren. By the Fates, he couldn't let that happen.

"Ramie, you must leave. The faster you go the better."

Ramie noted Fraul's singular reference. He looked at his captain, knowing Fraul would remain behind until he knew Ren was safe.

"You must leave. Now, my lord."

Ramie opened his mouth to speak but decided against it. Fraul was right. He had to leave before Ista discovered he had the Quy. Fraul ushered him to the gates of the castle. No guards were anywhere to be seen. Ramie was glad his troops had camped outside Stardom's walls. It would allow a much easier escape. When he reached the gate Ramie paused to look back, but his captain was already sprinting in the opposite direction.

- - -

"She's still asleep?" Sim whispered in his mind.

"Yes," his inner companion thought in reply.

"She hurt less than you did."

"She doesn't have magic. She's more easily merged with you," the other voice answered with fatherly patience.

"Will she live?"

"It appears that way."

"Good."

"Have we become sentimental, my friend?"

"Don't call me friend, bane of my existence. You're not my friend. As soon as I'm rid of you, I've decided to kill you. You've awoken the wrath of Sim."

"Now, Similian," the Bane chastised with good humor.

"Roasted bane will be my most treasured memory."

The Bane was silent, but Similian could feel him retreat, doing whatever it was the Bane did when he was silent. Sim felt the other inside him, the woman. She would be different from the Bane. She would care. The Bane didn't care. The Bane had never befriended him. That was all Sim had wanted, the only reason he had allowed the Bane inside. Sim yearned for knowledge, unlike others of his kind. He wanted to understand, to find a purpose. The Bane had promised Sim those things if Sim would allow him inside. Sim had thought the Bane would teach him what he knew and become a companion, but the Bane taught less and slept more. Similian was lonelier with someone than he had ever been without someone. He wished he hadn't let the Bane inside. Although he wouldn't have the answers he searched for, at least he would have lived.

"I like her. I don't like you."

"I like you, Similian." The Bane's thought was pleasant, but it didn't fool Similian.

"You lied to me."

The Bane heaved an inner sigh. "I didn't lie to you. We've been through this before."

"You lied to me."

"I told you we were going on one flight, and we went on one flight. I didn't lie about that."

Sim grunted and veered east, away from Stardom. "The flight lasted nine centuries, and you were asleep the entire time."

"I told you I would sleep."

"Not the entire time." Similian growled in frustration.

"But you didn't ask, Similian. You must learn you can't interpret someone else's replies without confirming them with your own words. All creatures believe what they want to believe. You believed what you wanted to believe. But it's of no consequence. I'm awake now."

Sim almost roared his reply. "You wake as soon as the door opens, when I'm finally happy again. You didn't wake in nine hundred years of flying through nothingness. I think that's rather rude. I don't want you anymore. I want you out."

"There's only one way I can get out, Similian. You know that," the Bane thought. "If you are patient, I'll be out of you soon enough."

"Or so you say. I'm beginning to believe you just want to be Similian the Silver and this saving the Lands affair is another of your lies."

"Believe what you will, Similian. Your belief won't matter. You'll be there when the opportunity arises."

"Why did I let you in?" Similian silently roared. "I didn't like you then either. Similian should have known better. Similian is smarter than that."

"I discussed this with you when we first met. I told you I could make you the most famous dragon in history if you would let me inside you."

"I'm not famous. I'm just a popular home."

"But you will be, Similian. You will be."

Chapter 5

Manda fell off her horse and kicked it in the flank. The horse bolted. Evann cursed and pulled back his mount before Manda was crushed beneath its hooves. When Vos and Yov turned, Evann motioned for them to reclaim Manda's horse. Evann watched the twins disappear over the horizon. If he wanted to talk to Manda, now was his chance.

He was living a nightmare. He felt like he was betraying everything he was; but when the twins refused to yield he had insisted on accompanying them, no matter how much he disagreed.

Manda looked past Evann in stark desperation. Evann turned and cursed the fates for his stupidity. He was so involved in trying to think of a way to free the heirs of Crape he had failed to notice Chris' spasms. Evann quickly cut Chris' restraints and pulled him off the saddle.

Then Manda was beside him, broken ropes dangling from her ankles and wrists. The rage in her soft green eyes, more so than the dagger in her hand, forced Evann back a step. Even though he knew he would feel the tip of her blade at any time, he was consumed by an overwhelming pride. Manda had escaped without his help. Nothing could stand in the way of something she wanted. But instead of turning his way, Manda collapsed beside Chris and placed the dagger in his mouth, forcing him to bite down on its leather casing.

Chris stilled, as if Manda's touch had cured him.

"Please, Evann, bring me some water."

Evann nodded and went to his horse, glad she had given him something to do. He felt helpless, both in body and in spirit. He unhooked the leather water bag and watched Manda dab Chris' feverish forehead. Chris moaned painfully. Manda's soft whispers of encouragement floated to Evann, emptying any doubts he still held of her innocence.

Evann's heart broke anew. He loved Manda, always had. Although he was ten years her senior she had such vibrancy he had become enamored with her years ago. He knew it was foolish. Manda was an heir. He was just a swordsman in her father's army. But the fact remained he loved her, and he had been in turmoil since leaving Stardom.

The sound of galloping horses tore him from his thoughts. Vos and Yov topped the ridge, leading Manda's mount. Evann raised his hands, indicating he could explain. The twins needed to hear what Manda had to say.

"Evann, Manda has to be tied —"

Before Evann could react, Manda's dagger sailed past his right ear, missing him by a hair, and impaled Yov in the neck. Vos released a yelp as he plunged off his horse to catch his brother, but Yov was dead before he hit the ground. Vos's eyes darted to each side as the Mar immediately began to take hold. Evann watched in revulsion as Vos rocked back and forth in the grass with his brother in his arms, the rest of them forgotten.

Evann spun, expecting a knife aimed at his own back, but Manda's biting green eyes only flashed a warning.

"I'm not going to harm you, Evann. We are, or were, friends." Her words stung, but he deserved them. "I know more than you do about the twins. They were under orders to kill us. I really don't care if you believe me. I just want to save my brother."

Manda's eyes were fire. Evann glanced back at Vos. The twin's body quivered as the Mar continued to tighten its grip. Evann repressed a shudder. Although twins were respected throughout the Lands, he wouldn't ever dream that horror on himself. Twins never married, never had a life of their own. If one twin ventured into a room without the other the Mar would claim them. Vos would die, not because of any hurt to himself but because Yov's death had opened a black void inside him, drawing Vos to it, claiming him for its own. A twin couldn't survive without his other half, as if he was connected in body and not in mind. Vos would die a gruesome, yet unexplainable death.

Manda watched Vos with both regret and acceptance. It was either her life or theirs, but her eyes betrayed her sorrow. Although Evann knew he should kill Vos and put the second twin out of his misery, he had never taken a life before. He didn't even know if he could.

Manda's knife still protruded from Yov's throat, shaming Evann even more. Not many soldiers could have made that throw. He wouldn't have been able to make that throw. But Manda had studied under her cousin Jolin. Unlike most women, she had learned how to wield most weapons from the back of a horse, knives included.

Evann suddenly recalled the soldier from Fest who had read Valor's order. He hadn't sensed anything unusual at the time, but the soldier must have given Manda the knife. Evann's shame grew. He should have been the one to save her, not a passing stranger.

When Evann turned back to Manda her green eyes cut through his soul.

"I believed in you, Evann," Manda said. "How could you think ill of me?"

Evann knelt and busied himself with a twig. "Manda, believe me when I say I've been trying to find a way to release you, to hear your side, but with the twins. . . " He glanced behind his shoulder at Vos. "I was trying to find a way to free you. Believe that."

Manda studied him with penetrating eyes before taking a deep breath and pulling Chris closer. "There are secret passages around Stardom. Ren told us about them a few years ago. He reasoned if there was ever trouble and he was taken or killed we might be able to save the Zier people by sending soldiers through the tunnels. When we arrived at Stardom we overheard our father plotting to frame Ren for Wyrick's death." Manda paused to glance back at Stardom, a fearful look on her face. "We went through the tunnels to try to warn Ren but we weren't fast enough. Valor found us in Ren's chambers.

"Ista's a sorceress, Evann. She was able to move past the guards unseen well after Ren left Wyrick's chambers." Manda closed her eyes and shivered. Evann's hackles stood on end, but he was unsure if it was due to Manda's words or Vos's haunting moan.

"Our father is using us to prove his loyalty to the Collective. Upon Ista's request he ordered our deaths. It was only a matter of time before the twins killed you. They were only keeping you alive to aid in watching us."

Evann remained silent for some time. When he spoke his voice sounded like stone on granite. "Your own father agreed to your deaths?"

Though she tried to hide it, a tremor of pain shook Manda's body. The thought of someone hurting Manda ignited a boiling rage inside Evann. He had the sudden urge to ride back to Zier and kill Valor himself.

"I'm sorry I've put you through what I have, Manda. Know my heart wasn't in it."

"You believe me then?"

"Yes, I believe you. I don't understand it, but I believe you."

She offered him a small smile. "Magic is being reborn, Evann. Ista said Chris would have the power." Manda paused to glance down at Chris. "I think it's just happened. With the herb in Chris, the shock of magic's rebirth may have been too much."

A chill went up Evann's spine as Manda fell to silence. She dabbed some water on Chris' face. Chris' eyes fluttered open.

"Where are we?" he whispered.

"A day's ride outside of Zier," Evann said. "Your sister has just told me what she knows."

Chris sighed. "It's true then." His eyes widened. "The twins!"

Manda placed a hand on Chris' chest, forcing him to calm. "I killed Yov."

Chris studied her for a few heartbeats, but instead of questioning, he nodded. "Maybe your training will come in useful after all, sis."

Manda's lips lifted into a sad smile. "It seems it already has."

- - -

The guards shoved Quinton into the cell. His eyes were so swollen he could only make out shadows.

"Fates, Quinton," came a voice. Strong hands caught him and lowered him to the floor.

"Michel?"

"The one and only."

Michel put a damp cloth to his forehead. Before Quinton could ask Ren's uncle what he knew of Ren, Michel spoke. "What happened to you?"

Quinton winced as Michel continued cleaning. "One of Valor's guard went after Ren. I stopped him. The man didn't take too kindly to my interruption." Michel dipped the rag back into the water. Quinton could only imagine the blood. He felt it all over him. The soldier had been beating him to death, not to unconsciousness. Quinton hesitated, unsure if he really wanted to hear the news. "Ren?"

"Escaped. No one knows where he is."

Quinton smiled. "That's my Ren."

Michel chuckled.

Quinton heard the whisk of a belt and stiffened, knowing what was to come. He had done the same to many of his own men. He held his breath, trying to brace for the contact, but when the end of the metal spike was thrust into his swollen eyelid he jerked on instinct. A gentle hand steadied him as Michel finished prodding. When the blood and puss had been drained, Michel handed him a clean rag. Quinton wiped his face and squinted in the sudden light. Michel was bruised, and a long gash ran the length of his face, but it wasn't deep and would heal soon enough.

They were at the end of the cellblock, guarded by five soldiers. If they were to escape they would have to travel the length of the dungeon. The odds weren't good.

54

"What else have you heard?" Quinton asked.

One of the guards turned in their direction. "Quiet! We said no talking!"

Michel and Quinton exchanged glances before sitting back against the cold stone. Quinton turned his attention to the others who had acted in Ren's defense. Bentzen stood by the cell door. Bentzen nodded in greeting and put his fist to his forehead and then to his heart, a sign Ren used often. It was an ancient blessing of the fates. It meant *truth above all.*

Quinton glanced at the others in the cell. Good men, all of them. Galvin stood beside Bentzen, shoulder bleeding from a knife wound, but although Galvin looked sluggish he wasn't injured severely. The silver teardrop hanging from the loop encircling his ear danced dangerously. Ren had given Galvin the teardrop insignia after Galvin had sworn the soldier's fidelity. It was an ancient oath, rarely given. Galvin had pledged complete homage to Ren, vowing to never take a wife, touch strong drink, or other such liberties enjoyed by most. In essence Galvin had no identity outside of his duty to his prince. Ren had been stunned when Galvin had knelt before him and spoken the oath, but once given it couldn't be refused. Since then Ren and Galvin had become inseparable. Quinton smiled at his friend. Galvin nodded back.

Neki, a new recruit in Ren's guard, leaned nonchalantly against the wall. The tall, wire-thin man looked to be watching the morning's sunrise instead of his captors.

Quinton let his worries drain from him. If Ren had escaped he had used the tunnels. He wouldn't be found. Quinton only hoped Ren wouldn't be fool enough to look for them, but as soon as the thought was out Quinton knew it was too much to wish for. Ren would come after them, and they would have to be ready to act. As he looked around the cell again, his hopes rose. They would win this war. It may not be that day, or the next, but they would win. Each man in the cell would fight to the death for Ren. And there were more out there, even people in the city whom Ren had never met.

The people who fought for Ren fought because they believed in the man he was, not because he was the heir to the throne. Although most would be blinded for a time they would soon realize as the men in the cell did: Ren was still Ren, and his beliefs did not waver. It may take time, but the people would see the truth.

- - -

Marva walked to the last cellblock, silently praying Quinton would be there. She had been at home when the chaos started, and before she had time to think a searing pain had forced her to her knees. After it subsided she heard the fighting and quickly ran to the keep, knowing full well if there was trouble her husband would be right in the middle of it.

There were whispers of Ren's betrayal throughout the keep, and different variations already abounded. She soon shut her ears and began attending those who had fallen, all the while looking for Quinton.

She didn't bother searching the remote section of the castle. If Ren had been brought to the courtyard Quinton wouldn't have been more than fifty paces from him. Her husband would have been the first to leap to Ren's defense.

She was determined not to worry. Quinton wasn't fast, but he was strong, and he would have fought like a dragon deprived of its last meal. Besides, his body wasn't in the courtyard so he had to be one of the soldiers they were holding to flush Ren out.

A death at dawn and a death at twilight, those were the orders. They came from Valor himself. Since dawn had already passed they had to execute a man in the heat of the day. When she had seen who swung from the gallows near the gates her fury had heightened. It was Eli, Stardom's priest. Eli was a man of peace, a man loved and respected by all who knew him. Marva hoped the Abyss opened up and swallowed Valor and his deformed accomplice.

Marva shivered. Ista touched everyone she passed with her wrinkled fingers, urging them to stay and train to become soldiers of magic. Marva couldn't quite peg what was behind Ista's glare. It wasn't arrogance or greed, as most leaders possessed. It was a type of irreverence, almost apathy that sent a quiver down Marva's spine. Although Ista would stop at nothing to gain the support of the Lands, she cared little for them. Ista may promise peace but her peace treaties would bring war. Couldn't the people see the Collective's glorification of magic would send the Lands into slavery? The future elite would disregard morality for gluttonousness and they would sacrifice their dignity for gold.

Marva's face darkened and her blue eyes flashed a warning to the stones beneath her feet. The more she thought the more vehement she became. She hoped Quinton had bloodied his sword on so many it was permanently stained.

As she approached the last room in the dungeon she smoothed her face, stuck out her chest and sauntered in as if she belonged there. It had worked so far. Men were aroused if the breeze blew. She was sure she had their heads spinning, but that was what she wanted – something to give her undisputed entrance.

A cluster of guards played astragali in front of her, oblivious to her approach. She put on a cajoling grin and cleared her throat. The head guard threw the elongated dice before looking up. "What do we have here?"

She tried to look as dumb as she could and smiled in feigned attraction. She had learned if she showed any intelligence at all men became suspicious and quickly distanced themselves, but if she batted her eyelashes like a young girl in heat they flocked in like lambs to slaughter. The guard's eyes flickered down her form. She had dolled up in a serving woman's dress, making sure it was a few sizes too small. It suited her purpose nicely. Men could be so easily distracted. It amazed her sometimes.

"So many guards for a handful of men?" She forced her eyes to survey the guard's body as she shifted her medical supplies on her hip. Her breasts swelled at the effort.

"Orders," he said, moving closer. The remaining men stopped the game and watched with interest.

She breathed a sigh as if she tired of bringing the message. "Ista and Valor are in search of everyone with the power, even those down here. Ista will be coming to test them soon." She licked her lips and turned her gaze to the area below the guard's waist. "I'm ordered to tend to the most critical parts of the injured, just in case they have the Quy. We need every defense to defeat the prince." She winked at him.

"We'll have to search you," the guard said, mouth lifting into a grin. His teeth were crooked, a few of them rotten. She hated men with bad teeth. Quinton's were a white fortress of defense, hard and commanding. They had served her well many a night.

"By all means," she said, harboring her disgust. She set down her medicine kit and spread her legs, holding her hands to each side.

The guard chuckled and moved with carnal purpose. She ground her teeth and closed her eyes. She could take it better if she didn't see what they were doing. His hands lingered on her breasts before slowly inching down to her stomach. When he leaned in closer to wrap his hands around her backside, she peeked over his shoulder.

She spotted Quinton immediately. Relief passed though her despite the vehement fury etched in his eyes. She gave him a flirtatious wink. His face turned crimson as his eyes followed the guard's hands.

The guard continued down her length but managed to remain on her upper thighs, missing the only part she wanted him to ignore. The other guards snickered at the show. She gave them a sultry smile before she turned her gaze to the man who searched her.

"You done, sweet thing? I don't want Ista upset with me for not tending to these men. Magic sounds real good until it's focused on you."

The lust on the guard's face dissipated into concern. When he rose he smiled down at her like she was a piece of meat at dinner. "I would say you're harmless, although those legs of yours could certainly be a weapon."

She walked her fingers up his uniform and glanced at Quinton. His hands were gripping the bars, knuckles white. She turned back to the guard, talking loud enough to spur her husband a little further. "Maybe sometime . . . "

He smiled as another guard handed her the basket and led her to the cell.

As soon as the lock clicked shut Quinton grabbed her wrist, mouth twisting with worried reproof. Her eyes flashed a warning. "My lord, you seem to be badly beaten. Is there something I can do for you?" She tried to sound apathetic, but Quinton looked like death. Someone had slit his eyelids and his left cheek had swollen to twice its normal size.

He pointed to Galvin. "He has a knife wound. Help him first."

Nodding, she quickly made her way to Galvin and motioned for him to sit. She tore Galvin's shirt as she looked him in the eye and kept her voice low. "There's a knife sewn into the bottom hem of my dress. Rip it out. Someone has got to save my brave yet reckless husband."

Quinton suppressed a smile. "I love you, my sweet."

"You better," she said, surprised she had to force the tears away.

Quinton was about to respond when she hushed him with a glance. She applied salve to the wound on Galvin's shoulder. Although the wound was deep, the knife had impaled a section of flesh directly between muscle and bone, as if the Maker himself had directed the blade. She glanced at Quinton.

"I have two other knives in my shoes. I'm leaving them while I attend the others. Please, my dear, be prepared to hide them."

Galvin flinched as she secured a compress around his shoulder but the less the wound was exposed to the elements the faster it would heal, and the faster Galvin would be able to wield a sword. She told him so as she pinned the cloth in place. He didn't argue. When she finished she turned to Quinton. Fates, how she loved him. His steel eyes were twin blades to her heart. He was the first man she had ever let court her. He was everything she had always yearned for – domineering, forceful, influential – but a man unafraid to love a woman with everything he had. She had never been one to show her emotions, but she knew he sensed her fear.

"Be careful," she whispered.

Standing, she slipped off her shoes before she bent to pick up her basket. The cloth she had wrapped around her feet hadn't insulated her flesh from the blades, but her adrenaline was pumping so high she felt no pain. Quinton and Galvin put one leg over each shoe, concealing some of the blood. Feigning an itch, she bent and stuffed two rags under her feet, hoping they would be enough to cover her tracks.

She inspected the others one by one, patching slight wounds and whispering encouraging words. When she finished she glanced at the guards. They were once again absorbed in their game. She breathed a sigh of relief and retraced her steps, trying to sop up the remaining blood. Quinton looked at her with worry as she eased her feet back into her shoes and hid a grimace.

Before she could whisper a goodbye, Quinton's head shifted and his eyes filled with an inner light. His hand gripped her arm, warning her to stay back. Michel was already rising and she sensed Bentzen shift positions. She heaved the basket on her hip, feigning disinterest, and turned.

Ren skirted the corridor, keeping in the shadows. His copper eyes shone with a fury befitting a dragon under attack. She didn't have to think long.

"Hello there," she said, offering the diversion Ren needed. "Would you be kind enough to let me out?"

The head guard smiled and motioned for one of the others to unlock the cell. Ren didn't hesitate. Bounding forward he ran a guard through before the man saw his attacker. The guard approaching their cell started to turn when a knife whizzed past Marva and embedded in his throat. Blood seeped from the wound in a sickening pulse before he toppled, spilling the keys paces away. Marva fell to the ground and reached for the keys through the bars. They were barely out of reach.

Another knife shot past, then another. One hit its target but the other missed as the guard with the rotten teeth scurried down the passage, shouting for assistance. Heartbeats later, echoing footfalls of reinforcements drifted to them. Marva shifted positions and tried again for the keys. Neki slid next to her. His fingers brushed them.

The footfalls grew louder.

Neki grasped the keys and fumbled for the lock. When the door swung open the men ran for the fallen weapons, but Marva knew they wouldn't be fast enough.

Ren impaled another guard and turned in time to see the reinforcements storming the corridor. He lowered his sword, a calm expression on his face, but Marva froze in terror. There were over twenty guards. They would never be able to fight so many.

Before Quinton or any of Ren's men could reach their prince, the air around them become dense. Ren began to glow with a silver sheen. The castle walls began to shake. The approaching men screamed as the walls caved inward, others ran back, but none came any farther, and within a heartbeat the entire passageway was blocked with rubble.

"That's for Eli," Ren whispered as he studied the rubble with both regret and absolution. His eyes were still lit with an inner power. Marva shivered in spite of herself. She never wanted to get between Ren and someone he loved.

Ren pulled back a hinged stone in the wall, revealing a passage. "Everyone in, quickly!"

They all filed in without question. A torch lay in the distance. It flickered sinisterly against the tall, narrow walls. Muffled curses and shouts arose from the other side, then an explosion. They all started down the passage. Quinton picked Marva up. Before she could protest, her eyes met his. He didn't carry her for love, but for speed. They needed to get out of the castle – quickly.

- - -

Renee leaned back against the chill earth, her squire asleep at her feet. The outside wall of Zier stood cubits from her. It amazed her how much she didn't know about the Stardom Castle. She had lived here over twenty years and each year she discovered a new secret. Thank the Maker Lazo had told her about the tunnels.

Renee stroked her squire's feverish forehead. Tol wasn't well. Ever since he had arrived at Stardom he had complained of head pains. When a fit overcame him he would shriek in anguish and clutch his head like it was about to explode. Time and again she had taken him to the healer, but the healer only gave him tanga roots to chew. Even tanga, an intense medicine that numbed the subject into feeling almost nothing, hadn't helped.

His last fit had come just after Ren's escape. Tol's screams were harrowing, shriller than they had ever been before, and without another thought she had scooped him up and fled, desperate to reach the tunnels that could take them to safety.

When she entered the tunnels Tol had passed out in her arms.

It was cold, so it had to be approaching late afternoon. Silver striations decorated the walls and ceiling. An old iron pike lay abandoned across from her, its wooden handle rotten and its iron rusty. Although the Stardom mines had once been the largest silver deposits in Zier, they had been dormant for over half a century.

Renee touched the silver band of rule encircling her head. Wyrick always wanted her to wear the band when other lands came to Stardom. She thought the tradition foolish, but when Valor had gained control of Zier she had worn it out of defiance. She didn't have to worry about that anymore. She tossed the band on the ground.

Tol's blue eyes slowly fluttered open and filled with fear. Before she could ask how he felt he scampered out of her arms and swung his slight form in all directions, chest heaving. Renee stood, a little uneasy.

"Tol," she said. "How are you feeling?"

Tol blinked and lowered his arms. "I'm not dead?"

He said it with such apathy she started. She knew Tol had been abused. He was skin and bones when she had first found him abandoned outside the city walls. The boy jumped at every movement, but responded like a flower in the morning's dew to any type of affection.

She stepped forward, wanting to comfort him, but unsure how. His eyes vacillated between boy and animal. When his lower lip quivered and his shoulders sagged, she quickly closed the distance and scooped him up in her arms. He clung to her as if he had been absolved a great debt.

She rocked him, smoothing his blond hair and whispering reassurances. Tol wiped his tear-streaked face with the back of his hand. Tears still clung to his eyelashes, but as he surveyed the abandoned mine his blue eyes flashed with the curiosity of a child.

"The fit was bad this time, wasn't it?" Renee asked, needing reassurance the pain had dissipated. She knew it had been deadly. Maybe Tol knew that too.

"Yes," he said, squirming out of her arms and trotting over to examine the abandoned pike.

"Careful. It's rusty."

Tol stepped back. Renee marveled. She had never met a child who obeyed as well as Tol.

"Where are we?" Tol asked as he climbed into her lap.

"We're in a tunnel at the edge of the castle that was once a shaft in an old silver mine. Now it acts as an escape passage."

Tol looked around. "I like it here. I feel safe."

Renee relaxed. "I feel a lot better myself. I'm just worried about my friends back at Stardom."

Tol turned in her arms. "Don't go back."

"I won't. Valor would only use me to harm those I love. I can't go back."

The fervor went out of Tol's eyes as he snuggled against her. "Good. I don't want to hurt you."

Renee opened her mouth to speak, but no words came. Was his comment just his way of showing her he didn't want her to leave? Surely that was it. Tol would never do anything to harm her.

Renee closed her eyes and pulled Tol closer, condemning her apprehension as foolishness. Tol had been abused and neglected, and he feared she would abandon him too. She kissed his head, eyes welling with tears.

It was approaching dusk. The only light crept through a small crack in the outer wall. The silver streaks surrounding them reminded her of thin trails of slugs, careening this way and that, transforming the dreary tunnel into a marvel of beauty.

Renee closed her eyes and silently prayed to the Maker Ren was safe, but not even thoughts of Ren could stop images of Michel creeping into her head. When Lazo had first told her about Michel's presence her knees had almost given way. Had Michel come to hate her over the years? Although they had both betrayed Wyrick, in a way, she had also betrayed Michel. She thought it had been the right thing to do at the time, the only answer to a love that had been stifled, but now she wasn't so sure. Michel had suffered far more than she. Soon now she may be facing her past. She could only pray Ren would forgive her.

Chapter 6

Zorc looked up from the book he had read many times before. The binding was so old some of its leather hung in shreds. There was something in the air he hadn't sensed a breath ago, something familiar . . .

He heaved a sigh, chastising himself. It was his imagination . . . only imagination. Turning the page he focused on the words. The air tingled. Zorc straightened. Did he really feel it? Closing his eyes, he breathed in the damp air.

Magic.

Zorc swallowed his excitement and hurried to the mirror propped against the far side of the cavern. He bent forward to inspect himself. Still the same, nothing had changed: the same dark eyes, the same widow's peak, the same ebony hair. Zorc frowned, silently cursing his foolishness. He was too eager, much too eager. Zorc drew a disappointed breath, but before he turned he noticed something glimmering in the torchlight.

"I'll be staggered," Zorc said as he gently touched the gray hair above his right temple. He was beginning to age!

Zorc spun with arms wide, waist-long dark hair twirling around him like a war banner. He felt so good he drew up his robes and began to dance the way he had in the Alcazar. For three hundred ninety-eight years he had been waiting. That was far longer than any of the great ones had expected and far longer then he thought he could bear. Waiting wasn't bad when you had someone to wait with, but only two of those years had been spent with another. Zorc wondered for the thousandth time what had happened to Galor. He could almost imagine the seer's excitement at the thought of his foretelling coming to life. Zorc felt a pang of sadness as he thought of his friend but brightened at the thought of seeing the sun, feeling the breeze in his hair, smelling a flower, and feeling the gentle ache of hunger.

After almost four centuries in a lonely, dismal cave he would have contact with the outside world, with people, and with the Chosen.

His smile withered. His time in isolation may be over but now he would be faced with challenges too terrifying to dwell on. He needed to consult the crystal again. He needed to be sure.

Zorc glanced back at his reflection. "You're here because the world is at risk once more, but this time the threat can't be stopped in the same way. Never forget that. You can't be the way you were.

You must be the way you are, the way you need to be. You're here for the Chosen."

He turned and hurried down the dark expanse that led to the crystal cavern. It had been a long time since he had made the trip, years even. He looked down at the impressions in the gray stone. His own footfalls had made them from his frequent pacing and many trips to the crystal in his early years of isolation.

When he reached the darker section of the passage he slowed to appreciate the beauty of the nightmoss glowing an illustrious yellow. Nightmoss had been his only indication of the passage of time. In the summer months the moss was yellow; in the spring, green; in the fall, orange; and in the winter without color.

His mind turned to the issue at hand, the Chosen and the prophecy. Zorc hoped he hadn't overlooked any interpretation of the prophecy. He had analyzed every contingency he could imagine, and there had been ample time to think. What else was there to do? After Galor had left the silence had almost driven him mad, but he had slowly grown accustomed to the quiet. It amazed him how much he had adapted to being alone. At times he thought he could remain alone forever, and that frightened him more than the quest he had been assigned. Now with magic's rebirth he yearned to leave the confines of the cave and experience life again. He was determined not to fail.

He entered the chamber where the crystal resided. Large stalactites and stalagmites glistened in the gloom. The Silver Eye sat in the middle of the cavern, glowing a soft silvery-blue, casting shadows over the cave and causing the white formations to glow with a haunting sheen. The crystal had an aura about it, an awareness that caused Zorc's skin to prickle. Even the base seemed real. Three silver dragons formed it, their sapphire eyes shinning with a rage befitting the silver dragon. Everywhere you walked those blue eyes watched you. Zorc often wondered if those eyes were guarding you from the secrets in the Eye or guarding the secrets in the Eye from you.

The crystal, formed at the beginning of magical times, had been passed down to each Calvet, the wizard director, as a stark reminder of how powerful the Quy could be. Until the Wizard War the Silver Eye was just one more mystery of the Alcazar. Now he knew its purpose. The Silver Eye held the goodness of the Quy. Zorc liked to think of it as holding part of magic's soul, but although the Eye contained goodness that goodness could be fatal and needed to be feared.

To his knowledge he was the only wizard who had ever seen the Silver Eye in use, even if that use was superficial. Zorc only used the crystal to speak with the mind inside. He would never unlock the Silver Eye's true power.

As Zorc approached the Eye, he opened his mind and whispered Krov's name. The crystal immediately began to glow with a bright silver light, transforming the cryptic cave into a crystal palace.

"It's time, Krov."

"Yes, it's time," his old master's voice echoed from the ball. Although it was Krov's voice it contained none of Krov's emotion. The voice was monotone, dull and lifeless. It had disturbed Zorc when he had first heard it, but he had grown numb to it years ago.

Zorc paused, trying to phrase his question carefully. The crystal didn't offer any information on its own accord. You had to ask the right questions for it to answer, and if you asked the right questions in the wrong way it could lead you off on a divergent path. Zorc had learned to think before he spoke. It saved time.

"The Chosen has rebirthed the power?"

"Yes."

"How did he rebirth it?"

"His love had great need."

"I see," Zorc replied, contemplating his next question. The crystal pulsated with life, patiently waiting for Zorc to continue.

"The dragon awakened his need?"

"Yes."

Zorc replayed the prophecy in his mind. "Was Barracus the traitor?"

"You know that, Zorc."

Zorc waved his hands in frustration at the crystal's reprimand. "Yes, I know. I'm the One?"

"You know that as well."

"We were the ones?"

"Yes."

"Dragons are the thorn?"

"No."

Zorc froze with mouth agape. Dragons weren't the thorn? After three hundred ninety-eight years the thorn had changed? Zorc stared at the Silver Eye, mind racing. On multiple occasions Galor had dreamed of a silver dragon crashing through the Eye of the Dragon, bellowing a warning and bringing the darkness. They had discussed it amongst themselves and with the crystal. Silver dragons had been destroyed years ago. When Galor had seen the rebirth of silver dragons they were sure to be the prophecy's thorn. Although silver dragons didn't use magic they possessed magical traits that could create magic, powerful magic, and if silver dragons were to come back into existence. . .

What other explanation could there be? It was the only one that made any sense, and Krov had agreed – until now.

Zorc stepped closer, hoping he had misunderstood. "Are dragons the thorn, Krov?"

"No."

"Krov, you've agreed with me for almost four centuries. Now you tell me dragons aren't the thorn?"

"Dragons aren't the thorn."

"How can you agree one day and not the next?" Zorc's voice rose in a frenzy.

"Because I know differently now."

Zorc had based all his theories on dragons being the thorn. From those theories he had decided what the darkness could be. Now all those theories were wrong and he was out of time. Panic swelled in his chest. He had been assigned the task of helping the Chosen and he may have failed before he had even begun. No. He couldn't think that way. He was the Chosen's only chance. Zorc studied the crystal. Krov said he knew differently now.

"Krov, do you mean you've been giving me your best guess all these years?"

"In a way."

"In a way! That's nonsense, Krov! You either did or you didn't, one of the two."

The crystal remained silent. Zorc began to pace, trying desperately to surmise a rational explanation. After a few heartbeats, he faced the silver glow once more.

"In your guesses you don't know otherwise at the time?"

"Correct."

"So, you think they're fact but also know they could be a guess?"

"Correct."

"Why don't you tell me if it's a fact that could be a guess and not a pure fact?"

"You don't ask."

Zorc sighed, frustration coursing through his old veins that had been frozen at forty-one. Zorc rubbed the bridge of his nose in order to calm the headache he knew would surely come. He didn't know who or what the thorn was, and the Chosen had already rebirthed the power. He had no time for guesses. He had no time for games.

Zorc knew his next question but hesitated, not wanting to be disappointed when the crystal claimed ignorance. "Can you see this thorn now, Krov?"

"Yes, I can see her."

Zorc's stared at the crystal. Krov had said "her." The thorn was human. Panic surged inside Zorc once again. All these centuries he had thought a creature would force the Chosen to reconnect the thread and in some way cause those with magic to begin a battle for power.

Now the thorn's definition had become human. A human with magic could cause much more disruption than a creature. A human could have already begun to seize control of the Lands.

Zorc moved closer to the crystal, eyes narrowing. "Can you name her?"

"Yes."

"What's her name?"

"Ista."

Zorc closed his eyes. "May the Maker's fates be with us. May the Maker's chance smile upon us. May Ista's choices condemn her soul."

Then the rage came. It emitted from him like smoke, taking him back in time. But this time he saw it clearly. He saw how Ista had survived.

- - -

Ista stared down at her kingdom. She drew in a breath, relishing the scent – magic. It was all around her. Multiple people were milling about the courtyard, talking in excited whispers. She heard her name recited repeatedly. If it wasn't spoken with reverence, it was spoken with awe. At last her plans were beginning. Wouldn't Zorc be surprised to see her again?

A throaty chuckle escaped her lips. Zorc should have killed her as soon as he discovered she was a spy for Barracus. Instead, Zorc played by the rules. He had chained her in the dungeon, allowing her a week to repent of her crimes, but then Barracus had attacked the keep. When magic was destroyed, the magical chains binding her had broken, and before Christa had cast the time weave Ista had conjured a summoning weave. It was strong enough to direct some of Christa's life away from Zorc. Wouldn't Zorc be pleased to discover part of his beloved Christa was now joined with the woman he had condemned?

Ista's brow furrowed as she thought of her escape. Fire was everywhere. She had run through walls of molten flame before she had broken free. A low moan escaped her lips as she dipped her hand in the washbasin and brushed her face. The cool air in the Zier castle doused the reminiscent flames just like the Yor Lake had centuries before. She had stayed in the mud for days, allowing the lake's water to soothe her skin.

But she had survived. Oh yes, she had survived.

She longed for the mist of her former home, the ever-present drizzle of water ensuring her no fire would ever touch her again. Although the Zier region had cool breezes it lacked the mist of the Cliffs.

Her eyes flickered to the lone torch lighting the room. She dipped her hand in the washbasin once again, cooling her brow. She felt her face. She had been beautiful once. Now she was condemned to live in a hideous body . . . all because of Zorc.

Years ago men had shaken with need as soon as she entered the room. Many in the keep had given their life to lay with her. From the couplings she took what she wanted. Each was different and unique. The one man who evaded her was Barracus.

But Barracus had whispered of his plans in the bedchamber. He knew she had evaded the tests and tricked the wizards into believing she was loyal to the Code. The metal plate in her head blocked the test's validity. Barracus had taken that knowledge and begun to build the future of the Lands – the needles.

But where Barracus had failed, she would not. Soon, very soon, Zorc would bow before her, begging for mercy: Zorc, one of the most powerful wizards in centuries, not quite a mage, but close, so close. A small smile touched her deformed lips.

To think the very cause the wizards of the Alcazar had died for was the very cause they had allowed to escape – Barracus' destruction. But this time Barracus would be under her control, not the other way around.

After her escape from the Alcazar, she had discovered she was carrying Barracus' son. From Barracus' line she had bred multiple children. Now she had a legion supporting her. And she had found the Red Eye hidden among the banished Maritium. As soon as she captured the Chosen he would be the first host for the Red Eye's power. She would control the most powerful mage in history, not to mention the rest of the Lands.

Ista chuckled. "It's funny only you and I are left, Zorc. Just think, my friend, I'll be the one to destroy you and your world when you thought you were going to destroy mine."

A knock on the door shattered her thoughts. She turned, not bothering to change into her beautiful guise. She knew whom the guards admitted. She placed her hand on the Red Eye. She could feel its power residing within, hungering for release. "Come."

The door opened and Lazo entered. Although his eyes were hard she could sense his terror. The twins remained in the dungeon, far below. If he didn't return soon the Mar would claim them. "Good evening, Lazo. I have a special request of you."

- - -

The creatures' howls were growing louder. Zorc gritted his teeth as the sound of the battering ram boomed in the stillness of the Orb, the centermost room in the keep.

All around him the wizards began to chant, softly at first, but soon their voices rose in intensity, drowning out the creatures' howls. Zorc tried to search for Christa, but all were robed and cowled on the Calvet's order. Krov knew it would be harder if Zorc saw his friends' faces, but Zorc wished he could see his betrothed one last time.

A lone figure stepped forward for a final blessing. Krov brushed the shaded face before turning to Zorc, eyes filled with sorrowful compassion.

"Remember, Zorc, when you look though wizard's eyes, he'll be like an eclipse – so dark he'll be blinding, so light he'll be unseen. His hate will be noble, his pain will be deep, and his love will be immeasurable. If he realizes the second truth he will succeed."

Zorc nodded. Krov had told him this before, but how was he to help a man seek a truth if he didn't even know the truth himself?

"You won't fail, Zorc. You don't know how to fail. That's why it must be you who remains behind." Krov gripped his shoulder. "Be strong, my son."

Zorc opened his mouth to speak, but Krov turned from him, body wavering like the summer heat, and faded from vision as he gave his body to dust and his mind to the Silver Eye.

An explosion echoed around them. The walls had fallen. In a few breaths Barracus' creatures would be upon them. Almost on cue the wizards' pitch began to rise, and soon their voices weren't individual voices at all, but one shrill voice, rising higher, moving faster, until their words were lost in one piercing scream.

Zorc covered his ears and fell to his knees, willing his mind not to shatter. Just when he thought his mind would burst, there was silence.

The circle was gone. The shouts, the screams, the chanting, all had silenced. The wizards who had surrounded him were now dust, their lives wrapped up in the emotional weave they had woven. But there were no howls either. The only ones with magic remaining were himself and the cowled figure before him.

A gloved hand came out of the robe, holding the well-measured time weave. Zorc drew in a devastated breath. The time weave was the most painful magic to invoke. The one conducting the weave relinquished his life so another could live until a future time. Although the granter of life would die, their spirit would live inside the vessel and continue to suffer until the time weave was broken. He didn't deserve the sacrifice the man was about to make.

Then he saw it. A tattered, red velvet pouch lay on the ground beside the cowled figure. His eyes went wide.

"Christa!"

He started to run, but it was too late. Christa flung her cowl back at the same time she hurled the dust into the air. A multitude of fiery-red hair cascaded over her shoulders as the dust fell upon her. Her eyes said it all. She wanted to be with him, and this was the only way.

Her body disintegrated as it joined the dust that fell around her. Zorc's entire body shook as her lifeforce found a home, wrapping around his life matter and carefully protecting his years ahead. He sensed his blood and bones become something unexplainable, something that slowed to almost ceasing. Then Christa's life took over, forming life as his own life was halted, but hers worked so slowly that for a precious heartbeats he thought he might not live.

He fell to the floor, desperate to reach inside and bring her back. Each time he drew a breath he felt her in every pore. When he felt a hand steady him, he looked up into Galor's worried eyes.

"Hurry, Zorc, we don't have much time."

The seer had warned him the peasants would storm the keep, desperate to destroy anything remaining of magic. Zorc quickly bent to retrieve the tattered pouch. After brushing all of Christa's ash inside, Zorc went to the crystal, shrunk its size and placed it in his robe.

Just before the door to the keep burst open Zorc and Galor plunged down the passage leading to freedom, turning over torches along the way. Almost immediately flames exploded skyward as the fire touched the black ashes of the wizards, ensuring complete destruction.

Zorc glanced to the side dungeon where Ista's body lay. Fire had already enveloped her cell. The destructive weave had granted her an easy death, unlike the death she deserved.

When he heard a lone whimper he thought it was his imagination. Now he knew better. Ista had survived and she had received some of the time weave. Ista had taken part of Christa – his Christa.

Zorc's vision blurred to a vehement red. His Christa was now part of that vile, corrupt woman he had condemned to death, a sentence that had never been carried out because of the war. Ista's aim wasn't control. It was revenge. He knew her mind. She wanted him to bow before her. She wouldn't stop until he did.

"Try to make me do so, Ista," Zorc said, as his widow's peak quivered with rage. "If you do you'll have a surprise waiting for you." He turned to the Silver Eye. He had to begin his questions. But soon he would have to go in search of the Chosen.

Very soon.

Chapter 7

They had walked fifty dragon's tails and had already passed the wall surrounding the keep where the first passage ended. It dipped under the thick stone layer and opened into a closet-like haven inside the wall itself, where a hollowed, hinged stone allowed access to the main road of the city. Ren had often used the first passage in order to escape to the city without fanfare. The second passage led to the wine cellar in the *Dragon's Bane*, an old pub in the city's center. Elderec, the pub's owner, knew about the passageway and kept it well hidden.

They were almost at the end of the third passage, which careened through an abandoned silver mine to the wall surrounding the entire city of Ziera, the main city of Zier and home of the Stardom Castle. Years ago Michel had hidden weapons and provisions in the wall's hollow in case quick escape was needed. Ren made sure to check the stash frequently, trading out rusted weapons with fresh and restocking the food supply. Now Ren was glad he had listened to Michel. The provisions would be invaluable in the days ahead.

The ground sloped down, signifying the passage's end. The silver streaks in the earth became more prominent, and the torch Ren carried brought them to life, bathing the tunnel in beauty.

A slight movement caused Ren to stop in his tracks. Michel gripped Ren's arm, forcing him back a step. The air filled with the sharp ringing of steel as the men drew their swords. Ren lifted the torch higher. Its rays cut the shadows. A sharp cry of delight lit the confusion of the group as Renee jumped to her feet and ran toward them.

Ren scooped his mother up in his arms. Renee clung to him. "Ren, I was so worried. Valor wouldn't let me near you. I tried everything to reach you – "

Ren chuckled. "You would have succeeded if both guards had liked raspberries. When the first passed out from your little trick the second warned the replacements you had slipped a sleeping herb into the tarts."

Renee pulled away and grinned mischievously. "That wasn't even my best attempt."

Before Ren could reply, Renee's eyes drifted to Michel. Ren found himself holding his breath. Everyone knew the rumors, and everyone knew why Michel had left Stardom. Although Renee had never voiced her sorrow, Ren sensed it. Wyrick was a king, and for years Renee had played the queen, but her heart was wild and her spirit free. Michel had called to those urgings. Wyrick had stifled them. As the men watched, the silence in the tunnel deepened, but it was a hopeful silence, one in which friendships grew and rekindled.

Renee stepped past Ren and offered Michel her hand. Michel started to bow, but Renee stopped him.

Michel's already widening smile grew wider. "It's good to see you."

"It's good to be seen," Renee said as the corners of her lips lifted into a grin. She kept hold of Michel's hand as she surveyed the others. "Thank you for defending Ren."

There were murmurs of 'My queen' and a shuffling of feet. Bentzen even blushed. Ren chuckled, fully aware the effect his mother had on men.

Hearing a slight noise, Ren turned to find Markum and Tol standing in the shadows.

"Markum, thank the Maker! Lazo and the twins, have you seen . . ." Ren's words faded with Markum's concerned look. "Markum?"

Markum's eyes locked on Michel. "Have you told him about the prophecy?"

"No," Michel said. "There's been no time."

Ren glanced between his friends' concerned faces. "What prophecy?"

Markum drew a worn book out of his tunic and handed it to Ren. "It belonged to my ancestor, a survivor of the Wizard War. It's been handed down through my family ever since. It's blank, save for the first page. Read it. It will explain a lot."

Ren could almost feel the concerned gazes of his friends as he took the book. He fingered the silver dragon on the cover, noticing it had blue eyes.

Ren read the passage aloud as Neki peered over his shoulder.

Magic must be demolished to conquer the traitor of the law
But One must live to show the Chosen how to unlock his inner call
For a thorn will go unnoticed by those who reap destruction on the masses
And permeate the Lands.

The Chosen's love will shatter, igniting an inner raging storm
When the dragon will rip open his mind and the power will be born
And if he can't destroy the silver form the darkness will begin
And darkness will live on.

The thorn will try to prick him as the righteous deed is done
And the prick will cause a rain of red to grow into a flood
And if the Dragon Tamer will not search to find the One
The world will drown in blood.

The crown will be demolished before it can be whole
And the Chosen will have to willingly sacrifice his soul
For only through the Chosen will the demon spike be flawed
And hope will grow again.

Neki gave a low whistle as Ren's voice faded.

"Ista suspected you were the Chosen, Ren," Markum said. "She framed you for your father's murder so Valor could order your execution. If you were the Chosen you'd tame the dragon. If you weren't she'd still have your kingdom."

Ren leaned against the damp earth as a shudder shook him. His eyes kept returning to one verse. *And if the Dragon Tamer will not search to find the One, the world will drown in blood.*

He forced his eyes to move back to the first verse. "It's talking about the Wizard War."

"Yes," Michel said. "Barracus was the traitor of the law. Magic was destroyed because of him. The wizards kept the One alive to teach you. This One is quite possibly unaware of who or what the thorn is. Ista, the thorn, somehow evaded the wizards. It seems she's been waiting to discover who would reconnect the thread to reveal herself."

"But how could they have survived for almost four hundred years?" Ren said, looking down at the prophecy. "Wait, a time weave."

Michel nodded. "That's what the advisors think. If the One received a time weave, Ista might have received one as well. The prophecy says a thorn will go unnoticed. She's just waited until magic's rebirth to reveal herself."

"Why?" Quinton cut in. "If she has magic, why would she care about its rebirth?"

"She's a sorceress," Markum said. "Sorceresses don't have the power wizards do. The only magic they can invoke at whim is something called the 'sorceress death.' It allows them to die without pain, but also without any tie to magic. Other weaves they evoke take time, perhaps days of preparation, to mold their emotions to induce the effects they desire. She was waiting for magic's rebirth to be able to lure others to her side, to build an army of magic.

"The Collective," Ren said. The Collective had already helped Ista rid the world of the Maker's chosen so the masses would flock to magic's call. Without the Maritium's basic ideology a new moral code could be imposed.

Ren closed his eyes. He was opposing a sorceress who had the knowledge of over four centuries. He knew nothing about the Quy. She knew everything. He recalled Aidan's warning about the crystal Ista carried.

At the thought of Aidan, Ren's heart stung. He looked back at the prophecy. It told him to destroy the silver form.

Ren's stomach curled. He would never harm the silver dragon. Now, with Aidan's life hanging in the balance, he had a driving need to protect it. Ren leaned back against the wall, suddenly understanding Ista's purpose. She didn't want him to kill the dragon, and she had used Aidan to ensure he never would.

But if Ista ever discovered the secret of the crystal she would have to capture the dragon once more.

Maker of Fates, he needed to find the One, not only to counter Ista but also to save Aidan.

"How do we stop her?" Quinton asked, a slight edge to his voice. "No one knows the slightest thing about magic."

"I do."

Ren turned to find Tol giving him a widening smile. Tol turned to look at a discarded pike. Heartbeats later the pike spun through the air and impaled the wall with a hollow thud.

Renee released a sharp cry of alarm as Michel stepped in front of her. Tol smiled at Ren, but his demonstration caused his grin to appear demonic.

"I know how to use magic." He tapped his head. "But she's gone."

Renee gently moved Michel aside. When he protested, she gave him a look of reproach. "Who's gone, Tol?"

Tol looked at her with slight confusion. A few strands of blond hair clung to the corners of his eyes, and when he blinked the hairs jerked in quick response. "Ista."

Ren put a hand on his mother's shoulder, urging her to stand back. Renee shook him off and pushed an errant strand of hair behind Tol's ear.

"How do you know Ista?"

"She raised me."

Renee's back stiffened. Michel and Ren exchanged troubled glances. Ren felt foolish being fearful of a boy, but he couldn't shake the feeling. Renee, however, was undeterred. "What do you mean she's gone?"

"I feel safe now. She can't call me anymore." Tol traced the lines of silver sediment with tentative fingers. "She kills all of them without magic, first thing." He shrugged as if what he said was natural. "She told me to kill you up there, but I didn't want to. Then she sent me bad pain. I'm supposed to be dead now. But I don't feel her anymore."

Ren met his mother's frightened eyes.

"How did Ista call you?" Renee asked. "I was with you. Ista wasn't there."

"In here," Tol said, tapping his head once again. "She screams in here and then I have to look at this." Tol pulled a hazy blue ball from his pocket.

Ren's breath caught. It was a crystal ball, the type wizards used for communication.

Tol turned to Ren. "When she told me to kill the queen and I didn't she sent me the bad pain." Tol bit his lower lip, suddenly understanding he had said too much. He lowered his voice to a whisper. "But the bad pain is better than the other way."

Despite his better judgment Ren knelt beside Renee. "What's the other way, Tol?"

Tol turned and pointed to the pike.

"May the Maker have mercy," Galvin whispered. "Ista deserves every death she finds in this war."

Ren silently agreed. He studied Tol, trying to make sense of it all. Although magic was powerful he didn't know anyone who could call to the mind of another.

Someone tapped his shoulder. Ren turned to see Markum holding up a thin needle.

- - -

They were trying to reason through what they should do, but no solution seemed a good one. Manda was exhausted. She wanted to go home, but home was the one place she couldn't seek refuge. Zier was out of the question.

They had traveled just far enough away from Vos to let him grieve in peace. Manda felt a pang of regret for harming a twin. The thought of Lazo under the Mar's influence sent chills to every fiber of her being.

"I'm fine, Manda," Chris said, voice barely above a whisper. "I can travel. We need to help Ren." Manda turned toward her brother. 'Fine' was a fabrication. Chris was not fine, and neither was she. Their father had betrayed them.

Chris rested against a large tree, paces from her, still incredibly weak. He would have passed for a ghost if his straw-colored hair wasn't matted with fever. When he glanced at her the pain in his eyes reignited her anger. The herb administered him was from the reston vine. Chris always had a negative reaction to the herb. As a child he had nearly died from it.

"We can't return to Zier, Chris. Although I'd like to help Ren, we can't. Ren may not even be there." She didn't want to voice the fact that Ren may already be dead. She didn't even want to think it.

"We can go to Ketes," Evann said, looking between them. "We can try to warn Bostic of this."

"Yes, Ketes, that's the best suggestion I've heard."

Chris nodded his approval, but when he opened his mouth to speak no words followed.

Manda silently entreated the Maker to save her brother. She had done everything she could to keep him comfortable. The herb had been in his system too long to counter the negative reaction. Chris just had to fight. He should have pulled out of it by now, but something had given him a jolt during the ride. Manda had a bad feeling that something was magic.

Manda turned to find Evann looking northeast, toward Ketes. If Zier had been taken someone may have already sent word to Bostic about Ren's alleged treachery. Manda shook those thoughts off. Ren's cousin would never believe anything dubious about Ren. Bostic loved the crown prince almost as much as his own children.

"Manda?" Evann asked softly. "Can you ever forgive me?"

"I already have," Manda said, holding his gaze to assure him of her sincerity. Evann had the most unusual eyes she had ever seen. They were dark blue around the edges but tapered into the color of the sky. She thought of Ren's eyes: copper pools of determination and caring. The past few years she had hoped she and Ren would grow closer. She had always cared for him, and the Fates knew he was far from ugly.

Evann smiled, but his smile was strained. Even if she forgave him it would be a long time until Evann forgave himself. Shoving aside all thoughts of Ren, Manda took Evann's hand. Evann smiled before turning back to the horizon. They stayed there for a time, watching the twin moons rise higher in the sky before they turned and silently began to make camp.

Chris was asleep, but he still burned with fever. They were in the foothills of the mountains and the night would grow cold. Manda made a quick decision to leave all the blankets around him. She kissed him on the check before she turned to find Evann watching her. He had already unrolled their two bedrolls.

"I don't want to take the blankets off him, Evann. He's still feverish."

Evann nodded. "I wouldn't have thought otherwise."

Manda lay on her mat and shifted until she found a position devoid of cumbersome roots. She could sense Evann behind her and knew he would wait until she slept before he allowed himself to drift off. She evened her breaths and tried to feign sleep, knowing it would take her some time to actually lose consciousness. Within a few heartbeats, Evann began to snore.

Manda found herself hating her father, and that frightened her. Surely hating one's own blood was a sin. When she was a girl, Valor had showered affections on her. She had always been Valor's favorite, as Chris was their mother's. As a child she had been athletic and strong, where Chris had been plagued with sickness and forced to watch her successes in the games he should have played.

When Chris turned ten his body miraculously strengthened and Valor sent him to Zier to become Wyrick's squire. With Chris gone Manda grew terribly depressed, and after years of pleading, Valor finally conceded to allow her to train in the finer points of horsemanship.

The day she left Valor had given her the sword he had carried since his marriage to their mother and requested she learn to wield it on the back of a horse. She had been overwhelmed. The sword was something Chris should have received, but she knew Chris would want her to have it. Now she could use a sword like an extension of herself. When she had come back and shown Valor her skill his face had lit like a summer morn.

What had happened to him? He had betrayed them for the Newlan throne. Now all she wanted to do was use the sword on him.

She heard a sound and realized it was her own cries mingled with the drumming of her chattering teeth. Chris lay shivering under the blankets, still breathing as if every breath would be his last. Her vision clouded. Her father had given them over as if they were nothing!

Rubbing her shoulders she tried to think of better thoughts, but none would come. It was going to be a long night.

"Manda?" Evann's hand was suddenly on her arm. She closed her eyes, cursing herself for waking him.

"I'm fine. Go back to sleep."

Evann's hand lingered for a few breaths, then lifted away. Manda felt a twinge of disappointment. She wasn't the kind to ask for help. Besides, Evann needed his sleep. Tomorrow would be a long day.

Then Evann's hand was back, and she felt him place his bedroll next to hers. Manda closed her eyes and turned, burying her head in his chest. Evann's grip tightened and soon the night wasn't so cold.

Although she slept, she was well aware of Chris' pained breaths and the cool breeze on her back. She had images of riding beside Evann's mare, hoping he would decide to help. The sound of horses' hooves echoed in her ears, pounding a rhythm that seemed foreign in her dream. The sound was heavy, fast, and it didn't coincide with her mount. Confused, she tried to turn her head, but her ropes didn't allow free movement. She twisted as much as she could, straining her neck, but she could only see her horse's flank. She tried to yell for Evann but only managed a moan. Her brow furrowed . . . something was wrong.

She opened her eyes, mind suddenly clear. A troop of horses stood before her, shadows eclipsing the light of the twin moons. Before she could shout in alarm she and Evann were yanked from the ground.

The three men holding Evann quickly beat him to the ground. Beside her, Chris groaned as another man hauled him to his feet. Panic seized her. Ista knew they had escaped and had sent a troop after them. The same helplessness she had felt during her father's betrayal crashed upon her with the force of a thousand storms, but when she noticed the red and blue brocade of her captors' uniforms confusion overcame her fear. Her father's colors were green and gray.

Drenched in shadow, a lady approached. The light of the twin moons fell behind her, crowning her in a halo of gold. When the heir of Quar came into view she scrutinized Manda with a deadly glare.

Alezza was beautiful, with lily-white skin and hair as dark as midnight. Her lips were red and full, her nose thin and dainty, and her cheekbones high and broad. She was the picture of perfection, but when Manda looked into her dark eyes Alezza's long hair became snakes and her smile became poison.

Manda and Chris had met the Quar party on the road to Zier. Alezza had every intention of luring Ren into her web and becoming queen of half the Lands. When she realized Manda's interest in the crown prince they had fought like two cats in a burlap sack until they reached Stardom. With Ren accused of his father's murder Alezza's dreams had been foiled. Manda's mind spun. What did Alezza want with them, revenge for her quick tongue? Manda didn't think so. The look in Alezza's eyes was far more dangerous.

"Well, well, what do we have here? Why would the heirs of Crape be running about in the dark?"

"Alezza, release us at once."

"Do you think Valor would pay for his children's safe return?" Alezza asked, turning to the men behind her, ignoring Manda's frantic protests. "Oh, I forgot. How silly of me. Valor sent his children off to die. Why ever would he want them back?"

Manda forgot to breathe. How did Alezza know?

"Oh, Manda, you're as good as dead. Valor announced your deaths this morning. You're disinherited. You're nothing."

Manda lunged. The man who held her stumbled, allowing Manda to come dreadfully close to hitting the viper. A slow, crazed laugh escaped Alezza's lips. "Dead people have no rights, Manda. I can do with you whatever I wish."

Alezza took a piece of Manda's hair and twirled it between her fingers. "And let me assure you, your beloved prince won't come to your aid. No, I don't think the traitor of the Lands even knows you're still alive."

Manda drew in a full breath. That meant Ren had escaped. Manda calmed. At least she knew Ren was safe. She risked a glance at Chris. He still looked pallid, but his shoulders had straightened and a small gleam lit his eye. He had been more worried about Ren than himself. Now, Manda hoped, Chris would fight his own battle and heal.

"But if I found Christopher Erik Kahn, the prince of Crape, alive and returned him to his home, how revered I would be by the Crape people!" Alezza chuckled, sensing Manda's puzzlement. "Oh, my dear, don't you see? Your father would be convicted of treason. Chris would inherit Newlan!"

Manda's eyes flickered to Chris, still not seeing the connection. Chris' confused look only emphasized her frown.

"Why my dear, you don't seem excited about having me as your sister."

"My sister?" Manda raised an eyebrow. "I know you're desperate, but surely you won't stoop low enough to marry a dead man? Whatever makes you think a dead man would think differently than a live one?"

Alezza paled and turned, but before Manda could think of another biting remark, Alezza spun with catlike quickness and slapped her.

Evann lunged, breaking free from the men who held him. A large, burly man bounded off his horse and hit Evann in the back of the neck, causing his knees to buckle.

"Bort," Alezza said, eyes locked on Manda, "why don't you bring Manda the peace offering I have for her."

The burley man turned, a lopsided grin on his meaty face, and untied a bundle from his horse. When Bort placed the bundle on the ground, Manda's eyes went wide.

It was Vos.

The twin was barely recognizable. His split head and gutted remains turned Manda's stomach, but it was his eyes that broke her heart. They stared up at her in stark terror. The Mar had killed him. Vos had barely felt the knife that had finally taken his life. Manda looked away. She had committed a horrible atrocity. She had killed his brother. No one, not even Vos, deserved the death of the Mar.

"Not grateful, Manda? Well now, I thought you would be." Alezza's voice came from a vacuum. Manda could barely breathe.

Alezza waved her fist under Manda's nose. "Ista didn't command the twins, Manda. She controlled them. Do you want to know how?" Alezza opened her fist. Three silver needles rolled back and forth in her palm, glimmering wickedly in the twin moons' light.

Alezza patted the top of Manda's head with a sole finger. "She inserts the needles inside the brain and controls her subjects through intense emotion. Vos knew everything about Ista's deception. When I found Vos dying of the Mar he was more than willing to tell me what he knew."

Alezza looked down at Vos. "I did you a favor. He betrayed you. He got what he deserved." Alezza smiled. "But don't worry, I won't make you do anything you would find distasteful."

Manda ripped her arm free and lunged for Chris. The guard holding her put his knee in her back, forcing her to the ground. Behind her, Evann howled in pain. Helpless desperation claimed her. When her eyes met Chris' her vision blurred. Chris was terrified, but not for himself. He was worried about her. Blessed Maker!

Alezza's red dress brushed the side of her face. The heir of Quar's voice wafted down with honeyed ice. "Now, I need to know which of you experienced a mind-numbing pain early this morning. Tell me now and I may reconsider the needles as your fate."

Manda's head spun. Her instincts had left her. "Chris, only Chris. Please, Alezza, he isn't strong. Use them on me first."

Alezza chuckled. "Thank you, Manda. You've saved me a lot of time." Alezza turned to her guards. "Saddle them up. I want to ride farther from Zier. When we stop, shave the prince's head. I'll see if I remember how the needles were placed."

Manda's mouth dropped open. "No! Me first!"

When Alezza smiled, death was in her eyes. "The needles only work on those with magic, my dear. But don't worry, I'll use you in other ways."

Chris' eyes burned with fever as he leaned his weight against the guard who held him. "I'll be fine, sis." He smiled in reassurance. Manda didn't know what to do. It would be suicide to try to escape, and Chris was too weak to run.

"If you misbehave, my prince," Alezza said, "I'll use the needles on your sister, with or without the gift."

Bort's lips parted into a grin, sending malodorous breath into Manda's face. "I like redheads, my lady. Let her ride with me."

Evann squirmed, frantic to reach her. One of the men holding him beat him until he fell unconscious. Manda tried to stifle her rising terror as her arms were lashed together and she was handed to Bort. When she hit the saddle a riveting pain shot through her abdomen. She struggled, but it was no use. She heard Evann's moans but couldn't twist her body far enough to find him.

The hem of Alezza's riding dress came into view. "It seems these two men want to protect you. Don't do anything foolish or I'll have to hurt them."

Alezza's soft chuckle violated the cool night air. Bort mounted behind Manda. She almost vomited as one of his hairy hands wiggled under her chest. Soon her blouse was torn. He scooted closer and she shut her eyes in disgust as she felt him on her back. The horse started moving and he moved with it, not bothering to conceal his grunts of satisfaction. Soon her back was wet from Bort's frolic. At times his hand left, but every time she thought it was over his hand came back.

She didn't know how long it continued, but before dawn broke they stopped. Rough hands grabbed her and hauled her off the horse. When her feet touched the ground her knees gave way. Bort hooked a hand under her shoulder and dragged her to a nearby tree, dropping her like a sack of grain.

Chris lay on the ground near the fire. Evann was thrown to the ground beside her. He was badly beaten and one arm looked broken. His face colored when his eyes flickered to her torn dress.

Alezza walked to the fire and dropped the needles in the water. She couldn't let this happen. She turned to Evann, determination filling her. He was only a short distance away.

She scooted toward him. Evann shook his head, eyes whispering of danger, but she pushed on and collapsed against his shoulder.

"We can't let them do this, Evann. In his state, Chris could die."

Evann heaved a sigh. "I've been trying to think of a way to convince them I have the gift."

"No, don't even think that," Manda said, twisting until her hands brushed Evann's ropes.

"Manda, they'll hurt you if they see."

Manda didn't care. She began working Evann's ropes, trying to feel the knots with her numb hands. Just as she was about to slide a rope free Alezza looked up from the water and shouted for them to be separated. Manda's stomach sank as tears blurred her vision.

Her hands were ripped from Evann as Bort took her by the hair and pulled her away. With a complacent grin, he kicked her in the stomach. Manda formed a ball as she fought to stay conscious. When her vision finally cleared, Alezza stood beside Evann with a knife to his chin.

"I told you to behave, Manda." With the flick of her wrist Alezza ran the knife down Evann's arm, slicing his flesh to the bone.

- - -

Carter watched from under the shade of the surrounding trees as Alezza cut the man's arm. Every fiber in his being wanted to attack, but he knew acting now would be as foolhardy as petting a dragon. He had to think of a strategy that would give the heirs of Crape a reasonable chance of survival. An attack would just get them all killed. He was the Kahn's only hope.

Carter shuddered. When Quinton had ordered Carter's squad to leave Stardom and follow the trail of the Crape party they had moved fast, all concerned about Manda and Chris. Chris was well liked among the guard because of his days at Stardom, and Manda's winsome disposition had won their hearts years ago.

Almost immediately after leaving the tunnels and entering the forest some of his men had shrieked in anguish. Carter had spurred his mount to a stop when suddenly, from out of nowhere, the wolves had come. No, not wolves – wolven, the two-headed magical creatures he used to read about as a child. His men slashed at them, but each cut only made the beasts stronger. When he yelled for his men to stop, it was too late. Most had been ripped to shreds, their horses with them. Carter had ordered anyone remaining to follow him to the light, but only one rider came after him, and that rider had died from a chest wound a sun's click later.

The thought of the wolvens' powerful jaws sent shivers down Carter's spine. The daylight had been his salvation. He had broken into a clearing just as the wolven attacked. While the new dawn shined down upon him, his men were still in the dark of the woods. Wolven never entered the light, only the darkness, and when ravished they frequented the shade of the forest.

Carter scanned the Quar camp, his plight bleak without backup. He had failed his prince. No, he hadn't failed yet. He could hear Manda's sobs even from this distance. He gritted his teeth, vowing to rescue Manda or die trying.

Chapter 8

Although the night wasn't over it was slipping further and further away. They needed to be away from Zier by daybreak, but Ren didn't know what to do about Tol. If Ista called him again she may be able to decipher their location.

The others looked as uneasy as he felt. The silence in the chamber seemed to deepen as everyone surveyed Tol with impassive faces. Even Neki, the jovial one, had his jaw set in resolve. Ren glanced at Quinton to find him with his sword already drawn.

Ren understood Quinton's silent demand. They couldn't let Tol travel with them. His very presence was a threat. Ren became uneasy as he looked into his captain's eyes. Quinton was prepared to kill the child. Quinton was thinking of the group, as all guards had been trained to do. And Quinton was right. Ren had seen the madness in Tol's eyes. Tol would be forced to do acts Ren couldn't allow. Tol was the enemy. No matter how innocent, Tol was the enemy.

But fates, how could he order such a thing?

After Tol's confession his blue eyes vacillated between fear and trust, between salvation and despair. Tol had come to Zier and found a home. His loyalty was with Renee but his body belonged to Ista. By his look, Tol knew that. He also knew Ren had to make a decision. Even before Ren spoke, tears welled up in Tol's eyes. Ren's heart ached. What had Ista done to this child? And how many others did Ista control with the needles?

"I need to ask you some very important questions, Tol. Can you answer them truthfully?"

Tol nodded, managing to add a formal, "Yes, my lord," after a brief span of silence.

Ren ruffled Tol's hair. "Call me Ren. You're a friend, not a subject."

The boy smiled, but his smile quickly vanished. The change was startling. Ren heaved a breath. "Have you been in any pain since you woke?"

"No," Tol answered. His grin broadened as he added, "Ren."

"Can Ista sense you if she doesn't send you pain?"

Tol 'chewed his bottom lip. Ren could tell the boy wanted to please him by his response and was therefore unsure how to reply.

"Tell me the truth, Tol," Ren said. "Anything you know will be a great help. If you know enough, I'll grant you a knighthood. You'd be the youngest knight in the history of this kingdom. You'd like that, wouldn't you?"

Tol's face lit with delight, and he nodded vigorously. "She sends us pain to know where we are. If she does, she knows. One time some of the others left and she got real mad. She sent the pain and when we found them they were dead. She always kills us when she gets real mad."

"When was the last time you sensed her?"

"In the castle."

"Before the tunnels?"

Tol nodded, pleased he was able to answer Ren's questions.

"Maybe she can't find him, Ren," Michel said a little skeptically.

Ren chewed his lower lip in thought. "Perhaps," he said, unsatisfied.

Tol wrapped his arms around Renee's legs and smiled up at her.

"You did well, Tol. Thank you," she said.

Ren tried to sense the needles inside Tol's head. He couldn't. He didn't feel the slightest twinge of magic.

"I want those of you who have the Quy to try to find the needles. I've tried but can't. Try to see how they work. If it brings Tol pain stop at once."

Quinton, Bentzen, and Galvin stepped back, allowing the others with the power to step closer. Michel bent down to eye level with the boy, Marva crossed her arms with grim determination, and Neki peered at Tol with none of the nervousness Ren had detected a heartbeat before. Ren shifted his weight, silently praying to the Maker one of the others would be able to find the needles. Tol couldn't travel with them if they didn't know how to block Ista's hold. The risks were just too great.

Just as Ren was about to give up hope, Tol squirmed.

Neki cocked an eyebrow. "I've got them."

Tol continued to squirm. Ren opened his mouth to tell Neki to release his hold, but then Tol surprised him – he giggled.

"That tickles."

Neki's grin widened. Tol's giggles increased. A few of the men chuckled at the scene.

Quinton raised an eyebrow. "Neki the sorcerer?"

If it was possible, Neki's smile rose higher. "Just call me Sorcerer Neki, the mighty wizard of Zier."

The tenseness quickly shattered as the men broke into laughter. Even Bentzen's lips twitched into a grin.

Ren turned to Neki. "How do you feel the needles?"

"I don't really know. I just reach out with my feelings and, well," Neki shrugged, "I can almost see them. Not truly, but if I concentrate I can feel something there."

Ren sat back on his heels. If Neki could sense the needles inside Tol, Ista should as well.

"Tol, before, in the castle, was Ista's presence always there even when she didn't send you any pain?"

"Yes, she was waiting."

"You mean you could always sense her, and now you can't?"

Tol nodded. Renee frowned. Ren didn't know what to think. Something had to be different, something . . .

Ren stood and quickly made his way to the hinged stone that granted access to the outside. After swinging it open he turned to Tol. "Step outside."

Tol glanced up at Renee. When Renee nodded, Tol did what Ren asked. Tol immediately crumbled to his knees.

Ren snatched Tol up and quickly closed the stone.

Tol's eyes cleared. "She was back. But she's gone now."

"Fates," Ren said. "Magic can't get through silver."

Ren stood and slapped Bentzen on the shoulder. The swordsman looked confused but smiled anyway.

Renee frowned. "I don't understand."

"Silver must absorb magic," Ren said with a grin. "We're in the silver mines. The silver is blocking Ista's call. Ista doesn't think Tol's dead. She just can't find him. I think we've found a cure for the needles!"

Ren's eyes landed on Renee's silver band of rule lying discarded at the far side of the passage.

After retrieving the band, he motioned for Tol to kneel. Ren placed the silver band of rule around the boy's head. Ren nodded at Neki, wanting to prove his theory true.

Neki knelt beside Tol and creased his brows in concentration. After a few breaths Neki shifted his weight and leaned closer. When he finally looked up, a slow grin stole over his face. "Nothing. Absolutely nothing."

Ren turned serious. "Tol, don't ever take that band off. Do you hear? Never take it off, not even when you sleep. Do you understand?"

Tol touched the band with tentative fingers. "Yes, my lord."

"Tol of Zier, squire of Renee, beloved by the crown," Ren said. "You've excelled in your duty, had faith in times of oppression and aided in times of need. For your loyalty we reward you with a knighthood, but with this knighthood comes grave responsibilities. Sir Tol, Knight of Ren and Knight of Renee, I charge you to have courage in your heart, to think of others before yourself and to speak the truth at all times. Do you accept these duties?"

Ren made sure to change the last line to be about truth instead of gallantry. He knew if he emphasized truth Tol wouldn't hesitate to speak if Ista called him. By the look in Tol's eyes Ren had nothing to fear. The boy's jaw clenched with a determination Ren had yet to see in a grown man. Renee had given Tol a home and a family. Tol would do nothing to jeopardize that.

"I accept," Tol said in a soft voice.

"Then rise, Sir Tol, and may the Maker shower his blessings on you from this day forth."

Ren turned to Bentzen. He had always worried about the silent guard. After years of Bentzen going above and beyond his duties, Ren had knighted him. It was one of the few times Ren had seen emotion cross Bentzen's face. Someone or something in Bentzen's past had hurt him deeply. Ren wanted his loyal guard to enjoy life, to love and be loved. Maybe Tol could teach Bentzen just that.

"Sir Bentzen, please step forward."

Confusion rippled across Bentzen's face, but he obeyed without question. "Bentzen, I charge you with the training of Sir Tol. See that Tol learns your ways."

Bentzen opened his mouth to protest but quickly closed it and nodded a silent assent.

Tol stared up at Bentzen with a mixture of awe and fear. Bentzen was an imposing man, tall and broad shouldered, with a look of wildness that, mixed with his silence, caused many to fear him.

"Tol, Bentzen is a fellow knight. He'll teach you duty and purpose. You'll ride with him when we leave." With Ren's words, Tol's awe overcame his fear as he reached out his thin arms. After a few heartbeats, Bentzen bent to pick Tol up.

Quinton motioned everyone outside. With one last look at Ren, he followed the men out the narrow opening in the wall.

At first Ren had planned to ride to the ruins of the Alcazar. He thought the One might have left some clue as to where he could be found, but then Tol had told them Ista's camp was in the Cliffs of Crape. He didn't believe in coincidences. The Maker had sent Tol to them for a reason.

Besides, the One could be anywhere. Any direction they went could be the right one.

When Ren finally stepped into the night, all the men had mounted one of Michel's horses, hiding under the shelter of the apple trees. Neki munched one of the apples and the smell of the fruit's sweet juice made Ren's mouth water. He hadn't eaten in days and was beginning to feel the hollow ache in his stomach.

There weren't enough horses to hold everyone. Tol sat in front of Bentzen and Renee sat in front of Michel. His mother and Michel were already engrossed in conversation. Ren felt a strange sense of completeness as he watched them.

Ren glanced back at the distant lights of Stardom. He had never hungered for the throne. At times he even yearned for the type of life Michel led. A man shouldn't rule because of name alone. Royalty was a privilege, not an inheritance. He had plans to give the throne back to the people, allowing them to elect their rulers, not be ruled by the elect. Now, the throne had been taken, but he would return to claim what had been taken from him. Ista had made a grave error. Although she had taken something he planned to relinquish that was the very reason he had to take it back.

- - -

Ren rode more on instinct than sight. The cloudy night smelled of rain, but if rain did come it would help hide their trail. At dawn he would begin to conceal their tracks in the Epigec River, otherwise known as the Tear of the Sierras. The Epigec ran from the base of the Sierra Mountains to the Black Ocean. It was so wide and shallow a horse could run the river and barely wet its fetlock.

Surrounded by the Sierra Mountain's naked peeks, Zier's boundaries consisted of dusty plains and tumbleweed, but the interior of Zier was a lush, verdant redwood forest. As they rode through the tall redwoods Ren silently said goodbye to the land he loved. Michel had taught him to appreciate nature and guided him in understanding the silent words of the forest. Now it seemed the massive redwoods hovered over him in protection and the gusting wind cried for haste.

When morning finally dawned and the Epigec River came into view, Neki rode to flank him.

"My prince," Neki said, eyes darting nervously behind him, "I don't know if this will be of use, but Grauss' home is on the way to Ista's camp. He's always talked about magic's rebirth. You may want to speak to him."

Ren could only stare as Neki's words dissipated. Even though Grauss was well respected in name, he was something of an enigma, and to Ren's knowledge had never been seen.

Quinton spoke from behind him. "Grauss the Sage? No one knows were he lives."

Neki grinned. "I, unfortunately, do."

The rest of the group moved closer. Grauss' name was a legend to old and young alike. He was well known for his discoveries, from when a comet would appear in the sky to when an ant would die. He was a mathematician, astrologer, poet, scholar, and much more. If anyone in the Lands knew anything at all about magic or where the One could be found it would be Grauss the Sage, but no one knew where he lived, much less what he looked like.

Ren pulled his horse to a stop. "Neki, that would be an incredible help, but how do you know he's still there and will see you?"

Neki's dark eyes darted between Ren and the others. "He's still there, and he'll see me again. He's my grandfather."

"Your grandfather!"

Neki winced as if he had just revealed a disquieting secret.

Ren looked back at Quinton, who shrugged.

"Where is he?" Ren asked.

"Southwest," Neki said, pointing to the Sierras on the distant horizon. Looking up at the first light of dawn, Neki paused. "We should arrive by nightfall."

Quinton pointed to the river. "Let's turn north until we hit the river and then ride south in its wake for as long as we can. If anyone follows, they might be fooled."

The clouds continued to roll in, and soon a light rain began to fall. Only Michel and Renee seemed oblivious to their surroundings as they whispered quietly, faces never once deepening into worry or concern.

When the sun was low in the sky Neki stopped and began searching for a safe place to leave the river. The banks were largely grass and small brush, but soon Neki discovered a rocky area. Although it wouldn't hide their trail, with a little luck, and more rain, their tracks would be harder to spot from the river.

With the river behind them, they pushed their horses as hard as they dared, intent on reaching Grauss by nightfall. The hills gave way to a more desolate area of sparse grass and tumbleweed. Though the landscape was still beautiful, it allowed no cover to shelter them from watchful eyes. Bentzen and Galvin took turns watching for any sign of pursuit.

The dust from the ground billowed around them until Ren was sure anyone within eyesight would swear they were a cyclone riding the wind. Soon they were all covered in dust, and constant curses from Quinton indicated his displeasure. When the sun was setting Neki led them up one of the smaller mountains in the Sierras. Neki pointed to an old, worn path, well hidden behind a few bushes that looked not only foreign on the mountain's slope but also suspiciously well watered for the season.

With Neki's knowledge of the narrow path's odd turns it was easy to travel, and when the swordsman finally dismounted he nodded toward the flattened slope where a large rock jutted out into the fading sun.

"There's a path behind that rock that leads into the mountain. Grauss lives inside. I'd suggest we only take one or two with us. Grauss doesn't care for visitors."

Ren turned and surveyed the group. He wanted to take Michel, but his uncle was deep in conversation with Renee. He glanced at Quinton only briefly. His captain needed to stay here in case they were discovered. He finally settled on Galvin.

Ren swung down and motioned for Galvin to do the same. He told Quinton he'd be back as soon as he could and to stay out of view. Quinton nodded his understanding, gray eyes holding the same intensity they'd carried since leaving Stardom.

Neki led them around the edge of the protruding rock to a narrow opening no bigger than a man's girth. As they eased into it Ren felt the cool air from the interior of the mountain drift over him. Neki pointed to the ground and then ducked down and disappeared. Ren found an opening in the mountain's face just below his waistline. Not only was Grauss' entrance well hidden, if Neki hadn't been leading Ren would have walked right by the hollow, probably reaching a dead end farther back inside the aperture. As soon as he cleared the stone overhang Neki put out a hand, indicating for him to wait, and rumbled in the dark, muttering a few colorful curses under his breath.

Ren heard the sound of flint being struck as a torch roared to life. Neki passed the torch to Ren and then quickly lit two more. When Ren's eyes adjusted to the light, he took a step back. Neki stood dangerously close to a ledge that seemed to drop to the depths of the earth. On the right the mountain cut off any path, but on the left a narrow trail wound its way around the mountain's interior. It appeared as if the mountain had caved in, leaving only a dangerous thread holding onto safety.

Neki broke into a grin. "I call it 'The Ledge of Lunacy' for only a madman would dare walk it." His grin broadened when they didn't reply. "Around the first bend, the path widens. I've walked it for over ten years. I assure you, it's sturdy."

Ren released an unsteady breath and carefully followed Neki. As Neki predicted, when they twisted around the first bend the ledge widened into something tolerable, although not tolerable enough to walk two abreast. Sensing the mountain's peak above him, Ren lifted his torch, trying to glimpse it, but only darkness greeted him.

Even though they had descended a fair amount Ren still couldn't see the bottom of the gorge, but he heard the faint sound of running water. In the past the water could have risen much higher and formed the very ledge on which they walked, but there was no sign water had touched the ledge in years. Only the nightmoss, glowing a brilliant yellow, could claim life at all.

Above them Ren could see more paths cut into the mountain. If paths existed within other mountains people could disappear for centuries and never be discovered.

A sharp clanking reverberated against the rock. As they moved closer to the noise, a distant cursing wafted to them, along with a clank and more colorful invectives. "Grauss," Neki said, as if that was explanation enough.

Neki walked around one last hook in the mountain and ambled into a huge cavern. Strategically placed torches, whose light ricocheted off multiple mirrors, lit the cavern and created a crystal ravine out of stark shadow. The fires brought life to the cave's natural formations and cast a formidable light in the large enclave. Two huge apertures at the top of the chamber were covered with a lattice, opening the night sky to full view. Ren frowned, wondering why Grauss, after all the trouble to conceal his alcove, would risk the openings.

Almost in reply to his thoughts, Neki leaned toward him. "That side of the chamber is impossible to reach from the outside. It's a sheer drop in the mountain and each window is invisible to outsiders, even in broad daylight. Other formations in the mountain cast the openings in shadow no matter the time of day or year."

Ren nodded, just now taking in the entirety of the chamber. It was immense, and chalk marks coated every wall. Words, numbers, drawings and agendas were scrawled with frantic precision, displaying steps of sagery but nothing Ren could discern. Gadgets of all sorts carpeted the floor. On Ren's right a clear liquid bubbled in a glass tube above a small fire; on his left a wooden shaft held a metal string that ended in a small pebble and swung in a continuous circle over a pail of water; in front a pit of bubbling black liquid simmered without fire or any other stimulus.

"Burning cinders!" yelled a voice.

Ren searched the cavern until he found a man perched in a metal chair dangling from a rope beside the first window. The rope hung suspended from a thick wire extending from the cavern's entrance to the high window on the opposite side of the chamber. Ren noticed a similar apparatus for the second window.

Neki walked forward, casually stepping over the pit where the black liquid boiled. "Grauss, I've brought someone for you to meet."

The skeletal body spun at the sound of Neki's voice. Although Grauss' head was bathed in shadow, Ren could sense the scowl on his face.

"Dear boy, I've no time," Grauss said, spinning back to the wall and writing something in chalk by the window. After a few breaths, Grauss spun back around.

"You brought someone to the chamber? Have you gone mad? You know the rules! No one can know where I live. My home would become a haven for wolves. Kings would demand answers. Peasants would demand cures. I wouldn't be able to deal with anything important, only resolve noble bickering and the world's petty problems!"

"Grandfather, I brought the one you call the synergy."

Grauss stopped raving. His bony legs dangled in the air like two twigs blowing in the wind. Reaching above him, he released a lever. The chair shot down the wire with lightning speed. Neki stood in its path, hands planted on his hips in complete disinterest. Ren drew in a breath to shout a warning when the chair lurched to a stop. Grauss swung from side to side, his stern face glaring down at his grandson. The chair's metal parts clicked in the silence. Neki seemed unconcerned, but Ren grew nervous as Grauss' face turned a brilliant shade of red. The chair bobbed a few more times and then went still.

Grauss leaned forward. "Don't toy with me, my boy. The synergy is too important, and he isn't yet complete." Grauss' sharp blue eyes glanced up at the latticed window. His voice became low, almost reverent. "The three aren't yet in a perfect alignment with the one. But it's begun. Did you feel the earth move?" Grauss turned back to Neki. "Don't toy with me about the synergy. You know how important he is to me."

"The synergy doesn't have to be complete to be alive, does he? Humor me, Gramps. No harm can come of it."

"Cinders, boy!" Grauss exclaimed, knitting together his thick white eyebrows and pushing Neki out of his path. Grauss released the lever and zipped forward, scant white hair billowing behind him. The chair lurched to a halt beside Galvin. Grauss leaned forward until his long nose hit Galvin's chin.

"Mmmm, no." Grauss jumped off the chair and scurried to a section of the wall with minimal chalk marks. "Synergy will look like this." The sage's thin arm worked with fervent intent. When he finished the drawing he shoved the chalk into his brown tunic and stepped back to study his masterpiece.

Ren emerged from the shadows to examine the picture. It was a simple sketch, but it did resemble him. How could Grauss know what he would look like? He cleared his throat. Grauss spun, but before the sage could open his mouth to bark his displeasure his thick white eyebrows shot up in surprise. The sage flipped down a glass eyepiece from the wide silver band encircling his head. One large blue eye stared up at Ren with a spark of hope and a twinge of belief. After quick examination Grauss flipped the glass back up and tapped the side of Ren's face.

"Born on the equinox?"

Ren was surprised by the question. "Yes." He was born on the day where day equaled night. Not many people even knew of the day. He barely gave it a second thought.

"The balance, the synergy." Grauss mumbled under his breath, whispering numbers and calculating the exact time frame. "Were you the one who caused all of the rumbling two mornings ago?"

Ren nodded.

"Was the rumble magic being reborn?"

"Yes."

Grauss grinned and took a step back. In a flourish of skin and bone, he bowed. "I'm humbly in your service, my lord. . . ?"

"Ren, Ren Razon."

Grauss paused in mid bow and peered up at him. "Ren Razon, the crown prince?"

"The very same."

Grauss straightened and scurried over to some scrolls on a nearby table. Heartbeats later scrolls were flung this way and that, curses were uttered and the glass eyepiece was slammed back down. "How could I have overlooked something so important? How could I have overlooked . . ." Grauss paused. "Ah, yes. I missed the split!

"Here, Neki! Here it is!" Grauss held up two scrolls with a wide-toothed grin. Neki nodded in slight boredom. Grauss turned and began scribbling notes on the pages.

"These go together, and I missed it, but you. . . " Grauss grinned up at Neki. "My dear boy, you have just solved the most significant event since the beginning of time."

Neki shrugged, but his eyes lit with pride. "I had a good teacher."

Ren suddenly understood why Neki approached things with a calm demeanor and constant humor. Grauss was a boiling pot of trouble. No one could get a word in edgewise.

"But wait," Grauss said, scrambling through the pages again. "If you're here and magic is reborn, then why aren't the other stars in alignment? Unless . . . " Grauss' eyes widened into saucers. "There are three others who will assist the synergy. Burning cinders!"

"What do you mean?" Ren asked, stooping to examine Grauss' charts.

"Lots, my prince. Look," Grauss said, shoving Ren back into the swinging chair. Before Ren could protest, Grauss pulled the lever and Ren was hoisted into the air toward the latticed windows.

"Grauss, we don't have much time. We're on the run from – "

"The thorn, yes. I just thought it would begin as soon as the stars had aligned, not before. But they shouldn't be long in aligning. At this rate it should be . . . " Grauss paused, counting on his fingers and mumbling something Ren couldn't make out, ". . . approximately one full moon. But cinders, I thought it would take months or even years for the quest to begin." Grauss waved his hands in the air as he ran up a narrow wooden ledge that rose from the chamber's floor, around the wall, only to stretch below the latticed windows for closer observation. Even before Ren had reached the windows, Grauss was waiting, bony arm outstretched to catch him.

Ren's brow furrowed. "How do you know about the thorn?"

"The Maker's stars told me." Grauss leaned over and pulled the rope above Ren, bringing him closer to the window. Grauss pointed to the night sky. "Do you see the triangular shaped constellation?"

Ren had seen the constellation multiple times before. When the constellation was first born there had only been the middle star. Over the years three other stars had been birthed from that star and were slowly moving outward to form a triangle. Ren knew Grauss had written about the constellation's movement. The sage conjectured the three stars would stop when they reached equilateral points.

"Yes, I see," Ren said, keeping in mind the sage had yet to fully answer the question about Ista.

"The constellation didn't exist twenty-five years ago. You're twenty-five are you not?"

"Yes, but I have nothing to do with the constellation."

"You're wrong, my prince. The middle star is you," Grauss said, glancing out the metal partitions in the lattice. "Twenty-five years ago that star was born, on the equinox, on the balance. Over the past twenty-five years the three outlying stars have emerged from the middle star, slowly moving to their positions until they'll finally reach equal distance between each other and the center star. When that happens they'll be in perfect alignment, tied to the one that birthed them.

"But, the middle star hasn't dwindled since they separated. On the contrary, it's grown. Can you believe it? That's a theoretical impossibility!"

Ren frowned. "I don't see what this has to do with me."

"Your birth created the star, caused it to be. You're the synergy, the union. Because of you, other things will begin to live, to be, to exist. All these years I thought the stars would have to be in alignment for you to exist, but that isn't so. You're here, you're whole, and you've already rebirthed the power. The stars that came from you aren't you. On the contrary, they're independent of you, but because of you, they are. It's convoluted but that's the case.

"You, the middle star, the one who grows larger though things are taken from him, can bring light or can bring dark. You, born on the equinox, will have to balance the light and dark inside you. Which side you choose will determine the fate of all mankind." Grauss clapped his hands together as if he had just discovered the secret to life.

Ren shook his head in horror, causing the swing to creak and grown under his weight. Grauss clamped his hand over Ren's mouth before Ren could speak.

"We are influenced by three external elements: choice, chance, and fate. Their influence affects what we do, as well as limits what we can do. However, the Maker also gave us an individual soul that has its own three internal elements: love, hate, and pain. Our internal elements influence the external elements, causing all six to be very unpredictable, hence chaotic. Though what appears like chaos to you to us theologians is underlying order. Yet the underlying order is very hard to predict for there're many ways we can view the interaction. That's why prophecies change. Some branch off, have different meanings, throw us a curve if you will. That's why each roll of the dice influences something else. One thing influences other things.

"People are normally born with only one dominant external element. Although all are fated for an end, some are more fated than others. Meaning, some people's fate can't be easily altered. Others are more prone to chance and either luckily or unluckily spin through life. Still others are deeply impacted by their choices. Just as we are born under dominant external elements, we are also born through and develop dominant internal elements. The internal elements influence and react unpredictably when the outer elements are affecting our life. People rashly turn from the correct choice, or run from their fate, hence making prophecy something that needs to be read with caution.

"But the synergy was created through all the elements, both internal and external. That's rare, almost impossible in fact, and powerful, extremely powerful, powerful enough to change the course of our world, to change history, and to even change the fate of all. You're that person. You're that power: the synergy, the balance, the union of all the elements into one.

"I don't know the method of your birth, but you were created with the external elements of choice, chance, and fate as well as the internal elements of love, pain, and hate." Grauss stuck one bony finger in the air. "But all six were in balance, weighted equally. They had to be, or you couldn't have rebirthed the power. You will, if you haven't already, grow the internal elements to be equal in you. This will make you even more powerful.

"Only one other thing in history was born from all the internal and external elements," Grauss said.

"The Quy," Ren said.

"Good, good!" Grauss said. "Only someone created with all the elements could be strong enough to rebirth something as powerful as magic. I've been studying the Maker's stars for many years. The middle star is you. The triangle points are the external elements: choice, chance, and fate. These elements will help guide you, but they will also influence you. That's why they separated. They don't make you up, but they helped bring you to existence. They're part of you, but they're also external. They're not easily changed, not easily altered. All these external points contain the internal elements because they were born through you, the synergy, which was born of all the internal elements as well: love, hate, and pain. This will make them strong. They'll be strong for you to draw upon, for it's the internal elements that allow you to use the power and allow you to have control and influence over the external elements. One person can be many, my prince, and you are all. You're the synergy."

Ren stared at Grauss, unsure if he should be honored or frightened. "Then what did you mean by three others?"

Grauss turned to gaze out the latticed window before his lips widened into a jester's grin. "I'm a fool. All these years I thought magic's rebirth would occur when all the stars were in alignment, but you've released the power. That can only mean three others will help you and give you power from which to draw. Once they're in alignment, that's when you'll be, in some way, joined with them and able to draw from them."

Grauss plopped down on the ledge and looked at Ren with a huge grin, happy for a listener and ecstatic the listener was the synergy.

"Everyone is born with a fate. However, choice and chance come into play. Choice provides different paths you can take, chance is the choices others make. Others choices are your chance and these chances influence your choices, which can eventually alter your fate. In your case, three others also heavily influence the fate you've been born with. If the others choose a wrong path, you may also, and then the world is lost, hence the union, my prince. You're all somehow connected, though you don't know it. You'll find each other when the time is right. If," Grauss said, holding up a finger, "you all choose the correct path."

"That's a lot of uncertainty, Grauss. My fate is affected by three other people?"

Grauss nodded. "Just like you have all six elements, the others will as well, all in varying degrees. Although all will have the three internal elements, I predict that each will have a unique way they were born or have come to be. Each one should have his or her own dominant external element of choice, chance, or fate and their own dominant internal element of love, pain, or hate."

"So how do you know about the thorn, or what the prophets have called the darkness?"

Grauss pulled Ren to the ledge. "Must get off and come with me to the next window."

Ren was careful to test the wooden ledge before he stepped out of the chair. His footing felt stable and he relaxed as he followed Grauss. The wooden ledge widened at the next window, allowing Ren ample kneeling room to peer into the night sky.

Grauss hunkered over, heels dangling dangerously off the ledge, and pointed. "There, do you see the dark spot in the sky, the spot with no stars?"

Ren nodded. He had seen the dark patch since birth. "It's called the. . ." Ren hesitated, thinking about what he was about to say. It couldn't be.

"The Raven, the darkness, devouring all the stars around it," Grauss whispered with something between awe and intrigue. "Do you know when it appeared?'

"The Wizard War."

"Good! And there's a star, a red one, precariously close to the darkness, so close in fact it looks like it's the very thing leaking the darkness into the sky, pricking it, if you will. It's called 'The Thorn.' The Maker designed the stars to mirror the world, my prince, to warn us. Stars, like prophecy, tell a story. I've been studying the sky all my life. The Maker is telling us the thorn will bring the darkness and only the Maker's gift of the synergy can stop it."

Grauss lowered his voice, brows furrowing in concentration. "The star wasn't red yesterday. Whatever she's planning she's begun to put into motion."

Something tickled Ren's mind. When he glanced at the star his breath caught. Ren stood and lost his balance. Grauss was suddenly beside him, pushing him toward the mountain's face. Ren managed to breathe his thanks even though he had broken into a cold sweat.

"Grauss, do you know anything about a red crystal or what it could be used for?"

Grauss' eyes opened wide. "A red crystal?"

Ren nodded, not liking the sound of Grauss' voice.

"Oh dear. Does the thorn have it?"

Ren glanced out the window. "Yes."

Grauss paled. "All crystals are blue or white if they're the crystals wizards used for communication. The only other crystal was the Silver Eye. The Silver Eye was passed down to each Calvet, the wizard director of the Alcazar. The Silver Eye held the love of the Quy, magic's soul so to speak, and was believed to hold power over life itself. For a crystal to exist it must have a twin. Twin crystals are opposite phenomena. One crystal can call to its twin, but no other. They are two in one – a balance – but also an opposing force. The Silver Eye can be no exception. Its twin is the Red Eye, and if the Silver Eye is the Quy's love and holds power over life, the Red Eye is they Quy's hate and holds power over death."

Ren took a step back, desperate to escape Grauss' revelation.

"People use the Quy for good as well as evil, for love as well as hate. If the Eyes are controlled the world is controlled, and the fate of the Lands is in the hands of the one who wields them. If you've found a red crystal it must be the twin to the Silver Eye, and it will be the balance of love. It will be hate."

"What could she use it for?"

Grauss drifted closer. "The Silver Eye can be used to call to good spirits, speak with them, but this power is forbidden by the Maker and should never be used. It also holds the secret to life, meaning whoever controls the Eye can create life. But the Silver Eye doesn't have to create life that's good. Although the Eye itself is the Quy's love, it's unconditional, ubiquitous. It's like a mother loving her murderous son. There's no hate, and the one who controls the Eye controls the aftermath."

Grauss gripped Ren's arm with such force Ren's hand went numb. "My prince, the Silver Eye can bring death in the form of life." He paused to let the words sink in. Ren remained frozen. "The Red Eye would be the opposite extreme. It can be used to speak to evil spirits, and it can be used to bring life in the form of death."

Ren was suddenly in dire need of a glass of water. His mouth felt like the desert at high sun. "What do you mean?"

Grauss glanced at the red star and the darkness before turning back to Ren. "The Maker has forbidden us to call to any spirit, good or bad. The realm of the dead is forbidden to us. To bring a good spirit into the Eye would mean to bring them pain, something the Maker clearly forbids. However, calling to evil spirits brings them relief."

Ren took another step back. Grauss followed, oblivious to Ren's sudden need to escape any knowledge of the Eyes.

"When you call evil spirits to the Red Eye," Grauss continued, "they become stronger. It's then possible for these spirits to pass through to the world of the living. They'll be able to live again."

"How could she bring a spirit through?"

"A vessel. The spirit would enter another's body and take control."

"Like a merging," Ren said, thinking of Aidan.

"No, not like a merging," Grauss said, eyes never leaving Ren's face. "In a merging a spirit of a living being is torn from its body and transferred directly to another live body. The spirit and the body's spirit battle for control and merge to create someone who's different from both. Hence the spirit hasn't passed through death. When a spirit that's been dead enters a live soul that spirit will consume the soul, eat it alive, leaving nothing of the former occupant."

Ren drew a deep breath. If Grauss was right any wizard who went to the lower Plains could rise again and fulfill Ista's commands.

She already had vessels awaiting them, vessels under her control. If she used the Red Eye she could have an army at her command almost immediately.

"Holy Maker," Ren whispered, turning to start the descent to the floor. He had to return to Zier and find the crystal.

Grauss put a hand on his shoulder. "You can't go back for it, my prince. It's far too dangerous. She's already bonded the Eye. Sorceresses can do such – bond things to them in a way that will cause your death if you physically touch it. And if you kill her before the bond has been broken . . . the Eye will be locked open or locked closed for eternity."

"But don't we want it locked closed?"

Grauss shook his head, white hair flying in every direction. "No, never do such. To lock something closed would be disastrous. I told you, the Silver Eye is the Quy's love, so the Red Eye is the Quy's hate. Both can be used for good and evil. We don't know why the Eyes were created, but without hate magic would be binary, not trilateral. I don't know the repercussions of such, but they can't be good. If you closed one Eye what would happen to its twin? Just as a human twin can't live without the other twin, could an Eye live without the other Eye?"

"But the Silver Eye can be used for ill as well. Why not destroy them both?"

Grauss leaned forward, eyes narrowing. "You'd want to risk closing not only hate but love? What if closing the Eyes takes love and hate from the world, leaving only pain?"

Ren's hackles stood on end. Grauss was right. He didn't know enough about the Eyes to destroy them. The silver dragon was the same notion. Just because a prophecy said to destroy the silver form didn't justify destroying the dragon without reason.

Grauss wet his fingers and smoothed back his hair. "There's only one way to stifle the threat of the Red Eye and that's to neutralize what Ista's begun. The only way you can neutralize the Red Eye is with the Silver Eye."

The prophecy echoed in his mind: *And if the Dragon Tamer will not search to find the One, the world will drown in blood.*

Ren's heartbeat quickened as he realized the importance of the quest before him. The darkness was bringing death to life. The darkness was bringing the wizards of old back from the dead and merging them with vessels. He had to find the One, for the One would have the Silver Eye, and the Silver Eye was their only hope.

"Grauss, there's someone I'm supposed to look for. Do you know where I could find him? Have you read anything in the stars?"

Grauss' brow crinkled in thought. The sage mumbled something under his breath and ran back to the other window.

Grauss looked over at him, blue eyes reflecting profound intelligence and depth. Ren had a feeling Grauss knew far more than what he revealed. Ren was about to voice his concern when Grauss pointed to the sky. "Look there, beside the synergy."

Ren peered into the dark expanse of sky, trying to discern what Grauss wanted him to see. Just when he was about to give up he saw it. A hazy white light, almost invisible to the naked eye, twinkled on and off as it moved slowly and steadily toward the triangular constellation.

"Do you have a current plan?" Grauss asked, still staring out the window.

"Yes, though I don't know – "

Grauss held up a hand for silence. "Follow it. That light means one of two things: either you're moving in the right direction or the One you seek will find you no matter where you go."

They were silent for a time as both of them watched the misty light. Ren could scarcely believe his life was in the stars for all to see. He wondered if Ista knew about the constellation or what it meant.

"Grauss, thank you, and rest assured I'll tell no one of your home. Your grandson meant no disrespect."

Grauss eyes softened with regret. "I know. He's special. I've always known that."

"He has the Quy, Grauss," Ren said, watching he old man's reaction. At first Ren's comment didn't seem to register, but then Grauss' face lit with fatherly pride.

Grauss spun, Ren forgotten, and ran down the path. Ren watched him go, and after deciding the path was better than the hanging chair, followed at a much slower pace.

"Neki! Neki!" Grauss shouted, waving his arms in the air.

Neki ambled over from where he had been talking to Galvin, brows furrowing in confusion. Ren reached the ground just as Grauss flung his arms around his grandson.

Grauss stepped back and put his finger in the air, indicating for Neki to wait, and scurried to a trunk at the far side of the cavern. Heartbeats later Grauss came back holding a long, sheathed saber. He handed his grandson the blade. Neki's eyes widened as he unsheathed it.

It was the finest blade Ren had ever seen. The thick, silver arc was decorated with ancient runes. Embedded on the hilt and surrounded by golden braiding were three large stones: a ruby, an emerald, and a sardonyx. The stones winked in the firelight, as if awakening from a deep sleep. Ren wondered if they truly had.

"This sword was used in the Dark Ages by your ancestor, Taurus," Grauss said, "one of the greatest wizards of his time. Taurus enchanted each stone to protect the one who wielded the weapon. The ruby is for luck in battle, the emerald wards off evil doings, and the sardonyx wards off things not of this world." Ren thought about the spirits Ista could bring through the Red Eye. The sardonyx may come in more helpful than any of them knew. Dark as midnight, brilliant red striations cut the stone. Ren could feel its power emanating within.

"Grandfather," Neki said, "Ren should have it."

Before Ren could object, Grauss held up his hand. "No, only an descendant of Taurus can wield it. Its power would be useless to your prince, but you can guard him well with it. The stones will glow when they're working and will be able to warn you if trouble is near.

"And remember," Grauss said, turning fierce blue eyes to Ren. "Watch the stars. They can help guide you and they can warn you of danger. Watch the Raven. Its darkness will grow larger, and it will begin devouring everything around it. You need to crush it before it hides the synergy from the sky. Once it hides your star from view, you'll have no guidance, no power, and no hope."

Chapter 9

Once word of Ren's escape had reached Fraul's ears he purchased a fast mare and left without so much as packing his things. He wanted out of Zier, and he wanted out yesterday.

He couldn't look at Ista without a thousand prickles of warning rippling across his skin, but it appeared as if everyone else was welcoming her with open arms. At least everyone except the Zier people. The Zier citizens he had passed on the road to Port Les were a little less than enthusiastic. Many were in tears. Fraul's lips twisted into a pensive smile. The Zier people still believed in Ren, but what they could do about the charges against him was a different matter altogether. Ista had magic, and magic was something no one understood.

Fraul squinted into the morning's light, hoping Ramie had made it to the docks with all his pieces. Surely Ista couldn't hinder the king of Oldan from leaving Zier, or so he hoped. How much power could she force inside the mind of another? Fraul shivered at the thought of the needles. He had told Lazo of their discovery and urged the triplets to leave, but Lazo had refused, insisting Ista would follow. Fraul discerned the truth in Lazo's terrified gaze. The triplets had lived in luxury their entire lives. Fleeing into the wilderness would be worse than death. Still, Fraul worried about his new friends.

As Fraul topped the final hill overlooking the small port city, his heart jumped. The outline of Ramie's ship could be seen in the distance, but it was already too far out to reach. Ramie had waited for him for as long as he dared. Fraul cursed, for now not only was Ramie unreachable, but his king was also steering the massive ship into the ten winds to make up for lost time.

"Damnedable cocky-ass king," Fraul said. "Just don't get yourself killed."

Fraul reined in his dappled mare and watched the distant ship. He let the chill breeze cool him as he patted his mare's side. She hadn't protested when he had pushed her to her limits, and now that he had missed the ship she deserved some pampering. Fraul rubbed his goatee and mulled over his options. He desperately wanted to reach his king, but there was no fast solution.

If he tried to obtain passage on the next boat to Oldan it would be on a merchant ship that would make frequent stops, delaying his homecoming for over a month. If he rode on land it would take him almost as long, but he would be moving, doing something. Just the thought of sailing for weeks on end nauseated him. He was a man of action. Sitting to him meant sitting in the saddle and going somewhere. Besides, if he traveled by land he might be able to detect Ren's trail, and if he had to bet, Ren would begin his search at the ruins of the Alcazar. The ruins of the Alcazar were near Yor.

With the decision made, Fraul turned the mare toward the small port town. He would need supplies. Patting the large bag of gold in his pocket, Fraul muttered small curses when he realized he would have to wait a degree or two of the sun before market activities commenced. Although he hadn't slept, he was far from tired and itched to get started. A trek across country would be an adventure. Although his old bones were rickety, they weren't buried yet.

When he reached the main road he scanned the town for any sign of life. It was a typical port city, the largest buildings being inns and bars. Most were well tended, and some were painted in bright, cheerful colors. The streets were clean and lanterns lit the area in a soft orange glow. Heavy flat stones were placed at intervals beside the shops so patrons could keep their ankles free of mud and debris on rainy days. Peddlers were beginning to set up their booths for the day's market. A few stopped long enough to nod as he passed.

People were just beginning to emerge from the inns and outlying houses as Fraul rode down the street, stealing quick glances into the shops, mentally keeping tally of where he would return. First, he needed a tailor. Traveling clothes could be fitted to his specific measurements while he purchased other supplies. He didn't want to travel in uniform; he wanted to be inconspicuous, and his uniform was far from that.

At the end of the street Fraul surveyed an inn and an adjoining bar called *The Crown Prince*. A few of its boards appeared recently replaced. The light pink of the new wood stood out from the old, grayish structure like two war wounds. He liked places with character, and by the look of it, *The Crown Prince* was a favorite among the rougher crowd. He chuckled. In his younger days he had seen the insides of even rougher places.

A stout whiskey suddenly sounded good to him. His mouth began to water.

Fraul dismounted and tied the mare to the railing outside, pausing to scratch the animal behind the ears in silent thanks for the quick journey. As he walked inside the smell of malt ale emanated from the floorboards. At first he didn't see anyone in the small room, but after a few heartbeats a young woman popped up from behind the bar, washrag in hand.

Fraul inclined his head. "I've had a long night. Would you be able to supply me with a stout whiskey?"

The barmaid looked as run-down as the place. Some of her dull brown hair fell out of her cap and a few dirt smudges graced her left cheek. She surveyed him with a quick glance before reaching behind her for a whiskey bottle.

Fraul sat at one of the tables and stretched his legs. He had been right about the bar being raucous. Two fallen tables and a broken chair from the previous night's fray lay in the far corner. The chair next to him had a battle-scarred arm, reattached with heavy burlap and wire. Testing the arm for strength, he was pleasantly surprised to find it sturdy if not altogether comfortable.

The barmaid set down a glass and poured the whiskey. "These days, not many people ask for a whiskey that way," she said. Her voice was soft but slightly rough, like silk across granite. Fraul liked a coarse texture to a woman's voice. It gave her character. He let her question linger to ingrain her voice to memory.

"How do they ask for a whiskey then?" he asked, taking a sip of the liquid, relishing the trail of fire it left as it slid down his throat. It wasn't as strong as he would have liked, but most of the rougher places watered down their whiskey in the hopes of keeping the patrons restrained for as long as possible.

"They usually just demand it." The barmaid tucked a strand of hair back inside her cap and surveyed him again. Finding what she saw acceptable, she nodded. "Just holler if you want another. I'll be in back."

Fraul lifted his glass in thanks and watched the woman disappear though a back door. He was glad she didn't want to make small talk. He felt like being alone with his thoughts. He took another sip, tallying everything he would need for the trek cross-country. The supplies would be tricky. He didn't like the idea of venturing into another city to restock. He needed to estimate future needs to precision. Chaos was sure to break loose now that Ista had declared the training of the Collective. People would be mad to learn the Quy.

He rose, draining the last of his whiskey. Although another would be to his satisfaction, the stores were sure to be open. As he threw down a gold piece and turned to leave, a shrill scream came from the back. Fraul spun, unsheathing his sword in one swift motion, and darted toward the sound, all the while wondering how he always landed right in the middle of trouble.

As he rushed through the back door he looked around for a disturbance, but saw none. The barmaid stood before an open door that led to the outside alley, a large bag of garbage dropped at her feet. The bag, bursting at the seams, was beginning to leak a thin trail of liquid, smelling of stale ale and day-old meat. The girl put a quivering hand to her face and slowly backed away. When her dress moved out of the doorframe, Fraul's eyes went wide.

A man, shaking and slightly damp from the morning's mist, crouched in the doorway without garments or covering. Wavy black hair reached just below his shoulders, and his forehead rested against the hilt of a golden sword. As Fraul watched in stupefaction the man raised his head and looked at the woman. His hazel eyes, so light they appeared golden, held no malice or evil intent, much less any recollection.

Fraul's looked from the golden eyes to the hilt of the sword. Etched on its surface was a woman, bound in shackles and bleeding from the heart: the sign of one betrayed. Without a doubt, Fraul knew what was on the other side of the hilt. A portrait of a man with a handful of money, dying as a golden blade drank the lifeblood from his heart, the very golden blade now before Fraul: the sign of the Avenger.

Fraul glanced back to the man's eyes. There could be no mistaking their power.

The Avenger had been born again.

- - -

Lorlier glanced back toward Stardom and chewed his lower lip. "May the Maker have mercy," he said for the thousandth time as he mounted his warhorse. When Ista had suggested everyone with the Quy remain behind, he had ordered his men to return to camp. He wasn't about to release his soldiers, not until he had done a great deal of thinking.

After magic's rebirth, he craved the long ride. He needed the wind in his hair, the smell of horses, solid ground, something he understood, not all of this humbuggery of magic.

But the Quy was something he had to face sooner or later. He was no fool. He knew many of his men wanted to train under the sorceress. Could he blame them? Magic was enticing.

The Quy, it was something he thought he would never have to deal with in his lifetime.

Turning, he scanned the troops for Marianne and Alise. Alise was talking to a of group high-ranking soldiers, batting her eyelashes with newfound confidence, not that she had lacked any before. Lorlier sighed. Alise was a boiling pot of trouble. Now she would be downright incorrigible. When the power had been reborn Alise's scream had scared the holy dragon's dung out of him, but the Maker had blessed the right child with the gift. Alise was the strongest of his children, and if he could have his pick would be the child who inherited the throne. Not even Davis matched her fire. But she was the youngest, and a daughter besides.

He scanned the throng for Marianne. As normal, Mari was off by herself, well away from the soldiers. Praise the Fates his Mari had nothing of the Quy, but even without the burden of the gift he still worried about her. Since leaving Zier a haunted look had lingered in her eyes. He had disregarded it at first, thinking it was just her nervousness about the ball. Marianne was extremely shy, like her mother Desra, and always grew nervous at such events, but now Lorlier thought her frightened look may be related to the Quy.

Lorlier heaved a sigh. Marianne was over twenty-one, past due for a husband, but he couldn't bring himself to agree to any proposals for her hand. Marianne needed someone special, someone who loved her completely. If Marianne were Alise he would have accepted a proposal long ago, for some of Mari's suitors held a spark in their eye when they looked at her. But he knew there was no love in those looks, only attraction. Alise would have nabbed the first attractive, powerful man she could find, but Mari shied away from everyone.

Well, everyone except Korin. Lorlier sought the white-gold hair of Korin. As usual, Korin was off by himself, and every so often his tender eyes sought Mari, making sure she was out of harm's way. Despite Korin's quiet manner he was extremely popular among the men, and one of the first sought for fun or sport. When Korin put his all into a job it was more like ten men than one. At times Korin wouldn't stop working until Lorlier himself ordered him away. It was as if Korin were trying to work off a debt or punish himself for some past deed.

If it was Korin's persistence that had first caught Lorlier's eye it wasn't what had won his heart. Korin loved Mari with everything he had. Mari didn't know of course, but Lorlier did. A father could always spot a man who would lay down his life for a daughter, and Lorlier was convinced Korin would lay down his life if it would save Mari a broken finger.

Although Lorlier couldn't be certain, he thought Mari loved Korin as well. Mari was an enigma, even more so than her mother. Lorlier had never understood how one could be so shy, so scared, and be a daughter of a king, and beautiful besides. Lorlier decided to talk to Mari soon. If his daughter loved Korin she would be the first heir to marry someone without title. He glanced at Korin, an idea forming in his mind. Korin had the gift, and Lorlier may be able to create a position that would guarantee Korin even greater respect among the guard. If Korin did well Lorlier could grant him land and a knighthood. Yes, that was exactly what he would do. Korin would become a lord, a knight of Lorlier of Fest, and he would wed Mari and love her completely.

Davis rode out of the woods with some wild chickens tied to his saddle. Lorlier smiled. At least Davis still acted normal. At twenty, Davis already matched Lorlier's size and had a mind as sharp as a double-edged sword. His dimpled chin and boyish good looks had already won every female heart in Fest. Lorlier had caught his son stealing kisses from almost every attractive maid in the keep. But how could he scold the boy when he had done the same at Davis's age? Davis glanced his way, smiled and saluted. Lorlier laughed and saluted back.

An approaching horse caused Lorlier to turn. His captain, Gregory, rubbed his long dark beard and nodded in Davis' direction. "Davis seems unaffected by the recent events, does he not?"

Lorlier chuckled. "Lucky for him."

Gregory raised a thick eyebrow. "Is the great Lorlier a little shaken?"

Lorlier shook his head, smile withering. "I just don't know what to make of it, Gregory. I want to push magic away, hoping it will leave, but I can't do that, especially with Alise and a quarter of my men under its power."

"I know, my lord. What are your thoughts?"

Lorlier sighed. He neither understood nor liked his thoughts. He didn't like being indecisive and that was precisely how he felt. Lorlier spurred his horse into a canter and motioned for Gregory to follow. When they were a fair distance from the men, Lorlier stopped and looked over at his captain.

"Gregory, you saw what happened. Ren attacked Valor and all the guard went after him. Although I have a bad feeling about Ista, how could all the guard be wrong?"

Gregory cleared his throat. "Excuse me, my lord, but I didn't see that. I saw chaos: men running to protect their prince, men running to protect their king, and men from other nations acting instinctively to save the king. I also saw many hesitate, due to the fact they believed in Ren but were loyal to the king, or because they believed in the king and feared Ren."

"That doesn't help me, Gregory."

A small smile spread to Gregory's thin lips. "No, my lord."

They rode in silence. After a time Lorlier nodded, thinking of his plans for Korin. "I believe I'll be neutral for now."

Gregory's dark eyes flashed with mild amusement. "Neutral? I don't know if you have it in you."

Lorlier didn't respond. How could he tell Gregory his mind told him Ren was a power-hungry young man? After all, the prince had killed his father, used the calling power to escape justice and fled, but in his heart Lorlier felt something wasn't quite right with that scenario. The man he had seen fighting the dragon was one of two things: being used as a scapegoat or putting on an incredibly good show.

Lorlier didn't like being neutral, but what else could he be? Until he had more of an inclination that was all he could be.

- - -

Manda watched Alezza boil the needles. Alezza didn't know what she was doing, and she didn't care. What did it matter if Chris died? He was presumed dead anyway. Alezza wouldn't be blamed for his death, and if he lived Alezza would control him. Chris was just a convenient experiment.

When Alezza had tried to insert the needles the previous day Chris had lost consciousness. Thankfully, Alezza had decided to wait until he had regained some strength. Although Manda was relieved, the waiting was just as bad, if not worse, than the threat.

Chris sat ten paces away, and although he still looked feverish he sat up straight and tall. The herb had finally left his body, but he was weak from fighting it. When he turned to look at her his face was devoid of emotion.

"Be strong," he mouthed.

She nodded and looked away, afraid he would detect her fear. Alezza would use magic to push the needles in place. She had been practicing on other objects during the day. Before Vos had died he must have shown Alezza how to touch the power for she was more adept than she should have been after a few days of tinkering.

Manda felt Evann's eyes on her and turned. He sat beside her, tied as she was: hands behind his back, feet bound beneath him, and a rope linking feet and hands together. His eyes conveyed his sorrow. She smiled her thanks and glanced at his arm, asking her own forgiveness. He shrugged as if there was nothing to forgive, but she could sense his pain. Nothing had been done for the wound. Flies circled his exposed flesh like vultures.

Four of Alezza's men held Chris still as Alezza reached into the bowl with a pair of tongs and brought out the first needle. Manda closed her eyes, willing the sight away. Chris told her to be strong, but she couldn't be strong. He was her brother. She couldn't be strong for this.

When Chris' first scream ripped through the air she was unprepared. It sounded more like a wild animal than her brother. It was a high-pitched wail of anguish that hovered in the air like a fog. A thin stream of blood seeped down Chris' cheek, marring his ashen face. His eyes were crazed and he heaved breaths as if he had just run from a pack of wolves. Manda shouted for Alezza to stop, but Alezza ignored her. Alezza reached into the bowl for another needle.

If Chris' first screams were a wild animal's, his second screams were from the Abyss. How a scream could be more terrible Manda didn't know. By the time the third needle was inserted his screams had stopped. The silence was even more terrifying. Manda cried his name to fill the void, begging him to hold on. Finally, the guards released him. He dropped to the ground, eyes wide with unspeakable horror. Alezza stood above him and watched his spasms until he stilled.

Manda swore to the Fates she would kill Alezza with slow precision. Her own words sent tremors of repugnance through her, but she couldn't stop. She knew she spoke the truth. She would make it her mission in life to destroy Alezza. Manda lunged for the viper, trying desperately to break free. The Maker knew she wasn't that strong, but Manda knew she would be able to slay the woman with her bare hands if given the chance. Alezza laughed and walked away.

Manda forced her remaining words to die on her lips. Words wouldn't help her brother. Although Chris made no sound and was deathly pale, his chest rose and fell in a steady rhythm. Manda contented herself with counting his breaths and listening to the silence. Slowly, calmness settled over her. She felt neither rage nor anger. Her only thought was escape.

Chris would be unable to move. She and Evann would have to leave him, seek help, and come back with force. She didn't like the idea of leaving her brother but if she stayed none of them had a chance.

Something beside Chris twinkled in the light of the fading sun. She shifted for a better view. It was a razor. One of the guards must have dropped it after they had shaved the top of Chris' head. Manda's mind spun. If she could reach it she could use it to cut her ropes. Soon night would fall and the men would sleep. Manda scanned the camp. Only one man hadn't unpacked his bedroll. It appeared Alezza would only post one guard.

As night fell the lone guard started to make his rounds. Manda counted how long it took him to circumnavigate the camp – ten, twenty, thirty, forty, fifty-two counts. That had to be enough time. She watched him pass again and shifted positions, getting as close as she dared to Chris, waiting for full night to fall.

The clouds were thick and blocked most of the moons' light. Occasionally Chris convulsed and moaned, only deepening her conviction. When full night fell she waited for the guard to pass. After five counts she began to roll, praying no one would hear the soft patting of earth. Evann whispered warnings but she didn't acknowledge them. This may be their only chance. The razor had gone unnoticed, but by morning it would be found.

When she reached Chris, Manda spun her body in an arc and searched behind her for the thin blade. After a few short breaths she clasped it. She almost gagged as Chris' hair and blood stuck to her fingers, but she blocked out the horrific images and quickly rolled back. When she saw Evann to her left she stopped, breathless. Heartbeats later the guard passed her without a second glance. She struggled to a sitting position and began slicing her ropes.

Her hands were numb, the ropes tight, so each thrust was sluggish and weak. Whenever the guard began to pass Evann's fervent whispers warned her and she paused in her work. Soon her wrists and fingers were wet with sweat and blood. The razor slipped out of her hands more than she could count, but after a time one of the ropes loosened and she could tighten her grip on the blade. Soon her hands were free.

She waited until the guard walked past before she swiveled her feet and started working again, heedless of the razor slicing the tender part of her ankles. When the ropes broke she pivoted to her former stance and waited for the guard to pass, then she ran to Evann.

Just as she was about to slice his ropes, his eyes stopped her.

"Manda, leave me the razor and go. One alive now is better than two dead later."

Although Manda fought Evann's words, she knew he was right. She dropped the razor in his hand and kissed his cheek.

Then she was running through the woods as branches slapped her face and slashed her bare arms. She stumbled a few times over the hem of her dress but never missed a stride, pushing hard, tasting freedom.

Her frantic breaths created voices in her head. She thought she heard someone whisper her name. She ignored the whisper, telling herself it was only her imagination. It came again, this time with more urgency. She ran faster, suddenly fearful her escape had already been discovered. Then she saw a shadow running beside her. Panic overtook her caution and she opened her mouth to scream just as the shadow sprung. It tackled her, knocking the wind from her lungs. Her assailant pinned her to the ground and covered her mouth.

"My lady, I'm from Ren's guard!"

When she heard Ren's name her body went slack. Ren knew. Ren would help them. Tears stung her eyes as the man on top of her continued. "I've been waiting for a chance to help."

"Ren?"

"I know nothing of what happened, my lady. Quinton sent us . . . me to find you." The man offered a small smile. His face was dirty but his eyes were kind. They pleaded for her forgiveness, for being unable to come sooner. "First Lieutenant Carter Meal at your service. Come, I have a horse."

Without further question he hauled her to her feet just as cries of alarm erupted from the camp. Manda glanced behind her, praying Evann had managed to escape. Blessed Chance let him be safe!

Manda paused as a shrill scream reverberated through the trees. "Hurry, Manda," Carter whispered, a worried glint to his eyes.

Another scream resounded through the night. Manda fell to her knees, covering her ears. Evann! Once again they were punishing him for her actions. The black horse stood silently in the brush only paces from her.

The third scream was far worse than the first.

Manda closed her eyes. She would never forgive herself if she didn't go back. Evann was expendable. Alezza would kill him. Carter shook his head, compassion in his eyes.

"He's already dead, Manda. There's nothing you can do but get to safety and try to save your brother from further torment."

Evann's next scream chilled her to the bone. She broke from Carter's hold. She couldn't leave with a death on her hands. Evann's kind eyes kept appearing in her mind. They were eyes she wanted to see again.

When she broke though the forest she saw Evann kneeling before Alezza and Bort. Evann's left hand was severed. Bort's sword dripped blood. Evann was pale, very pale, but when he saw her, the color returned to his face. He screamed for her to leave him and run. Alezza brought a knife to his heart.

"No!" Manda sprinted forward, watching in horror as Alezza plunged the knife into Evann's chest. Manda fell to her knees just in time to break Evann's fall.

"Evann, blessed fates!"

"Manda," he whispered as a small smile touched his lips. "You're so beautiful." The light left his eyes as his arms went slack.

Someone grabbed her from behind. She ripped free and lunged for Alezza. Bort's arm rammed her neck. She fell back, gasping for air. Alezza put the bloody dagger to her face. With calm precision she trailed the knife's tip down Manda's cheekbone, not cutting her flesh but leaving a thin line of Evann's blood. She wiped the remaining blood on Manda's sleeve, placing blame.

"When will you learn, Manda? Every time you do something I find disagreeable I'll hurt both you and your friends." Alezza paused and glanced down at Evann's lifeless body. "Well, now it will just be your brother. He's weak, Manda. Don't anger me again."

- - -

The port city bustled with commerce. Fraul wasted no time buying supplies, the man at the inn being foremost in his mind. People looked at him curiously. His navy uniform, beaded with glittering decorations, branded him as someone of profound importance. On another day his status would have served its purpose with the women, but a frolic was the last thing Fraul wanted, although his loins told him differently. Albeit he still flashed the handsome women his best smile, pleased to observe most blushed like teenage girls. He had always had a way with women. Most in the Lands were imbeciles, treating women as they would a man or, at the opposite extreme, a fragile flower. Women were neither. Women were complex, beautiful creatures who had to be treated as if they were more precious than gold. In Fraul's mind, if he had one in his arms, that wasn't too far from the truth.

After paying the tailor, a short, squat man with ruddy lips and a pleasant smile, Fraul hurried back to the inn where he had taken a room. The barmaid scurried out just as he walked in. Her eyes went wide at the sight of him, and as if he alone had caused her reason to flee, she brushed past him and trotted down the main street, heedless of anything else around her. Fraul shifted the weight of his packages and watched her departure before turning to proceed up the stairs.

He was unsure if the girl would tell others about her earlier encounter or deny the event ever took place. In either case he wanted to leave the port town as quickly as possible. He was sure the man upstairs would feel the same.

When Fraul opened the door to his room he found things exactly as he had left them. The Avenger still sat on the bed, staring out a side window where the only thing visible was another inn's wall. He was still naked, and he still clutched the betrayal sword. He was in the Avenger daze and would probably remain so for a while longer.

After stacking the supplies, Fraul stretched and sat in an old wooden chair. The room was simple but comfortable enough. The chair, like the ones downstairs, had been mended with burlap and wire. Other furnishings appeared in a similar shoddy condition, but the room had a pleasant feel to it. Whoever tended it took pains to keep it as comfortable as possible. The linens on the bed were crisp, despite their singed color, and a bowl of fruit sat on a small table in welcome. A broken mirror hung above the wash basin, but instead of making the small room look inferior, it gave it character. The bed looked inviting but Fraul remained content to sit and watch the man who stared at nothing.

Fraul thought back to his arrival in Zier. The simple trip had turned into an adventure of a lifetime. First came Ren's conviction, then magic's rebirth, and now he sat in the same room with a magical mystery still revered as being the most terrifying tale of all time. He wondered what the next day would hold, but after a few heartbeats Fraul decided nothing could shock him more than the man sitting before him.

Fraul still couldn't believe it. When the Aaron the Avenger was born it meant someone had been brutally betrayed by a loved one. The Avenger's duty was to find the betrayer and slay him, thus avenging the betrayed.

The Avenger was always born naked, clutching his betrayal sword, far from the object of his interest. The distance was one of the mysteries surrounding Aaron. The pain of the betrayed was said to awaken Aaron's magic. Why then did his magic not take him directly to the betrayed?

Fraul had read a great deal about the myths of the Avenger. The man had always fascinated him, but now, even with Aaron sitting before him, Fraul was unsure he would be able to unlock Aaron's mystery. He didn't recall one story where Aaron communicated with anyone other than the betrayed. Well, that may have been understandable. Once the Avenger discovered the betrayer the electrifying current surrounding him intensified, and if anyone tried to stop him death was instantaneous. Even now Fraul could see the effervescent light circling Aaron, spinning over his skin and making him glow a golden bronze.

Fraul leaned forward, tapping his foot with impatience. When the Avenger was born he had to surmise who he was and what his purpose was before he awoke from the Avenger daze. Most of the time this introspection didn't take longer than a sun's click, but this time it would take Aaron far longer to wake. After all, Aaron hadn't been born since magic's destruction almost four hundred years before.

Although the Avenger's mission sent terror into the bravest of hearts, Fraul had never thought of Aaron as someone who needed to be feared. The story of the Avenger always brought Fraul more sadness than terror. The legend read the Avenger was free to live a normal life after fulfilling his duty. In other words, when Aaron's last mission was over he could live a full life, never to be reborn as the Avenger.

But no one knew when or if Aaron's duty would ever be complete. Over the ages Aaron continued to appear with no sign the legend was factual. Each time, after Aaron killed the betrayer Aaron only lived a brief time before he killed himself. No one knew why Aaron did so. Some thought Aaron had to kill himself in order to be born the next time someone was bitterly betrayed. Others thought Aaron took his own life because after the avenging he had no purpose, and thus no will to live. Still others believed the Avenger loved the people of the world too much to continue witnessing the pain they caused each other.

Fraul had his own theory. He believed the Avenger had too much pain inside, so much so the very pain he avenged ended up driving him mad. The Avenger needed a way to banish the pain. Fraul hoped he would be able to help the man find a way to do just that. He wanted to help Aaron live. Fraul was sure the Avenger would be extremely important in the war about to begin.

As if on its own accord, his foot began tapping the rhythm of the Avenger's song. Fraul began humming to himself:

When the earth moves beneath your feet
And rebirth is in the hearts of men
The betrayer will walk upon the land
And the Avenger will come again.

His love will lead him to the one
His pain will lead him to his prey
But as the betrayed reveals her twin
Will the Avenger be strong enough to stay?

If he can't find the purpose there
If he can't give his love away
The Avenger will walk the land no more
And the world will be betrayed.

Leaning back in the chair, Fraul stroked his goatee and thought about the first stanza. He had always considered the "rebirth" as the rebirth of the Avenger. Now he wasn't so sure. It was clear *The Legend of the Silver Dragon* was truly prophecy. Could the Avenger's song be prophecy as well? If the song was prophecy the "rebirth" could refer to magic's rebirth. This could be the Avenger's last mission, unless he could find a purpose.

Fraul had always firmly believed that things happened for a reason. Had the Maker allowed him to miss Ramie's ship in order to find Aaron, and help him, somehow, find a purpose?

Fraul heaved a sigh and tucked an onerous strand of gray hair back behind his ear. "Hang tight, Ramie, I'm coming. I'm just going to be delayed a little longer than I thought."

As the twin moons rose higher in the sky, shadows crept into the small room. Fraul crossed the floor to the oil lamp beside the bed, noting Aaron's electrifying current emitted the only light in the room.

Although Fraul didn't fear Aaron, he also felt uneasy with something he didn't understand. Before reaching the lamp he stopped and cocked his head to the side. Aaron's breathing had changed. Instead of being soft and disjointed it was smooth and rhythmic, like one just waking from a deep sleep. Aaron heaved a tremendous sigh. The luminous current surrounding him became more frantic with his deepening breaths.

Aaron stood and went to the window. "It begins again, doesn't it?" he whispered, deep voice sounding strange in the silence of the room. "Maybe this time I won't fail."

Fraul cleared his throat, unsure of how to announce himself to the legend before him. When Aaron turned Fraul wasn't staring into the eyes of the Avenger, but into the eyes of Aaron, full of resignation and regret, torment and agony, caring and love. The intensity of the emotions shocked Fraul, but when the shock subsided Fraul decided the emotions fit the face. Fraul's theory of Aaron's life re-formed in his mind. Aaron's pain was too great for him to bear.

Aaron's shoulders relax as he recognized Fraul from the downstairs bar. As he looked around the room a small smile threatened his somber face. "It seems I owe you my thanks."

Fraul nodded as best he could, suddenly overcome with reverent awe. After a brief pause he managed to find his voice. "I'm Captain Fraul Joste of the Yor army."

"Why are you here?"

The look in Aaron's eyes was frightening, but when Fraul realized their severity held no anger, but disbelief, he managed a small smile. "To help you."

Aaron raised his eyebrows. "You touched me?"

"Yes, I touched you. Why?"

Aaron laughed a deep, rich laugh. It echoed around the room with the same intensity as the current flowing over his body. "Either you're a very dumb man or a very smart one. I thought everyone believed if they touched me they would die."

Fraul smiled, Aaron's joy contagious. "I like to think I'm on the side of very smart, but some may have a different opinion." Aaron's laughter boomed louder. Fraul chuckled in mirth, his prior hesitation fleeting. "The legend claims if someone tries to stop you they'll die. It says nothing of helping you. Besides, I've never believed the Avenger would kill innocents. It would go against everything you are. I took my chances."

Aaron extended his arm in greeting. Fraul gripped it under the elbow, allowing Aaron to grip his own. It was an ancient greeting, but one still used on formal occasions. "My name is Aaron Goodenspy, and it's a pleasure. I've never had a friend as I am now. I hope you'll be the first."

The Avenger's conscious touch felt different from when Fraul had helped him to the room. Before, Aaron's current of power glistened off his skin like a mist. Now, Aaron's grip was much more concentrated, and it sent a pulse of energy throughout Fraul. It wasn't unpleasant, but profound.

"I hope you'll allow me to be. The honor would be mine."

A smile lit Aaron's face, and Fraul found himself grinning like a child being offered a taffy.

After a short time of standing with their arms locked in a silent promise of friendship, Fraul became increasingly aware of Aaron's unfurnished wardrobe. Fraul picked up the package the tailor had given him and handed it to Aaron. "I took the liberty of guessing your size. I don't know how you managed to buy your clothes on previous occasions but – "

"I didn't buy them," Aaron said, smile withering, "they were normally thrown at me. Thank you. I'm in your debt."

When the clothes were on a few sparks of power sizzled off Aaron's hands and ran the length of the black fabric with frightening speed. Fraul winced. He had purchased a solid black outfit. The only color adorning the ensemble was a golden clasp securing the cape.

Aaron stepped to the mirror to inspect himself. He raised his eyebrow and looked at Fraul's reflection. "Your favorite color?"

Fraul chuckled and scratched the back of his neck. "Just thought it was fitting."

Aaron didn't respond. He merely sat down and pulled on the black doeskin boots Fraul had purchased. "I must go. The power won't let me rest long. I must find the betrayed."

Fraul wondered how Aaron had become the Avenger. Something tickled his mind but he quickly disregarded it, now intent on traveling with Aaron. "It would be an honor if you would allow me to accompany you. I need to leave as well, and I might be able to provide you with a fair amount of companionship you as you travel."

"I know not where I go."

"That's all right, neither do I."

Aaron stood and sheathed his golden sword. When the betrayed had been avenged the blade would once again turn silver. Aaron studied him for a short time. "I would enjoy company, but I can't allow it. The power isn't dangerous to you now, but as I approach the betrayer it will be."

Fraul shifted his weight and planted his hands on his hips, determined to leave with Aaron. "I understand your concern, but I believe our paths have crossed for a reason. We need each other in some way. Call me superstitious, but that's what I believe."

Aaron studied Fraul for a long time before he spoke. "I was once told I would find a friend who would help me and I him. If you want to accompany me, I will welcome you." As Aaron spoke, the lightning threads rippled faster and the avenging power came into his eyes. "But I warn you, the closer I move toward the betrayed the more focused I become. When I know the betrayer I don't want you near me. If you touch me then, you'll die."

Fraul nodded without fear. He knew he was supposed to be with Aaron. He thought of the song again. There could be no mistaking it. This would be Aaron's last mission, or it would begin his life.

"You said you hoped you wouldn't fail this time. What did you mean? I don't recall you ever failing."

Aaron's face twisted with an indescribable emotion. "I fail every time," he said softly.

A shiver ran down Fraul's spine. "How?" Fraul's voice was so low he almost doubted he had voiced the question at all. The air in the room had filled with something sacred and Fraul didn't want to disturb it.

Aaron straightened, shouldering a bag of supplies. "I can't betray the one I love."

"That doesn't sound like failing to me."

"It's the only way I'll be released from this fate, the only way I can live again."

Fraul felt the sanctity of the room intensify. He glanced about him, a little uneasy. "But that goes against who you are. The Avenger can't betray – "

Aaron held up his hand. "No more. There is time yet before I must make the choice again. I don't want to think of it now. I can't. Love is pain, Fraul. Love is pain."

The saying hung in the air like a cold rain. The suffering in Aaron's voice was an arrow through Fraul's heart. He couldn't imagine what the Avenger felt if Aaron could invoke such intense emotions with only a phrase.

Chapter 10

"Ren."

Quinton's voice was almost unrecognizable. It was low, muffled, and contrary to his usual boisterousness. Ren turned to see his captain pointing to a creature twenty cubits from them. It was the size of a bobcat, standing on its hind legs and rocking its head from side to side, smelling the air. It had large golden eyes and a golden coat that would be hard to see in a sandy setting.

"I've never seen that creature before," Quinton said, an edge of fear to his voice.

Ren took a quick step back. "Markum?"

"It's a nesbit," Markum said.

"Let's get out of here," Quinton said. "Now."

Ren nodded as he studied the weasel-like creature with a rising sense of danger. He had read about the magical creature before. It didn't have good eyesight, but when it locked on its prey's position, it could freeze its quarry in place. Once something was frozen, there was no defense. The nesbit's jaw would open like a dragon and shatter the prey's neck, while its powerful claws dug into the prey's flesh, allowing no means of escape. Nesbits would lock on their carcass and slowly drain the juices over days, leaving the rest to rot.

Ren looked behind him. Some of the men were already taking provisions off their horses. Just as he was about to shout a warning, the creature bounded forward, mouth opening into a vicious snarl, eyes crazed with hunger. Where before the nesbit appeared a harmless scavenger, now it seemed to be something from the Abyss. Its jaws were huge; its teeth, long and yellow; its eyes, intent on the kill. Ren mouth went dry. The nesbit had locked onto something.

"Everybody move! Get on your horses! Leave everything and move! Now!"

The desperation in Michel's voice left no room for question. No one hesitated. A few of the horses screamed a warning as they caught the nesbit's sent. Ren jumped on his mount's back as she reared. Just when he was about to urge her forward, Galvin screamed Neki's name.

Fates, not Neki! Ren couldn't spin his mount fast enough.

Neki sat on the back of his horse, watching as the nesbit's lithe form bounded toward him. Ren was too far away to reach his friend in time. A cry came from his lips as Michel screamed for Neki to jump.

Neki glanced Michel's direction, seeming to wake from a dream. Neki's mount, not Neki, was frozen.

"Move Neki!" Ren's cry seemed to come from far away.

As Neki slid off his horse, the nesbit took to the air. Neki's leg moved over the horse's neck, directly in line with the nesbit's attack. Neki wouldn't be able to move fast enough. Ren watched in horror as the nesbit's gaping jaws began to widen only a hand's width from Neki's calf.

Galvin galloped toward Neki, battle-ax high. Just as the nesbit's jaws were about to clamp hold of Neki's leg, Galvin let the battle-ax fly. The aim was true, and the ax severed the nesbit's head with a hollow "thunk."

As the ax hit the ground, Neki crumbled from the saddle, barely able to catch hold of his horse's reins as it came out of its daze and reared in terror. Galvin skidded to a stop beside him and helped steady the terrified creature.

It took a few heartbeats for Ren to remember to breathe. The men were silent, their faces drained of color. The body of the nesbit lay discarded in the field, its blood staining the lush grass crimson. Galvin's battle-ax looked as foreign in the terrain as snow would in the desert. The playful call of a few birds echoed overhead, oblivious to the terror below them. Their cackling cries sounded perverse as Ren gazed at the blood-soaked field. A soft, warm breeze blew, but instead of providing comfort, it caused Ren's flesh to prickle.

Without a word, Galvin held Neki's horse steady as Neki remounted. Ren waited until Galvin retrieved his battle-ax before turning. He didn't trust himself to speak. No words seemed worthy of his feelings. In the stillness, he knew everyone felt the same. The group's silence was a blanket of protective solace.

If Neki had been taken, the strength of the group would have dwindled, and hope would have been hard to retain. Each person had become a part of the mission, part of the hope of the Lands. No one felt that more so than Ren.

How many magical creatures were already alive? And how many more would appear? Ren shivered as he thought of his worst childhood fear: the Adderiss. She appeared to the wealthiest kings and the most meager beggars. Everywhere the Adderiss went, adders followed. When the Adderiss came for you, she would coat your body with snakes and make demands. If you refused her demands, or if you tried to escape the adders, you would die. It was that simple.

Because the Adderiss was part human, it was unlikely she would be reborn like the nesbit. She was one being, not a breed of creature. Or at least, that was what Ren kept telling himself.

- - -

"Marianne?"

Marianne jumped. Korin grinned as if he knew her thoughts. She blushed and looked down at her hands. She had been daydreaming about him again, and his scrutiny of her only flustered her.

With a glance toward the main party she discovered why Korin had ridden over to her, or why, she thought with a pang of sadness, her father had commanded he do so. She had wandered a fair distance from the main group. She was always daydreaming and wandering. She had never been comfortable among large crowds, much less a troop of soldiers. To think Korin had come to her because he found her charming was ludicrous. Korin was just checking on her, by her father's command.

Korin had lost his smile and was looking at her with what appeared to be genuine concern. He was handsome, with long golden hair, suntanned skin and midnight-blue eyes, so dark they appeared brown in scant light.

Korin had spoken with her many times over the past few months, for reason's that escaped her. At first she held hopes he harbored feelings for her, but she soon discarded the idea. Korin could have anyone he wanted. Why would he want her?

"I saw you at the banquet," Korin said, cheeks flushed from the ride. "You were the prettiest one there."

She blinked in surprise, her shyness briefly forgotten. "How did you see me? Weren't you camped outside the walls?"

His strong eyes turned toward her, causing her stomach to twist into knots. "Yes, but I told the guards I had a message for your father. They let me pass and I peeked inside."

Marianne's heart raced. "You told them you had a message just to look in on the guests?"

Korin blushed and turned away. "Actually, I wanted to make sure you were all right."

"Me?"

Korin shrugged. "I just had a bad taste in my mouth. Maybe I was right after all that happened the next day."

She wanted to say something, do something that would keep him talking, but she didn't know what, so she just sat there gripping the reins like a fool, hoping he wouldn't ride away. When he turned to her again she blinked in shock at the panic in his eyes.

"Did you see what happened, Marianne? Did you see the prince do all those things they say?"

His voice pleaded with her to speak the truth. She twisted the reins and nodded, remembering the dragon's roar, the prince's mad determination, and the woman falling. Yes, she had seen everything.

"So, you believe the sorceress?"

The question took her off guard. She wasn't accustomed to anyone asking her opinion. Could she tell Korin her feelings? She thought of the crown prince's pain and rage as he ran for Valor and Ista. It was terrible. She had never seen anyone so furious, but she didn't believe the accusations. She didn't know why, and she wouldn't voice her feelings to anyone, especially her father. Lorlier was rigorous in his judgments, and if she spoke of believing in Ren, and he did not, he would look at her with disappointment.

Korin's eyes searched her face, stripping her. "Please, Marianne, don't be fearful of me. I'm just concerned people are accepting this woman blindly. Was what you saw so condemning no one will question her intentions?"

He reached over and placed his hand over hers. His thumb absently stroked her forearm, sending a tingling warmth to her heart, melting away any apprehension.

She drew in a breath, unable to turn from his eyes. "I don't doubt Ren went after Valor and Ista. No one does, Korin, but I doubt the charges."

As soon as her words were out, Korin's eyes closed. She glanced down at his hand, still holding hers. His grip was strong; his touch, gentle. She laid her palm over his lower arm, feeling his taut muscles. She blinked, shocked at the way his touch made her forget her reason, and turned to see if he had noticed her caress. He was watching her with eyes filled with something she couldn't describe. It was as if the ocean had come into them. She blushed and took her hand away. His hand stayed where it was, clutching hers with what seemed to be an entreaty for salvation.

"Marianne, I don't know how to tell you this." He paused and turned away. "I'm in love with you."

She opened her mouth to speak, but no words came. She felt dizzy and was barely able to focus on his words.

"You're so unlike me, so gentle and kind. You don't even see how beautiful you are. I know I'll never be able to be with you, but I'll protect you for the rest of my days. Please know I would never intentionally hurt you. Hold me in your heart as you see me now. Know that this is who I truly am."

Korin released her hand, spun his horse, and galloped back to the main group. Marianne watched his departure in a stupor. The warmth of his hand lingered like a fleeting wish. Had she heard him right? A rising sense of elation filled her. Closing her eyes she tilted her head back and let the sun shine down on her face.

He loved her?

Then she remembered his words. Why did he think she would hold him in ill regard? Her elation turned to worry. What was wrong with him? He had been acting strange since leaving Stardom. She had even overheard a few of the men talking about his pensiveness, like he had been sentenced to death.

She scanned the group, unable to find him. Alise would know what to say to him. Alise always knew what to say. Marianne found her sister easily, flirting with a few of the guards. She loved her sister with all her heart, but she had always lived in Alise's shadow. Although she was the eldest, Alise's personality was a bonfire. Hers was only a small spark.

Alise was everything: attractive, outgoing, and intelligent. Marianne was none of the above. Her hopes dwindled.

Korin wouldn't continue to feel as he did. He couldn't love her. How could he?

- - -

"Are you sure she believes you?" Brice asked, raising a dubious eyebrow like he always did when it was up to Korin to complete an assigned task. Brice's pitted face had haunted Korin's nightmares since he arrived in Fest. Korin had never seen another who looked the part of evil as much as Brice. It was the reason, Korin was sure, why Brice had never risen above a lowly stable hand. Many of the men still steered clear of Brice, with good reason. Brice was Ista's eyes in Fest. He saw everything. Although the men didn't know Brice's true profession they felt uncomfortable under Brice's watchful stare, hooded under a veil of dark brows.

"I'm sure."

Korin took the saddle off his white steed, Salve. He loved his horse. Salve was the first thing of value he had ever owned. Lorlier had given Salve to him after he had earned a position in the king's guard. Korin found it ironic the horse didn't have an ounce of color on him since its rider had enough stains to taint all the water in the Lands.

When people questioned the stallion's name Korin would say the horse calmed him, but Salve's name had nothing to do with tranquility. Salve was short for salvation. One day he planned to ride free on Salve, free from the pain, the suspicion, and the guilt.

Brice watched Korin rub Salve's flank. Korin felt like a mouse under a hawk's glare, but he had learned to live with it long ago. Brice wasn't as nefarious as some, and Korin forced himself to be pacified that Brice, instead of one of the others, had been assigned to Fest. After a long silence, Brice grinned and nodded.

"We're in a good position."

Korin leaned against Salve and glared at the man. "It won't matter, Brice. My confession will only gain us a little information, nothing more. Lorlier would never marry one of his daughters to a commoner."

"But the king likes you, Korin. You've been promoted from a serving boy to a castle guard, to a swordsman in the king's guard, all within two years. It isn't unheard of for a king to give one of his valuable subjects some land, and if you have land – "

"Dragon's dung, Brice!" It was a phrase Korin had picked up from Lorlier. "Even if Lorlier granted me land that alone wouldn't be enough to bargain for marriage. I still wouldn't be in line for the throne. Davis will take control once Lorlier's gone."

Brice, whittling on a stick, continued to stare at Korin with devious eyes. "But Davis won't be here."

Korin tried to hide his shocked expression. He should have guessed killing Davis was Ista's plan. Taking a life was nothing to her. Korin forced up the emotionless mask he always wore around the Collective. "I see," he said, but not too quickly, too quickly would mean suspicion of his loyalty. "But I won't harbor any vain hopes I'll be allowed her hand."

"That's wise," Brice said, turning his attention back to the piece of wood he was carving into the shape of a voluptuous woman.

Korin whispered words to Salve, suppressing the urge to retreat from Brice. If he left immediately Brice would question him. So Korin waited a degree of the sun, the shadow of Ista's hold hovering over him like a promise of death, before ambling toward a nearby stream. Dipping his water sack in the chill water, he released a loud breath. He sat for a time, watching the water trickle over the rocks and wind its way back into the forest. From an overhanging branch a raven shrieked its displeasure at his presence. Korin's lips twisted into a grimace.

"I know I don't belong, my friend. I know that all too well."

Korin sat back on the grass as he felt Ista's invisible noose around his neck tighten with each breath. All he wanted was escape. When he left Ista's camp over two years prior he had hoped he could find a way to rid himself of the pain. Now he knew escape was impossible. He would never be free of the needles.

Korin choked back his terror as he thought of digging up Bor's grave. When the dragon had ripped open Bor's chest at the dragon match, Korin hoped if he just saw Bor's body he would discover the answer he was looking for: how Ista controlled the Collective. He had discovered the truth. Needles were in his mind. Death was his only escape.

When he had been at the camp there had been no talk of the Maker, only of the Watcher, and pain and hurt and anguish. His life seemed to be something out of a nightmare, a nightmare from which no one ever woke, only fought to survive. But during those years he had trusted something else existed, something opposite of pain.

Then he had witnessed what he knew in his heart was real: goodness, love, and laughter. He had found it when Ista finally allowed him to leave the camp: in Lorlier, in Marianne, in the men who called him friend. Where before he wanted escape, now he wanted salvation: salvation so one day he would be able to look those he loved in the eye and feel no remorse; salvation so he could have a chance to atone for his crimes; salvation so he could finally touch a woman in love, have a friend without secrets, and exist without fear of discovery.

But how could he ever have that? Even if he gained his freedom he had committed so many acts that would damn his soul he didn't know if salvation was possible for him.

He had played a part, looked out of his own eyes, but repressed his soul, trusting he would one day be able to freely choose what he did and did not do. He had worn a mask of survival that had fooled them all. He had told himself he was only the instrument, not the offender.

But was he? How did fighting for survival, for life, make it right to do what he had done? He could argue he hadn't known better, but he knew if he was sent back in time he would do those unspeakable horrors again if one day he thought he could be free.

No, there was no salvation for him. He was a fool to believe it. "Forgive me, Marianne." It was over. Ista had won. Only she knew the secret behind the needles, and that knowledge would never be revealed.

He had witnessed how life could be with Lorlier and his family. The king thought him a friend; Marianne looked at him as a man. Now, because he knew the meaning of love, it was harder to release the hope of salvation he had clung to for so long.

Lorlier's family had given him love, honor, duty, and friendship. They had given him the strength he needed to face death. He couldn't let Ista destroy their family. Lorlier would be devastated if Davis was killed, and Marianne . . .

Praise the Fates he loved her! She was everything he was not. Her heart was pure. She had never harmed another, even by words, and would die before she did so.

He wet his hand and rubbed his face until it stung, wishing it were as easy to cleanse himself on the inside. It was time for him to decide his fate.

As he saw it he had three options: to give in to the pain and follow Ista, to reveal all he knew and be killed by the people he loved, or to kill himself.

Giving in to the pain was something he couldn't conceive. He had never done so, and now that he knew how to feel other emotions he would never consider converting to Ista's side. He knew the righteous thing would be to reveal all he knew to Lorlier, but how could he reveal his knowledge when he would be looked upon with disgust and vanquished or killed by the only person who had ever put any faith in him? No matter how much pain he had felt in his life he couldn't handle the pain of Lorlier's shame.

Korin released a breath, expelling his last hope. He knew what he had to do. He had to end the threat to Lorlier and his family. He had to kill Brice, and then kill himself. It was the only way to die with some honor. Ista wouldn't claim him, and the people he loved would never know him to be the vile person he was.

His life would end without one truth. He would die before he was allowed to prove he was capable of love. He thought of the Stardom guard he had seen the night he had dug up Bor's grave. The man had looked just like him. Korin didn't know how, but maybe in some way, the guard knew the truth.

"Korin, I need to talk to you."

Korin bolted up in alarm and spun to see Lorlier's shocked expression at his fright.

"Did you use magic just then, Korin?" Lorlier grinned. "I don't think anyone could move that fast on his own accord." Lorlier hazel's eyes danced with mirth. Korin's chest tightened. The king only revealed his winsome humor to a chosen few.

"No, my lord," Korin replied, bending to pick up the water bag that was now leaking on his boots. He didn't want to think about magic. Magic was something he had wished for his entire life if only to learn how to escape the presence and the pain. Now he knew escape was impossible.

Lorlier lost his smile, causing the shadow cast by his vast height to shiver on the forest floor. Many of Lorlier's soldiers feared their king, but Korin had grown to understand Lorlier's actions stemmed from love: the love of his family, the love of the land. If you spoke the truth and had good intentions you had nothing to fear from Lorlier.

"I heard you felt the pain when the Quy was reborn."

Korin's heart quickened. "Yes, my lord." Although Korin knew Lorlier wouldn't hold him in ill regard because of magic, he was unsure how the man would react to it. The king relied on physical strength and cunning. Korin suspected magic's rebirth wouldn't settle well with Lorlier.

"What do you think?"

"My lord?"

"I know it's an odd question, Korin, but I'm just a little, shall I say . . . unnerved by the entire affair. I don't like battling unforeseeable enemies. Magic's rebirth will cause far more than battles. It will bring war. War is something I know about but war and magic together? I don't like it. And I don't know what to think."

"I don't know if anyone knows what to think, my lord."

Lorlier sat on a large rock and looked at Korin with a touch of unease. "The people at Stardom seem to."

Korin almost smiled. The king looked foreign in the serene setting. Korin was used to seeing Lorlier in the castle surrounded by fine things, or on the back of a horse with weapons in hand. The calm trickling of the water and the gentle sway of the trees was lost on Lorlier. Lorlier didn't heed the peaceful things of nature. Lorlier was a man of action.

"They knew, and I don't like it. It's almost as if they knew too much."

Korin ground his teeth, desperately wanting to reveal the truth but fearing it more than death itself. "What does your instinct tell you, my king?"

Lorlier heaved a tremendous sigh. "My instinct goes back and forth. First it says Valor was full of dragon's piss to pronounce Ren a traitor but when I look at the evidence, well, let's just say I don't know how long a man can deny his own eyes."

Korin hid his disappointment. He wanted to tell Lorlier Ren wasn't the one to fear, but if Brice suspected his deceit he would be the first to die. Then he would be unable to save Lorlier the heartache of losing his only son. Korin risked a glance in Brice's direction. The man was watching, and the presence inside Korin's mind tightened as if aware of his thoughts. Korin's insides twisted into knots. He had an obligation to steer Lorlier in the right direction. Although he needed to be cautious, he could still offer Lorlier some semblance of the truth and hope the king would take it to heart.

"My lord, I wasn't there when the power was reborn but I've overheard talk. Ren has never been portrayed as someone who hungered for power. On the contrary, he was the antithesis of Wyrick. Still, most of the men in your guard believe the woman. I don't know if their belief is due to their hunger for the Quy or if they truly believe the accusations, but I can tell you this . . . "

Lorlier leaned forward, intent on what Korin was about to reveal. Korin felt his gut wrench. He didn't deserve the trust in Lorlier's eyes.

"I'm questioning the validity of her claim. If she's a four hundred year old sorceress she could have staged everything. She could have charmed the guards who confirmed Ren's presence in Wyrick's chamber, she could have charmed Ren himself, and you mustn't forget she's ruling by Valor's side. Peaceful? I have my doubts."

Lorlier studied him in silence. A band of sweat broke out on Korin's forehead. He felt as if he were being stripped of all knowledge, searched for verity. After a few dragon's breaths, Lorlier chuckled and Korin relaxed.

The king slapped his thigh. "How is it the most obvious thing was never challenged? Maker curse it! Ista can't be trusted."

Dread inched up Korin's spine. He wanted Lorlier to disbelieve Ista, but not adamantly. Lorlier was the type to give credit where credit was due.

"You'll be honored for this, Korin."

"No!"

Lorlier took a step back, surprised. Korin flushed and cleared his throat. "My apologies, my lord. I just feel caution would be wise. Openly denying Ista will cause her to rise against you. If you announce your belief in the crown prince your kingdom will be her next target."

The king creased his brow. "I don't like being neutral, but you're right again." Korin expelled a relieved breath. Lorlier didn't seem to notice Korin's worry. Instead, he smiled like a proud father. "Do you think you could learn the Quy without training under anyone else?"

Korin tried to decipher Lorlier's words. What was the king asking? How could he reply? He already knew how to use it. Although he had never put it into practice, he knew. "I suppose I could try, but I don't know how successful I'd be."

"I have books on how to use the Quy."

Korin blinked in surprise. To his knowledge no training book remained except for the few Ista had taken before the Alcazar burned. "I thought only some minor histories remained."

"That's what people think. During the Wizard War Barracus destroyed all the training books he could find, those at the Alcazar burned in the fire, but the wizard in Fest hid some books before Barracus captured the castle. They weren't enough to cause Barracus suspicion, but enough, I'm sure, to begin powerful training."

Korin couldn't speak as his hopes of escape resurfaced. Those books might be able to tell him how to counter the needles. Maybe, just maybe, he wouldn't have to do what he had previously planned.

"Korin, if it's as you suspect, and my soldiers are hungry to learn, they'll soon grow restless if I don't give them leave to train in Zier. I need to teach them here. The sooner the better."

Korin could barely focus on Lorlier's words as his mind spun with possibilities, but in the next breath his hopes sank to the pit of his stomach. Ista would never allow him to teach others if she knew about the books.

"I want you to learn the power and teach my people, especially Alise. I know she'll begin on her own, and it worries me. She's headstrong and may go too far too fast. I don't want her to injure herself. When we reach Fest, please begin research. The Maker knows I never knew I would need the books, never even wanted to think about them, but it looks like the time is upon us."

Korin nodded, mind reeling. "Yes, my lord, it would be my honor."

Lorlier smiled. "I knew I could count on you, Korin."

When the king turned away Korin became desperate. He needed those books, but if Ista discovered them he wouldn't be long for this world.

Before he lost his nerve, Korin cleared his throat. "My lord, I do have a request."

Lorlier turned to face him. "Ask."

"I don't think anyone else should know about the books, not even the soldiers I teach. They could be dangerous in the wrong hands."

Lorlier nodded. "I agree. The knowledge of them ends here."

Korin almost cried out in relief. He had a chance. At last, no matter how small, he had a chance.

After Lorlier had taken a few steps toward camp he paused and turned back, worry spreading over his strong features. "Korin, I'm concerned about Marianne."

Korin felt the heat rise to his face. The king would never approve of a man such as himself yearning for one of his daughters. "My lord, she doesn't have the power. Why are you worried about her?"

Lorlier heaved a weary sigh. "I fear she may one day take her life. Depression runs in her mother's line. It has claimed many of them."

Korin's eyes widened. Ista had told him to befriend one of Lorlier's daughters, and he had chosen Marianne because she intrigued him. She was shy and distant, but also caring and gentle. She was terrified of strangers, but when someone needed help or was fraught with anguish Marianne would reach past her fear and touch them in some way. When he had first arrived in Fest one of the guard had lost his wife and child to a sickness. Marianne had gone to his home, heedless of the contamination, and sat with him while he mourned. Her compassion had touched something in Korin he couldn't begin to explain, but he had never been held when he cried or comforted when he feared. To him, Marianne was an angel, a beautiful, gentle angel.

He hadn't known about the depression. Had he in some way caused it?

"Depression? My lord, I had no idea. I fear I may have caused it."

Lorlier's brows furrowed. "Korin, I've seen you with her. You seem to calm her, bring her out of her shell. You caused nothing of the sort."

Korin shifted his weight, heart laden with worry. "My lord, I didn't have a good feeling about the ball. I may have caused her distress when I voiced my concerns. I had no idea she suffered from depression. Please, forgive me if I caused her worry."

"Nonsense, Korin. I think it has something to do with this magic business. She doesn't have the power, but she may have something related. Can you look into it for me?"

"I would be honored, my lord."

"Please, call me Lorlier in private." Instead of turning to go, Lorlier walked forward and clasp Korin's shoulder. "Thank you, Korin. When we arrive in Fest I will give you a new rank and title, something to make you proud."

Korin watched as Lorlier walked back to camp, unsure of what to focus on first: magic, Marianne, the needles, Brice or Davis. But before he could focus on anything Lorlier turned once again.

"I would be happy if you would spend more time with Marianne, if you . . . well, you're good for her. Try to give her more confidence, like you. She's very dear to me. I worry about her more than anyone knows."

Korin was left standing with an ache in his chest. He didn't want to fail Lorlier, but Ista was powerful and he felt impending doom gathering around him. He struggled against the presence to cling to the peace, to the hope of life, but he knew his time was short. He would be unable to fool Ista much longer. His time was coming. The rope was tightening. But he vowed, before the rope hung him, he would do his best to cripple the monster that had raised him.

- - -

Ista stepped forward and ran her hands over the Red Eye. She could feel its power residing within, churning for release. A small smile lit her face. Soon, everything would begin. Although she had underestimated the Chosen's power she had predicted his actions with flawless precision. He was far too concerned about his friends, far too predictable.

After Ren's escape she hadn't tried to follow him. His power required her to begin the second phase of her plan. She had thought of every contingency long ago. With each step Ren moved closer to his demise. The prophecy the wizards had placed so much faith in would be his undoing. A hollow laugh escaped her throat. When Zorc came out of hiding he would find the Chosen a broken man. She would crush Zorc's last hope and force him to bow at her feet to reclaim what had been stolen from him – his precious Christa.

Ista chuckled as the spirit inside her stirred in discomfort. If Christa's spirit dispersed without first rejoining with her other revenant held in Zorc's body, Christa's soul would be forever trapped in the Realm of Shadows, forever searching for her other self. Christa would become a soul without completion, a soul with no place to go.

Imagine Zorc's reaction when he discovered his redhead beauty could be lost for eternity! But Ista would be kind. Zorc would have a choice. Oh yes, he would have a choice. Ista's festering hand moved over the Red Eye as if caressing a long-lost lover.

"Soon I'll call and you'll come, Barracus. Soon you'll be mine to command."

Ista dipped her hand in the basin of water and wiped her brow as her thoughts turned back to the Chosen. The poor prince, thinking he had escaped her. He would be surprised to discover she knew exactly where he was, and exactly where he was going. Did he think she was fool enough to leave anything of importance at the camp? Did he think she wouldn't have had the foresight to leave something behind that would aid in his undoing?

All in the castle, and soon all in the Lands, would believe the accusations against Ren. In fact, those with the Quy would agree to anything if only to be thrown one morsel of knowledge. Yes, things were working out much better than planned.

Already all of Newlan was hers. Soon all of Oldan would be as well. Pity Ramie hadn't wished to join her, but that was of no concern. Before long one of her pawns would declare Ramie an ally of the prince and attack the Augustus empire. The throne of Yor would fall and Ramie Augustus would fall with it.

Ista pushed those thoughts aside. It was foolish to dwell on subjects of little concern. She needed to focus on the Red Eye. She caressed its form, sensing the power within yearning for freedom.

"Soon, Barracus," she whispered, gazing into its fiery depths. The cloudy interior shifted in response. Ista licked her lips and yelled for a guard.

When the door behind her opened she didn't turn. She didn't need to see the guard to know his face teemed with apprehension. Although she was revered as the savior, everyone cowered in her presence. A small sneer formed on Ista's lips as the slight glow of the Red Eye illuminated her molten face with crimson flame.

The next day she would begin inserting the needles in those with magic who had chosen to remain behind. But that was the next day.

Now she wanted to concentrate on the Red Eye.

"Bring Lazo to me. I need to question him again."

The door clicked shut behind her.

Soon now, she would be unstoppable.

Chapter 11

As Sass slowed her mount, she wiped her brow with her forearm and licked her lips. After a few attempts at swallowing she finally managed to send some saliva down her parched throat. She squinted up at the sun, wishing she had paid more attention to her pedagogues when they discussed navigation and geography. Streams were scarce in the territory between Zier and Ketes, but they did exist if you knew where to look.

Her mount nickered and Sass sent a silent prayer to the Maker she would arrive in Ketes before her horse collapsed. She didn't know much about horses, but she did know they couldn't ride forever, especially without water. Whispering praises for its efforts, Sass patted the roan's neck and surveyed the landscape: no stream, no sign of life and nothing in either direction that looked any different than the terrain of the past day.

The Nolands, the lands north of the Sierra Mountains, consisted of rocky soil with sporadic, spindly, knee-high plants displaying exquisite purple flowers. Despite the land's rugged beauty it held no promise of water, food or shade. The Nolands went for leagues only to end abruptly where the coastal mountains became low enough to allow the moisture of the Neoteric Sea to escape the mountains' peaks and settle in to replenish the dry soil. But the Nolands were vast and she was sure she had yet to cross half their length.

When she had left Stardom she was in such a hurry she had neglected to grab water skins, food or any other item she might need. She chastised herself for being so stupid. No matter how hard she rode she wouldn't arrive in Ketes for days. What if she got lost? She had no weapon, and she knew nothing about catching game. How was she supposed to survive?

Tears stained her eyes before she blinked them away. She couldn't give in to her emotions. She had to focus, not only for her brother but also for Ren and the Newlan nation.

When Paul had seen the gates of Stardom swinging open after Ren's escape, he had ordered her to flee to their father. She had pleaded with Paul to come with her but he insisted on staying behind. Their conversation wasn't long, but Paul's eyes said it all: their cousin was fighting for his life and they would be too if they stayed inside the gates of Stardom.

Sass blinked back her fear and prayed to the Maker to keep Ren safe. Her father would know what to do. Bostic always knew what to do.

The sun beat down with a vengeance and as the day progressed she began to see water that wasn't there. She chased after streams that turned out to be nothing more than barren earth, and soon she had little idea of where she was. All she could do was try to stay north, hoping she moved in the general vicinity of Ketes.

The day turned to night, and although she found relief from the sun the darkness did nothing to help her thirst. Her roan pushed on, but Sass could tell the animal was tiring. She would have been afraid if she weren't bone weary. As the night deepened Sass leaned on the horse's neck, letting its movement lull her into a fitful sleep.

Just as dawn broke and the scorching sun rose to scrape her blistered neck, the roan lurched into a gallop. Sass jerked awake and yanked the spirited animal to a halt. Sass gaped at the vast expanse of trees rising before her, jetting from the rocky soil in stark contrast to the landscape as if daring the thistles of the Nolands to violate their domain. She could see no end to the trees to either side or ahead.

Although they weren't wide, they were tall, and because their branches were only as long as a man's arm and climbed the trunks in a ladder-like fashion they appeared to be prodigious even in width. Their rich bronze bark soaked up the sunlight and sparkled with alluring charm. Their bare branches ended in a bud of three long, thick, dark leaves, almost two hand spans in length. The vision was almost too magnificent to believe.

The cool breeze from the depths of the trees continued to hit her face, and after blinking a few times the image became even more vivid.

Sass dismounted and cautiously approached the trees, sure their image would soon disappear. It did not. She heard running water in the distance as her horse pawed the ground in irritation. Sass touched the closest tree with a tentative hand. The bark was smooth, not rough like most trees, and a slight tingle shivered through her fingers and up her arm. Sass jumped back, startled.

She yearned to plunge into the shadows and find the water she so desperately needed, but the forest hadn't been there on her way to Zier. No forest existed in the Nolands. Sass chewed her lower lip as she peered through the trees. Her mount continued to paw the ground, snorting in annoyance at her hesitation. She cooed to it, trying to calm its anxious movements.

The forest stretched endlessly in both directions. It almost appeared as if the ground had cracked and a whole new world had erupted with its breaking. Tears of frustration stung her eyes. Traveling around it would waste days, possibly weeks. She had no food or water. She couldn't risk being in the Nolands for that long.

The bronze trees shimmered in the sunlight. The longer she looked at them the less apprehension she felt. Why was she so fearful? It was just a forest. And it had water. When a small doubt tickled her mind the forest's cool breeze touched her face and the doubt floated away. She stepped forward, leading her horse by the reins, and touched one of the trees. This time the tingle that shivered throughout her body was welcoming. She smiled. Her apprehension was silly.

As soon as she made her decision to enter the forest, she felt elated, almost drunk. Stepping into the trees she saw a path she hadn't noticed before. It was well worn, with only a slight amount of grass and clover dotting its dusty trail. The sunlight filtered through the treetops and lit the path in a golden glow. Sass smiled and quickly mounted the roan. There was nothing to fear.

The roan cantered down the path without instruction. The smell in the woods wasn't unpleasant but it was different from the open air. It smelled of heat, almost a burning, and was tinged with a trace of honeysuckle. She found that odd because she saw no honeysuckle, but the dense trees made it impossible to see beyond the path before her. The sweet-smelling vines were probably prevalent away from the path.

A clear stream appeared in the distance. Its echoing caress on the rocks made her shiver with delight. Her mount surged forward and soon they were both gulping the water as if it would soon disappear. When she finally took a breath Sass laughed with pleasure. Water had never tasted so sweet! It even tasted of honeysuckle! She couldn't get enough. As soon as her thirst was quenched, she bent to drink again.

The sunlight brushed her skin with comforting warmth. She leaned back against a tree and let the sounds of the woods drift over her. Every few heartbeats she brought a handful of the sweet water to her lips. Her back tingled with the same sensuous sensation she had experienced before, and the soft breeze on her bare neck whispered for her to give in to sleep. Her brows furrowed as a wisp of a thought escaped her. There was something she was supposed to do, wasn't there? Her eyes became heavy as she allowed her body to melt into the tree.

Sleep came quickly, and she dreamed of Paul riding with her on the roan. Paul sat behind her, humming a tune, but then Paul became Ren and –

Sass's eyes flew open. Her mission crashed over her with the force of the ten winds. She had to reach Ketes! She had to warn her father!

The day had almost escaped her. She had been asleep for some time. The tingling in her body became a dull pain when she moved from the tree. The faster she walked to her horse the more severe the pain became. When she finally reached the roan she had almost lost consciousness, but the roan seemed to know her thoughts and quickly trotted down the path. She had to dismount frequently to get sick in the trees. The sweet smell of the water was now replaced with the other smell of the forest, a burning. Sass gagged time and again, hungering for more water, but passing every stream she happened upon with grim determination.

The breeze began to feel rough even though it moved without force, and the shimmering trees taunted her to give in to her desires of rest and sleep. Sass began to panic, spurring her horse faster, wondering how far the woods continued. She had been riding for what seemed like days, and the path just went on and on, but she knew she traveled north. She kept the setting sun at her left shoulder.

She slowed her mount and tried to calm her rising sense of dread. When she noticed fresh tracks on the path her hopes lifted. She followed them, hoping they would lead her out of the forest. Luckily, they were bearing north as well.

Another stream came into view. The craving began again. She leaned over to heave what little of the water remained. She slowed the roan to a stop and tried to regain her composure. Her body trembled, hungering for the sweet liquid, yet she was determined to push on. When her eyes landed on the large tree beside the stream her breath caught.

It looked familiar. Her throat tightened as she looked down. Hoof prints dotted the bank. They continued through the stream to the other side. She jumped the creek, stifling a cry, and forced the roan into a gallop. She continued until she reached another stream.

Sass looked at the tracks. They were fresh tracks on top of fresh tracks.

They were her tracks.

She was going in circles.

A rustling sounded next to her. She spun, peering through the dense trees. Although she knew it was still light out it was darker than death in the woods.

Without warning her horse reared, releasing a shrill wail, and she was thrown. Her horse galloped onward down the path.

Something knocked her down. She turned and jerked on instinct, tossing whatever it was off, and quickly regained her footing. Plunging into the heart of the forest, she tried to lose whatever had attacked her.

Something caught her ankle and she fell. Her attacker locked its arms around her neck and squeezed. A scream escaped her lips but it was truncated by the creature's tightening grip. Sass flailed on the ground, trying to tear free, but the creature held on. She felt the tingling warmth of the trees flow through her body, making her weak. She collapsed, sobbing into the cool earth, knowing it was hopeless to resist.

"Calmed thee, haven't we?" came a raspy voice.

Sass didn't want to look. She didn't want to know what kind of creature had that voice. The burning smell had become more potent. She realized it seeped from whatever spoke.

"Up then and look at me," the creature whispered in her ear.

The creature moved off, but Sass remained frozen on the ground, face in the dirt.

"Look at me now!"

The creature's shout echoed through the forest with such force Sass turned to defend against the blow she knew would come. When her eyes fell on the being above her, her screams followed. The man was small, only about waist high, and he was burnt an ebony black, with wrinkles covering his naked body. He had waist-length white hair and white eyes. His lips bared fangs bigger than any creature she had ever seen.

His thin body leaned closer. She pushed herself backwards, but she couldn't move fast enough. The creature straddled her chest, locking her in place. Sass closed her eyes and turned her head.

The creature's hot breath exploded in her ear. "What do you hunger for, my lust?" he asked, lips brushing against her skin. "I can grant you anything you wish, anything at all. You're a beauty. I can give you all."

The creature began to sing, softly at first, but then his song escalated into a high pitch that drifted through the air with a life of its own. It was the most beautiful voice Sass had ever heard. She felt it weaving its way through her, caressing her body from the inside. She twisted in the creature's grip, trying to resist the seduction of the song, but soon her inhibitions gave way. She leaned back into the earth as the man sung of her beauty and shape. His hands brushed her bare neck. She forced her eyes shut, not wanting to end the feelings inside her by looking at the small, wrinkled man. An ache began to burn in her loins and she stifled a cry when the song took her to heights she hadn't known existed.

The breeze sent a shiver over her as the creature's hands explored her. Sass tried to focus on her mission but quickly shoved it aside. The song crashed over her, praising her shape, referring to parts of her body she yearned to know better. When the explosion came her eyes flew open, but instead of the blackened horror she remembered, the man standing above her was the most exquisite being she had ever envisioned.

The last of the sun's rays fell behind him, caressing his taut form. Blond hair fell around his face, tickling his shoulders. His movements were fluid, graceful. He studied her with the most beautiful green eyes she had ever seen. Still humming the tune he engulfed her mouth in his own. The song moved inside her with more force. She almost lost consciousness as the pleasure heightened.

"Do you want me, my desire?" he hummed into her neck.

"Yes, please." Sass tried to say more but it took all her strength to pull him closer.

He smiled as he caressed her cheek and moved his lips to her neck. She neared the apex and remained there, almost touching, close enough not to care about anything else. All that mattered was the apex. She had to have it. She heard herself begging, pleading for him to begin. And then he did. She broke through the apex, and climbed higher and higher – soaring. There was no end.

When he tore away she was unprepared. The tingling became a searing pain. The song seemed hollow as he rose above her, face masked in shadow. She writhed on the ground, frantic.

"Please," she whispered.

He stepped back, letting his voice fade to nothing. The pain inside her was breathtaking. She reached for him but he retreated, and when the moonlight stole over his face, his green eyes shone with rabid longing. His smooth chest heaved, muscles rippling. "I want you now," he sang.

She nodded, unable to find the words to respond as the need welled within her.

"Will you give me all of you?"

His song began again as he engulfed her lips in his own. The song inside her was moving high, but remained just below the peak, tantalizing. She moaned in confusion.

"Can you give me your life, my love?" he sang.

She struggled to grasp his words. She clawed at him, shaking with need. She would give him anything, do anything to see how high she could go.

Something tugged at her mind, something she had to do, but she lost sight of her other aim as she allowed the magic of him to seduce her – magic. She had to do something about magic – and Ren. Ren was in trouble.

"I just need to give my father a message," Sass said. "Then the rest of my life is yours, is ours."

"Give your father a message?"

She pulled him closer. "Yes, just give him a message."

"I can send you to your father," he whispered in her ear, "if you will give me the rest of your life."

She reached the peak. "Yes," she mumbled. She crested the peak, rising higher and higher until she forgot everything else. Higher she went, so high her screams were silenced by her own lips as the pleasure sucked her dry of everything but breath.

When it was over, it wasn't over. It continued as she lay shivering on the ground, clinging to the waves breaking inside her, but then the song ended and he started to laugh. The laugh was in the raspy voice she had first heard. It intensified until all the waves were pulled from her. When she was able to force her eyes open, she cowered back. The man above her was the blackened form she had first seen, only younger. He was still small but now had a more muscular build, with white-blond hair and piercing green eyes. Something was wrong. An ominous feeling inched up her spine. All feeling was gone from her limbs. Sass's eyes moved over her body. Her skin was ashen, wrinkled – old.

He had taken her life. Maker of Fates, he had taken her life!

She rolled to her side and sobbed in the dirt. Triumphant laughter echoed around her like thundering rain. She opened her mouth to scream.

But nothing would come. All breath and life were draining from her with terrifying speed. As soon as she thought she could take no more, his laughter was gone. Sass lifted her head and found herself in front of her father's castle. The man had kept his end of the bargain. Now she could deliver her message.

An alarm sounded as guards hovered above her, demanding she reveal herself and her purpose. She recognized Raymond, her father's most trusted guardian and her own second father. His face was hard, but when their eyes met a flash of fear touched his strong brow.

"Reveal yourself."

"Raymond, it's me." Her voice was so soft she could barely distinguish it from the other sounds around her. "Please, Raymond, take me to my father."

Raymond's dark eyes widened as he recognized her features. When he opened his mouth to speak, no words came. She heaved a sigh as he lifted her in his strong arms. The guards around them fell back as Raymond moved with quick, careful steps to the castle entrance.

She was tired, so very tired. She wanted to close her eyes, but she did not, knowing as soon as she yielded to sleep she would die. She had to deliver the message to her father, and then she could give up. Resting her head on Raymond's broad shoulder, she watched the memories of childhood pass her by. She felt like crying but couldn't. There wasn't that much strength in her.

Raymond bent and opened the door to her father's study. She turned her head in time to see her father rising from his chair, surprised at the interruption without announcement. She loved her father with every fiber of her being. He was tall and strong, with gentle brown eyes that lit like the dawn whenever she entered the room. The beard he had grown the past year suited him well. It gave him a powerful appearance while softening the lines of his face. Sass felt Raymond draw a breath to speak, but nothing came. A drop of moisture fell on Sass's cheek, but she barely felt it. She felt very little of anything.

When Raymond stopped before of the king, Sass felt a sense of dignity rise inside her. She hadn't failed her brother. She hadn't failed Ren. She had reached her father, and now everything would be all right.

Bostic's face drained of color.

"Sass?" His voice was soft. If she hadn't been looking directly at him she may have been unable to make out her name.

Bostic took her from Raymond and sat down. He brushed the hair away from her face and smiled down at her, a silent tear trickling down his check.

"Oh, Sass, my precious, my gorgeous, what's happened to you?"

Sass fought the urge to tell him all the things she had neglected to tell him over the years: how much she loved him, how much she admired him, and how much each day she had spent with him meant to her. But she couldn't. With each breath she took she drew closer to death. The longer she delayed the less she could reveal.

"Father, I don't have much time. I must tell you why I've come. Ren's in trouble. Valor said he murdered Wyrick. Valor has taken over Stardom. When I fled the castle was in chaos. Ren's men were captured or killed, and other lands were joining in the fight. Magic has been reborn, Papa, but Ren is the one to trust. Don't believe anyone who says otherwise. I, your only daughter, am telling you to trust in your only son who is still fighting for Ren, and me, who now dies for him. I love you, Father. I love you more than anything I've ever known."

Bostic screamed his daughter's name as her eyelids slipped closed.

"I love you too, Sass, my puppet." Bostic rocked his lifeless daughter back and forth. "I love you too."

Chapter 12

"She's waking, Bane," Similian thought, careful not to disturb the other presence inside him. He didn't want her to be frightened. He wanted her to like him. She had a beautiful soul, like Mezuzah. He was glad he had flown over nine centuries to meet Mezuzah, although he would never admit that to the Bane.

"Don't scare her. Let her approach us," the Bane thought in reply.

"Where am I?" The girl's voice was soft yet strong. The dragon liked it. He liked it multiples better than the lying Bane's voice.

"You're in Similian the Vicious Silver Dragon!" Sim declared, almost too loudly. He shuddered, hoping he hadn't scared her. He knew he could be frightening. After all, he was the most ferocious beast in existence.

"Similian," the Bane chastised. "Don't try to claim her. Although I didn't foresee it, she will be critical to the quest. Until I know her role you mustn't let her begin to merge with you. Child, you must fight for who you are."

Sim felt the turmoil inside the girl's presence. He knew her thoughts. She was thinking about the man who had saved her individuality by merging her body with her spirit, the one Sim found himself almost liking, the one who had looked at him with no fear or desire to kill. Sim had never had anyone look at him like that, with the respect he deserved.

The girl tried to make her body move as she remembered her life. The dragon knew she couldn't move because she was in him now, but the action of her trying to leave shook him with discomfort. The Bane never tried to leave, so Sim had never known the feeling, but it was extremely unpleasant.

"Be still, child. Don't fight," the Bane silently commanded. "You must use your energy to remember your identity or you'll be forever lost inside Similian. The man who sent your body in after you saved you, but that's all he can do. You must do the rest. If you don't fight to remember, you'll become the dragon. Tell me about yourself. If you begin to forget, I'll remind you."

The girl was silent for a short time. "How do you remember then?"

"I have the Quy. It helps me remember. You have nothing to help you."

The girl shifted. Similian could feel her determination. "I have my faith."

Sim almost chuckled. He knew he liked her. She was already defying the Bane.

"I hope it's enough, my dear. I hope it's enough."

Sim scowled. The Bane never gave encouraging words, only harped on the negative. The Bane thought he knew everything and never missed an opportunity to speak his mind. Sim growled. He wouldn't allow the Bane to discourage the girl.

The girl began telling the Bane about herself. Sim listened with interest as he flew above the treetops, steering for the lake below. Although he disliked the Bane, the Bane had instructed him to open himself for the girl. Sim scowled. He had to give the Bane a small piece of credit. Without the Bane he wouldn't have known what was happening, and the girl would have been lost. His silver skin naturally absorbed all magic. He had to consciously open his pores to allow magic inside him. He never thought he would open himself up again after his experience with the Bane, but he had liked the girl immediately, and some part of him also liked this Ren. Although the pain on Ren's face as he held the girl confused Sim – there was no wound on the man, nothing that should have caused any pain – his look caused Sim's intrigue to stir. And that, more so than the Bane's warning, compelled him to allow the girl inside.

Normally, magic was directed at him for evil, so Sim had never associated it with good. He scowled again. The Bane hadn't improved his opinion of magic, but Aidan may. Sim heaved a sigh. He supposed the Bane did have his uses.

"Will I ever be whole again?" Aidan's voice was hesitant, worried. Sim felt a stab of jealousy. He didn't want Aidan to want out. She was what he had been looking for when he foolishly allowed the Bane inside. Sim knew Aidan would become comfortable in his darkness, but he sensed her resisting his warmth. She wanted to help this Ren. Sim didn't understand it. He was powerful and humans weren't. They let their emotions interfere with life.

"You're whole now, my child. You just exist in another time and space. One day, in the not so distant future, you could be released from the dragon, but you must hold onto you."

"It's much better to be Sim the Silver!" Sim internally roared.

"Hush, Similian, let the child be."

Similian growled deep in his throat. He didn't like it when the Bane chastised him. The Bane had no right to chastise him. Sim thought again about roasted Bane. The Bane didn't think he was serious, but he was.

"Sim?" Aidan thought.

"Yes, dear heart." Sim liked the fact she called him Sim and not Similian like the Bane. The Bane used his formal title to stay distanced from him. The girl used Sim. Similian smiled, even though it came out a sneer.

"Where am I inside you?"

Sim bristled with pride. "You're everywhere inside me."

"Then why can't I see?"

The question took Sim off guard. Why couldn't she see? He had never considered it before. He supposed it was because he didn't direct her to see. "Would you like to see?"

"I would like to see Ren."

"I don't see him," Sim thought, disappointed.

The Bane had never asked to see anything, but Sim could feel the Bane's power in his eyes, somehow telling the Bane what occurred, even in sleep. Sim scowled. If the Bane was going to be rude enough to share his body, he could try to be a friend. Now Aidan wanted to see, but she wanted to see the reason she wanted out.

"Then I would like to see what you see."

Sim's heart leapt with her words. He snickered. He had learned snickering from the Bane. He liked snickering.

"Then focus inward but outward at the same time. Focus everything, every strength, on one spot inside you. Tell me when you have done so."

Aidan released a satisfied breath. "I've done so."

"Now, with that focus reach out. Put your strength into something that exists in another point in time."

Sim felt Aidan's strength soaring through him. She landed in his eyes and looked with him as he flew over the lake. He began to circle and made a point to look around so Aidan could appreciate the entire view. She laughed. Sim couldn't help doing the same as they looked out of the same eyes – it almost tickled. As he landed by the lake, he barked a greeting to the other dragons. His mate rolled on her back in a submissive, yet attractive stance. The missing scales on her neck marked her as the dragon that loved the same human Aidan loved. Sim gurgled an affectionate greeting.

"Is that your mate?"

Sim snickered. "Yes. I have named her Mezuzah."

"Mezuzah?"

"She has great faith. Mezuzah means faith."

"Why does she have great faith?"

Sim hesitated, unsure if he should tell Aidan. "She believes in the kindness of man."

"Then she's Ren's dragon."

"I know." Sim sighed, jealous of Ren once again.

"You'd like Ren, Sim."

"Similian the Vicious wouldn't like Ren." Sim lied, wanting to rid the girl of her need to escape him. He leaned forward and nudged Mezuzah. She gurgled with pleasure. Sim puffed out his chest so she could admire his attractive features. Mezuzah's mate had died years ago, and although most dragons never chose another mate, Mezuzah had reconsidered. After all, Sim was a silver.

"Then you're losing a good friend."

Sim felt Aidan retract inside him. He heaved a sigh, wondering why he would want a man as a friend. Sim could tell he had upset Aidan, and although he didn't want her to be upset, he also wanted her to stay with him. He was lonely. Sim thought of Ren. He knew the man liked him, but dragons didn't have human friends. Sim glanced at Mezuzah and heaved a sigh. Mezuzah was a strong dragon. No dragon had told her she was weak for trusting a human. Maybe he could have a human friend on the outside. After all, it was the same human Mezuzah trusted, and it may make Mezuzah like him more than she already did. He decided he would be honest with the girl.

"I did find myself liking him. He isn't like others."

Aidan stirred a little. "No, he isn't." She paused. "Can we go on another flight? I want to see the places you like to go . . . and I'd like to see Stardom again."

Sim stopped eating, surprised. The Bane had never been interested in what he liked to do. Sim puffed his chest out further. This day was going well. Even though he knew the girl wanted to fly to Stardom to see Ren, Sim decided he would take her. Besides, Ren was probably being held inside. He had seen Ren surrounded by guards before he flew off. Although he had hurled fire over the men pursuing Ren, it wasn't enough to stop them all. Ren couldn't have escaped.

Mezuzah licked Sim's face. Sim gurgled with pleasure and licked her back. Yes, this day was going well.

"Yes, dear heart. I'll fly high and fast . . . although the Bane will be highly agitated." Sim spread his large wings and took to the air.

"Why will he be agitated?"

"He hates it when I fly fast. He says it disturbs his plan-forming."

"Where is the Bane?"

Sim sighed. "Asleep. He's always asleep."

- - -

Ramie leaned against the railing of the boat. The sun's rays were just beginning to kiss the deep cerulean water, causing the tips of the waves to dance around the hull. They had sailed far into the Neoteric Sea. At times the upper sails dipped to drink the water as opposing currents threatened to capsize the ship. Ramie barely noticed. His eyes were locked on the misty atmosphere leagues away – the ten winds.

Most ship's crews refused to sail out far enough to catch the current of the winds, but this time Ramie had paid their price, and then some. The winds' current could help them reach the Divi River in a mere day, not the weeks it would have taken in normal waters.

His advisors had warned against it, and all had called him mad, but Ramie hadn't listened. Somehow he knew the Maker's fates were with him. He knew they would make it through the winds' currents. He just knew.

The misty panel of water rose before him like a sheet of ice. He felt its power and heard its roar. No one knew exactly what the ten winds were, or why, or how they existed, but as close as anyone could tell the ten winds were a thick wall of water rising from the seas to the heavens: a waterfall, no doubt, but one that had no rock or mountain to tumble from. The wall of water had been named the ten winds because of the gusts existing the closer you steered toward it. The winds came from everywhere: north, south, east, west, northeast, northwest, southeast, southwest, up, down, everywhere. No ship could survive the winds, and no ship could sail into the ten winds' depths and ever sail out again.

Ramie's ship was only close enough to catch the beginning of the currents. The ship's crew had to be careful not to steer too far into the winds and keep a tight grip on the controls. If the crew released the wheel the ship would spin into the deadly currents and every person on board would perish.

The ten winds surrounded the Lands, encompassing them in a wall of water. Ramie had often wondered if some sort of magic had put the winds there, but when magic was reborn and nothing had changed he doubted his theory. The ten winds were the ten winds, magic or no magic.

Only marauders or occasional bards ventured into the winds' outlying currents. Ramie was sure no king had ever tried. He wondered if he would hear a song about his journey in the future. A small smile lit his face. Fraul would tease him unmercifully if a bard ever sang his name.

The ship lurched to the side and a cry of adulation lifted to the Maker. They had broken from the currents and were now venturing to the calm waters of the Divi that would lead them inland to Yor. The ship's crew began banging on anything they could find, shouting about their deftness against the winds. One of the crew pulled out a flute and began a peppy tune. Others began to dance and sing. The cabin door opened and Ramie turned to see members of his guard resurfacing on deck, faces pale from either sickness or fear, but eyes bright and smiles wide as they clapped along to the tune in celebration of their near-death escape.

Other crewman handed out food and drink. Ramie's stomach turned. Food was the last thing on his mind. After leaving Zier he had been unable to keep down more than vegetable broth. He had never been queasy before. He had never been scared before. It infuriated him that he felt both queasy and scared now. And it wasn't the winds that had frightened him. It was magic. May the Maker help them all.

He turned back to the sea. The ship sliced through the still waters, the current of the winds sending it off like a catapult. At least their speed was a small comfort. They would arrive in Byn far sooner than expected. He had been up for days, trying to decide what he should do and how he should do it. He had come to only one conclusion. He was in the midst of one large trap.

Ista had planned her strategy to perfection. She had taken over Zier peacefully and she had done it so well no one could doubt her story. Why have war when you could triumph through skill? Now Ista had the people's trust, and she had created something that couldn't be controlled: people's hunger to learn the Quy.

The internal power inside him was a constant feather brushing his conscious, incessant and demanding. Ramie found himself yearning to touch the feather and feel its power alive and burning inside him. Others would feel the same, and they would flock to Ista.

One wrong move and he would be opposing her without any knowledge of the Quy or how to defend his family or his lands. He would stall for as long as he could, but sooner or later he would have to choose a side. Until then, the people would be restless. They would want to leave for Zier and he would deny them. He would have to think of a bloody fine excuse to forbid the people's passage. One false move on his part would cause Ista to retaliate. How? He didn't know and that scared him most of all. He was up against something he had no idea how to fight. Give him a sword and lead him to battle with something tangible. But magic? A shiver went down his spine.

He patted his coat, assuring himself the message was still with him. He had written it himself. Normally he had one of the advisors draft his messages, but he was unsure of whom to currently trust. An image of the needles flashed through his mind. Ramie inwardly cringed. How many did Ista control? How many were in Yor?

Ramie looked to the horizon. The city of Byn topped a small rise overlooking the sea. Farther inland, the rugged peaks of the Jaguar mountain range dominated the landscape. Ramie drew a deep breath, gathering his courage.

During his sleepless nights he had been unable to form a plan to help his kingdom, but he had decided on a course of action to help Ren, or so he thought. Not only would Ren be hunted by Ista, he would also be hunted by Druids.

There was only one man who would dare oppose the Druids.

Chapter 13

They were over the Sierras and well on their way to the Cliffs. Although cover was a concern, for the rolling hills leading to Crape had few trees, the men's spirits were up.

Galvin left the group every degree of the sun to double back and check for any sign of pursuit. He said he was just being cautious, but Ren saw the concern in his eyes. Ren felt it as well. Ista should have discovered their trail by now. He had trouble believing Ista was so easily fooled.

Aidan was constantly on his mind. Whenever he read the prophecy his gut twisted into knots. Destroy the silver form, it said. In a way, he supposed he had. Any type of merging altered the beings involved. But the more he read the prophecy the more he thought it referred to something more, something in the future. The joining of Aidan's body with her spirit had been an instinctive reaction. He never doubted what he had to do or how he had to do it. The prophecy said, "If he couldn't." The "if" indicated a conscious decision, not instinct.

A sheer scream caused him to turn. Markum sat on the back of his horse, face twisted in anguish. As Markum's horse reared Galvin caught the reins, steadying the terrified creature. The others drew their swords, searching for whatever had caused Markum's distress.

Ren dropped to the ground, concerned. "Markum?"

When Markum's eyes cleared, color rose to his cheeks. "It's Sass, Ren."

Ren blinked in confusion. "My cousin? What do you mean?"

"She's dead."

Renee drew a sharp breath. Ren opened his mouth to speak but no words came. Had he heard Markum right? "How do you know?"

Markum let the question hang in the air. Ren could sense his terror. Then Ren instantly knew why Markum liked to keep to himself, why Markum shunned close human contact, and why he buried himself in books.

Markum was a seer. Ren could almost see the visions dancing in Markum's eyes.

"Why didn't you tell me?"

Markum shook his head. "Would you have believed me?"

Ren opened his mouth to speak but quickly thought better of it. Now, with magic's rebirth, prophecies and visions were easy to believe. But before? He was ashamed to say he would have been doubtful. Markum saw the truth in Ren's eyes and offered him a forgiving smile before describing the shriveled, blackened man he had seen, Sass's terror, and her ultimate sacrifice.

Ren closed his eyes. "The Reaper."

Neki peered between Ren and Markum with unsteady eyes. "What's the Reaper?"

Markum cleared his throat. "The Reaper is a magical being. He's a small man, only about waist high, but when he sings he can appear to be anyone or anything you desire. The only way he stays alive is to feed off others, or essentially drain another's life."

Renee put a hand to her mouth as her eyes welled with tears. Ren put his arm around her, trying to give her some small comfort.

As the grassy fields shivered in the breeze, Ren tried to concentrate on his mother, but his mind kept imagining the Reaper with Sass. Gritting his teeth, he let out a slow breath.

"Is it a year for a year?" Neki finally asked.

"No one knows," Markum said. "Sometimes the Reaper isn't heard from for decades, other times it's years or days. I don't know if the Reaper takes a year for a year, some fractional amount, or some other formula.

"All anyone knows is to avoid the forest that appears between Zier and Ketes. That's the only place the Reaper has ever been seen. The forest appears huge, wide in every direction and impossible to circumvent, but it's all an illusion. If you steer from it, it only takes a degree of the sun to bypass. The Reaper's magic is what causes you to see something more."

"May the Maker have mercy," Ren said, "how could the Reaper be reborn? The Reaper isn't a bread of creature, Markum. It is one being."

Markum exchanged a worried glance with Michel. "We discussed the possibilities of magical creatures reappearing when you went to see Grauss. I don't know if the wizards could have distinguished between a breed of creature or an isolated magical being. Although many creatures were feared, others were loved and cherished."

"Like the Avenger," Ren said, thinking about the stories he had read as a child. He had always loved the Avenger's righteous judgments. He had always prayed to the Maker to be as discerning as the Avenger when he inherited the throne.

Michel brushed back his sun-bleached hair. "In other words, when the wizards unleashed magic's destruction they probably wove another underlying emotional weave with that destruction, one that would call to those things destroyed in the Wizard War when the thread of the power was reformed. Now that magic's alive, magical creatures like the Reaper will begin to appear."

"All of them?" Although Quinton's voice was calm, his eyes betrayed him.

"I don't think they could have distinguished between those feared and those loved," Markum said. "I think the Reaper is proof we can't rule out anything."

Ren stared in the direction of Ketes, horrified. Sass was an innocent child. How could the Maker allow such a thing? Anger burned in his gut. He turned back to Markum. The seer was already watching him.

"Have you had any more visions?"

Markum nodded. "I've seen the One you seek."

Ren gripped Markum's arm. "Where?"

Markum shook his head. "In a lake, in a forest, he could be anywhere, Ren. But he's real."

Ren closed his eyes, overcome with relief mingled with fear. Until then he hadn't known he doubted the truth of the prophecy. He still couldn't understand his role in the darkness or how he could stop it. The One was the key.

Ren turned and looked in the distant foothills of the Cliffs of Crape. Their rocky form rose in stark contrast to the plains. Under the darkening sky the small trees jutting over the sides of the cliffs looked like spiked weapons, warning all away. The Cliffs were rarely visited. Most travelers steered days out of their way to avoid becoming trapped amidst their haunted caverns. The Cliffs' constant winds created shrill cries so eerie many would swear they heard children's screams from leagues away.

Ren suddenly realized those tales were probably true. He was sure Ista's camp was never without screams of torture. Ren vowed once again to stop the woman. What she had done to Tol was unforgivable. What she had done to Aidan she would die for.

He wanted to push on and reach Ista's camp, but they all needed a good night's rest before they undertook the Cliffs. He didn't know how long it would take to find the One, and he didn't know how long it would take for Ista to unlock the Red Eye's power, but he also knew his men's limits. After Markum's vision, approaching the Cliffs would only emphasize the dangers the quest may hold.

They were in a large clearing with distant trees surrounding them on three sides. It was a good place to make camp. They didn't need to be surprised by any magical creature. The clearing would provide them ample warning if something approached. As soon as Ren motioned for everyone to dismount, he sensed the men's gratitude.

They erected the camp in a sun's click: bedrolls undone, blankets unfolded, fire lit, horses brushed, food prepared. Neki even hummed as he sharpened his saber. Galvin commented that if Neki sharpened the sword any longer he might sharpen the blade clear off the hilt. There were a few chuckles, and for the first time since Markum's vision Ren felt his muscles relax.

Ren turned to watch his mother unpack her bedroll. After the story of the Reaper, Renee looked fearful. Her eyes darted around for any sign of danger. Ren knew he needed to send his mother to safety, Marva and Tol with her. The wilderness was no place for them, especially with magic's rebirth.

After the evening meal of stew and dried berries, Ren called the men to him. He nodded to Bentzen. "At first light I want you to ride to Ketes. Do what you can to help Bostic create a force to counter Ista. Take Renee, Marva and Tol with you. Be as quick as you can, but be wary of everything. The Reaper isn't the only creature that's been reborn."

Bentzen drew in a breath, disappointment in his eyes, but when he looked at Tol he nodded with understanding. Ren felt slightly nervous about sending Tol with his mother and Marva, but the silver band did seem to block Ista's hold. Although he was taking a risk, it was slight.

"I've been having dreams about wolven, Ren," Markum said as he looked toward the Cliffs, a worried glint in his eyes. "In magical times wolven thrived on the Cliffs, and if Ista is as shrewd as we believe, she could have laid a trap for us. I think we should split up. A few of us should ride to the camp while you and the others ride toward the Alcazar.

"I'll go," Neki said. "I'm not tired. I could ride tonight and be back by morning."

Ren shook his head. "Wolven thrive at night, Neki. Now isn't the time to approach the Cliffs." He glanced at Markum. The seer was still staring off in the distance, a frown dominating his amiable features. Something was different about Markum, something Ren could almost touch. Where before Markum stood in the shadows, now he dared to venture into the light. His dreams were taking over, forcing him to become the protector of the group. Tonight he would ask Markum more about his dreams.

"At first light then," Neki said.

"No," Michel said. "I'll go. You can find the power with little problem. Ren may need you."

Neki was about to argue when Quinton cut him off. "Michel is right, Neki. We need you here."

Neki scowled but didn't protest.

Ren wanted to ride with Michel, but Quinton's stare stopped him from even making the suggestion. And Quinton was right. He needed to focus on finding the One, not ride into the unknown.

"I'll go with Michel," Galvin said, casually rested his broadsword on his shoulder. In the light of the fire Galvin looked like death itself. Although Galvin was soft-spoken, he was fiercely protective, and he could wield a sword better than any man Ren knew.

Ren nodded in acceptance. "I don't like sending any of you away, but so be it. In the morning we split in three directions. My group will ride northwest toward the Alcazar, Galvin and Michel will ride to the Cliffs, and Bentzen's group will ride to Ketes." Ren paused and turned to Galvin and Michel. "But be quick. If you aren't back in two days time I'll personally come after you."

"That won't be necessary, my prince," Galvin said, his voice soft yet fierce.

Ren felt almost sorry for any man who tangled with the swordsman. The only blood he had ever seen on Galvin was someone else's.

If Ista had left any traps for them Galvin would be the first to notice.

- - -

The wolven were behind him again. Markum ran so fast he could barely feel his feet touching the ground. He could hear the beasts' howls above his own rapid breath. He couldn't outrun them this time.

He felt something grow hot in his hand and looked down at the prophecy book. The silver dragon's blue eyes were glowing with a light hotter than the bluest flame.

His mind said to keep running, to put all the distance he could between himself and the wolven, but his heart said to stop and read the book. The book would tell him what to do.

Markum skidded to a stop and opened the book's cover. The howls were closing in, but he made himself concentrate on the page before him. It was the prophecy he had read at Stardom. It didn't help. Panic rose in his gut. He forced himself not to look back.

He turned the page. More words began to appear, words that hadn't existed before. His heart leapt as the apparitions formed before his eyes. They formed not only prophetic verse but also notes in the corners and margins.

One word on the top of the page glowed with an eerie blue light.

Jump!

Markum didn't hesitate. He jumped with all his strength just as the wolven's hot breath exploded on the back of his thigh.

He soared upwards so high he was able to grab hold of a tree limb. The wolven jumped and snapped below him, but they couldn't reach him. Swinging one leg over the branch, he propelled himself up only to come face to face with the man he had seen before, the one with the ageless eyes. The One turned to look at him, long, dark hair reaching his waist, dark eyes soaking up every ounce of light. His widow's peak gave him a look of grave intelligence, but he held no smile.

The One reached for him. Markum tried to scoot away, but he couldn't move fast enough. The man gripped his upper arm, and Markum could only watch as he was shoved off the branch.

As his body plunged toward the wolven, Markum screamed. . . and woke up, shuddering.

Night had long since fallen. Beside him, Neki snored with contentment, saber resting by his side. The emerald twinkled in the light of the dying flames and cast a green glow on the figure sitting by the fire.

Ren was supposed to wake him for the second watch but Markum knew his watch was long overdue. Ren stared out into the night, muscles tense. Markum knew Ren worried for their safety. Markum suddenly realized why he respected Ren as much as he did. The people surrounding Ren weren't his subjects. They were his family.

When Markum shifted, Ren turned and motioned for silence. His copper eyes reflected the golden light of the fire, sending urgency with the message. Markum froze and peered into the night, suddenly aware of another presence.

The campfire sent gossamer shadows into the woods, bringing stones to life. Out of the depths of the forest a hollow screech rose to the heavens. Markum leaped from his pad as Quinton, Galvin, and Bentzen jerked awake and bounded to their feet, swords in hand. Quinton was about to step forward to guard his prince when Ren caught his wrist.

"Put your weapon away, Quinton."

Quinton's jaw sagged in shock. "Ren – "

"Now."

Neki moaned in his sleep, unaware of the commotion surrounding him. Renee and Marva stood together behind the men. Although Marva tried to put on a fearless front, her eyes betrayed her.

Quinton sheathed his sword, Bentzen and Galvin following. Markum looked at the trio in disbelief.

"It could be wolven, Ren," Markum said.

"It's not."

Markum didn't know how Ren could be so sure. In the distance, a shadow swayed violently. Its large eyes glowed orange in the firelight. The hollow screech came again.

Markum glanced at Ren, but his prince looked calm as a frozen pond.

The eyes blinked and moved closer. Whatever it was had on an armor of ivory. Markum could see the soft texture of the design in the chest region.

Ren took a step forward. Quinton's fierce whisper urged him back, but Ren didn't listen.

The eyes watched Ren sink to his knees and dig into his pack. After a dragon's breath, Ren withdrew a piece of dried apple and tossed it to the creature. The eyes disappeared as the creature bent to sniff the bounty.

Taking a fallen branch, Ren ignited the tip and swung it out before of him. The clearing was immediately illuminated, revealing what stood only cubits away.

Wide, brown eyes blinked in the sudden light. Ivory scales coating the creature's sides and front shimmered a pearly radiance. Rust-colored fur grew long around the creature's feet and neck, short around its muzzle, and shivered in the slight breeze. Its long tail curved upward in curiosity.

It was a kota, one of the most loved magical creatures of all time.

The men stood still as Ren took another step forward, holding out another piece of dried fruit. The kota started to prance. Its ivory hooves glistened in the night, drumming a beautiful rhythm.

As Ren moved closer Quinton came out of his daze and urged him back, but Ren paid him no heed. Markum touched Quinton's arm, silently telling him all would be well. Kotas were gentle, beautiful animals that only used magic when attacked. Their magic was a stunning ray that emitted from a curved horn on the crown of their head. As of yet the horn of the small creature was only a short stump. It would soon grow to be almost the length of a man's forearm.

When Ren knelt before the creature, the kota leaned against him and gently lifted another piece of apple out of Ren's hand.

Chapter 14

The sun had yet to rise but all the men were up. With the group splitting three ways the lighthearted banter was strained. Everyone worried about what would happen after they parted ways, Ren especially. Michel watched as Ren's eyes darted from Bentzen's group to Renee and then back again, brooding over the dangers with a furrowed brow.

Michel went back to stuffing his pack. It was going to be a hot day. The morning's air was muggy and the clouds were heavy with rain. Summer was coming to an end, but it was ending in full force.

Years ago, after leaving Stardom, he had become fearful of goodbyes, even good ones. If he poured a cup of water he never finished it. He always left a sip or two. He knew it was foolish, but it was who he had become. Endings didn't bode well for him, and he had a sick feeling in his stomach that when he and Renee parted this time he would never see her again.

Stealing a glance at her, his breath caught. The morning's light outlined the shape of her body against her thin smock, but she was still the queen. Even though Wyrick was dead he had nothing to offer her. She deserved castles and riches, nothing he could possibly provide.

He forced his eyes back on his pack and shoved some dried meat inside. The past few days had been wonderful. He was with Renee, gazing into her soft blue eyes, the scent of her hair filling his lungs. They had talked about each other's lives, of the landscape, of Ren. They had shared dreams and visions of the future. Never once had they discussed their goodbye, and never once had she insinuated he would become part of her life, but he was with her, and that was all that mattered.

He hadn't touched her other than to help her off the horse, but when he held the reins her arms rubbed his hands and her hair brushed his chest. He had never loved another, and he never would. Razons were known for their loyalty, and stubbornness.

Ren was a Razon as well, in every way. Ren felt as much or more for Aidan as Michel did for Renee. The men had questioned Ren about Aidan, and he had responded to their questions as best he could without divulging his true feelings, but Michel knew Ren's heart. He saw the truth in Ren's eyes.

The girl had given her life to Ren without even knowing him. The bond of the Maritium was sacred and complete. Michel didn't know if Ren knew the sacrifice Aidan had made. Now the bond was growing without Ren even realizing it. Michel could only pray Aidan could be made whole again or Ren would never be complete. But as much as Michel hoped for Aidan's restoration, he also feared it. Ren and Aidan could never become more than what they were now. It was forbidden.

Michel glanced at Ren and smiled. The kota hadn't left Ren's side all night. The creature leaned against Ren's leg as if it were a dog and not a creature that would grow to be the size of a large horse. Ren's hand casually rested on the kota's head as if it was the most natural thing in the world. Michel shook his head, chuckling.

Although half-starved, thin, and fairly weak the kota was more beautiful than Michel had ever imagined it could be. The head of the animal was flatter than a horse, almost like a deer. Its neck was full, with a thick mane of the rust-colored fur curling in all directions and running down and under its chest. Its muzzle was the same color as the scales, and a lighter fur surrounded its eyes, accentuating its gentle observation.

When Michel turned back to Renee he was surprised to find her looking in his direction. His heart swelled when she blushed and turned away like a young girl, but sunk again as he remembered what the morning would bring. He was leaving her again, and he hadn't even begun to tell her how he felt.

Michel shoved his apprehensions aside and quickly tied his pack. He may never see her again. He couldn't let his misgivings and concerns mask the truth. His life, or hers, could be taken at any time. He had to show her how much he loved her.

When his pack was tied he looped it over his shoulder and walked to her. Her back was turned and her soft voice tickled his ear as she whispered to her new mount. With a tentative hand, he brushed her shoulder. Her lips parted in surprise when she turned, but she quickly lowered her eyelids and reached for his hand. He barely heard Bentzen say they were ready to depart.

He opened his mouth to speak. Nothing came out.

She knew how he felt. Couldn't she read it in his eyes?

He squeezed her hand, trying to convey all the love he held inside. He felt empty, knowing his action wasn't enough. But what else could he do? Renee studied him, eyes questioning. Then, without warning, she kissed him.

It was so quick he questioned if it had happened at all. When he was finally able to take the air into his lungs he drew in her warm breath. Every breath he had ever thought of her, every time he had ever dreamed of kissing her, he hadn't expected it to be so sweet. Nothing and everything had changed since he left. Now her touch meant more to him than it ever had before. He loved her with all his soul. Every breath he had ever taken was because of her.

Her blue eyes searched his face. Did he love her? May the Maker help him.

He pulled her to him, hands running over her face and down her arms. He didn't care who saw. He was with the woman he loved and it may be the last time he would ever see her. He pulled her tighter. Her nails dug into his back with reckless need. Their embrace was more sensual than anything he could have ever imagined.

When they finally parted Michel ran his hand down her cheek, too overcome to speak.

"I love you, Michel, with everything I was and am. I love you and only you," Renee said.

"You don't know how much I've thought of you," Michel said, "wished you were there beside me. Blessed Fates, how I love you still."

Renee closed her eyes, ingraining his words to memory. He kissed her forehead, once again feeling the bitter ache of goodbye.

"I want you to be safe. I would never forgive myself if you came to harm."

Renee nodded, clutching his arm as if he were trying to pull away.

Bentzen rode up beside them. Michel swallowed back his emotions and helped Renee on her horse. When she was settled she looked down at him, lips twisting into a flirtatious grin. "Soon, my lord, you'll stop sending me away."

Michel chuckled and stepped closer. He tugged on her hand until she leaned down and met his lips in another kiss. This time it was soft, and lingered between pain and sadness. He held her to him, forcing her eyes to linger on his own. "Soon, my queen, you'll be begging me to leave."

"Not on your life," Renee whispered before she raised a mischievous eyebrow. "I'm not the one who'll be begging."

Before he could reply, she spurred her horse forward to meet Marva, stopping only to say a few words to Ren. Michel watched with mixed emotions. Part of him was exuberant Renee held thoughts of being with him in the future, but somehow the other part of him knew they may never have the chance.

Tol sat in front of Bentzen, face lit with excitement. He was going on another adventure as a knight of the crown prince. Michel couldn't help but chuckle as Tol bowed to the men with pride. Ren had given the boy hope, in more ways than one.

Although Ren smiled, Michel saw the worry in his eyes. But Marva, Renee, and Tol would be safer away from the main party, and Bentzen would keep them from harm.

Ren heaved a worried sigh. Michel felt a pang of remorse when he realized he hadn't been there for Ren the past few days. Although he commented when asked, he had been too focused on Renee to offer much support.

"It's better they leave, Ren. Bentzen will see they arrive safely, and the band will work. We tested it."

"Correction, the band works with the experience we have."

A chill went up Michel's spine. Ren was right. Although Neki couldn't sense the needles in Tol's mind when the band was on that didn't mean Ista couldn't. What if Ista could still sense Tol without Tol knowing?

No, they couldn't second-guess every decision they made. The needles were probably made of partial silver, and because silver absorbed magic they acted like a conductor inside the brain. The silver part of them absorbed the magic and transmitted the power down the needle's shaft, stimulating the brain to feel a certain way. The band, because it was solid silver, blocked the magic Ista sent, absorbing it before it reached the needles inside Tol's mind.

Tol would be fine. So would Renee. So why did he have a sense of foreboding?

A passing cloud suddenly dampened the light of the rising sun. A distant rumble of thunder rolled past.

Renee turned. When she found his eyes her face lit in a beautiful smile, but there was something else scrawled in her features. It was the same look he had seen that day so long ago. With sudden revelation he saw in her eyes what he too felt inside.

He would never see her again.

His legs tensed to run after her, but before he could do so she turned and spurred her horse into a canter.

His heart melted inside him.

- - -

"My lord, a messenger from Zier just arrived. He wishes to gain an audience."

Raymond studied Bostic. The king's eyes were sullen. Sass's death had driven him almost to the point of insanity. Her body still rested in an adjoining room. The burial would be the next day.

Raymond was slightly nervous about the burial. It had shaken him when Sass had come to them an old woman, but what was happening to her now shook him even more so.

She was getting younger.

He had just seen her body. She was far younger than when she had first appeared. If he stood with her long enough he could almost see her skin smoothing, her curves accentuating, her hair lightening. It scared him more than the ten winds.

Sass was dead. Her body was cold. How could she be changing back into what she was before?

It had something to do with whatever had happened to her, but he had no idea what that was. Part of him thought they should burn her body, just in case something was in her that could cause harm, but he didn't want to mention his thoughts to Bostic. Although the release of a body by fire was common, he knew the king wouldn't want Sass taken by flames. Bostic needed a tangible place to visit her. She had been taken too early as it was. How could Raymond suggest an incineration?

"Please, by all means, send the man in. We always like to hear from Wyrick and Ren."

Raymond caught the sarcasm in Bostic's voice. The sentry did as well.

"My lord," the sentry replied, visibly nervous, "the man comes with a message from Valor."

Bostic's eyebrows rose as he cleared his throat. "Valor? Well this should prove interesting."

The sentry departed and soon a tall, thin man dressed in Crape's colors of green and gray stepped through the door. His hair was slicked back and he wore a sly grin Raymond didn't trust. He bowed with pompous confidence before coming to stand at attention. Bostic observed the man for several long breaths before nodding.

"My lord," the man began. "I'm here to deliver grave news. Wyrick, the king of Zier and supreme ruler of Newlan, is dead. Sadly, his only son, the crown prince, Ren Razon, has been accused of his murder.

"The crown prince has long plotted to overtake the Lands. A sorceress from the old Alcazar detected Ren's deception and emerged from hiding to help defeat him. I'm sure you, or some of your people, felt an acute pain days ago. This pain was the Quy being reborn. The sorceress had to rebirth the power in order to fight the crown prince.

"Although the guards of many kingdoms tried to subdue Ren, he escaped. Valor Kahn, the new supreme ruler of Newlan, has declared the crown prince a traitor and requests you send word if you see or hear from the prince."

The messenger paused, but when Bostic made no comment, he continued. "Valor now petitions your assistance in stomping out the tyranny Ren will try to bring to fruition. Ren is sure to regroup and attack the throne. Ren needs to be found and stopped before he can gain in both strength and number. The sorceress, Ista, has offered to train the Lands in magic. The sorceress is now seeking an army of people with the Quy to defeat the prince. Valor strongly extends Ista's invitation to your people in Ketes. She will begin training immediately.

"My lord, that isn't all the news I have." Raymond noticed a thin line of sweat had broken out on the messenger's brow. The man licked his lips. "A battle ensued after Ren's escape. Some men fought for Ren, others for the crown, but many died. Your son, Paul, was among the tragedies. It isn't known for whom he fought, but he died with honor, fighting for what he believed."

Raymond's breath caught. Both of Bostic's children were gone. It wasn't right. How could the Maker allow such a thing?

Bostic didn't move. He just sat staring at the messenger without any sign of emotion. If Raymond didn't know the king he would have sworn the man in the chair was a statue. The messenger cleared his throat. The tenseness in the room deepened. Raymond placed a hand on Bostic's shoulder, trying to send the king some small comfort. After a long pause, Bostic rose and walked to the messenger.

"Let me see if I understand," Bostic said, looking past the messenger at some distant scene. His tone was apathetic but the muscles in his back quivered with his words. Bostic wasn't a small man. The king could pin the messenger in a heartbeat if he was so inclined. The messenger looked at Raymond with uncertainty. Raymond stepped closer, suddenly uneasy, but before Raymond could speak Bostic's voice sliced through the air like a saber.

"Newlan wasn't enough for the crown prince, so years ago Ren began plotting to kill his father." Bostic paused and casually rubbed his beard. "So Ren kills Wyrick to gain control of Newlan, something he already had by the way. After the king's death, Valor, the thorn in Wyrick's side, seizes control of Zier along with this woman who has magic." Bostic looked over at the sentry and smiled. "And now Valor has strongly extended an invitation for me to send my men to him and leave my own lands unprotected?"

"My lord, um, I only come with the message."

Bostic tensed. "Do you believe your message, soldier?"

The messenger turned to Raymond with questioning eyes.

"I asked you a question! Do you believe your message?"

"Yes, I believe –"

The messenger didn't have a chance to reply, and Raymond didn't have a chance to reach Bostic. As soon as the answer had been given Bostic plunged his knife into the man's chest. The messenger barely had a chance to register shock before his face went slack in death.

Raymond stopped by the king, watching helplessly as the messenger's blood began to stain the marble floor.

"That's for Ren," Bostic said, voice breaking. "May he come back safely."

The helplessness in Bostic's voice was suddenly gone. He turned to Raymond, eyes lit with revenge. "Seal the walls. No one leaves Ketes. No one enters. Now."

- - -

They had ridden hard since they had left Ren, each wanting to reach Ista's camp as quickly as possible. In the beginning rain had poured down, heightening Michel's sense of foreboding. In his mind he knew the group's separation was the best choice, but his heart kept insisting something was amiss.

Bentzen was a skilled swordsman and fiercely determined. If something were to happen, Renee would be as safe with him as she would in Ren's larger group. And Ren was with Neki and Quinton, two loyal and exceptional men. Still, Michel's feeling of dread persisted.

As they approached the Cliffs, cover was scant, and it was hard for them to remain hidden. The Cliffs were hauntingly beautiful, with skeletal trees and red-tipped ferns covering their peaks. A plethora of caves were said to reside among them, but none were used, for when magic was prevalent the Cliffs had been the home of the wolven. Those daring to venture inside the caves after magic's destruction said they were haunted by the screams of the souls the wolven had killed.

As they rode closer an eerie whistle spun in the muggy breeze, and Michel knew it would only increase the closer they rode to the Cliffs. The Cliffs were famous for their high-pitched trilling. The scholar inside him knew the Cliff's caverns fed air through holes and around angles that forced the current faster, causing the trill, but a shiver shot up Michel's spine just the same. Although he had never believed the bewitching tales of the Cliffs, he now knew the effects the trilling could have.

Tol had grown up with that sound. He wondered how the boy had retained his sanity.

A light mist began to fall, adding to the eeriness of the area. The red-tipped ferns looked like blood against the green vegetation and the skeletal trees seemed to droop in death.

Their horses heaved deep snorts as they began to climb the steep terrain. The rocky ground soon changed to a lush landscape where red-leaf ferns and silk-leaf trees swayed gently in the breeze.

The Cliffs never lacked water, the Old Sea sending mist and light rain almost every day. The plants surviving on top of the Cliffs thrived in rocky soil and continuous drizzle. Michel recognized many of them.

Galvin slowed and dismounted.

Michel frowned. "We aren't near the camp, Galvin."

"I know, but we need to ride in with our full wits about us."

Michel understood. Now that the swordsman had seen the area and listened to the eerie trill, he wanted to access any unforeseen dangers before moving forward. Michel liked that about Galvin. The soft-spoken swordsman was never taken off guard.

Michel dismounted and reached inside his pack for some dried meat. He wasn't hungry, but he needed something to do. He disliked waiting even more than endings. When he turned back to Galvin, he found the swordsman studying him.

"There's one thing I can't figure."

Michel cocked an eyebrow, curious. "That is?"

"You left Stardom taking nothing but your name. Why didn't you take her with you?"

Michel blinked in shock before he smiled. "You were there?"

"No," Galvin said, "but the men still talk."

Michel had suspected as much. "If I had taken Renee, Wyrick would have followed. He had first rights."

Galvin didn't speak for a short time. Michel tensed, fearing the question he knew would come.

"How is it Ren is so much like you and nothing like Wyrick?"

Michel forced his face into a mask of stone. "Good blood."

Galvin broke out into a rare grin. The silver teardrop on the loop encircling his ear shivered as he chuckled. "Good blood," he repeated before turning serious again. "You never married?"

Michel tore off a piece of meat, wondering if Galvin would give the underlying question voice. "No, never married. You?"

Galvin pointed to the silver teardrop. "No. Many feel my vow rash, but until you I've never witnessed anything that would cause me to think marriage would be anything but trouble. What you and Renee have is rare."

The feeling he would never see her again stole over Michel like a shadow. "I know."

"You're a rare man, Michel. You love yet you don't take. You're taken from yet you don't ask for anything in return." The dark eyes of the swordsman softened as if already aware of his sacrifice.

Michel released a breath. "But I did, Galvin. I took everything."

Galvin remained silent, appraising him. "In the end, Michel, only in the end." Galvin shook his head and turned to check his horse.

Michel hoped Galvin was right. He hoped he would have everything in the end. The shadow danced over him again, brushing his heart with ice-cold fingertips. Michel sat where he stood, not bothering to seek shelter from the mist. The drizzle suited his feelings.

The distant howl of the Cliffs distressed him even more. It was a constant presence, too far away to be worth pondering but too disturbing to disregard. Michel wondered if that was the way Tol felt with the silver band off his head.

Galvin shifted, absently brushing his broadsword. Michel rubbed his arms and listened to the distant howl, sensing Galvin's concern to hurry back to Ren. He felt the same. Ren was a like a magnet drawing the course of the world along with him. Ren didn't have to find anything. Things would find him. Michel wanted to be there when they did.

Galvin stood. "Ready."

It was more of a statement than a question, and Michel didn't bother to reply. Soon they were riding through the trees with hurried caution. Michel had to commend Ista: she had picked the one place in the Lands few would ever approach. Not only were the Cliff's howls uncanny, but the mist was maddening, and stories of the wolven sparked terror into the bravest of hearts. Michel almost expected to see one of the two-headed wolves rise before him, but none appeared.

Galvin slowed and motioned him ahead, dark eyes disturbed. Michel moved beside him and saw a well-worn path in the dense forest. Although it was muggy, Michel shivered. It was the path Ista had used for almost four centuries.

Once the horses slowed he could hear the whispering howls of the Cliffs with more intensity. Michel drew his sword, more for comfort than protection. Beside him he heard the "swish" of Galvin's battle-ax. At least he wasn't the only one on edge.

The path was deep, almost a trench, with scant water standing in its center. When they turned a slight bend, the path split in two directions. The main path was clear, and Michel pressed forward.

The stench caught them before they broke through the trees. Michel's stomach tightened into knots, unsure if he would be able to keep down the small amount of meat he had eaten. They heard the slight undercurrent of humming.

"Death," Galvin said.

Michel nodded, suddenly wondering why he had volunteered to come. As the path widened, the silk-woods cleared and Michel spotted the overhanging rock Tol had described as his home. It was sheltered from the naked eye by thick red maples and dogwood. Ironically, the setting was beautiful. The pink and white dogwoods stood in stark contrast to the red maple.

But as they approached the humming amplified, and the stench became even more profound.

Michel tore a piece of cloth from his mount's blanket and covered his nose. The smell of the horse's sweat did more good than the cloth, but nothing could shelter the stench from filtering in.

After looping his reins around a low branch Michel dismounted and cautiously approached the overhang. The droning grew louder until it became one continuous ringing in his ears. Even the sweat of the horse was useless to combat the smell. He kept the cloth over his nose anyway, as if breathing the air would somehow taint him. Michel tensed before he stepped around the rock, trying to prepare himself for whatever sight he was about to see.

But nothing could have prepared him. His insides shook with revulsion and he quickly looked away. Flies pelted his arms and face like drops of rain. He shook them off, disgusted, and turned back to the abomination. Galvin whispered an oath behind him.

There were seven small boys lying against the far wall, their legs chained to large spikes in the ground. A swarm of flies buzzed around the bodies, feasting on the exposed flesh. Beside the children were five older women, all with only one foot, but there was little left of them. Their skin hung in shreds from where the children had stripped off meat to survive. One of the cripples was clearly with child.

Michel swallowed in horror, Ista's scheme all too clear. She crippled women with the power. In her eyes women were weak, only good for childbearing. The boys with the power were the ones she trained. They were now the Collective, stationed across the Lands answering her call.

The children hadn't died of hunger. They had died of disease and lack of water. There were a few overturned buckets beside them. Water had been supplied, but it was gone. Anger surged inside him. Rain was plentiful in the Cliffs. How the children must have felt to sit under the overhang and watch the misty rain outside, rain they desperately needed but couldn't reach.

"Fates," Michel whispered in abhorrence.

Galvin surveyed the children with a dark look. "Ista deserves every death she finds in this war."

Michel nodded, noting the swordsman's dark eyes didn't miss anything that moved, even the slightest rustle of leaves.

Michel forced his mind on the task at hand and appraised the overhang. At the back was an entrance to a deeper cavern. Michel drew a hesitant breath and ran through the darkened air, unnerved by the incessant droning, and broke though to a smaller chamber. Wind billowed down from above, taking most of the stench with it. Michel lowered the cloth. An overhead broken section of rock allowed scant light into the chamber, but it was more than enough to inspect the room's contents.

A lone shelf held a few books. Full bags rested below the shelf, some large, others smaller than a traveling pouch. A broken mirror was propped against a far corner, a poorly made chair sitting before it. A crude bed sat to the left of the chair, and a long, stone slab stood in the center of the chamber and dominated the room. As Michel approached the slab, he noticed the bloodstains. Somehow they looked more ominous than the children. Michel recalled Tol's words. *"She kills all of them without magic, first thing."*

Galvin stooped beside the bags.

"Careful," Michel cautioned.

"Dirt," Galvin declared as he peered into the first bag.

Michel reached in, scooped up a handful and held it up to the light. The grain sparkled silver. "Magic dirt, Galvin. Silver dust."

Galvin looked a little uneasy as he went to the next bag. Michel untied a large burlap sack from his belt and shoved some books inside. His skin crawled as he did so, as if the books were stained with Ista's sins, but as he surveyed the titles one appeared to be a basic training book of the Quy.

"There's black sand also. Is that different from silver?"

Michel shoved the last of the books into the sack. "Yes. It can do different things. See if there's any white sand as well."

Galvin went back to the bags as Michel circled the room, looking for anything else Ista might have left. He looked at the lone bed and thought of Tol. No wonder the boy almost worshiped Renee. He had been denied every comfort until he arrived at Stardom.

He bent to lift the bed, wanting to assure himself nothing lay hidden underneath. When he straightened, his back hit the stone slab and he felt something touch his right elbow. Galvin said he found some white sand just as a small vial, previously bathed in shadow, hit the floor. The glass burst, releasing the liquid it contained. A baby's scream echoed around them. Galvin spun, holding some of the white sand in his palm, a strange look on his face. Michel's throat constricted – something was wrong. Looking down at the broken vial, his vision blurred.

"Michel? Did you hear that?"

When Michel looked back at Galvin he saw the strange look again. Some white sand trickled from his palm and twirled around him in a hazy cloud. When their eyes met, Michel knew Galvin felt it too –evil.

"Let's get out of here."

Galvin slapped the back of his neck. White sand spun around him, marring his black tunic.

Michel bent to pick up two bags of sand before jogging down the corridor. Galvin already had four bags thrown over his shoulder. As soon as they left the small chamber the stench impaled them, but Michel didn't bother to put the cloth over his nose. He could almost feel the hands of hate reaching out to claim him.

A distant echo of howls reached their ears, but it wasn't the trill of the Cliffs. Galvin turned to him, dark eyes intense. "Wolven."

Galvin broke into a run. Michel followed, jumping on his horse and slashing the reins with his sword. His mount needed no encouragement. The horse sprang forward, instinctively reaching for the light of day.

The wolven's howls were getting closer. Michel spun in the saddle, almost feeling their hot breath on his neck.

The trees of the Cliffs provided plenty of shade. The wolven could attack at any time of day here. He leaned down, giving his horse free rein, sending a silent prayer to the Maker that the edge of the Cliffs would come quickly.

Just as he heard the wolven beside him, he broke through the trees and fled down a steep path into bright sunlight. He had never been so glad to see the sun. It beat down unmercifully, but he welcomed it. Soon the trill of the Cliffs and the howls of the wolven were just a distant memory. When he finally slowed, Galvin rode to flank him. White sand still clung to his eyelashes.

Michel breathed in deep, desperate to rid his body of the smell and taste of death, but he knew it was too much to wish for. The memory of the camp would never leave him.

- - -

Bentzen's voice droned on in the darkness, reciting the legend of the Avenger by memory. It had been his favorite as a child. Although the Avenger was death, he was also righteous judgment. Tol sat with eyes wide and mouth open in rapt attention. Tol's mind was like a sponge. He absorbed information within heartbeats and was willing and able to soak up much more.

They had ridden until well past dark, all anxious to reach Ketes as quickly as possible. They decided not to bother with either a bath or a hot meal. They managed to pool enough dried fruit from their pouches to satisfy their grinding hunger. Perhaps in a few days he would feel safe enough to take the time to catch a rabbit for a stew. Until then they would push on.

Tol's fruit lay untouched beside him. Renee kept shooing the flies away. Tol barely noticed, his mind wrapped up in the story of the Avenger.

Bentzen leaned against his pack and delayed the story's end for as long as possible. He enjoyed teaching Tol. The boy was remarkable. Even after the horrors Tol had witnessed the boy always aimed to please. Bentzen knew part of that obedience stemmed from the needles, but although Tol understood Ista couldn't harm him, he exerted all his energy even in the smallest task assigned.

When the story was complete Bentzen smiled at Tol's astonished expression.

"That really happens?"

Bentzen nodded, heart warming. "That really happens."

Marva's eyes widened with childlike wonder. "Just think, Tol, he might even be here now."

Tol remained transfixed. "I'd like to be the Avenger, to kill those who hurt."

Renee eyes flickered with worry as she pulled Tol into her lap. He snuggled close as she fussed with his hair.

Just imagining the torture Tol had endured enraged Bentzen. A child was defenseless, trusting in those older to provide love and affection. When affection was denied it was unforgivable. Tol had not only been denied, he had also been asked to hurt others.

Bentzen tossed another stick on the fire and watched the flames flicker to new heights. He never dreamed his rage could ascend past the anger he held for his own father, but it had, with Ista it had.

As Tol sat in Renee's arms, so open and innocent, Bentzen's chest filled with new emotions. Tol had been through the abyss and back, but to be with him you would have never known. What had Bentzen done? He had been through his own perdition but he was beginning to think it was an abyss of his own making. If Tol could open up his heart and soul to the world after what he had experienced, why couldn't Bentzen?

Tol was everything Bentzen was not: open, happy, loving and eager to learn. Bentzen had been rebellious and angry. It was humbling to Bentzen. He needed to be more like Tol. Even though he was teaching Tol, the boy was also teaching him.

Bentzen knew his heart was pure, and although he was inherently liked and held in high regard he never revealed his emotions. He was Bentzen, alone by choice. Duty was all he lived for.

Bentzen thought about his childhood. He had held onto his anger for so long he didn't know who he would be if he let it go. Why did Fate always hurt the innocent and leave the rest to be? Why did Fate always punish those she shouldn't and not those she should? Why was Ista allowed to give pain to someone so defenseless, so innocent?

The world didn't make sense to Bentzen, and it never would. That was why he hid from the world. He didn't want to know the world, and he didn't want the world to know him.

Now he felt that changing. He found himself laughing; he found himself giving; he found himself loving a child. And that child was stirring emotions inside him so quickly he couldn't evaluate them fast enough.

Bentzen ran his hands through his hair, undoing the small ponytail he always wore. The fire had dwindled so he threw a few more sticks on the flames and stood to gather more wood. He made a quick decision to keep the fire alive that night. They all needed its comfort. If Ista found them he would be ready. He would never let anyone hurt Tol again.

He felt a gentle tug on his tunic and looked down to find Tol staring up at him.

"What, little one?" he asked, ruffling Tol's blond hair.

Tol frowned. "Renee said I have to go to bed."

"Well, she's the queen, and knights never question the queen."

Tol thought about Bentzen's words before he smiled and reached out his arms. "Good night."

At first Bentzen didn't understand what Tol wanted, but after another tug Bentzen knelt to Tol's level. Tol wrapped his small arms around Bentzen's neck before darting to his bedroll.

Bentzen turned to the darkness, not wanting anyone to see the tears in his eyes. He stayed there for a time, ingraining his new emotions to memory. A whisper or two from Renee told him she was wishing Tol sweet dreams. Tol's soft laughter filled the air as Bentzen went to gather more wood. Bentzen vowed once again nothing would ever harm the boy.

When Bentzen finally lay down, he couldn't go to sleep. He just stared up at the stars, thinking about how much his life had changed. He suddenly realized why Ren had put Tol in his care. Although Ren didn't know Bentzen's history or the reason behind his detachment, Bentzen knew Ren had sensed his distance long ago.

When he had auditioned for the castle guard he had little or no weapons training. During the tryouts he had failed miserably at the scrimmages, but Ren had sensed something in him no one else had. Bentzen still didn't know what that something was, nor did he care. Ren had helped him find dignity and pride in himself. That was all that mattered.

Benton sighed and put his arms behind his head. It was a clear night, a fresh night. That was how Bentzen felt inside too. This was the start of a new life. Magic frightened him, but magic had brought Tol and a new beginning.

"My prince," he whispered, "thank you for giving me something I didn't know I needed."

Then, in the starlight, Bentzen put his fist to his forehead and then to his heart.

Chapter 15

Ramie rode down the plank on his favorite steed, Mortar. Mortar was the fastest horse Ramie had ever seen, not to mention beautiful. His dark gray coat shone like polished silver. Ramie reached down and patted Mortar's neck, whispering things he would rather not have his men hear. Although he longed to do things with an unconventional flair, he did not. His young age, along with his small stature, had forced him to become the model king. Appearances were everything, and as of yet no one had challenged his leadership.

He heard the two guards he had chosen take their positions behind him. Although many on the ship had protested, Ramie refused more of an escort. No one could know what occurred that day. If anyone suspected he might arrive home in a box.

Ramie looked into the distance and frowned. It was a hazy morning. The Jaguar mountain range couldn't be seen and that made him nervous. He didn't have time for a long journey. He knew his trip to the mountains would take him, in good time, two sun cycles. If he could just see them it would make the ride easier.

The heavy bags of gold hidden in his cloak jingled as he shifted in the saddle. He fingered the dagger in his belt. If gold failed to buy secrecy the dagger would. He had purposely ordered two of the younger men aboard the ship to accompany him. He didn't want to kill someone he knew, a stranger was bad enough.

He spurred Mortar into a gallop. The two guards followed close behind. Port Bynni was bustling with people. Roads made of pebbles wound through the town, sprouting only cubits from the dock. The strong smell of fish drifted from two large fishing boats that had just unloaded their morning's catch. The workers on the dock separated the fish with dexterous hands before hauling them in small carts to the market.

The people of Byn barely gave them a second glance, all intent on their work or bartering. The city was alive with talk of the Quy. He heard the word "magic" repeatedly. Sometimes he even heard "Ista." When he did he was loath to realize the people spoke Ista's name in reverence. Surprisingly, he heard no mention of Ren or his supposed betrayal. It was as if no one cared.

The more Ramie heard the more worried he became. He wasn't up against Ista's claim; he was up against Ista's knowledge. Even if the people believed in Ren's innocence they still wanted to learn the Quy. They would still travel to Zier.

As he wove his way through the market his mood diminished rapidly, not that it had a high level to diminish from. Many of the townsfolk had packs on their backs. Not packs from a morning at market but packs foretelling of a journey. By the time he reached the crossroad veering southeast toward Zier Ramie's mood hadn't only diminished it had reached rock bottom. The road was awash with people, some walking, some riding, some men, some women, and some small children, but all carried a mask of hope.

Ramie's chest tightened. People were migrating, chattering about the power and how they would soon be able to turn stones into gold.

He passed the road and started down a dirt trail that led southeast toward the Jaguars. He could barely see their shape in the distance, the morning's haze still thick, but just the sight of his destination soothed his nerves. The two guards exchanged confused glances as Ramie slowed Mortar to a stop. The men thought they were staying in the market, not traveling across country.

Ramie had told his crew he had forgotten to order the Ketes crystal he had promised his wife Javi. He insisted on disembarking in Byn to send the order to Ketes himself. Since he hadn't sent word as soon as he arrived in Zier, the crystal would take months to reach Yor, much to Javi's chagrin. Ordering it from Byn would reduce the time by half. To apologize for his oversight he would also search the Byn market for a trinket Javi would favor.

Ramie turned to the guard who had introduced himself as Tec and motioned him forward. The lanky boy followed as Ramie moved out of hearing range of the other guard.

Ramie lowered his voice. "Take this message to Ketes. Don't let anyone read it except Bostic himself. Do you understand?"

A flash of surprise swept across Tec's boyish features. Although Tec knew a message would be sent to Ketes, it was supposed to be delivered to a crystal merchant, not the king, and normally a messenger was used, not a personal guard. But Tec didn't flinch. He took the message without question and saluted.

Before Tec could spur his horse east Ramie put a hand on Tec's arm and pulled one bag of gold from his cloak. It could have supported a man for an entire lifetime. "Take this. I want you to know how important this is to me. If you come back to Oldan I'll welcome you, but if you breathe one word of this message to anyone other than to whom it is intended you'll be hunted like a dog. Do you understand?" Ramie searched Tec's face for any disloyalty. He saw none.

Tec flushed as his horse pranced with excitement. "Yes, my lord."

"Now go, and may the Maker go with you."

Tec's flush deepened, causing his blond hair to appear white as he spurred his horse into a canter and held the message close to his chest. Ramie was glad he had chosen Tec; he was a good lad. Ramie shook his head and smiled. That "lad" was only a few years his junior.

He motioned the remaining guard forward. Lynn was stocky, and unlike Tec had the look of a man twice his age. He studied Ramie with mild confusion.

"Lynn, please search the market for a beautiful golden broach. Money is no object. I'll meet you back here tomorrow at high sun." Ramie handed Lynn another bag of gold, far more than a broach would cost in three lifetimes. Lynn's eyes widened, but after the initial shock they flickered back to Ramie.

"I can't leave you alone, my lord. It's against code."

Ramie heaved a tired sigh. In all his days he never thought he would say what he was about to say. "Starting now, you must break code. I must attend to something private. Go to the ship tonight and announce I haven't found anything I fancy. Tell them I will search in the morning and may not return before the setting sun. But Lynn, make your lies believable. If you don't you'll have no place in my army and no place in life. Do you understand?"

Lynn straightened to attention and nodded. "As you wish, my lord."

Ramie spurred his mount forward, trying not to analyze all the things that could go wrong. He knew it was asinine to attempt to ride to the Jaguars and back within a day and a half, but he had to try – for Ren.

At least that's what he kept telling himself.

He rode hard, forcing his mind to clear. If he thought about his destination it would shatter his resolve. So, for the first time in his life, Ramie let his mind go blank. He didn't think of magic; he didn't think of Ista; he tried not to think at all.

Byn was a beautiful area, its rocky landscape not only sensual, but haunting. Huge boulders dotted the terrain, some twice as tall as Mortar. Trees were sparse, but lush long grass danced in the breeze. In heavy storms the grass would flatten, only to rise when the breeze beckoned it once again. A painfully aching loneliness crept inside Ramie as he galloped past the boulders. Although he forced his mind not to focus on his destination his heart still knew, and in response the hurt and anger rose inside him like a summer storm.

The sun inched higher in the sky and not one splash of shade invaded his path. Sweat glided down his skin, creating a constant itch. As the haze dissipated, the rugged peaks of the Jaguars dominated his vision.

Ramie had never been to the Jaguars in body, but he had been there many times in spirit. The Jaguar's snowcapped peaks seemed to disappear into the atmosphere. He had heard of some trying to climb those peaks, but had never heard of anyone returning. The peaks were steep, with air too thin to breathe. Year-round snow and ice warded off any sign of life.

Ramie stopped Mortar and unstrung his water skin. He took a swig and then poured a scant amount of water over his head. The water dissipated quickly, but a cool breeze from the mountains dove past him, chilling him despite the oppressive heat. After he wiped the sweat from his upper lip he spurred Mortar into full gallop. He was making good time, but he needed to make better. He still had to find the place described to him almost ten years prior, and descriptions were rarely representative of actuality. Fortunately, he did know the mountain he needed to climb. It was easily spotted by the naked eye. It was the only peak that had a flat top, as if the Maker himself had come down and slapped off the mountain's crest in anger.

Within a degree of the sun he reached the mountain's base, and Ramie guided Mortar up the first path he found. The rocky mountain terrain was dense with evergreen trees. The smell reminded Ramie of Nigel's habit of gathering pine boughs from the surrounding forests of Oldan. Year round, Nigel's room smelled like it sat in the middle of the woods and not in the middle of a castle. Although Ramie teased his brother unmercifully he had inwardly loved Nigel's passion for the outdoors. He missed the ritual of the boughs but refused to gather them himself. It just wouldn't be right without his brother.

The higher he went the less rocky the soil and the denser the trees. The forest continued until the naked, snow-covered peaks began, leagues up the mountain. The sun was fading fast. He quickened his pace.

Trees brushed against him as he rode, and although he felt nervous about the imminent encounter the rugged terrain gave him a sense of peace. The growth around him became heavy, bending inward over the path in protective shelter. The comforting smell of sweet lemon-bud vines wound their way through the pines, further easing his nerves.

When he reached a bend in the trail he slowed, knowing he was approaching the place he sought. He had seen it in his dreams many times, but it had been revealed to him in late fall. It was still summer, the vegetation full. He needed to be cautious. He had no time for mistakes. He was cutting it close already.

When a rock wall rose before him he stopped and let the path disappear into the unknown. This was the place. Turning, he went back through the pines. He dismounted and led Mortar closer to the trees. After bending a few branches and peering over rocks, he found what he was looking for: trampled grass and a slight marring of the landscape. The well-hidden path began beneath a spidery pine whose branches had been carefully cut to cover the entrance. Ramie pulled the branches away and led Mortar through the brush only to discover the path led straight to a large boulder and disappeared from view.

Ramie walked around the boulder. Sure enough, the main path veered away from the rock. There were small, chiseled indentions in and around the gray stone. The man he sought didn't want to be found. He deliberately climbed the stone to hide the main path from view, and Ramie was sure the man didn't use the same trail past the stone for more than a few days at a time.

It was inventive but sad. At one time the man he sought loved human companionship; now the man isolated himself out of fear and loathing. As Ramie led Mortar down the worn, narrow trail that skirted around the mountain's edge, he grew nervous. He didn't mind heights, but as he looked down the slope he knew one misstep could mean his death. The path continued around the edge far longer than Ramie cared, but soon ventured back into the heart of the mountain where vegetation was thick.

The sun had set but the twin moons emitted ample light. He tried to enjoy the walk but he was too jittery. His mind was awash with fears, regrets and memories.

After a time he came to the beautiful clearing he had only seen in his dreams: a sea of grass and clover surrounded on three sides by tall, rugged pines that skirted the mountain's face and looped out and around a small wooden house. Smoke rose from the chimney. The man he searched for was sure to be home.

Ramie tied Mortar to a nearby tree and walked toward the house, heart pounding as if the Watcher himself were after him. He stopped at the door, marveling at the design. It was elaborately carved, with a star-shaped pattern adorning every inch. Ramie drew a deep breath, knocked, and waited. The slight echo of the knock made him uneasy. After all, who had ever knocked on this man's door?

When there was no reply, he twisted the handle and stepped inside. The stone fireplace immediately caught his attention. It was made with stones Ramie knew weren't found in the Jaguars. They were a beautiful array of colors: some red, others cream, others a deep cobalt. A pot of stew bubbled over dwindling flames and the smell of spices filled the room.

A lone wooden chair sat before the fire, worn but well crafted. Ramie felt a pang of sadness at the sight but quickly repressed his deepening empathy. The man had chosen isolation. He had sought help of no one. He deserved all the loneliness the solitary chair symbolized.

A small bed rested in the corner, animal pelts covering it. Even though it was still summer Ramie could already feel the chill in the night. He knew he could never survive the winter in the Jaguars and knew of no one but this man who could.

Logs were stacked five thick against the far wall, ready for the beginning of winter. Above the bed, wooden shelves were replete with bows, arrows and spikes for hunting fish and prey. A large bearskin rug made the room appear fuller than it really was.

Then Ramie noticed the carvings. They were everywhere, nestled in every corner, donning the mantle, set in windows and hung on walls. As Ramie scanned the work he almost forgot the purpose of his visit, for everywhere he turned he looked into his own eyes. One carving portrayed his fifteenth birthday, when his father had knighted him. He sat on a horse holding a sword, a large, cocky smile playing on his lips. It was that very year his world came crashing down. He wondered if he had ever smiled like that since. He had grown old at a young age.

Ramie wanted to push away the pain but he knew he was only delaying what he would have to face. At the sound of splitting wood, Ramie's eyes found a back door. It stood slightly ajar.

Ramie shoved all apprehensions aside and stepped onto the threshold. A man stood in front of a wide stump, ax in hand. There were already two layers of wood, from ground to roof, stacked against the house, but Ramie knew those layers would only last weeks in a Jaguar winter.

Sweat ran off the man's back like rivers, causing his long, wavy brown hair to stick to his skin. He wore only a pair of doeskin trousers. The muscles in his arms and chest barely strained as he lifted the ax and impaled a log. A sword Ramie recognized, for it matched his own, leaned against the tree stump. He wondered how often the man had been without a sword, even in sleep.

Although he had always believed the man was alive he had no solid evidence, only a word of a scout he had sent to find a homestead in the Jaguars. Ramie's anger evaporated. All that remained was a blinding fear. He thought of Ren, swallowed his feelings, and took a step forward.

"Nigel?"

The man spun, dropped his ax and grabbed the sword within heartbeats. Nigel's bright blue eyes glimmered with ferocity. His hair whipped across his chest and clung to heaving muscles. Although Ramie saw alarm in Nigel's demeanor he also saw savage determination. Nigel squatted in an attack stance as Ramie took another hesitant step forward, arms hanging defenseless at his sides.

"Nigel, it's me."

Nigel looked at him without emotion. His eyes were those of a hunted animal, depraved and stripped of everything but the need for survival. This wasn't the man Ramie knew.

This was not his brother.

Ramie backed away. It was a mistake he had come. He had been right all along. Nigel would have never done what this man had done. Nigel would have never abandoned him. Ramie backed into the house, turned, and fumbled for the door.

"Rye? Is that you?"

The pain in Nigel's voice froze him in place. Rye had been Nigel's nickname for him. It was a shortened form of Ramie, meaning "little king." The tears in Nigel's eyes took Ramie off guard. His brother's chest rose and fell in a quick rhythm, but it was no longer with deadly intent. It was with profound hope.

When Ramie finally nodded his reply, Nigel laughed and dropped his sword. Before Ramie knew it, his brother was embracing him.

All of Ramie's fears evaporated. He never thought he could be so happy again, and when they finally broke apart they were both smiling like the children they had left behind so long ago.

"How did you know? I mean." Nigel stiffened. He turned, looking in all directions.

"I'm alone, Nigel," Ramie said. "I suspected your deception and sent a scout ten years ago to search for a man in these mountains. He came back and informed only me. He didn't know who your were, only that I searched. The scout died a few years ago. He told no one, and neither did I."

Nigel straightened, eyes questioning. "You knew I was alive ten years ago?" His voice was quiet, hurt.

Ramie's anger came back in a rush. "You knew where I was, Nigel. You chose this life. I was just granting your wishes."

When Nigel's face twisted in anguish, Ramie regretted his harshness, but he spoke the truth.

"How did you know I was alive, Rye?"

Ramie's chest tightened at the sound of his nickname but made no effort to acknowledge it. He closed his eyes, remembering the day years before. It was amazing how one choice, one day, one breath, could affect the rest of life. But it had – Nigel's choice, that day, that breath. Ramie sighed and turned from his brother's gaze, wanting to block the memory from his mind, but it was a scene that had plagued his nightmares for years. "When they discovered your body, I refused to believe it. They tried to keep me from seeing you, but I broke free."

"You're always the pigheaded, stubborn one," Nigel said, trying to lighten the mood. It was Nigel's way of trying to banish the scene himself.

"Megglan and Sherri were easily identifiable. Their faces were whole, their bodies intact. But you had been ripped to shreds." Ramie's voice quivered. He fought to gain control. Nigel touched his arm but Ramie retreated, anger bubbling to the surface once again.

"I'm sorry I couldn't say goodbye."

Ramie glared at Nigel. "Did you think I wouldn't honor your wishes, Nigel? Did you think I wouldn't understand? All these years I needed you and you haven't been there! Father had to train me to be the leader you should have been!"

"You were always the king, Rye. We both knew it. Father knew it. I was just born first." The pain in Nigel's voice rained down on Ramie, calming him. He hadn't come here to reveal how much his brother had hurt him. He had come here on duty.

"What gave me away?"

Ramie grabbed Nigel's hand and held it up between them. Three bands, made of gold, silver, and bronze, were intertwined on his little finger. "The ring you gave Sherri was missing from her hand. Druids don't wear jewelry, Nigel. Druids wouldn't have taken it from her."

Tears filled Nigel's eyes at the reference to the promise. He nodded and blinked them back. "They killed them because of me." Nigel's voice held so much anguish Ramie almost reached out to him, but held his ground. The crazed look passed through Nigel's eyes once again. When it subsided all that was left was hate.

"Why?"

Ramie could almost feel Nigel's rage filtering through the air. It frightened him. His brother had always been quick to love. Now he was bound by hate.

Nigel motioned Ramie inside the house. He pulled a wooden jug from a shelf and poured two cups of wine. Ramie accepted one and went to stand by the fire. He almost felt as if he were dreaming the entire encounter, but just as he thought he would wake his brother's voice cut through the silence.

"Please sit. I'm sorry I have only one chair, I just – "

"Never expected visitors." Ramie turned to meet his brother's piercing gaze. "No, thank you. I've been in the saddle all day. I prefer to stand."

Nigel sat in silence. Blame and guilt stole into Nigel's eyes. At first Ramie thought Nigel was thinking about his vocation, but then he realized Nigel was thinking about Megglan and Sherri. Nigel blamed himself for their deaths.

"It wasn't your fault, Nigel."

Nigel stiffened. "You can't say that. You don't know what happened. You weren't there."

"I know enough to say it wasn't your fault. You knew the Druids might come when you discovered you could . . . move things. They did and you resisted. They killed Megglan and Sherri. You killed them. Simple."

Nigel discovered he had the calling power at the height of the Druid terror. Ramie and Nigel knew the Druids would come and try to change Nigel forever. They had been terrified. Everyone with the telekinesis ability was a threat to the Druids, no matter your political affiliation.

Nigel rocked back in the chair. His hair fell over him like a mane. Nigel was like their mother in every way: tall, slender, with thick brown hair and blue eyes. Ramie had their father's features: shorter, stockier, and darker. He had envied Nigel growing up, his stature and looks, but now Ramie was glad he was like his father, both in body and in mind. Ramie knew castle life had been hard on Nigel. Nigel was a free spirit, one who desired neither wealth nor title. Nigel would have preferred to be a knight for a king, not a king himself. Ramie was stable, a rock, like their father, and although he didn't necessarily desire rule, it was who he was.

When Nigel began to speak his voice was so soft, Ramie had to step closer to hear.

"It was a beautiful spring day and we decided to go to the far side of the lake to be alone. You were training for the upcoming sword competition. You almost skipped it to join us. Thank the Maker you didn't.

"Three Druids appeared as soon as we rode into the forest. Meg's horse reared and she was thrown. I ran to her, Sherri following. Meg had hit her head on a large stone but was unharmed. Then they entered my mind. Without even asking or speaking they entered it!" Nigel pounded the arm of the chair.

Ramie tensed, reliving the terror as if it were happening again. He sensed the pain his brother felt; he saw Druids standing as impassive as stone; he felt the sun on his back; he smelled the girls' fear.

"I fought so hard. It hurt, Rye. It felt like my mind was about to rupture. I remember falling to my knees, barely able to stand, throwing all my efforts into pushing them out.

"Suddenly, the pressure became bearable and I looked up to find Sherri and Megglan beside the Druids. They had tried to stop them." Nigel's voice was soft as his brow knit with pain. "They had no weapons. They were only imploring the Druids to wait. But the Druids stabbed them. Without hesitation, the Druids stabbed them."

Nigel's chest heaved with the memory, and his muscles rippled as if he were in combat. Ramie held his breath.

"I was filled with such rage when they tried to enter me again I blocked them somehow. I ran to the one holding Meg. I don't remember what I did to him but he fell in death.

"With only two Druids I knew I had a chance. I knocked the second one down and stabbed him with my dagger. The third one, well, he was the one I butchered.

"I dressed him in my clothes and I took his. I knew I could never go back. They would come for me again. They would kill others I loved until I let them have my mind. They would kill you, kill father."

Nigel drained his glass before he continued. "I would never be able to rule with the threat of the Druids, and if I left you would be safe. I decided to let the Druids, let everyone believe me dead and disappear. I've never used the calling power again and somehow I have literally blocked it away behind a door of my own making."

"Then why the isolation? Why not live where people are?"

Nigel looked at Ramie for a long time without replying. Although Ramie knew the answer, he wanted to hear it from Nigel.

"Because I'm hunted."

"You're the Black Knight, aren't you?"

"Yes, I am."

Nigel observed Ramie with deathly calm eyes, devoid of emotion or feeling. They were the Black Knight's eyes. The Black Knight was the sword of justice. The Druids were the violators of justice.

Ramie knew Nigel thought his little brother wouldn't understand. Nigel was wrong.

Near the end of the Black Knight's ride, the Drek, the Druid leader, had placed a price on the Knight's head. The reward for the Black Knight would purchase kingdoms. The reward for accurate information could support an entire family for ten lifetimes.

"Do you remember a man warning you there was a price on your head?"

"Yes, he came right before I went into hiding."

"I sent him."

Nigel studied Ramie before breaking out into a boyish grin, prior tenseness forgotten. Ramie smiled back, feeling better than he had in years.

"Why didn't he tell me it was you?"

"The messenger didn't know who had given him the message. The Druids would have retaliated against Yor if they suspected I warned you. When you went into hiding I thought it was in this area. You always talked about wanting to see these mountains. I've wanted to come for years."

"But?" Nigel asked, rising to his feet.

"I waited for you to send word Nigel, to me, your only brother, that you were alive!" Ramie paused, forcing himself to calm. "When nothing ever came, I thought . . . "

"Thought what?"

Ramie's eyes were hard as they held his brother's gaze. "That you wanted to forget your life, everything about it, me included. That hurt me more than you know, Nigel. When someone sends a message like that I don't go after them."

Nigel looked away and heaved a sigh. "I wanted to send word but I didn't want to endanger you or your family. If anyone discovered my identity you would have had the entire clan of Druids fighting against Oldan. You know that."

Ramie shook his head. He had been waiting for this for fifteen years. "But you've changed, Nigel. No one would suspect you if you came back, except those who knew you well, and I could let them go, send them to another city to work. At least you would be with those who love you."

In response, Nigel slowly raised his left hand. In his palm was a brand: a hollow circle with two horned spikes curving up and inward from the top. It was the mark of evil and hatred. Ramie remembered the story. The last Druid remaining on the mainland managed to brand the Black Knight, ensuring all who saw him would know the truth. The brand looked wicked, like it had been done just yesterday.

Nigel raised an eyebrow. "I don't think this would go unnoticed, do you?"

"Gloves, Nigel, you could wear gloves."

"And if the king wanted me to go for a swim, what then? Do I wear my gloves in the water?"

It was an exaggeration on Nigel's part, but Ramie knew what he meant. Sooner or later someone would suspect him, see the brand, and connect the story. No matter how much the Black Knight was admired, even loved, not many could refuse the money the Druids offered.

"So why did you come if you decided not to find me?" Nigel asked with a slight hint of annoyance.

"A man I care a great deal about is in trouble."

"What does that have to do with me?"

"The Druids will hunt him."

Hatred filled Nigel's eyes once again, but after a brief time the hate faded into scorn. "The Druids haven't set foot on the mainland since I rode, and they won't until I've been found." Nigel turned to pour himself another chalice of wine. "They won't come again for many years."

"Magic has been reborn, Nigel."

The Black Knight stopped in mid-stance, wooden carafe poised over his chalice. After a few breaths, he proceeded to pour. "I suspected as much."

"You have it, don't you?"

"Yes, but I won't use it, just like I won't use the power of the Druids."

"This man has to use it, and he also has the power of the Druids." Ramie paused to watch an array of emotions flicker across Nigel's tan features: hatred, revenge, and curiosity. But also one Ramie hoped to see, and it dominated the others: a strong desire to help all those hunted by the Druid clan. Ramie sat on the hearth and began to relay what he knew of magic's rebirth.

"They'll come for him. They won't allow someone as powerful as Ren to walk free. The Druids have always considered themselves superior to the normal man. They won't like magic's rebirth, and they'll interfere. Ren will be the first they seek, and he's the only one who can stop Ista."

Nigel remained silent for a long time. Ramie rose and circled the room, inspecting each carving. They were replicas of the things Nigel held dear: his horse, the Yor castle, trees, waterfalls, but most were of Ramie, Meg, and Sherri. Nigel had never given up on him. He had given up on Nigel. All these years he had been bitter because Nigel had never sent word to him. How could he have been so selfish? He could have sent word to Nigel just the same.

When he found his voice it came out a harsh whisper. He didn't like to admit he was wrong. "I'm sorry I didn't come sooner. I've hurt you. Forgive me."

"Don't regret the past, Rye. Let's hope for a better future."

Ramie smiled. Nigel smiled back.

"I must go. I have to make Port Bynni before anyone on my ship suspects. I can't trust anyone."

"Do you have the Quy?"

Nigel's question took Ramie by surprise. "Of course not," he lied. "You are the free spirit, not I."

Nigel studied him only briefly before turning to a closet and pulling out a thin cloak. "I'll walk you to the main path," he said, draping the cloak over his bare shoulders. Nigel hesitated, the light of the fire softening his features. When Nigel turned back, Ramie saw the brother he had lost over fifteen years ago. "I've missed you, Rye."

Ramie drew an unsteady breath. "And I you, more than you know."

When they walked out of the house a large black horse grazed near Mortar, not an ounce of color donning his sleek coat: the Black Knight's horse. He was loose, not bound by chain or rope. Ramie would have thought the horse would be wild by now, for it had been years since the Black Knight's last ride, but Nigel had always had a way with animals.

Ramie untied Mortar and they walked in silence, each just content the other was there. They had been close growing up, even though they were as different as two brothers could be. But they learned from each other, and in an odd way each found strength in the other's differences. Ramie let his anger drain until only a rueful peace remained. Nigel was his brother. And Nigel was alive. Nothing else mattered.

Nigel led him around the rock face. A few clouds had rolled in, allowing scant light to filter through, making the path dangerous to unfamiliar eyes. Nigel pointed out dips, rocks and sharp turns until they came to the second trail leading to the boulder.

Although the path was easy, they slowed even more, each not wanting to say goodbye.

"Will you help him?" Ramie finally asked.

"I'll think on it."

Ramie nodded, content with the answer. "That's all I ask."

When they reached the boulder Nigel turned, concern in his eyes. "Continue south, away from the city. There's a tributary that runs into the Divi. A ship leaves tomorrow at dawn. This time of year the river is swift and will reach Port Bynni by midday."

Ramie nodded, not willing to trust his voice.

Nigel leaned forward and embraced him. "Take care, little brother."

"Come home, Nigel. I'll find a way to hide your identity."

Nigel laughed. "That's Rye, always thinking large."

Nigel gave a little bow before he turned and ran into the night, thin cloak billowing behind him. Ramie shivered in the cold, wondering how his brother didn't go mad in the isolation.

Ramie waited until Nigel had disappeared from sight before he looked up at the moons and calculated the time. He had to hurry. If he didn't make the ship, he would never make the city at high sun. He led Mortar to the main path, mounted, and whispered a sharp command.

Mortar jumped into motion. Ramie held on, trusting Mortar's instincts to guide him safely down the mountain. But on this ride his mind was far from clear. He thought of the Druids claiming Ren and killing Nigel. He vowed that if they did so he would personally annihilate the entire Druid race.

- - -

Nigel didn't hurry back. Instead he sought strength in the mountain and allowed the chill air to sort his thoughts. There were so many emotions stirring inside him it was impossible to place them all. When Ramie had first appeared he had been so overjoyed he had lost all sense of who he had become. Ramie brought memories of love and laughter, of childish pranks and dreams, of things he had left long ago. The Druids had destroyed everything he had and everything he was. He hadn't told Ramie the entire story. He hadn't told Ramie how Meg had suffered.

Meg had been beautiful, with silk-fine brown hair, eyes as black as pearls and a heart like none other. All Meg had to do was look at you and you couldn't resist her request. But she had been as beautiful on the inside as the outside. She never demanded anything, was full of laughter and love. No, he didn't want Rye to know how she had cried for him to run away and hide. He didn't want Rye to know when Meg's eyes found her belly, where her guts were spilling, she had tried to put them back, murmuring she would be all right, that he should leave her and run so the Druids could never harm him. He didn't want Rye to know how Meg had died in his arms, so slowly.

Meg, the girl who had the whole family attend the burial of a cricket she had accidentally killed when she was five; the girl who never forgot to give her brothers a kiss before she went to bed; the girl who would sit for a degree of the sun just to watch a flower open; the girl who deserved every happiness, had died in terror and anguish, worrying about him.

And Sherri, she had become Megglan's best friend that summer. Sherri's father held one of the lesser holdings in Yor, but had managed to save enough to pay the price for her to train in all manners of court. Nigel had quickly fallen in love with her, and she him.

Sherri was pure as Meg, and although not as strikingly beautiful, Sherri possessed the one trait Nigel always found attractive in women – determination. Sherri would bite her lip in concentration when she studied. If she didn't master something one day she would stay up all night and have it mastered the next. Even his father was impressed with her, and little impressed their father. Jarek Augustus could do anything.

He had watched Sherri for weeks without speaking to her. He hadn't known how to approach her. All the men at the castle spoke of her fiery will and her eyes, her green eyes. They were as bright as the morning's grass. When she looked at him he always seemed to lose his voice. Then it happened. One day he was jogging to a nearby stream, hurrying to take a dip before the weekly dance. She was running from the water, in a hurry to dry her hair before she prepared for the night's festivities. They had collided. He had innocently reached out to catch her, but as soon as they touched time seemed to stop. He could still see her, wet blonde hair clinging to her skin, eyelashes damp from her swim, lips parting when she recognized the man holding her.

They hadn't attended the dance that night.

Nigel toyed with the ring he wore on his little finger. He had given it to her the morning before the Druids came, vowing to love her always. Then her life was taken from him. He hadn't even had a chance to say goodbye. The Druids had her blood on their hands. The age-old hatred whirled inside him like a gale, desperate for release.

His emotions always spun out of control when he thought of the Druids. What gave them the right to say who could have special abilities and who couldn't? What gave them the right to act like gods and rid the world of what they found unworthy? His hate for them ran as deep as the ocean and as high as the mountains. He would shed no tear if the Maker annihilated every single one of them.

Nigel forced his mind to clear. He hadn't wanted to become what he had become, but the Druids had left him no choice. Without the Black Knight the Druids would have taken over the Lands, closing out what they would when they wanted, demanding people bow to them as the supreme race. They would have brought the Dark Ages again. Magic didn't need to be present to have tyranny, only greed.

He felt no regret for his actions, but he did feel sorrow. He had killed many Druids, but none of their deaths would bring back Sherri or Meg.

Over the years he had dreamed of returning to Yor, but he knew his return would bring destruction on his brother and the kingdom. Eventually someone would see the brand and recognize his face. Then he would be taken to the Druids, dead or alive, for the reward.

He whistled as he walked into the clearing where his house was nestled. When he heard Rage whinny a greeting, he turned to find the black stallion cantering through the crescent curve of trees. Rage stopped before him and pawed the grass, kicking up clods of soil. Nigel leaned his head against Rage's nose and breathed in the familiar scent of dirt and sweat. Memories of riding wild and free, destroying every Druid who remained on the mainland, surfaced within him: the blood, the screams, and the terror. He had been mad with revenge. At times he thought he'd gone insane, but other times, when he rode through the streets and the people applauded his efforts, he knew he wasn't insane. He was justice, pure and simple.

When the colossal price had been placed on his head he had come to the Jaguars, knowing he could never leave. Over the years he had tried to will himself peace and just remember the happiness he had once known. That was when he started carving. At times, when he brought to life those he loved, he wept. At other times he felt great joy at seeing loving faces. And so he went on, focusing on the land, survival, and strength. In the Jaguars the summer was preparation for the rest of the year, and the rest of the year was a fight to stay alive. In the winter he fought creatures desperate for food, traveled in the snow-covered peaks to find nourishment and battled each day for the right to live. Thoughts of home and happiness were something he put at the back of his mind.

Ramie had stirred them up again, and along with those feelings came painful memories, and hate.

The Druid threat may be back.

Nigel thought of the man Ramie had mentioned. Ren reminded Nigel of himself. Ren and he were very similar creatures. Nigel found that to be a small comfort. Ramie still loved him, no matter the pain both of them had lived. And Ramie was right. The Druids would come for Ren. How could he allow that? The man had lost his home, his world, and the Druids would destroy him for it.

Nigel stroked Rage's shimmering black neck. "How would you like to ride again, Rage?"

Rage nickered as if to say he would do whatever Nigel decided. Nigel sighed and walked inside the house. He went directly to the chair he had crafted years ago, slid it over, lifted a loose board, and reached inside the hollow. His hand caught hold of familiar leather. Nigel gritted his teeth and drew out the large, black bundle. He pulled each piece apart and inspected them individually. The pants were rugged and worn but whole. The tunic was fashioned from fine black silk and tied at the shoulder and waist. He had purchased it only days before retreating to the Jaguars, his old tunic tossed when the seams had torn too much to mend. His cape came to the floor and encircled his body with ease. He had cured it until it was so loose it glided around him like a second skin, covering his form until he struck. The gloves were still as they had been, one whole, the other falling apart from the branding iron he had pushed away. If he rode again he would need new gloves. Those he would need for the rest of his life.

No padding remained on his black deerskin boots. He would have to fashion soles if he left. Although winter was two seasons away, it was coming, and the boots were in no condition to travel in ice or snow. Nigel placed the boots aside and reached back inside the hollow. This time he brought out a large burlap bag. After a few heartbeats he dumped its contents. Multiple tufts of black hair spilled over his lap: the hair of each Druid he had killed. Nigel gazed down at them with no joy or sorrow, no remorse or satisfaction. He felt nothing, absolutely nothing.

He looked at the clothes strung over the floor. The Black Knight. Nigel sat back on the hearth, letting the fire warm his sudden chill. The stew bubbled and spices filled the room, but Nigel had no appetite. Now he was worried about Ren, and Ramie. Nigel could always see right through Ramie's lies. Although Ramie said he didn't have the power, Nigel knew better, and he knew the Druids would hunt all those in high positions with the Quy. This time it would be a battle between wizard and Druid supremacy.

Ramie would be among the Druids' first targets.

Nigel knew his brother was smart enough to hide the ability, but Nigel also knew how much effort it took to block away something that was inherently part of you. It was only a matter of time before Ramie was discovered.

It had taken him a year to learn how to shove the calling power away: a year of running, and a year of prayer, but he had succeeded. Ramie wouldn't run, couldn't run, for Ramie was the king of Yor. Ramie was also stubborn, and would never allow the Black Knight to be his protector unless Ren was safe.

"Stubborn mule." Nigel's hand brushed something. He looked down to see two small burlap bags propped against the hearth. Picking one up, he peered inside. Just as he thought, the bag of bullion would feed the entire Lands for a week. Nigel sighed. He was tired of thinking about it.

"All right, little brother. You win."

Chapter 16

Ren sat by the fire as the twin moons rose higher, staring at the prophecy book. He opened it every moons' click, reading the prophecy time and again. The men were preparing dinner and talking in hushed whispers as if the very forest had ears.

Ren leaned back into his gear, instinctively petting the kota that had curled up beside him. Despite her small size she had kept the hurried pace of their horses. Since it looked like she had joined their group, Ren had decided to call her Keena. It meant "most beautiful" in the ancient tongue.

When he shifted, Keena placed her head on his knee and closed her lazy eyes, purring in contentment. He smiled and rubbed the tender area where her horn protruded. Her purr deepened into a thunderous legato.

Neki twisted around from the fire to see what had caused the disturbance. "If only I could make women purr like that."

Ren shrugged. Markum smiled and went back to the fire.

Quinton didn't pay any attention to the banter. He sat deeply involved with diagramming the area in the dirt, pondering which direction they should take in the morning. Ren was glad Quinton was with him. The last thing he wanted to do was worry about distance and direction.

The Alcazar had never been explored. It was a burnt ruin, collapsing inward, leaving a dangerous structure rumored to take any life that ventured inside. One month ago he would have laughed if someone had told him he would be intent on exploring the ruin, but now the Alcazar was his only link to the One.

Markum had described the man in his dreams with vivid detail: the widow's peak, the long hair, and the dark, midnight eyes. Ren could almost see the wizard's ageless eyes, frozen in the grips of time, searching for him through the ages. Ren didn't like the thought. Had he been born because of the prophecy, or had the prophecy been born because of him?

A distant rumbling broke Ren out of his thoughts. The kota's ears perked up. Markum and Neki sensed the change and ceased their chatter. Ren placed a hand on the hilt of his sword, eyes darting to the surrounding trees. The kota bounded to her feet, brown eyes wide with caution. Then they heard the pounding hooves of riders.

Quinton shouted a warning. Neki drew his saber. The horses sensed the tension and screamed in fear. Ren had chosen to camp in a clearing again, concerned the watch would be unable to spot a threat before it was too late. Now Ren chastised his foolishness. They had no shelter, and no place to hide. The hooves pounded closer, inundating the still night, but it sounded like only one or two riders, not a troop of soldiers.

Neki's curved blade glimmered in the firelight, but the stones on the hilt remained torpid. Ren recalled Grauss' words: *"The ruby is for luck in battle, the emerald wards off evil doings, and the sardonyx wards off things not of this world. The stones will glow when they're working and will be able to warn you if trouble is near."*

Ren lowered his blade as the pounding hooves drew closer. Neki saw his look and straightened, trusting his grandfather's word without any hesitation.

Then there were other sounds around them: rustling leaves, vehement snarls, and howls. The ruby and emerald began to glow with a brilliant intensity.

Ren raised his sword and lowered himself in an attack stance. The hooves pounded closer, heralding doom. The growls became more intense. Michel and Galvin broke through the forest at full speed, faces pallid masks of fear.

"Fire, Ren! Fire!" Markum shouted as soon as he saw the two-headed wolf snapping at Galvin's heals.

More wolven emerged from the forest, running at full speed, jaws dripping saliva and eyes glowing a golden green. Puissant muscles rippled underneath their dark gray coats as they bounded toward them. Neki was the first to act. Grabbing a few logs from the fire he tossed them paces away, forming a circle.

The kota began to prance. Her drumming hooves sounded like a declaration of war.

Markum ran for the horses as they bucked and screamed in terror, trying to flee from the predators' scent. Someone shouted Ren's name. When he turned a wolf was only paces away, poised to take to the air. Beside him the kota bowed her head. Ren tried to push her aside but she refused. A glow came from the small horn at the crown of her head. Within a heartbeat a thin ray of light shot from her horn, hitting the wolf in the flank. The creature halted in mid-stride, a heartbeat before it would have leapt for Ren's back. Before Ren had time to react another came from his left. Quinton grunted as he slung a fire-laden log and knocked the beast down. The wolf howled in pain and retreated. Ren grabbed another log, hurling it at the next one that came near. Michel's mount, eyes wide with terror, leapt the circle of flames and crashed into the center haven, Galvin close behind.

The wolven were everywhere. They surrounded them.

Michel jumped off his horse just in time to impale one of the beasts as it jumped the flames. The creature landed within the safety of the circle. Quinton threw a log in its direction but missed. Galvin kicked the beast into the circle of fire. It howled in pain but only rolled paces away. Its eyes glowed a vile green as it watched them through the flames. The thick fur behind its neck rose like needles.

When another leapt over the flames, Ren did the one thing he could to defend himself, all the while knowing it would only make the beast stronger; he sliced through it. The wolf fell near him. He forced the beast toward the fire. The fangs from the creature began to close around his arm, but as the flames touched the creature's flesh it howled and released him.

It lay limp beyond the circle, but Ren knew it would soon start to stir.

"More fire!" he yelled, eyes glued to the creature that had begun to grow.

Galvin lit more logs and filled the gaps in the flames. Soon the barrier was firm. The horses paced back and forth, eyes wide with fear, but they didn't bolt, fearing the wolven more than the flames.

"I count twenty-two, Ren," Quinton said, resting his bloody sword on the ground. Thick clods of gray fur clung to the edges. Quinton had fought back more than a few.

The wolven circled the fire. Their snarls could be heard over the crackling flames. The circle would hold the wolven at bay for a while, but not until dawn.

Quinton heaved an unsteady breath. "Fire is the only thing that deters them?"

"That's all I'm aware of," Ren replied. "Markum?"

"Yes," Markum said. "Swords are useless. Each cut only makes them stronger. Fire can't kill them, but it weakens them."

"I hate to bring this up," Neki said, "but the wood we have won't last long. We only have a few more branches."

Neki was right. Only a few stray branches lay discarded within reach, and the nearest trees were over a hundred paces away. It would be suicide to try to gather more. They were running out of time.

Galvin looked at Ren. "Can you use magic to bring in more wood?"

Ren looked at the surrounding trees and tried to concentrate on the force inside him. He found the light, reached for it, grasped it, and let the white-hot ferocity flood through him, but it dissipated as quickly as it came, almost as if it had a mind of its own. He frowned, frustration coursing though him.

Turning to Galvin, he shook his head. Neki stepped forward and focused on the distant woods. Ren held his breath. Neki had touched the Quy with ease back at Stardom. If he could do so now it would be their salvation.

After a few heartbeats, Neki's shoulders sagged. "I don't know how."

"We need more fire," Quinton mumbled under his breath.

"They're coming closer," Markum said

Galvin and Quinton immediately took the remaining branches to where the fire had begun to wane.

Ren walked to the far side of the circle, frustration coursing through his veins. How could he merge a body with a spirit and not move a piece of wood? Even the Druids' calling power was useless. Unless he could see a fallen log he couldn't call it to him.

The wolven continued to move closer. Now Ren could see the color of their eyes: brownish bronze with pinpricks of blue and gray. They circled the men one after the other, waiting for the fire to die. The few they had cut down were a hands-width taller than the rest, hair still bloodied from the men's swords.

He was the Chosen, the one who had rebirthed the power, and there was nothing he could do to save his men from the wolven. Only dragon's fire was lethal for the beasts, for it poisoned their blood internally. They would need nothing short of a miracle to survive until dawn.

"We need to find more things we can burn," Ren said. "Everyone start looking."

The others began searching their packs. Ren's eyes found the prophecy book. It lay on the ground where he had dropped it. It would be the last thing they would burn, but if need be it would be burnt with the rest.

Markum caught his look and shook his head. "No, more prophecy will appear. We can't burn it. It may guide you in the months to come."

Before Ren could voice that they may not have any time left, Michel shouted a warning. Ren spun in time to see one of the wolven jumping through the fire toward Neki. The svelte man reacted quickly, but not quickly enough. The wolf clamped down on his shoulder.

Rage surged through Ren. He couldn't allow this to happen. He wouldn't allow it.

He grabbed the whip-like thread in his mind and propelled his emotions forward with impetuous precision. A thunderous clap resonated around them as the wolf ignited into white-hot flame. Ren's mind exploded with heat as his world became dark. Just before he crashed to the ground he heard Galvin scream his name.

- - -

Total blackness surrounded him. It was a black so dense it hurt to see. It was as if the gates of Abyss had been opened and the world had been consumed in its tenebrous gloom. Was this the darkness?

Had he failed so soon?

From the depths of the darkness came a quiver of light. As he watched it began to grow larger, eating the darkness with a steady cadence. Then he realized the shimmer wasn't growing larger but gliding his way. It flickered with silver sparks as it came, daring the darkness to halt its approach.

As the light neared he decided it wasn't gliding but walking in smooth, rhythmic patterns. Instead of fearing the light's approach, he anticipated it, longed for it, but at the same time was humbled by its radiance. A soft peace began to grow inside him, and as the light drew closer it grew even more profound. Then he saw its beauty. He was almost blinded.

It was a woman. A long, white gown clung to her shape, tight enough to reveal exquisite curves but loose enough to be enticing. A silver chain circled her slender waist and dangled from her hips. Golden blonde hair cascaded down her back until it brushed the chain. She was so brilliant her very presence cursed the darkness and banished any hint of diablerie.

She smiled. It took his breath away, and when he looked into her solid silver eyes he had to turn away. They were filled with such compassion and caring he felt unworthy. She brushed his check in tender affection and turned his face to her own.

He trembled as the power of the Quy coursed through her, into him, and then back again. As he gazed into her heart-shaped face he slowly began to discern light particles, so minute they were barely detectable, coursing over her skin. They moved so fast she appeared fuzzy on the surface.

When he looked closer he realized her entire form consisted of the particles moving frantically to form her shape. There were so many of them she appeared solid, with only the extremes of her being noticeably illusory.

"You're strong, my Chosen." Her carillon voice carpeted the darkness with music. After she stopped speaking he waited, listening to its charms echoing in the void.

"Your Chosen?" His voice seemed far away, almost unreal. But it didn't matter. He was with her, and he loved her without even knowing her.

"Yes, my Chosen. Although I didn't make you, I've waited for you. I've been alone for so long." Her solid silver eyes peered past him into the black void.

He stood, transfixed by her beauty, hanging on her words as if they were wine. Her eyes cleared and she turned to him, smiling an apology for her inattentiveness. He smiled back, unable to feel anything but elation in her presence. When she spoke her voice was a harmonious whisper, tingling around him like rain.

"I want to feel people again. I want to be a part again. Although I fear it will be worse before it gets better." Her lips twisted into a tight frown.

An overwhelming desire to help her coursed through him. The loneliness and pain in her voice was more than he could bear. She deserved nothing less than laughter and light, and that couldn't even begin to describe what she deserved. He would have given his life to see her smile. "I'm sorry," he said, "but I don't understand. Who are you?"

She laughed. It sounded like a multitude of high notes perfectly in tune with one another. "I'm the Quy, Ren Razon. I'm what you're fighting to save."

Ren. That was his name. Her beauty had taken every memory from him.

She laughed again and cradled his face in her hands. He closed his eyes, savoring the sensation.

"You're the Quy?"

Her lips twisted into a grin. "Yes."

"You're beautiful."

She smiled and took his hand. "You make me beautiful, my Chosen."

They began to walk in the darkness. He felt as if he should do something to protect her, but there was no threat. He moved closer anyway, the nothingness disturbing him. Something so beautiful shouldn't be in a place so dark.

"Others make me ugly. They use me for glory, fame, or wealth. You use me for love. That's why you're my Chosen. You only use me in love."

Ren looped her hand through his arm and pondered her words. "Not all the time. I collapsed part of the castle in anger. I lit the fire on the wolf in rage."

She stopped and turned to face him. Her silver eyes glowed with extreme power. "You're wrong. You collapsed the castle because of your love for a man killed. You lit the fire on the wolf because of your love for a man about to be killed.

"Continue to fight this way, Ren, for only love can defeat those who strive to control me. Before you strike make sure you do so out of love. If you begin to use other emotions like hate, lust, envy, or desire you'll fail. Sometimes you'll strike in anger, or shun the one you strike at, but if you remember the love inside, if the love inside is what drives you, all will be well."

As they continued to walk in the darkness the last of her words lingered in his mind. He thought of Aidan. "Can you tell me how to use the power to help those I love?"

The Quy shook her head. "No. You use me, but I don't know how you use me. I'm not alive, but I exist. That's why I can't fight for me. You must fight for me."

"I'm fighting for you to be in the world again?"

"Yes and no," she said. "Yes, you fight for me to be connected to the minds and hearts of people. But no, you have already given me that. Soon this nothingness I'm in will be light as people begin to use me for good. You fight for that to happen, for this to be light. Others fight for this to be darkness."

"Would the darkness hurt you?"

"No, I'll still be the Quy. I'll still exist. I'll feel no pain, but I know others will feel pain. You'll feel pain, and I don't like the thought. If this place becomes darkness it will be just that – darkness. But there's no laughter in the darkness and there's no joy in the darkness. I'm not who I want to be in the darkness. I can't see what I want to see in the darkness. If complete darkness finds this place I'll become darkness, and light will cease to be."

Ren's heart constricted. He didn't want the musical beauty standing before him to become darkness. The thought terrified him. "What can I do?"

She stopped and turned to face him. "Be you, my Chosen." Her brow lifted in hope. "For you are the one who can defeat the darkness."

"I'll try."

"Don't try," she said, losing her smile. "You must do. If you do not, all those you love are lost. In a way, I'm lost. But you underestimate you. You don't see the love that drives you. Others do, that's why they follow."

The Quy stepped forward, silver eyes intense. "Only one other has ever seen me. That means your feelings are so strong they hurt you in here." She placed her hand over his heart. An array of emotion built within him: all his love he held for his kingdom, his mother, Michel, Aidan, the men with him. They overwhelmed and comforted at the same time. Then the pain came, the pain his love brought: the death of his men, Aidan unreachable, creatures attacking those he held dear. The pain ripped through him with breathtaking surety.

"The emotion stronger than love is the pain love brings," she continued. "Unless one is strong enough to release the pain to pursue love again, nothing can equal it. Together, love and pain produce the strongest emotion of all and can overwhelm anything evil produces."

She began walking again, but this time more slowly, as if anticipating her imminent departure. He fumbled for his next question, not wanting her to leave. "How did I come to see you?"

"Strength in your love. When you conjured fire your mind snapped. You instinctively reached inside yourself and found me to preserve the power inside you. No wizard, sorceress or mage has ever sparked fire. Doing so drained you almost to the point of death. Due to your strength and instinct you reached for me to have me help you rebuild your strength, to save your life.

"When you learn to use me and grow in the strength of your emotions, this ability won't affect you as it has now. You're still unused to me being inside you and the energy it takes to use me."

Ren thought of Neki. "So, Neki is safe?"

"Not yet."

Ren stopped in mid-stride, but when he gazed into her eyes her look melted his fear.

"You were there and then you were here. There is still happening, but here is so fast, one heartbeat there can be years here. Neki isn't safe yet. But don't worry. You'll go back to your men in the same heartbeat you left. Our talk is but a breath in your time, but that breath is long enough to give you what you need to live." She stopped and held out her hand. "Now, give me your sword."

Ren looked at her in confusion before handing over his sword.

The Quy took a step back. Her hair flowed around her shoulders, leaving her neck exposed. The small smile playing on her lips took his breath away. He vowed to lay down his life to protect her from the darkness.

"I may never get another opportunity to help you. I would like to give you something to assist you in the days to come and remind you of me."

Ren forced his lips to move. "There's not a chance I could forget you."

Her titillating laugh sent shivers down his spine. She held the sword straight above her, silver eyes glowing with power. Ren took a step back as he watched the blade grow longer and more lethal. The hilt bubbled with texture, the "T" becoming two silver dragons' heads: one with white-hot eyes and the other with twin pools of darkness. Their mouths opened into a roar and their scales reached back to merge with the handle. The blade separated at the dragons' scales, becoming a hollow teardrop that slid down the blade, forming an equilateral triangle between it and the silver dragons' heads.

The Quy began to sing. Her voice was so crystalline it sounded like the wind rippling among the tips of the tallest tree, bending the branches with gentle persuasion and caressing the leaves with its breath. It was so rich Ren could barely make out the words, but the more she sang the more distinct the words became until the tenor of her voice seared into his memory, repeating over and over words he would never forget:

May Choice, Chance, and Fate be with you
For all three play a part
Always choose the right
And when you roll the dice
Let life's kiss prove your heart.

When the sword was whole the Quy opened her silver eyes and looked at Ren. "Kneel, my Chosen."

Ren knelt without question, putting his right fist over his heart in the sign of complete submission.

He felt the cold blade of the sword hit his left shoulder and then his right, marking one who is to fulfill a quest.

"Mark my words, my Chosen. Love and pain go hand in hand, but hate exists through both. Beware of hate, for when hate consumes the soul darkness takes control."

He was frozen in place by her words. Her voice lingered in the nothingness.

"Arise, my Chosen."

As he looked into her eyes he felt her charge making the power grow stronger inside him. The sword disappeared. He felt its weight around his waist and glanced down at the sword's crest. It had two parallel lines slanting upward, with a third connecting the two, forming a backward Z, the symbol of victory. It glowed silver in the void.

The Quy walked forward and kissed him on both checks. "Victory, my Chosen."

Ren felt his love for her heighten as his vision began to blur. The silence of the void shifted and a whirlwind of sounds roared past. Ren opened his eyes to find Galvin and Michel leaning over him.

"Ren, are you all right?"

Ren nodded and pushed himself up. The fire surrounding them had grown taller and its flames were white.

"The wolf you lit on fire fell into the flames, Ren," Michel said. "When your magical flames exploded the circle the other wolven ran."

Ren turned, observing the waist-high white flames, a knot of fear in his chest. Markum lay paces from him, unconscious. Neki knelt beside him, pouring water over his head. Galvin followed Ren's gaze.

"Markum was too close to the flames. He was thrown backward."

Ren closed his eyes. He could have easily killed them all. He didn't understand the Quy or how he was using it. He needed to find the One. He needed to understand his own strength.

Markum stirred and Ren let his fear drain from him. Neki looked up and smiled. The wound on his shoulder seeped blood, but it didn't look severe and would heal soon enough.

His men were safe. That was all that mattered.

Ren rested his hand on the hilt of the Quy's sword. He could still feel her power lingering in the blade. He unsheathed it and examined the hilt. At the top, next to the crest, was the symbol for Choice: three arrows intersecting, meaning every decision you made directed you a certain way, either toward or away from the path you need to follow. Below Choice was the symbol for Chance: two astragali, or pieces of bone, carved with dots and used for gambling. Six dots showed on each astragali, the sonnez throw, or the luck roll as it was known. Finally, next to the beginning of the dragon's scales rested the symbol for Fate: a seemingly three-dimensional spiral, starting wide and collapsing inward, meaning at any point you start there was only one way to go.

"What does it say?" Galvin asked.

Ren's eyes flickered to the sword. Ancient script was carved on the silver blade repeating over and over a phrase Ren instantly recognized: *Truth Above All.* Ren lifted the sword until the light of the twin moons illuminated the script with vivid detail. A warm breeze blew past and Ren thought he heard the voice of the Quy rising above the treetops.

- - -

The circle of fire roared around them. The whiteness of the flames had faded and the wolven hadn't returned, but they had gathered more wood anyway. No one wanted to take any chances. The only one who slept was Neki, and although the grin normally dominating his features was gone, he slept peacefully.

The Quy's touch and voice still lingered in Ren's mind, but now he had even more unanswered questions. Ren shifted on his pad and looked up at the synergy constellation. He didn't know for sure, but he thought two of the stars were more aligned with the center. He wondered whom the three outlying stars represented and when or if he would ever find out.

Ren lifted his sword. The impressions of Choice, Chance and Fate called to the light, causing their emblems to blaze with golden fury. He wondered what the guardians of the Oracle would tell him if they were here.

Ren sat up, surprised at the thought. The prophecy book slipped off his stomach, pages flipping in the slight wind. The kota stirred beside him but didn't wake. Ren absently rubbed her neck in silent reassurance.

Since the quest began, he hadn't thought about the ancient temple where Choice, Chance, and Fate resided. When magic was first born the Maker had sent the Oracle to the Lands to help guide humanity. Although it was once a permanent temple, after the Dark Ages it disappeared and only showed itself to a select few. The Oracle hadn't been seen in four centuries, but with the rebirth of magic the Oracle was sure to return.

Ren fingered the hilt of his sword. The Quy had put Choice, Chance, and Fate's emblems there for a reason. He needed to seek the Oracle. Although the Oracle only appeared to a select few, he was the Chosen. Choice, Chance, and Fate may grant him entrance.

The Oracle would have the answers to the questions he desperately sought. The beings could tell him where to find the One and how to release Aidan. The quest was too important to deny searching for the Oracle.

"Ren, there's another prophecy."

Ren turned to find Markum staring down at the open prophecy book, a look of pure horror on his face.

On the page opposite the main prophecy more writing had appeared. It didn't look as methodical as the first. It was scrawled in haste, like someone had been fearful of losing the thought before putting it into words. There were even notes scribbled in the margins as if the composer of the verse had to decipher to whom or what the verse referred. In one margin there was a count of years totaling three hundred ninety eight, the exact time since the Wizard War.

Michel rose to his feet. "What does it say?"

Ren scanned the words as the men moved closer. Ren recited the verse out loud:

The dreamweaver will remain in death
When magic will choke his mind.
And he must choose only one
Door to open wide.
For if the wrong one he chooses,
The darkness will settle in
And the Chosen's heart and soul
Will be forever cold.

The dreamweaver could only refer to one person.

"Markum," Michel said, placing a concerned hand on the seer's shoulder. "Prophecy clouds the truth. It's probably not as bad as it sounds."

Chapter 17

"Similian," thought the Bane.

The Bane had just woken up, but Sim would rather he stay asleep. Foreboding was in all his talk.

Sim heaved a dragon's sigh. "Yes?"

"Where are we now?"

"We're over Stardom."

"Stardom?" Aidan stirred.

Sim's heart ached. He didn't know his heart could do that. He was jealous of this Ren, he knew. Sim wanted Aidan to forget Ren so they could talk of lakes and rivers and flying above sunshiny fields.

"Similian, the more she looks though your eyes, the more she breathes your air, the harder it will be for her to resist your influence. You don't want her to lose her identity."

"Please, I won't become the dragon. I need to know if Ren escaped."

"You must fight to keep your identity, my child," the Bane reemphasized. "The dragon is much stronger than you. If you give into every urge you'll be forever lost inside Similian. If your whole self wasn't with you, you already would be."

Similian heaved a grunt. "To forever be Similian isn't a bad thing, Bane."

Sim landed in an apple orchard on the outskirts of the city. "Focus, dear one, and you'll see." Sim bent to pluck an apple off one of the pink-blossomed trees. It was sweet, and some juice dribbled down his chin. He grinned as he thought of Mezuzah licking it off. He must find Mezuzah soon. It was, after all, still mating season.

He felt a slight tickling as Aidan moved inside him. He scratched his side, knowing it wouldn't do any good, but feeling the need to do so anyway. Heartbeats later Aidan looked through his eyes. The walls of the city were right beside him. He smelled the heavy scent of man but it was days old. No man had been in the orchard for some time.

Aidan sighed and Sim could almost sense her sadness. He wanted her to be happy inside him, but she was making it difficult. Although she laughed it was restrained, although she spoke nicely she was distant. But it still felt good to have her looking through his eyes.

The bees swarming around the trees made the air come alive with a rhythmic undertone. Sim looked around, allowing Aidan to observe the landscape. Not too far in the distance redwood trees started and continued north and west. The paths on this side of the city were well traveled, and pebbled roads led to both Crape and Ketes.

Sim drew another breath, granting a bee access to his nostrils. He snorted it out.

"My child, this can only cause you harm in the end."

Sim scowled. The Bane always took the fun out of everything with warnings about the future. The future wasn't here. The present was here. Sim thought the present entirely better than the future.

"Sim, will you move closer to the orchard?"

Sim was about to step forward when he caught Ren's familiar scent. Aidan would recognize it. Now she had a dragon's sense of smell.

Aidan drew a sharp breath.

"What?" Sim quickly moved past the place that smelled of Ren.

"Ren's alive, Sim! Please, follow his trail!"

Sim didn't want to find Ren. Man was man. Ren was man. Man was something he never sought. He wouldn't harm this Ren, but he wouldn't help him either, although Mezuzah would like him more if he liked Ren. Sim scowled. This was getting complicated.

"Please, Sim." Aidan's voice betrayed intense emotion. He didn't understand how someone could feel so much for another. Dragons never showed that kind of weakness, except to their young, and that was more from pride than anything else.

"My child, you shouldn't weaken yourself. It will take everything you have to retain your identity."

Sim almost breathed fire. Why did the Bane have to be so negative?

"I have no identity without him." Aidan retreated back into the darkness. "We are linked, he and I."

"You're Sim the Vicious!" Sim released an internal roar. "Do you know how many people would love to be Sim the Silver?"

"Similian, behave," the Bane chastised. "My child, then you wouldn't want to disappoint him. Don't give in to urges to see with dragon's eyes, and don't upset yourself. The more you focus on Sim the less of you there will be." The Bane paused. "Do you mean a one to one link?"

"Yes."

"What?" The Bane almost shouted. It was an odd sound. Sim had never heard the Bane raise his voice. The Bane always spoke in an even-tempered, almost tired drone that irritated Sim. Sim stopped moving. He let the bees begin to swarm around him as he listened to

Aidan's tale. The Bane remained silent, but Sim could feel his mind at work.

"Oh dear," the Bane thought when Aidan finished. "I hadn't foreseen this."

Sim rolled his eyes. How many times had he heard the Bane speak about things he had foreseen? Sim had accepted the Bane into his body because of things he said he had foreseen: greatest dragon, most loved dragon, Sim the Silver. Sim had yet to see any proof of the Bane's words. Although he knew he was the strongest dragon in the Lands, the most cunning, the most daring and the most dashingly handsome, he wanted more. Sim had always hungered for more. He wanted to know everything. He had thought the Bane would give him more wisdom, but all he had given was mystery, never finishing answers, or answering in a way that created more questions. Sim felt the Bane retreat and repressed a dragon's sigh. Sim was accustomed to the Bane leaving comments unexplained. Aidan was not.

Because of Aidan's story Sim found himself liking Ren more, but he still didn't want to find him. Man was man.

Sim scowled as Aidan's story brought back memories of his capture and how he had allowed the Bane's promises of glory to lure him once again. The Bane insisted his capture was necessary for him to become the greatest dragon. He didn't know why he felt the need to listen to the Bane, but the Bane did have magic, and the Bane could harm him. Although Sim was immune to magic on the outside he wasn't immune to it on the inside, and the Bane knew it. Sim suspected the Bane had used magic to make him more passive when the men shot him with arrows, causing him to slumber when all his instincts told him to fight. The Bane offered no explanation. He only said that through capture Sim would be there when the time came to remove the Bane. Sim supposed all the humiliation of capture was worth the chance to banish the Bane from his being, but now the Bane claimed Sim needed to be captured again. The Bane said the first capture wasn't the capture he had foreseen. A low growl escaped Sim's throat. Why should he trust the Bane again? The Bane was making him appear the dumb animal and not the cunning creature he was. But then the Bane was Bane, just as man was man.

Roasted Bane sounded dreadfully delightful to Sim.

"Sim?"

"Yes, dear heart?"

"Why do I feel your emotions and you don't feel mine?"

Sim hadn't been expecting that question. He thought for a dragon's breath, unsure of how to reply. "Because you're in me and you're weaker than me. I'm Sim the Vicious Silver Dragon. You're human. Dragons are stronger than humans; therefore, I don't feel your feelings."

Sim spread his wings and took to the air, pleased Aidan was asking him questions and ignoring the Bane. Ren's scent quickly faded. He wondered if she noticed.

"But if you want me in you, you're being selfish unless you feel what I feel. If we merge completely and you don't feel me, I lose me, and therefore I can't truly be with you, for I'll no longer exist."

Sim thought about her words as the chill air blew by him. To a lesser degree, Aidan felt the wind too. He was a strong dragon. He relayed his feelings to Aidan with no conscious effort. To feel hers he would have to want to feel hers, and he would never want to feel hers. She was woman. Woman was woman, just as man was man, and Bane was Bane. He tried to put his thoughts into words that wouldn't hurt.

"But your feelings are insignificant compared to a dragon's feelings. Our emotions are intense and strong. If I took your feelings for my own I would be less of a dragon. I would have weaker emotion, less hunger, and less power."

"That's where you're wrong, dragon." Sim noticed she called him dragon and not Sim. He didn't know whether to be angry or ignore her. "My feelings are stronger than yours."

Sim was getting irritated with the conversation. He didn't like a human telling him she was stronger. "You're lying."

"I know what you feel, Sim. My emotions are stronger. If you took my feelings inside you, you'd be the strongest dragon in the Lands."

Sim didn't like where the conversation was leading. It reminded him of the Bane: if this and if that he would be the greatest dragon; if this and if that he would be the strongest dragon; if, if, if. Sim was sick of ifs. He wanted action.

The girl was becoming a bane. There could be nothing more powerful than the emotions of a silver dragon. When Sim spoke it was almost a roar. "I'm already the strongest dragon. I'm Sim the Silver."

Aidan was silent for some time "If you're the strongest dragon even if I weaken you a little you'll still be the strongest, but if I make you stronger you'll be all the more powerful."

As Sim thought about Aidan's words the more confused he became. Although he hated to admit it, the Bane was right. If he let her merge with him, she would cease to be her and be him. He didn't want that. He wanted her to remain whole, but he also wanted her to enjoy being him. If Aidan continued to look through his eyes she would eventually lose her strength and begin to change into him. He decided to warn her the next time. He just hated the Bane being right.

But he knew his emotions were stronger. Hers would be so weak they would fizzle to nothing without affecting his current strength. So what was the harm in appeasing her? Maybe his sacrifice would bring them closer and somehow make her enjoy being him.

Sim cleared his throat and tried to sound ferocious. "If I don't feel what you say, I'll be angry."

"I don't lie, Sim." The conviction in Aidan's voice shook him. He thought of his dragon strength and quickly snorted out his apprehension. Woman was woman; dragon was dragon.

Sim opened himself up and forced himself to focus on Aidan. Her feelings would be so slight he may be unable to detect them. When he felt the slight trickle begin, he stifled a snicker and breathed in deeply, wanting Aidan to sense his efforts.

Sim screamed. His wings faltered as he spiraled toward the ground. The world was a blur of light and shade, blue and green, up and down. He flapped his wings, trying to regain altitude, but he only managed to get them tangled. Although the world was a blur he knew the ground was quickly approaching. With one last burst of strength he managed to regain his correct wingspan just before he crashed to the ground.

His entire body ached. Dirt and debris rained over him. He groaned as something foreign seeped from his eye. His chest swelled with profound loneliness, but on top of all the agony his heart filled with an indescribable emotion. He breathed it in. It was a good emotion, a pure emotion. It overcame the pain in his leg and the loneliness in his chest. He closed his eyes, letting more of the liquid run down his jaw, and lost consciousness.

- - -

Ickba surveyed the approaching riders with a smile and quickly invented a viable story. As they neared, Ickba studied the tall guard. The man appeared calm, but his eyes never left Ickba's face and his hand remained rooted to the hilt of his sword. Ickba had seen Bentzen about the castle but had never had a direct confrontation with him. The man would be tough to distract, but Ickba loved challenges.

Tol sat in front of Bentzen, smiling as if he were an ordinary boy. A silver band circled his head, blocking Ista's call. Ickba's smile widened, imagining Tol's terror when he took the band away.

The women surveyed Ickba with curiosity but they didn't seem too concerned. After all, he was just one man, and a small one at that. The queen was dressed in ordinary clothing, but Ickba wasn't fooled. He had looked into her commanding blue eyes on numerous occasions. Ickba swallowed in anticipation. He couldn't wait to show her how terrifying he could be.

"Hello there," Ickba said, lifting his hand in greeting. He nodded to Renee and quickly addressed her as, "my queen."

The group pulled their mounts to a stop. "You're one of the stable hands, aren't you," the queen said, cocking her head in recognition.

Ickba nodded, glad he wouldn't have to prove his connection to the Stardom castle. "Yes, my queen," he said respectfully. "I'm honored you remember."

"You've helped me on occasion," she said cautiously.

"You left Stardom?" Bentzen asked.

Ickba licked his lips. "Yes. I don't want anything to do with magic. I'd rather be rid of it." He quickly judged their direction. "I thought I would try my luck in Ketes."

The guard appraised him with distrusting eyes. "Why Ketes?"

"I don't want to go to Crape," Ickba said. "The magic woman came from there. Ketes is the only other option close by."

"We travel alone," the guard said.

"Then maybe I'll see you there." Ickba nodded politely and turned his mount, thinking swiftly. He hadn't seen many provisions on their horses. If he could get ahead of them and catch some meat, when they happened upon him that night they might be inclined to stay.

Ickba set a swift pace, stopping every so often to peer into the woodlands for rabbit or fox. The Sierras were to his right, jutting into the fading sun, reminding him of the need to hurry back to Zier.

The lands across the Sierras were flat, brushy and replete with streams. Small game flourished in the shrubby woodland growth. It didn't take long for him to come across a rabbit den.

He knew Bentzen would lead his group until well past dark. Ickba traveled hard until the sun was finally setting, then pitched camp beside a swiftly running stream and quickly set to work. Gathering water from the stream, he began to boil his catch in wild onions and garlic.

Night soon fell and Ickba settled back to wait. When he heard the group approaching he quickly feigned sleep.

Tol's soft voice wafted from the darkness. "I'm hungry."

Ickba scowled. Tol's weepy disposition had always infuriated him. In the years since he had seen the boy, Tol hadn't improved. He didn't know why Ista tolerated him but he supposed Tol had been the perfect choice to win the queen's heart.

When Tol had arrived in Zier, he hadn't recognized Ickba. Ickba had grown longer hair and a beard since the camp. But Tol would soon remember. Ickba smiled.

"I'm too, little one," Bentzen replied. "But we should keep moving."

Ickba rolled over and pretended to wake. "Hello again," he said. He motioned to the pot of bubbling stew. "If you're hungry, help yourself. There's plenty to spare."

"Please, Bentzen," Tol said.

"It should be fine, Bentzen."

The sound of the queen's voice aroused Ickba. He risked a glance. Renee was already dismounting, Marva behind her. Ickba could hardly wait until he had them. He had never been unsupervised with a woman before. He had ideas of what would bring intense pain.

Ickba fingered the crystal in his pocket. Once he had taken Bentzen and captured the queen he would call Ista. Ista was furious with Tol. The boy wasn't long for this world.

Ista had known Ren might send word to Ketes. Scouts were scattered this side of Zier, in the rolling hills leading to the Nolands. Ickba had just been the lucky one to come across the group. He was surprised the crown prince wasn't with them, but Ista had already begun the next phase of her plan. The crown prince would soon be hers, and with the Chosen under her command nothing could stop her.

Bentzen drew his sword as he dismounted. Ickba ignored him as he served the stew to the ladies.

Marva took the bowl and collapsed where she stood. "I'm starved. This child is going to be huge."

Renee looked down at Ickba and smiled. "Marva has just learned she's with child."

Ickba feigned interest as he glanced at Marva's stomach. She wasn't showing yet. That was good. Ickba hated fat women.

Bentzen took a bowl of stew and stood a few paces away, watching Ickba with ice-cold blue eyes. Ickba leaned back on his pack and studied the group, only speaking when spoken to. He studied their demeanor, what sounds alerted their attention, and the total softening of Bentzen's features when he looked at Tol.

Ickba refined his plan. He would make his move the next morning.

Chapter 18

"Have you thought of any names?" Renee asked, looking up from her hot tea. Ickba had rekindled the fire that morning, causing the group to tarry.

Marva smiled, a dreamy look in her eyes. "I'm considering Balin if it's a boy - my surname, and Magram if it's a girl."

Ickba wanted to gut Marva. She just wouldn't stop talking about her precious child. He licked his lips, forcing himself to calm. Soon now, he told himself, he could repay her as he saw fit.

"Balin?" Tol asked, crinkling up his nose.

Marva laughed. "Balin is a good name, Tol. Balin means 'fierce warrior.'"

Tol's brows furrowed. "What does my name mean?"

"It means 'one loved by the Maker,'" Benton said, looking up from where he was brushing the horses.

Tol smiled. "I like that better than a fierce warrior."

Bentzen winked at Marva, exposing his lie.

Renee and Marva chattered on about the baby while Bentzen continued rubbing the horses.

Now was the time to make his move.

The previous day Ickba had noticed wild berries growing at the edge of the woods. Tol loved wild berries.

Ickba stood from his pallet and pointed to the bushes. "I think I'll pick some berries before I start off this morning."

Tol raised his head from where he played in the dirt. "Can I help you pick them? I love wild berries."

Ickba nodded and started walking toward the brush. Bentzen's eyes followed them for a few heartbeats before returning to work.

Tol chatted about the Avenger, insisting he would return and kill Ista. Ickba frowned. He had questioned Ista's judgment when she had chosen Tol for the mission. Tol was young and had yet to advance into a loyal member of the Collective, but Ista had chosen him, and Tol had betrayed her. As soon as the silver band was off Tol's head he would be punished.

But Tol had served his purpose. He had told Ista everything before magic was reborn. Without Tol, Ista wouldn't have known about Ren's desire to save the Maritium or when he had returned to the castle. She wouldn't have known about Renee's attempt to see Ren in the dungeon or the advisors' plan to revolt. Thanks to Tol, Ista had woven a complex web that helped corroborate her claims.

Even now the crown prince was walking into a trap. Ista had taken every precaution. She had left a little treasure for the Chosen to find in case he escaped. Whomever the magic affected, be it one man or an army, Ista would command them. Wouldn't the Chosen be surprised when he found his men butchering each other? After the magic took hold the Chosen's men would be annihilated, until only the Chosen would remain – an easy target.

When they reached the brush Ickba led Tol deep into the shadows. Tol muttered under his breath, plopping every other berry he picked into his mouth. Ickba relished the suspense as he bent to Tol's level.

Ickba grabbed Tol's throat. Tol's eyes bulged as a few berries flew from his mouth.

"You don't remember me, do you, Tol?" Ickba said, leaning closer. "Take a real good look. We had some good times, you and I."

Madness rose in Tol's eyes. When the boy started to scream, Ickba clamped a hand over Tol's mouth and pulled him deep into the shadows. Distant laughter rolled in, making the deed all the more rewarding. Ickba chuckled in satisfaction as the odor of urine burned his nostrils. It appeared he was more than Tol could handle.

"Tol, it's a pleasure to see you again."

Tol thrashed in his hands. Ickba tightened his grip. His vision blurred as his arousal heightened. Blood pumped through him with blinding heat. Ista had taught him the rapture of control, as she had taught the entire Collective. The strong sacrificed the weaker, most of the time without weapons. The pleasure of ending a life with your own hands was much more pleasant than with aid. He wondered how Tol had managed to live this long. Rarely did one so weak live past the age of five.

Ickba bent forward, eyes a finger's width from Tol's own. "I think you've grown fond of Bentzen, haven't you?"

Tol nodded as snot bubbled from his nose.

"If you so much as make a sound, I'll gut him like I did the one back at camp. You remember that one, don't you?"

Tol nodded again. Ickba felt his arousal intensify. If he had the hunger he would be more powerful in his attack. His eyes flickered past the brush toward the women. Renee was bent over, packing her things. Ickba could see her shape through her thin smock. He licked his lips.

"Take off the silver band, Tol,"

Tol lifted the silver band and held it close to his chest. The madness intensified. Tol felt Ista's hold.

"Remember your friend, Bentzen?"

Tol nodded.

"If you don't do as I ask, I'll kill him. If you do, I'll let him live. Do you hear?"

Tol blinked in acceptance.

"While we're picking berries, you're going to cut yourself. When we get back to the others you'll ask Bentzen to take you to the creek to wash off. I'll kill him if he doesn't go with you. You're saving him by taking him away. Do you understand?"

Tol nodded.

"If you tell Bentzen who I am, I'll butcher Renee and Marva. I'm going to release you now, Tol. Don't scream."

When no ray of hope brushed Tol's face, Ickba took the silver band from Tol's grasp and looped it through his belt. Tol's legs quivered as he turned and began to pick berries. Ickba forced Tol's hand to close down on the thorny leaves until he could see blood dripping from Tol's small fist.

Ickba leaned closer. "Remember, Tol, only Bentzen."

Tol's cry echoed over the plains like a wild animal. Ickba shoved him toward the camp and waited in the shadows until Tol reached Bentzen. A look of genuine concern stole over the swordsman's face as he picked Tol up and hurried to the nearby stream. When Bentzen was a fair distance away, Ickba emerged from shelter of the brush.

Ducking behind the horses he bent to grab a rope out of his saddlebag. As he cut it into four shorter pieces he listened to the women's concerned speech.

"Poor thing," Renee said. "Those leaves are painful when they cut."

"Ickba should have been more careful," Marva said, voice hard.

Ickba peered around the horses as he formed a noose in one of the lengths of rope. He wouldn't have much time. The creek was just over the rise and Bentzen wasn't the type to leave the women alone for long periods.

Renee's back was turned. She gazed in the direction Bentzen had gone, shaking her head. Ickba tightened the noose. As Renee sighed, her chest rose, tightening the smock around her breasts. Ickba's member hardened. He broke free of the horses and threw the noose around Renee's neck. Yanking her to the ground, he turned to Marva. He felt Renee struggling but knew she couldn't cry out with the rope tightening, threatening to break her neck.

Marva heard him coming and spun. Her blue eyes widened in surprise, but before she could scream he struck her across the face, knocking the wind from her. She fell, clearing the fire by a hair's width. He jabbed his knee into her stomach and stuffed a rag into her mouth. He heard Renee gagging behind him and knew he'd have a few heartbeats if he released her.

Ickba tossed the rope aside and pushed the silver band on Marva's head. He didn't want her trying to use the power; Marva would be trouble enough without the power, and he also had the queen to contend with. He quickly tied Marva's hands together and looped a rope around her neck.

Marva kicked him in the groin. He was used to pain and only grunted before he hit her across the jaw, knocking her unconscious. Renee gasped behind him. He spun, grabbed Renee's rope and quickly pulled it taut. Taking another rag from his pocket, he stuffed it in her mouth and flipped her over. She inhaled deeply, the rope causing her face to splotch. He loosened the rope. She coughed out the rag. Ickba swore and knocked her in the head with his elbow just before she screamed. Her body went slack. A thin trail of blood oozed from where her head had hit a rock. Ickba licked his lips and ran his hands down the queen's sides. She was shapely but slender, just the way he liked them. He felt the pressure building inside him. Crouching, he lifted her flimsy dress and fingered her. He threw his head back and laughed. The queen was only the beginning of his rewards.

Bentzen still hadn't returned. Ickba quickly tied the women's hands and feet before he threw them over the horses. With spare rags he tied them to the stirrups. The longing to kill built inside him. He hungered to release his rage and lust upon the women, but Ista would want the queen. Marva he could have his way with. He may even leave her body as a warning for the Chosen.

Ickba grabbed the reins of the two horses and jogged to his stallion. Bentzen and Tol emerged from the creek just as Ickba mounted. Bentzen looked up. When their eyes met Bentzen broke into a run, lips opening in a silent scream.

Ickba spurred his horse into a trot, leading the other two mounts behind him. "Tell the Chosen his mother will be with Ista!" he shouted. "With each day that dawns the more she will suffer!"

He reached into his pocket and pulled out the crystal. Ista's image was already contained within its depths. Behind him he heard agonized moans of terror.

Ickba glanced back at the silver band on Marva's head and smiled.

- - -

Pine needles, nuts, leaves, sticks, twigs, and dirt twirled in small cyclones. Ren held his hands up to shield his eyes and shouted, "Neki! Stop!"

"I can't!" Neki choked on some of his own emotional weave. "I don't know how!"

After the wolven attack no one had slept and they had decided to stop early that day to gather ample amounts of wood. Galvin built the fire while Markum had begun searching through the books Michel had gathered at Ista's camp. The first was a history book dating back to the Dark Ages. The final two were training books: one containing lessons only useful to sorceresses, the other explaining the basics of the Quy. But one training book was all they needed.

Those with the Quy were trying to harness their emotions to elicit a specific response.

The four of them differed in both force and talent. Michel had only been able to do small things such as stir a small breeze or bend a flower.

Markum could do nothing. He had felt pain when Ren had reconnected the thread, but nothing happened when he tried to focus his emotions. Markum's eyes held a hint of fear. Although the books indicated those with the sight may be unable to do more than the smallest tasks with the Quy, the dreamweaver prophecy still haunted him and he feared being unable to do what he must without the aid of magic.

What surprised Ren, and everyone else, was the fact that he was also unable to make anything happen. He had thought once he had written instructions he would be able to use the power with ease, but it seemed his mind was blocked.

He tried to encourage the others, but he knew they could sense his worry. Galvin stayed close to him, offering a silent comfort.

Neki had the power like none other. He could do everything on the first try like it was an innate ability, sometimes without the instructions being finished. That was precisely what had happened with the storm of particles. Markum had been reading how to create a dust storm when Neki had sprung into action.

The particles whirled faster.

A small rock pounded Ren on the head. "Ouch!" He could barely see the others, too much debris spun about him. He could hear the kota's drumming hooves as she pranced nearby. "Neki!"

"I'm trying!"

Suddenly, the air calmed. Particles either dropped or whisked softly to the ground. When Ren was brave enough to open his eyes, he laughed.

Neki stood with Galvin's silver necklace looped around his head. Beside him, Galvin grinned like one who had just won a joust.

"Your theory is sound, Ren. Silver absorbs everything coming in *and out*," Galvin said, emphasizing the latter.

Neki looked at Galvin with disgust. "So I'm not an almighty sorcerer yet, but I will be."

"I have no doubt," Ren said.

Leaves and debris stuck to Neki's clothes. One small stick protruded from underneath the necklace. Ren chuckled again.

"Will you look at that," Quinton said.

Ren looked up from where he was dusting off his breeches. Quinton pointed to Ren's sword. The sun's rays siphoned through the trees and played on the emblems of Choice, Chance, and Fate, but instead of merely casting the hilt in a golden sheen, the light reflected a rainbow into the atmosphere, illuminating the depths of the forest in a spectrum of color. Ren slowly brushed the rainbow with his fingertips, marveling as the light moved with his touch.

"Burning cinders," Neki whispered, reaching toward the colors with a tentative hand.

"The Oracle," Ren whispered.

Neki's fingers caused the rainbow to flicker on his face, lighting him with blues, purples, and yellows.

"Don't go, Ren."

Ren turned to the sound of Markum's voice. The seer sat in the shadow of the woods, concerned etched into his tired eyes. Ren was surprised Markum had guessed his thoughts, but he supposed he shouldn't be. A seer could deduce a lot from his dreams.

"They Quy wants me to seek the Oracle, Markum. I can deny her nothing," Ren said. The rainbow continued to dance through the forest, but with the look in Markum's eyes it seemed ominous. Neki drew back his fingers.

Markum stood. "I haven't told you my dream. I had it the night you met the Quy." As Markum stepped into the clearing, he cut off the sun, vanquishing the rainbow. A blanket of darkness settled in, granting power to Markum's words.

"In my dream I followed you into the woods. You were in a trance and I was worried you would go astray, but before I reached you, you stopped at a fork in the path and tossed a pair of astragali on the ground. You took the path to the right. I tried to follow, but as soon as I stepped on the path, a stone sphinx came alive before me and stopped my entrance. You had already disappeared.

"I sat in the middle of the path and waited until I saw you coming back. Hearing a noise behind me, I turned. You walked down the other path as well. You emerged from the two paths at the same time. The you to the right looked like you did when you left, but you had a wound by your heart and it was bleeding black blood."

"And the me on the left?"

"Was deformed and hideous, snakes were slithering all over your body and. . ."

"And?"

"Half of your face wasn't yours."

Markum's words hung in the air like a stench.

"The Oracle plays with people's minds, Ren. Some come out crazy. Some don't come out."

"But some come out with answers," Ren said, thinking of Aidan. "If the Oracle shows itself to me, how can I deny it?"

"You would risk death?"

Markum's words chilled him, but didn't sway him. If the Oracle appeared to him he would have to answer a riddle given by the sphinx, the herald of the Oracle. Most didn't pass the challenge. If you failed to answer the riddle you died instantly.

Despite the danger, as Ren thought about the Oracle a sense of purpose filled him. The Quy wanted him to seek the Oracle; the Maker wanted him to seek the Oracle; and that was what he would do.

"Don't go," Markum said again. "Too many things could go wrong, Ren. You may never come out. That has happened."

The fear in Markum's eyes gave Ren pause, but he still felt the need to seek Choice, Chance, and Fate. They could help him. He was sure of it.

"Ren, even if you do make it out, people have been reported to return crazy."

"But they've done what they needed to do. They've altered the future," Ren said.

"Then they kill themselves or forget their names! Some who emerge from the Oracle never regain their complete sanity. Many die trying to enter, and many others have never returned."

The others stared at Markum with wide-eyed fear.

Markum's eyes flashed angrily. "I'm not going to convince you, am I?"

Ren shook his head, sure his decision was the right one. "I need to know what the guardians have to say. They are the Maker's messengers, Markum. The Maker isn't evil. He won't bring me harm. Those who die trying to enter or leave the Oracle are deserving of death. If I go with a true heart, seeking nothing but guidance, the guardians won't harm me. I'm certain of it."

"But they'll give you shadows of prophecy."

Ren shivered at Markum's words. But even if the Oracle spoke in riddles, he had to try. He had many questions.

Galvin shifted in worry. "Ren, I don't like this."

"I second that, Ren. I don't like this at all," Quinton said.

Ren sighed and fingered the hilt of the Quy's sword. "I know you're worried, but if the Quy gave me this sword it has to mean something. I need to find answers, and the Oracle can give me the answers I need."

No one objected. Everyone knew he was right. If the Quy had given him the sword, branded with Choice, Chance, and Fate's symbols, he had to try.

- - -

Bentzen took the knife from his belt and sliced his arm. Fresh blood poured over his other cuts, still throbbing in pain. He stumbled forward, weak from lack of blood. He had to find Ren. Then he could taste death.

It would feel good.

His eyes blurred as the thought of Tol, screaming as his small body was racked with pain. Bentzen had been desperate to find something solid silver, but there was nothing. The kettle at the fire was steel, his sword was steel, and his belt was made of pewter. He had nothing solid silver like the silver band Ren had given Tol.

Why hadn't he noticed the band was missing when Tol came to him, crying from the thistles on the bush? If he had he would have known something was wrong. He would have demanded Tol tell him where the band was. Now Tol was dead.

Bentzen sliced his arm again. As the blade entered a previous wound, his vision blurred. He caught himself before he fell and stumbled back to his feet. He had to reach Ren.

Tol was dead. Renee was taken. Marva, her unborn . . .

Why didn't he notice the missing band?

He kept seeing Tol's bright blue eyes looking up at him, pleading for help. The convulsions had been violent, and when the blood had begun to seep from Tol's ears all Bentzen could do was hold him, tell him it was going to be all right – lie to him.

Bentzen wasn't really sure where he was going. It was hard to see the landscape. All he knew was the sun was to his left shoulder. He was heading south, back to the others. He had to reach Ren.

He didn't deserve to live. He had let Tol die, let Renee and Marva be taken. How could he have been so stupid?

He sliced his arm again. He would keep punishing himself until he had suffered enough for his foolishness, for his vanity in thinking he could protect Tol from harm. But nothing would ever be enough. No pain would ever be enough.

He hoped he found Ren soon. He hoped he would really be able to feel the knife next time.

Chapter 19

Chris' screams were finally silenced. Manda opened her eyes. Two Quar soldiers lifted the tent's flap, dragging her brother behind them. Chris was unrecognizable. He had thinned to a skeleton, his skin was blistered and sun-worn, and the spark had disappeared from his eyes. If someone had shown her a picture of the broken body a week ago she wouldn't have dreamed it could be her brother. The soldiers tossed Chris in the corner and chained his hands and feet to iron stakes. Manda's own chains rubbed fresh wounds from where she had tried, time and again, to lift her stakes from the ground. The urgency to escape was now an inferno in her mind. Alezza didn't care if she or Chris lived or died, and if they lived Alezza would make each of their lives a living nightmare.

Every hour of the day Alezza practiced touching the needles in Chris' mind. Although Chris was now silent, Manda could still hear his screams ringing through her ears.

Chris rolled on the floor, still convulsing from Alezza's internal torment. Manda could almost feel his anguish. The look on his face reminded her of when she had witnessed a death by fire, but this time the fire was on the inside, not the outside. Exhaustion was etched in every line of his face, as if his torture had been going on for years and not days.

His eyes fluttered open. Their brilliant green was now dull and muted, and the pain lingering in their depths was more than she could fathom.

Chris sighed in contentment from the reprieve. Anger boiled inside her. Their father had allowed this to happen. His death wouldn't be kind; Alezza's would be brutal.

Almost on cue, Bort and Alezza sauntered into the tent, laughing at some private joke. Although it had only been days since their father had betrayed them, it seemed an eternity. She didn't know how much longer Chris could remain sane; she didn't know how much longer she could watch his torture.

Her eyes found Alezza's.

Alezza smiled as if in friendship. "Gag them both," she said to Bort. "I grow weary of their screams."

A rare smile stole over Bort's meaty face before he turned to Chris.

Manda closed her eyes, sending a silent prayer to the Maker. Chris couldn't bear more pain this evening. He would go mad. Maybe madness was what Alezza wanted.

Bort drew a rag out of his doublet and kicked Chris in the ribcage. Chris had no strength to resist. His entire body arched from the force of Bort's blow.

"Please," Manda heard herself say. "Don't hurt him anymore."

Alezza knelt beside her and stuffed a cloth smelling of horse dung into her mouth. Manda gagged as the thick, foul taste coated her tongue.

"Granted."

Manda blinked back her surprise and tried not to swallow her tainted saliva. What had already seeped down her throat left a rancid trail that would linger for days.

Alezza gathered her long, luxurious hair from her shoulders before leaning forward and brushing Manda's cheek with a kiss. "It's your turn, my dear."

Manda's eyes widened as Alezza released a throaty laugh. A multitude of horrors flashed through Manda's mind. She would be burned, beaten, gutted, or worse. Alezza was capable of anything. The heir felt neither compassion nor remorse. It was as if she was aroused by their torture. As Manda looked into Alezza's eyes she saw only enmity and revenge. Alezza hated her, not only because of Manda's own tongue but also because of her birth. Now that Valor was king of Newlan, Manda predominated Alezza.

A clamor of steel broke Manda out of her thoughts and soft grunts tore at her heart. Chris was fighting back. Manda tried to convey a warning with her eyes. Alezza would only send Chris more pain if he resisted. When his eyes found hers she recoiled from the severity of his desperation. He knew what they were going to do.

Chris twisted on the ground, straining on the chains. As his eyes flickered past Alezza, Manda followed his gaze. Alezza rocked back on her heels, a soft laugh escaping her lips as she watched Manda's reaction.

Bort stood, naked, pulsating with need and leering at her with lewd, dark eyes. Manda squirmed backwards, coughing as her scream was quenched in the rank cloth. The chains gnawed her wrists, slicing her flesh with each movement. Even though her mind whispered there would be ramifications she continued to try to pull free of the stakes in a feeble attempt to escape the inevitable.

Chris' screams came to her from a distant place, her own breath too heavy in her ears. The taste of dung and the smell of sweat made her lightheaded, as if she was looking in on another's nightmare.

Alezza reached down to unchain her legs. Manda kicked in desperation. A speck of blood seeped down her throat as she bit the inside of her mouth. It augmented not only her fear but also her rage. She kicked harder, and though she couldn't make out Chris' words she knew he urged her on.

Alezza's face twisted in malice just as Chris released a savage cry of torment. Manda ceased her struggle, understanding all too well. After agonizing heartbeats of painful screams, Chris collapsed. Without even glancing at Manda, Alezza finished unchaining her legs, patting Manda's shoulder as if in pride.

Manda's vision blurred as her rage heightened. She imagined herself breaking the chains and twisting Alezza's neck, watching it snap like a twig beneath her grip. As quickly as the rage came, it evaporated. If she acted rashly Alezza would punish Chris.

The night was warm, almost stifling, and Bort's massive body glistened with sweat as the lights of the torches licked the night air, giving no reprieve from the heat and casting ominous shadows around Bort's approaching bulk. Her struggle had caused old scabs on her wrists and ankles to reopen. The biting smell of blood overpowered the smells of sweat and dung.

As Bort continued his approach, her life grew more and more precious.

Fates, she was going to die.

Alezza towered over her, letting her ebony hair fall around her shoulders now that it was safe from Manda's contamination. Alezza's eyes flickered down Bort's massive form. "You may have her, but make sure she lives."

Manda choked back the tears. Why not kill her and be done with it? She was presumed dead anyway. What did Alezza have planned?

The words Alezza had uttered days ago came back to Manda with blinding force: *"Why my dear, you don't seem excited about having me as your sister?"*

Blessed Fates, Alezza was serious! Alezza planned to marry Chris. She intended to be queen of half the Lands. If Valor told everyone they were dead and Alezza found them alive she would be revered.

Manda's mind spun. How could Alezza force Chris into marriage? Sending him pain was futile. Chris wouldn't acquiesce because of his own suffering. Surely Alezza could see that already.

Did Alezza think Chris would relent because of his sister's suffering? Although the theory was sound surely Alezza would know Manda would speak the truth, no matter their torture. Chris would rather die before he married Alezza, and Chris knew Manda felt the same. Her mind searched for the answers but none were forthcoming.

As Bort walked forward the grin left his face. All that remained was carnal lust. She stiffened, forcing herself to still.

Manda tried to turn her gaze as Bort approached, but her eyes wouldn't leave him. He stretched his arms, crackling bones as if he were coming to combat and not rape. He was a huge man, the largest she had seen, with a barrel chest and burly arms. Coarse hairs carpeted his chest and shoulders, but when he moved pure muscle rippled beneath his skin. His short, black, curly hair brushed the top of the tent as he sauntered forward, grabbing himself as if to present a prize.

Chris fought to reach her, but she didn't turn. Her gaze remained locked on Bort. Her whimpers echoed in her ears like a knell of lost innocence, lost dreams, and lost hopes.

After this her life was never going to be the same.

Bort's scent hit her with the force of a brutal blow: sweat and dirt, horse and pig, sex and stench. She drew a deep breath of disgust as her chest heaved in panic.

Chris screamed into his gag, telling her to fight. She wouldn't. She couldn't. Alezza looked on, waiting for a reason to send Chris pain. His chains echoed in Manda's mind from far away. All she saw was Bort. All she smelled was Bort. All she heard was her own terrified moans.

She squeezed her eyes shut. She didn't want to remember anything about Bort when it was done. Something brushed her face. She recoiled, unable to help herself, but when she heard Chris begin to moan she forced her body to still.

She felt Bort next to her, heard him breathing, and smelled his stench. It seemed to last forever. Terror gripped every bone, wrapping its horrific darkness around her. There was no hope to cling to. This was her new life.

Bort's large hands grabbed her around the waist and tore her clothes. He pulled the gag from her mouth and tossed it aside. "I want to hear your screams, girl."

Manda lurched forward and bit Bort's inner thigh. When she heard his grunt she clamped down harder, briefly feeling the elation of the kill.

But when Chris' screams reached her ears she heard his agony even through his gag. Bort yanked her off and slapped her. The force of the blow sent her backward, causing her head to hit the iron stake. She felt one of her teeth dislodge. Before she could recover he struck her again. The hollow echo of the blows swam through the pain. Bort's grunts of effort reaffirmed the severity of each, but Chris' screams sent a terror inside her no blow could inflict.

The distant rumble of Alezza's laugher filtered through the stench with a foul odor of its own.

Chris' screams lingered in the night. Manda rolled on the floor, trying to move closer to her brother when another brutal blow landed across her jaw. She heard her bone crack as blood filled her mouth. She spit it out, gagging on the taste, thinking how ironic it was that she was grateful for her own blood. It drowned the taste of dung.

Chris' shrieks succumbed as soon as she lay still.

She forced herself not to move.

The still air hovered over her, condemning her blood to dry quickly. She felt Bort's heat and smelt his stench but couldn't exert the energy to open her eyes. An impetuous laugh sounded around her, deep and vicious. A large hand stole over her nakedness, smearing blood or sweat – she was unsure which – along with it.

Then Bort rammed into her, grunting with carnal lust.

Her world was filled with agony, over and over. She didn't hear. She didn't see. She was aware of the blows, of the iron stake, of the groping, but it all ran together in a nightmarish quality, burning into one horrific memory.

She tried to think of other things, telling herself it was only an illusion, that she would wake at any time, but her screams were too much, the pain was too much to rationalize away.

The night wore on. In time she became as limp as a rag doll. From a distance she heard Bort's savage cries, his grunts of pleasure and Alezza's laughter. She felt the blows but they didn't affect her. She was numb. She neither cried out nor resisted.

Her brother still screamed, but it was a different kind of scream. She knew they weren't screams of pain, and she knew they weren't because of her actions, so she didn't concentrate on them. She only prayed the Maker would be with him.

She didn't know how long it continued. At one point she turned to Chris. His screams had abated and he lay on his side without movement, eyes staring blankly ahead. A thin stream of drool trickled down his chin. Panic flooded through her.

He was dead. Alezza had killed him.

She reached for Chris' hand and clutched it with fervent desperation.

His skin was still warm. An immense relief washed over her despite what was happening to her own body. Her brother was alive! When his eyes cleared and he saw her for who she was and what was being done to her, a low moan escaped his lips.

"Be strong," she mouthed.

"Leave me," he whispered before his eyes clouded over and he began to convulse on the floor.

Manda watched in horror as Chris' face was washed not with pain, but with pleasure.

- - -

"Goodenspy," Fraul said. "Aaron Goodenspy?"

Aaron turned his piercing gaze toward Fraul. "Yes, that's my name."

They had left the port city as soon as they were able and had given Zier a wide girth. They had seen regiments traveling from the crown of Newlan, but it was from a safe distance.

Despite the ominous circumstances, Fraul was having the time of his life. He loved traveling across country, and the Avenger was an added bonus, one he was still relishing. Aaron didn't speak at great length, but Fraul had no problems keeping the conversation alive, and Aaron seemed to enjoy his stories.

Just being able to experience how the Avenger went about his quest was sometimes so stimulating Fraul found himself grinning like a madman. At times Aaron sensed his glee and chuckled at his mannerisms.

Even though Aaron chose not to speak without Fraul asking a direct question, Fraul had become very fond of Aaron. Aaron was upright and moral, judgmental but truthful, and very, very blunt.

When Fraul wasn't focused on Aaron, which sadly enough was almost constantly, he worried about Ramie. His king was cunning, but Ramie also had the rage of a hungry manacanard, and that rage could sometimes make him lose his senses.

Fraul rubbed his goatee and wondered if the manacanard had been reborn with the rebirth of magic. The manacanard had been his one fear as a child. When it did exist not even a dragon could escape harm. The manacanard's magic was its voice. It could wail a mournful cry, bewitching those who heard it into seeking the voice. When they were close enough the manacanard would strike.

Sometimes the manacanard continued to wail until entire legions of men had been ravaged. With a woman's face, a lion's body, and razor sharp teeth, it had an unnerving intelligence and a strength no human could escape. Once it had you the manacanard could tear your flesh like a ream of silk.

Shaking off the thought, Fraul turned to Aaron. Aaron said his name was Goodenspy.

There had been stories of a man with a very similar name almost since the beginning of time, although the name had probably been altered into different renditions and the modern tongue. The story of Ari Goodspeed was told to children when they were old enough to surmount its atrocities. It was a story of betrayal in the worst way, and children were told the story to have the sin of betrayal far removed from their hearts and minds.

Ari was the middle son of the third king of the Lands. In Ari's time the Lands were far from their current structure and modernization. The people were of small number, living in the region now known as Yor. Ari was a caring man, helping far more than his brothers, and putting himself in harm's way when those of lower classes were in need. Ari became a peacemaker between the different settlements, and was sought after to settle disputes, keeping peace for the Lands and also his father's rule.

During one of his peacemaking missions, Ari traveled to a small village that had decided to rebel against his father. At the edge of a village he met a girl named Kyra. It was said Kyra was so beautiful many couldn't look upon her because her beauty shone brighter than the sun.

Kyra knew her people were planning on taking Ari's life if he entered their boundaries so she took Ari into town herself. During the negotiations, Kyra and Ari fell in love. The outcome wasn't only peace but also the joining of the two lands in marriage.

Ari and Kyra's love was spoken of in reverent whispers. The two rarely parted. When Ari went on his missions Kyra was at his side, and the more they were together the deeper their love grew.

Ari's younger brother, Cyrus, coveted Kyra and wanted her for his own. One day Cyrus approached her and she denied him. She said she would never love any man but Ari and wouldn't even consider remarrying upon his death.

Once Kyra denied him, Cyrus's obsession grew. Cyrus began plotting to frame Ari for the death of their eldest brother, fantasizing he would have both the crown and Kyra for his own. After Cyrus murdered his elder brother he sent guards to Ari's house with proof of

Ari's guilt. When the guards arrested Ari, Kyra fought them, pointing to Cyrus as the true murderer. Cyrus flew into a rage and ordered the guards to chain Ari to the wall and beat him to the point of death. Cyrus raped Kyra in front of Ari, and then, before Ari's eyes, he skinned Kyra alive.

Fraul glanced over at Aaron. If Aaron and Ari were one in the same person the story would be a plausible explanation as to how Aaron had become the Avenger. Fraul shook the thought off. Surely it couldn't be. Aaron was magic, and magic hadn't been born during Ari's time. It had appeared decades later. Besides, the story of Ari Goodspeed was so horrible it couldn't be factual.

- - -

Manda could hear Bort snoring in the tent beside her. She had heard that contented sound as other men came to have their way with her.

She had lost count as to how many. There were too many. That was all she knew – far too many.

Alezza had watched the entire time. Her smile would be with Manda for the remainder of her days. At times, she had even heard Alezza's complacent chuckle.

Manda had ingrained Alezza's chuckle to memory. If she ever needed to find her inner strength, she would remember that chuckle. It would ignite a fervor that would send all other thoughts away.

If, she reminded herself, she was allowed to live. Chris was the one Alezza wanted. She was just someone the spider could play with before she bit. Manda was expendable, and she knew it.

During the night Manda had realized Alezza's plan. Throughout her demoralization Chris had grunted with erotic pleasure, not pain. Alezza had exhausted Chris' strength by sending him intense pain all day. All he could do was welcome the other sensations. Manda didn't blame him, but at times during the night she had almost gotten sick. Her brother sounded like the men on top of her.

Chris would soon be Alezza's puppet. He would hunger for the pleasure and do anything to avoid the pain. Chris would soon agree to Alezza's demands. Then Manda would no longer be needed. She was expendable.

Manda squeezed Chris' hand. He was unresponsive. She tried again as she whispered his name.

It hurt to move and it hurt to breathe. All she wanted to do was remain still, but her gut told her if she didn't force Chris to wake he would soon be unable to recognize her. Manda inched closer, feeling a new trickle of blood flow in response to her movement.

She hadn't bothered to re-dress. Her clothes were ripped to shreds and she didn't know if she had any strength to salvage anything. Besides, Alezza had promised more of the same the following night.

When Manda brushed his face, Chris' eyes opened and he let out a terrifying sound. It rent her heart.

"Chris." Her own voice sounded foreign, but she wasn't the same person she had been only days ago. Now she knew what pain could be, what terror could be.

Chris moaned again, but this time it was in more of a human tone. She squeezed his hand, trying to convey her love. Slowly, recognition came into his face.

His shoulders sunk in sorrow as he took her in his arms. Everywhere he touched it hurt, but she didn't care. Her brother was whole, and he remembered her. He whispered for forgiveness, saying he had tried to reach her, promising he would kill them all.

She looked into his face. He had aged years in only days. His face was taut, his eyes devoid of their former zest. All that remained was doleful abandon, mirrored in her own soul, and enmity, not for what had happened to him but what had been done to her.

Chris rolled to his side. Something shimmered in the dim light. Chris' hand caught whatever it was and lifted it to her chains. When her lock clicked open Manda gasped, her mind unable to grasp sudden freedom.

Manda replayed the night in her mind. Bort had undressed, leaving his keys in a heap of clothing. Chris had been near that pile. He had managed to take them.

She lifted his chains and tugged at them in expectation, but he stopped her with a look. When he spoke, his voice was so low she almost didn't hear. It was a different voice, a voice that knew torment and hate. "Manda, they'll come after me. They may not come after you."

"No. You're coming with me."

"Manda, you know what she plans. She'll hunt me. Besides, I have no strength. You must seek help. Find Ren. He'll know what to do."

Manda shook her head, her whole body aching. "If I leave she'll send you more pain. I can't do that too you."

"She has given me more pain than she ever could tonight."

A lone tear trickled down Manda's cheek when she realized he meant her rape and not his torture. Manda looked deeper into Chris' eyes. Her brother had known exactly what was being done to him. He had been in his own perdition while she was in hers. She wondered what was worse: being raped and abhorring it or being raped and relishing the sensations but loathing the price?

The soft crunch of leaves betrayed someone's movement. Manda jumped, the last of her chains falling from her ankles as a knife ripped down the back of the tent, its silver blade flashing in the moonlight. A black and gold band below the blade signified Zier's colors - Ren's colors. Heartbeats later Carter's face appeared. Manda was too shocked to react. Carter moved silently into the tent and placed a finger over his mouth.

He quickly looked away. "My lady, I'm sorry. May the Maker's fates condemn me for being unable to come sooner." Carter paused, heaving a sigh. "I have one horse. It's yours, my lady. Take it and get quickly away."

The anguish was evident in his voice. Manda looked down at herself. Bruises so deep they were almost black covered her body and dried blood was caked in places she hadn't realized she was harmed. She could feel the blood on her chin and chest from her shattered jaw, but she had paid little attention to the other parts that screamed every time she moved. A gash on her shoulder seeped blood, causing her entire left side to appear horrific, and cuts from the chains continued to ooze blood.

Carter's red-rimmed eyes locked on her face. "Guards have been surrounding your tent all night. There was no chance for me to come. Now they have all passed out from drink after the . . . " His voice broke. Chris' hand tightened on her own.

Carter's eyes flickered to the tent flap. "The patrol looks into your tent every moons' click. I made sure he passed before I came. We must hurry. We don't have much time."

Manda glanced behind her, expecting an alarm to sound. When none came she quickly turned back to Chris and tried to pull him up. "No, Manda, only you."

Carter took off his coat and draped it around her shoulders. His voice wafted to her, soft and sorrowful. "Your brother is right. If both of you aren't here an alarm will sound." His eyes bore into her with stark determination. "Both of you will be here."

A lump rose in her throat. Carter intended to take her place and fool the guards until morning. By dawn she could be safely away. Manda swallowed back her fear and opened her mouth to insist Chris be the one to go, but when her eyes met her brother's her words evaporated from her lips. If Manda remained without Chris she would die. If Chris remained without Manda he would live. Alezza's plans depended on Chris living, at least for a while.

Manda put her hands to her lips, revulsion filling her at the thought of what she was about to do.

Carter's voice floated to her, but she barely heard. Her eyes were riveted on Chris, knowing it may be the last time she would see him sane. Manda leaned down and wrapped her arms around him, barely listening to Carter's soft drone.

"Put on my uniform and run through the woods until you reach my horse. He's by the creek, tied to a sycamore. He's black and won't be easily seen. Take him and find help."

When she turned to Carter he stood in his undergarments, rubbing chunks of soil on his body.

He was a small man, not much taller than she, but he had a barrel chest and wide shoulders. His hair came to his chin and hung limp like a soiled rag. His sweat filtered through the air, causing her to remember her defilement. The smell became even more pronounced as she slowly pulled on Carter's uniform. With each movement her body screamed in pain, but when the outfit was assembled she found the pants fit loosely enough to hang around her hips, protecting her most painful area.

Carter bent to his knees and rolled the pants' legs up to free her movement. When he stood he looked at her without regret. "There's no more time, my lady. Go, and may the Maker go with you."

Manda bent down and kissed Chris on the check. He clutched her to him.

"I love you, Manda. Know I will try to remain whole. "

"I know. Stay strong. I'll come back for you and kill Alezza and every last one of her men."

Chris smiled a smile that conveyed his true spirit. "I know you will, sis."

Manda turned to Carter. He shook his head, silencing her before she could speak.

"No words are necessary. I took an oath to follow orders, and that's what I'm doing, no more and no less. Go and go quickly."

Although it hurt, Manda smiled. Carter smiled back. In that breath Manda knew and understood the man before her. She saw his dreams and his desires, his hopes and his fears, but dying for her wasn't one of those fears. In fact, it was an honor. For the remainder of her days she would never forget Carter's eyes gazing at her with a type of love she had never known. Manda turned to the back of the tent. She looked into the night, tasting freedom but feeling no joy. She was now a soldier in a war.

It was a war she intended to win.

"I'll never forget you," she whispered to Carter before she slipped into the night.

When the tent slit closed, she drew a deep breath, noting how much it hurt. Carter's rough uniform sent needle-like pricks into her skin with every movement.

Bort's snore ripped through the air. Manda turned to the sound. His tent was paces away. She peered into the night, calculating the time before dawn.

She was a soldier in a war.

She straightened and set her jaw as the pain of her steps evaporated from her mind. All that remained was intent – fervent intent.

- - -

"How do you know where to go?" Fraul asked, dipping his water skin into the creek and glancing at Aaron. The Avenger stared westward, eyes glowing with an internal strength that could only be a blessing from the Maker.

They hadn't been riding hard but they had been riding incessantly, starting in the early morning and continuing to well after dark. It suited Fraul fine. He had never been one to require a tremendous amount of sleep and it seemed he required even less of it with each passing year.

"I don't know the way you know things," Aaron said. "It's hard to put to words. I know when I'm going toward the betrayed and I know when I'm not. We're going toward the betrayed now. We'll find her soon."

Fraul shivered, not from the chill but from Aaron's augury words. The way Aaron's golden eyes flickered with divination sometimes made Fraul uncomfortable. He almost pitied those who fell on the wrong end of Aaron's sword. Almost.

"It's a woman then?"

"Yes, it's a woman. She's starting toward us, determined to find help. She'll find us, or we'll find her, but I don't know the distance separating us."

Fraul capped his water skin and looped it around one shoulder as they started back to camp. "Why aren't you born where the betrayed is, so you don't have to travel to find her?"

Aaron considered the question as he settled on his pallet. Fraul was now used to Aaron's spans of silent thought and had come to revere those few heartbeats of anticipation. They gave Fraul a profound sense of dignity. It was only because Aaron had never put his experiences to words that forced his silent introspection. The fact Aaron honored Fraul's questions at all gave Fraul a pride few possessed.

No breeze stirred, which was rare on the outskirts of the lush Zier region, but the stillness only accentuated Fraul's contentment. The crackling of the fire and the faint sounds of the nightbirds settled into the evening as if they were permanent fixtures of the area. It was a rare experience Fraul knew he would always remember. He leaned back onto his pack to soak it all in.

Aaron's face glowed in the firelight. His fingers absently brushed the hilt of his golden sword. When he spoke his eyes never focused on Fraul. They remained locked on some distant scene.

"To discover, to learn," he said, reverence resonating with every word. "Each time I'm reborn I learn something invaluable on my journey, so when I live again I won't die."

Fraul took a few heartbeats to analyze Aaron's words. "You mean when you're able to live a full life?"

"Correct."

Fraul rubbed his goatee as he studied the man across the fire, wondering if he was asking too many questions. Aaron didn't seem to mind, but Fraul had an odd sensation he drew close to approaching the point where Aaron would not, or could not answer.

He could see the emotions in Aaron's eyes: the pain, the love, but also Aaron's doubt of his own existence. That shook Fraul more than he would have thought possible. How terrible it must be to exist, yet not to know.

But did anyone really know his or her own significance? Why did he exist? Was there some ultimate purpose he was supposed to fulfill? Had he stumbled off course or was he still in line with his personal fate? Fraul shivered. Fate had always given him pause. The notion that he was to do one thing scared him more than the afterlife. Although he was no fool, if there was one purpose for his life he knew he had already passed it by. He had always been good at passing things by, rationalizing them away.

No matter how much he knew of fate, life would always be a mystery to him, as would the Avenger. He supposed most things were intended to remain that way. Mystery kept humanity striving to achieve. If everything were known no one would have the desire to do anything more, and all would fall to ruin. At least that's how he surmised human existence. Humans reached for reason and purpose behind everything. The more they reached the more they understood, but the more they understood the more they didn't understand. Who said the Maker didn't have a sense of humor?

"Tell me, Fraul, you aren't married?"

It was the first question Aaron had ever asked him, and it took Fraul by surprise. Aaron regarded him with golden eyes that held a pensive affinity. For the first time, Fraul realized Aaron truly liked him.

A small smile stole across Fraul's face as he fingered his goatee. "No, not with my life. I'm the leader of an army, like my father before me. There's no tomorrow for a warrior, only today."

"That's admirable of you." Aaron raised his eyebrows, lips lifting into a rare grin. "None you ever wanted to marry?"

Fraul chuckled at Aaron's expression. "There was one. Her name was Leslia. She was the most perfect woman I've ever seen."

"What happened?"

"Nothing, nothing at all happened." Fraul shifted on his pallet, pausing to relish the story. "I was traveling to Yor, to try out for the army. She was a farmer's daughter who gave me fresh fruit and bread to take with me. When I looked at her and she at me I knew she was the one. She asked me to stay for a few days, but I declined and walked away. I knew if I stayed I would eventually leave to join the army. I couldn't bear the thought of seeing her cry so I chose not to even know her. Our conversation was no longer than a sun's click, but I remember her like I've known her for a lifetime."

"You don't regret it?"

Fraul stared into the fire, remembering Leslia as she handed him the parcel of food. "I regret it every day, but I don't regret it for her. She's better off without me."

Aaron nodded as he threw another log on the fire. The fire flared, blinding Fraul for a few heartbeats and sending a torrent of heat in his direction. When the flames finally waned the night seemed even more still, as if their conversation warranted sanctity even from the nightbirds, whose incessant chatter continued until well past dawn. Fraul drank in the darkness so as to bring the memory back when he wanted.

"I sometimes wonder how we go on when there's so much pain. I've seen the worst of it," Aaron said. "I've held those dying because someone they trusted betrayed them. I've lived it. Every time I come back, love drives me to kill, but pain drives me to die. Love is pain, Fraul. I want to be through with pain. Therefore, I suppose, I want to be through with love."

Fraul bent toward the Avenger, not wanting to miss anything the man said. The plaintive quality of Aaron's tone, combined with the love in his eyes, reminded Fraul of the Maker looking down upon his beloved children who continually turned their backs on him. Fraul recognized the experience he now lived was far more than sacred – it was sanctity.

The silence continued. Fraul dared not speak. He had never been uncomfortable with silence, and he knew the Avenger was forming his thoughts into words that Fraul could better understand. A sudden warmth stole over him: a warmth for the man across the fire, and a warmth for the Maker who had sent the Avenger to him.

"Once I avenged a woman who had been pronounced an adulteress by her husband," the Avenger said. "Her husband, an important man in society, said he'd caught her in the act and killed the man with her. It was believed by the masses but it wasn't true. At that time the punishment for adultery was fire, and the woman was burned at the stake screaming out her love for her husband the entire time. But I knew the truth. The husband had committed the crime. He had taken a mistress and decided he wanted her over his wife.

"When I rode into town and heard the wife screaming for her husband's love, it broke my heart. Her husband was burning her alive and she begged for his love, for forgiveness for whatever she had done. I tried to reach her but I was too late. She died before she knew I was there."

The crackling fire suddenly sounded ominous. Without warning the wind gusted, blowing sparks into the night and throwing the flames higher. The still night was abruptly chaotic and the moaning breeze wailed in anguish. Fraul didn't move, wondering if the very wind was reacting to Aaron's mood.

"What did you learn on that mission?"

The Avenger slowly lifted his head from the flames. "I think the lesson was this: the woman would have chosen death rather than see me kill her husband. Love is pain, Fraul, but love is also stronger than death."

Chapter 20

Korin was running out of time and he knew it.

He strode through the early morning light, deep in thought. Davis' life was in danger. Korin was sure of it.

Nothing had been said, nothing even hinted at, but he had woken that morning bathed in a cold sweat, gut twisting like the Watcher himself had hold of him. He always had those feelings when something he dreaded was about to come to pass. It was almost as if he had the sight, but it could be he'd been among evil for so long he could smell it like the wolven smelled blood.

Korin stopped short and rubbed his forehead. Ista's presence was a constant. He clawed at his skull, desperate to rid himself of the needles.

For days he had searched the books Lorlier had given him. He had barely slept since returning to the keep, desperately searching for a way to free his mind. He had found nothing, and he was out of time.

He didn't know how Ista intended on taking Davis' life, but Korin had to stop it.

Korin swallowed back his fear and started for the stables. He needed a ride to clear his thoughts.

Lorlier had taken Korin's advice and announced his neutrality. Still, many in the Fest kingdom had journeyed to Zier, and many more were leaving. Unlike Ramie, Lorlier did nothing to stop them. Korin had convinced Lorlier that tolerating the departure of his citizens would pacify Ista.

Ista claimed the Collective would fight for all the Lands, but Korin knew the truth. Yes, the Collective would fight for the Lands, but within months the Collective would become the power. Kings would be helpless to resist such a force. Steel was nothing against magic. Kings would follow the Collective's demands out of force or necessity. They would be puppets on a string.

Most kingdoms would be hungry for a magical weapon. Men who left their homes to join the Collective thought they would return to defend their homeland. Korin knew better. By the time the men returned they wouldn't be loyal to their kingdom, but to the Collective.

Lorlier wanted Korin to teach the Fest guard the ways of magic. Lorlier wanted to build his own army with the Quy. He didn't want to be vulnerable to anyone. Korin thanked the fates he had been assigned a fighter rather than a pacifist.

It was a truce: Ista was ignorant of Lorlier's plans, satisfied with the men Lorlier allowed to leave Fest, and Lorlier was satisfied Korin would teach his soldiers.

Brice's suspicions had surfaced when Lorlier demanded all soldiers remain in Fest, but after Korin explained Lorlier's plans to replace his soldiers before those with the Quy were allowed to leave, Brice had been appeased. It was a good lie. It took months for men to complete the admission tests of the Fest guard and it had given Korin ample time to search for a counter to the needles. But today, his feeling of foreboding told him he was out of time.

Would Ista order Brice to take Davis' life? Or would she order him? Korin shivered. If Ista ordered him to complete the task Korin would be tempted to take his own life, but that in itself would not help Lorlier. If Korin ended his own life, he would be unable to help Lorlier train his men. Magic was the weapon Lorlier needed to defeat Ista. It was up to Korin to destroy Ista's plan.

Most people with the Quy were hungry to learn the power and had joined Ista with fiery enthusiasm. Korin could hear them in his mind: the Collective, their constant whispers. Soon it would be hard to hold onto sanity.

Before, the Collective were few, and Ista spoke with each individually. As they grew in number the stronger the web became and the less Ista relied on her individual hold. Now she could whisper her thoughts and they were conducted throughout the network like vibrations of raindrops on a spider's web.

The whispers currently vindicated Ista as being the savior of the Lands. It made Korin want to scream. Memories from the camp exploded inside him. He shoved them away, unwilling to remember the atrocities he had committed for a life that would never be his.

Korin opened the stable door and blinked in the sudden dimness. The scent of sawdust, oats, and horses floated to him. Although the smells didn't rejuvenate him, they lifted his spirits. Horses always made him feel more at peace. They symbolized salvation.

Ista had already begun building the New Alcazar in Zier. She would soon rule from its ramparts like the Calvet before her, but this time she would make the Alcazar the controlling influence in the Lands, not subservient to kings. In a matter of months Ista would be the controller of the Quy and the controller of lives.

Although Korin knew he couldn't stop her, he could hopefully slow her enough to allow the Chosen to crush her. If only the Chosen would act soon, Korin may have a chance at a normal life, but that was a fatuous hope. It was neither rational nor feasible.

When he stopped in front of Salve's stall the white steed nickered. Korin whispered a greeting and rubbed the untainted face. Salve pawed the ground, eager for a ride even though he had been ridden hard over the past few weeks.

"You don't know how lucky you have it, my friend. If only I were as spotless as you the world would look all the more beautiful," Korin whispered.

"Is father being hard on you, Korin?"

Korin knew who had spoken before he turned. Her voice always sent a warm chill down his spine. Marianne looked as if she hadn't slept since returning to the castle. Her eyes were dull, her lips faded. The buttons on her blouse were off by one, making her appear a little disheveled.

He hadn't spoken to her the rest of the trip, feigning to be busy discussing strategy with Gregory. Lorlier's request to spend more time with Mari bothered him. Although Korin would have given his right arm to do so, the closer they became the worse he would hurt her when he left, and leave he would have to do. Even if he found a reprieve from the needles Ista would hunt him. He would have to flee, take on a new identity and always be on guard for one of the Collective.

As he looked into Marianne's gentle brown eyes he once again wished he had chosen Alise to approach. Mari reminded him of a timid fawn. Alise would be able to handle his deception, but Mari? The concern in her eyes tugged at his heart. She stood before him, shy and perhaps a little fearful, but she had dared inquire because of his biting words. The mystery of her built inside him once again. How could one be so gentle by nature, so altruistic?

All his life he had been focused solely on himself. He had lived day in and day out by thinking of only Korin: how to survive, how to break free, how to deceive Ista, and how to deceive those who loved him. To find someone so opposite was extraordinary. Around Mari he felt like he was a speck of dust and she the mountain, he the weak soul and she the vibrant spirit. He deserved neither her kindness nor her worry. He was a creature sent from the Abyss; she was an angel sent from the Maker.

"No, Marianne, your father is exceptional to me. Have no fear. How are you?" he asked, growing more troubled as he continued to study her. "You look tired. Have you been able to rest?"

Mari bit her lip and glanced away, but not before he saw tears spring to her eyes. He wanted to reach for her, console her in some way, but he didn't know how. All he had done was hurt his entire life. He was incapable of anything else.

"I don't feel well, but I'm sure it will pass."

Korin saw her lie. She didn't think it would pass. His pulse raced as he thought about the depression Lorlier said ran in Marianne's line. "What do you mean? Are you ill?"

Her fawn-like eyes flickered back to him. "No, at least I don't think so. Oh, I shouldn't be troubling you. Father told me you were studying to teach the men. Alise has the power you know."

Korin shifted, disliking Mari's sudden change of subject. "Yes. Lorlier thinks she may hurt herself by trying to learn too fast."

Marianne smiled, transforming her face into something celestial. "She'll try, but she's strong. I don't think a bolt of lightning could harm her."

"Good morning to you both."

Brice sauntered down the dimly lit corridor to begin his morning patrol of the grounds. Eternal damnation! If Korin didn't ask Marianne to accompany him on his ride Brice would report back to Ista his dubious nature. Korin didn't want to cause suspicion, especially at this critical time.

When he glanced back at Marianne, his heart melted. She looked so alone, and Lorlier did say to spend more time with her.

Brice stopped beside them and raised an eyebrow. "Are we riding together this morning?" Brice's eyes held steady on Korin. Korin threw up his mask and tried to remain calm. Was Brice looking for something? Korin shoved the thought aside and turned to Marianne.

"If the lady will have me," Korin said.

Marianne searched his eyes. She frowned as if not seeing what she wanted. Korin dropped his mask, fearful she would refuse, and took her hand.

He drew in a breath to say something, but as he stood holding her hand a warmth stole through him. He had never held someone's hand, and Marianne's slender hand closed around his as if it belonged there.

"Please," he whispered. This time he let his feelings for her rise inside him until he could feel his face transform into someone he had always wanted to be.

Mari glanced away, face reddening. "It would be a pleasure."

Brice moved on without another word. Korin watched him leave, his sense of foreboding rekindling, but Davis was with his pedagogues until that afternoon, hence safe from Brice's hand.

When their horses were saddled, they rode in silence. The sun inched its way into the sky and the morning's dew brought the wispy grass to life. The sparse trees of the fields shivered in the slight breeze and rained down an occasional mist.

The ride was bittersweet. He was where he wanted to be, in the position he wanted to be in, with the only person he wanted to be with, and yet everything was out of his reach. He couldn't stay in Fest, he couldn't stay in his position, and he would never be with Mari.

But the wind, the ride, the fantasy that he was just Korin, without the needles or his secrets, was something unexplainable, untouchable, and beautiful.

After a time his thoughts wandered back to Brice. Brice had acted strangely. It was almost as if the man had expected Korin to blatantly deny Ista's wishes.

Did Ista know of his deception?

He thought back to what had occurred since leaving Zier. Ista hadn't called him. Ista enjoyed summoning members of the Collective with the pain. Why hadn't she summoned him?

He glanced at Marianne. Was it something to do with his relationship to Marianne and Lorlier? Korin's mind spun, frantic to think of every possible scenario.

If Ista knew he held feelings for Lorlier's family she would use it to her advantage. She would force him to do things by threatening the safety of Lorlier and his children. He felt the tendrils of Ista's hold tighten. With sickening dread Korin realized Ista had more control of him now than she ever had before. He had inadvertently given Ista the one thing that would keep him alive: the threat of harming those he loved.

As Marianne slowed, Korin's breath caught. Her long, brown hair had fallen loose of its clasp and cascaded around her shoulders in frantic disarray. Her cheeks were flushed from the chill breeze and her eyes shimmered with rare enthusiasm.

Korin swallowed past the lump in his throat. He couldn't take his eyes off her. He desperately wanted to reach over and bury his hands in her hair, pretend he was a normal man and she a normal woman. Korin turned away. He had to return to the keep. Mari would never be his.

Mari's soft cry made Korin turn back. She had doubled over. Her face was clinched with pain.

Korin jumped off his horse and steadied her mount. "Mari?"

She blinked, eyes clearing. After another breath she straightened and shook her head. "It has passed now."

He grabbed her hand, frantic for an answer. "What just happened, Mari?"

She looked at him with something between sorrow and apprehension. "I'll tell you if you swear you won't tell my father."

"I swear on my sword, please."

Marianne lifted her chin, as if warding off evil sprits. "I think I'm dying."

A chill colder than the Watcher's heart rushed through him. When he spoke his voice came out a harsh whisper. "What do you mean?"

"I don't know, Korin. My father would say it's the depression that runs in my mother's line. It's not. I've always been shy, not depressed as my father thinks."

"Marianne, stop talking like this," Korin said, voice rising in a panic. "You're scaring me."

Marianne turned her uneasy gaze his way. What he saw in her eyes seared his heart. Korin threw down the reins, giving the mare freedom to chop the lush grass, and helped Mari out of the saddle, leading her to a path that veered into the surrounding trees. There was an enclave a short distance down the path where he often went to think. Korin always felt the place wrapped him in a gentle embrace, sympathizing with him when he was melancholy and laughing with him when he felt joy.

He had never felt an embrace of a woman. He knew the enclave was the closest thing he would ever have to one.

They walked in silence. He hadn't let go of Mari's hand, and she hadn't taken it away. It felt so small in his own, so vulnerable. His very existence was a threat to Marianne and her family. Ista would use his love against him. It would be better if he just ended the fight and gave into death, but walking with Marianne stirred dreams inside him once again.

A smile lit Marianne's face as he led her into the small enclosure, chasing all signs of uneasiness from her countenance. She put a hand to her lips. "Korin! How did you find this place?"

Despite the circumstances, Korin grinned. It was beautiful. The towering rocks formed the shape of a horseshoe. A low ledge curved along one side, forming a natural seat. Purple and red wildflowers lined the rocks' edge, and creeping moss stole over the tops of the gray stone, careening down the interior sides, giving each rock a unique personality.

Marianne picked some flowers and placed them behind her ear. She was incredible. She looked better in disarray than she did dressed for a ball. When she turned to look at him she quickly turned away when she found his eyes on her. He could sense her nervousness, but his voice wouldn't come. Her fists clinched before she turned back. Although her eyes held a hint of fear, she started to hum and held out her hand for a dance.

"Marianne, I don't know how to dance, and we need to talk."

She clasped his hands and leaned into him. She began to sway.

Heat exploded inside him. He became disoriented. As her head dropped to his shoulder the scent of her drifted to him, causing his feelings to rise to the surface.

Everything became vivid: the wildflowers in his peripheral vision, the sun's rays dancing on the rocks, Marianne's hair tickling his chin, the soft breeze, the sun-warmed enclosure, the heat of his own body, and her soft humming, sending a low rumble inside his chest, chasing away all cares and memories.

He became just a man holding the person he loved. He would give his life for her. He would do anything to keep her from harm.

His head drooped. His eyes closed. He buried his face in her hair and breathed her in.

"You're dancing," she whispered.

He supposed he was. They were moving in rhythm. Her hips swayed under his touch, but slowly, so slowly. Before he knew what he was doing he grabbed a handful of her hair, brought it to his lips and kissed it.

It even tasted sweet.

His arms encircled her, drawing her closer. Her hand slid down to his waist. The cadence of a sparrow's song made him realize she had stopped humming.

A burst of sun-warmed wind gusted past, twirling the scent of wildflowers around them. Marianne tightened her grip. With sudden insight he realized she needed him just as much as he needed her. He reacted on instinct. Drawing her head from his shoulder, he found her lips.

His entire world exploded. She was so perfect, so innocent, and so beautiful. He couldn't get close enough. Everywhere he touched, he brought her closer. He wanted to make her feel everything she allowed him to feel. Moving his lips from her face, he kissed her neck and shoulders, marveling at their smoothness. Her hands burnt a trail of fire over his flesh. He was ravenous for her touch.

She whispered his name. He answered. Nothing else in the world mattered but her.

"Oh, Korin, you meant it." The pleading in her voice stopped him. His vision cleared. They were on the ground, surrounded by wildflowers, clinging to each other. Her smock was almost off, buttons torn.

The trust in her eyes terrified him.

He bounded to his feet and turned away. The entrapment of his life, the solitude and the lies tightened their hold once again. "I'm sorry, Mari. Oh, may the Maker forgive me."

How could he! He was a vile creature who had killed to avoid pain, who was only in Fest because of an order, and who may not be alive the next day.

He was hurting the one thing he swore he would never harm. Marianne didn't know him. She would be appalled to discover his true nature, and she would be crushed if he had to take his life.

When he felt a tentative hand on his shoulder, he turned to face her. The broken look in her eyes was too much for him to bear. She didn't understand his withdrawal, and there was nothing he could do to explain his reaction.

"You don't." It was a simple statement, but the weight in her voice hung in the air like lead. Korin watched her face go through a variety of emotions: first it was confirmation, then disappointment, and finally despair. He didn't understand. He tried to grasp her words but they evaded him, something about him not meaning . . .

He grabbed her wrist before she turned. The pain in her eyes would torment him for the remainder of his days.

"I love you." His voice broke with his words, but the conviction in his tone left no room for doubt. "I've loved you since the first time I saw you. Don't ever doubt my love for you, Marianne. It's unending."

Tears rained down upon her breast, but they fell out of elation. He didn't know how to feel. Part of him wanted to embrace what was happening but another part told him to hold back. He was the spawn of the lower plains, she of the upper. The twain would never meet.

"But why?" She turned a furtive glance to the crushed wildflowers at her feet.

Korin cupped her face in his hands, forcing her to look at him once again. "No," he said, searching her face, making sure she understood. "I want you. I want you more than anything in this life.

But it can't be. I'm no prince. Even if I were I'd be unworthy of you. You don't know me, Marianne. I'm not what you see. You wouldn't want me if you knew my life."

She placed a hand on his chest. "Yes, I would." Her smock fell open. Korin quickly closed it again.

"This isn't right. You'll marry a prince and you'll regret anything that happens between us. You deserve so much more than me, so much more than anything I could possibly give you."

Marianne lifted her chin. "You're more than you know, Korin. Even my father says so. And I love you."

Korin's knees gave way. He staggered backwards until he hit the rock wall of the enclosure, sliding down the warm stone until he rested on the ground. His heart pounded so hard he knew she could hear it. He rested his face in his hands and tried hard to hold onto his emotions. He couldn't. They were a torrent of pure, chill water welling inside him, cleansing his soul.

He reached for her, pulling her to him, clinging to the fountain that had purified his spirit. He buried his face in her chest and savored the experience, relishing the feel of her but knowing it could never be.

His life had been worth nothing. Now she had made everything worthwhile. Korin set his jaw, determined to end the pain Ista planned for Lorlier's family.

"I can't tell you what those words mean to me," he said.

Marianne's eyes filled with tears.

"What is it?" Korin whispered.

"I just want you to know me, to be able to remember me."

"I could never forget you. You're the only one I'll ever love, Mari. But you'll soon forget me, which is what you should do. You'll love another and bear fine children."

"No." She pulled away. "I'm dying, Korin."

Korin put his hands on her shoulders. "You aren't dying. You're just ill. I want you to see the healer. Promise me you will."

Mari remained silent. Korin's previous foreboding crept up his spine. A cloud passed over the sun, casting them in shadow.

"When the power was released at Stardom," Mari said, "I watched Alise crumble to the ground in pain. I saw others screaming, others dying. I felt nothing, but at the same time I felt everything. Something happened to me too. In the next breath I wasn't the same person I was just heartbeats before. I don't know how to explain it any better than that.

"All I know is something isn't right inside me. What, I don't know, but I know I won't be alive much longer, and I'm frightened."

"Mari, a lot changed when the Quy was born, for many people. You're compassionate. It's only logical you felt changed. People were dying, in pain, and you felt for them. You reached out with your feelings and felt so much it's now making you physically sick. Can't you admit that's a viable possibility?"

Marianne studied at him for a long time before replying. Korin held his breath. The look in her eyes was one of a fatally wounded animal full of quiet acceptance it was going to die.

"No. Something's inside me. It's eating away at my soul."

- - -

Keys clattered against the lock. Lazo squinted in the gloom but the slits at the top of the door were too high to reveal their visitor. Beside him, Jasta and Justin exchanged furtive glances.

Lazo put a gentle hand on the Jasta's shoulder. "Don't fear. I'll return before it claims you."

They had been confined to the isolation cell since capture. It was an individual confinement, devoid of any kind of opening, and encompassed by dreary gray stone. Four men guarded the cell at all times. The only light, night and day, was from a lone torch hanging behind the thick wooden door. It gave little light and little comfort.

Ista kept them secluded because of their close association with Ren. She knew they could reveal the truth to whoever would listen. No food was brought them, no light given, and the sanitation was theirs to control. Now the only thing keeping each of them from giving up on life and rejecting the dirty water the guards brought was the unspoken threat hanging around them like chains: if one of them died the Mar would claim the others. So they drank the water. And they ate rats.

Rats thrived in the dungeon, feeding off prisoners too weak to push them aside. They had gone for days until they could stand their hunger no longer. Jasta wept after they had eaten the first rat. Lazo had never seen his sister cry, not even as a child. It had shaken him more than he could have imagined.

By his calculations, it was early morning. He was never called during the day, only at night, when the castle was quiet and the Collective asleep. He had been taken every night since their confinement, Ista demanding he reveal the secrets of the Red Eye.

Ista had taught him a chant that called to the Red Eye's memories. Because he was a twin he had learned the chant within a moons' click, not the days it would have taken a normal man. Because he was a triplet he could leave the twins in small doses without the Mar claiming them. Ista was holding his siblings over his head. One day, if he didn't reveal the memories of the Eye he would be taken from the twins permanently and their deaths would be on his hands.

In the ritual all contact was lost with the outside, even for a twin. Each time the ritual began Jasta and Justin's lives hung in the balance. Lazo made sure to end the calling before his siblings were lost to the Mar.

So far, Lazo had been able to avoid the Red Eye's memories. When the ritual began he closed his eyes, never allowing himself to witness the Eye's secrets. The apparitions of the Red Eye were as real as an army of soldiers. The memories of the Eye could come alive, and they could kill. Because he originated the chant he was immune to the Eye's memories. The children, however, were not.

May the Maker forgive him. Ista had known he would try to protect the Red Eye's secrets so she had forced innocent children to be witnesses. Ista hadn't guessed Lazo would allow the children to die. Lazo might have been able to save them if he had seen the memories, but he had not. He couldn't allow Ista to discover the truth.

Each night he had wept in remorse and prayed a fervent prayer for the Maker's forgiveness. But what choice did he have? The Red Eye could not be awakened.

The door squeaked open. The glare of the torches almost blinded him, and Lazo shielded his eyes with a soiled hand. The outline of four burly guards could be seen in the doorway. Just in case anyone besides Ista could sense the power by touch, Lazo stepped forward so he would be the first one handled.

He had always been able to reach his other side. He was a triplet. It was in his nature. Since birth he had been able to enter another part of his mind and escape the constant chatter of the twins. That's how he could leave the twins and not feel the Mar, or the pain of separation. Because he could go to his other side he was able to hide his power from detection. It was next to impossible for Jasta and Justin. Thank the Maker Ista had only touched him when they had first been captured. She hadn't tested the twins. Ista knew if Lazo had the power the others would as well. That had given him the time he needed in the dungeon to teach Jasta and Justin how to enter the other side of their minds in order to conceal their power.

By night, Lazo was a soldier. By day he was an instructor, tutoring Jasta and Justin on how to find their other side. Although it had been a grueling task, both had learned. Lazo had to keep his own emotions under control as he ordered his siblings to give themselves over to the Mar. The Mar's effects were something the twins experienced even if each left the other for only a heartbeat. It was excruciating: as if one heartbeat you were floating in a sea of warm water, the buoyancy carrying your weight easily, and in the next you were drowning as a frigid undercurrent pulled you down, plunging you into a torrent of darkness.

There had been times in his life Lazo desperately wished he had the twins' closeness. This was not one of those times. The Mar was something he hoped to never feel.

Jasta was able to remain on the other side longer than Justin; Justin had always been the weakest of the three, but both could remain in the other part of themselves for as long as it would take for Ista to touch them and test them for the power. They had to be prepared at all times. If they went into their other sides too soon or too late Ista would have them.

A guard came forward and tethered Lazo's arms and legs. The other moved to Jasta and Justin. Lazo almost cried out in alarm. Jasta and Justin had never been taken. Did Ista know of his betrayal?

Lazo reached inside and found the light of the Quy. Although he was no fighter, he desperately wanted to try to break his chains and flee. His inner voice was never wrong, and it currently screamed for him to run. The same fear was mirrored in the twins' eyes, but they would never escape the guards. They knew nothing of the Quy and they were far from soldiers.

Lazo tried to recall if he had ever held a sword. He glanced at his hands. They were covered with grime. His fingernails were broken to the quick and there were a few bloody scabs where the rats had nipped him in sleep. He tried to recall the way his hands had looked before magic's rebirth: smooth, without calluses, murky white and unblemished. A sword would be as foreign in his hands as it would in the hands of a newborn child. He knew strategy, maps and tactics but nothing about physical combat. Escape was as fleeting as water through his fingers.

A guard jabbed Jasta in the back and shoved her forward. Jasta tripped over her chains and released a sharp cry of pain. Lazo watched as Jasta wavered precariously to regain her footing. He wanted to reach out to her but he knew the punishment for his aid would be worse than the punishment if she fell, so he remained where he was, whispering encouragement to her with his inner voice. When Jasta managed to stumble to an upright position, her hair was tousled, her cheeks were pallid and sunken, and her robe was torn from her falls. It was an image Lazo would have laughed at weeks ago. Jasta was steel:

hard, unemotional and almost cold. Now she was a fine silk thread, needing him and Justin more than they needed her.

And Justin: the twin whose eyes always shown with inner excitement now had eyes of granite; the twin whose incessant chatter almost drove Lazo mad was completely silent. Lazo found himself talking about anything he could bring to mind just to ensure Justin would hold on to sanity. Soon, Lazo knew, sanity would be the least of his worries. Disease would kill them. Rats were host to many illnesses. Jasta already had odd spots on her back, and Justin was losing his hair.

Jasta and Justin walked in front of him with one guard to each side. Lazo followed, the other two guards at his heels. A sharp spear butted him in the back. He barely noticed. He was intent on trying to decipher why Ista had summoned the twins. Did she suspect they had the power, or did she want to question them?

He settled on the latter. If he had judged Ista correctly she took little notice of those she deemed harmless. Just as a giant ignored a pebble, Ista ignored those who couldn't match her skill. Her arrogance could very well be her downfall. Even a pebble could arm a sling to down a giant, even a pebble.

But his observation did little to suppress his feeling of dread. Something terrible was about to happen, something treacherous. Sweat broke out on his brow, and despite his weak condition every fiber of his being tensed for battle.

From what Lazo had overheard, Ista had begun to rebuild the Alcazar and she was training those with magic with rigorous intent. She promised all her subjects glory and power beyond reason and had proclaimed the age of the Collective.

Lazo knew the real meaning behind those words. It would be an age of domination, an age that would defy all the Code of the Alcazar stood for, and an age that would herald wizards as rulers of the Lands. A silent rage ignited within him. He opened his mind to allow the others to feel it. He felt the twins grab on to his anger like a banner of hope. If they concentrated on rage, Jasta and Justin would have no time for fear.

His siblings began to murmur frantically. When Lazo refocused, his step faltered. They had reached the great room. Nothing could have prepared him for the sight. In all of his days and nights in the dungeon he hadn't imagined this.

A cry came to his lips but no voice would follow. Hundreds upon hundreds of migrants filled the lower chambers of Stardom, valises tossed over their backs or dropped by their sides. Children shouted in excitement as they filtered through the adults to reach the forefront of the throng. Soldiers' uniforms, not only from Crape, but also from Fyl and Byn, some even from Oldan, weaved in and out of the mob, trying to maintain order among the commoners.

Although the people were grains of sand on the shore, that wasn't what stunned Lazo to silence. It was the fact that every one of them, man, woman and child, had one thing in common – their heads were shaved. Although a few of the women wore snoods to keep their baldness hidden, most did not. Their baldness was a mark of their power. Lazo sent a silent prayer to the Maker, knowing the needles lay under the surface of their skulls. Ista already controlled them.

He felt as if he looked in on a nightmare. People glanced in their direction but gave them little notice. The chamber was filled with a current of titillation. Fervent voices infiltrated the air like a drone of bees, and bursts of laughter sent the ado to even higher levels. Lazo's stomach turned, sick with the reality before him.

A sentry posted at the bottom of the stairs sounded a trumpet. All quieted, and everyone, children included, fell to their knees and touched their heads to the floor. Lazo's eyes rose to the landing overhead where Ista stood in her glorious body. Her stoic green eyes looked straight through him.

One of the guards cursed and forced Lazo to the ground. With sudden realization, Lazo saw he was the only one who had remained standing. Jasta and Justin were already down. He was unsure if they had been forced to bow or if they had done so out of fear. They were silent, even in their minds.

His heart beat so frantically he was sure it could be heard in the hush that had settled over the crowd. He held his breath, wanting to look up but sensing Ista's eyes had yet to stray from him.

"Arise, my children." Ista's voice floated across the assembly. "As I have said, I'm your humble servant, you aren't mine. I welcome you to the Collective."

A roar went up from the crowd. The marble hall seemed to magnify the shouts and carry them to the depths of the Abyss.

Ista lifted her hands, stilling the throng to silence. The sunlight filtered in the windows and bathed her in sunlit glory. Her dark hair seemed to dance in its graces. A few men in the crowd spoke in admiration of her beauty. Ista smiled before she began.

"In my day wizards were under the Code of the Alcazar. They were forbidden to rule, forbidden to fight, and forbidden to embrace the Quy for all its power. My children, the wizards of old failed for one reason and one reason alone: they gave magic boundaries." Her face twisted in anguished disapproval. "I've had many years to think on magic's history and what rules need to be changed. Now I have a chance to mend the old ways. I'm honored and humbled to teach and guide you in something as powerful as the Quy."

The crowd was silent. Lazo closed his eyes, feeling Jasta and Justin's panic mingle with his own. The people were transfixed, hungering for every word and swallowing her ideology like life's water.

"Why did magic have to be destroyed, my children?"

Murmurs sifted throughout the great hall, but no one raised their voices to speak. After a few heartbeats the murmurs stilled and all waited in expectation.

"Because it was stifled," Ista said as her eyes grazed the crowd. "The wizards of the Alcazar forbade learning the Quy utterly and without bounds. They set limits by adhering to a Code that didn't allow wizards to use the Quy to kill, even for righteous reasons; that didn't allow wizards to join together for war, even for justice; that didn't allow wizards to reach for the outer boundaries of magic for fear of harming themselves."

Ista paused to lock her penetrating gaze on certain individuals in the crowd. "I've spoken to each of you, taken your vow for the Collective and blessed you with the ancient blessing. Most of you have asked me what I've learned in my years of isolation. I'll tell you what I've learned, my children. I've learned the Quy is a blessing that sets us above other people of the Lands. The wizards of old knew this but chose to humble themselves, yielding to the leadership of kings and administrators.

"I challenge you now, as children of the Collective, to use the Quy without limits, to use it without restraint, to become soldiers of the Quy, defending magic and leading the Lands into a new era! The Collective will rule without acquisition but will guide the kingdoms into the future. Magic will be upheld as a power to command respect and reverence. You're the elite, my children! Let us take this divination with open arms! Do you accept this challenge?"

The crowd roared their acceptance. Lazo and the twins were the only ones who didn't lift their voices to the sky. Ista's eyes found Lazo before she soothed the crowd to silence.

"The Collective force will be impenetrable. You'll belong to no Land. You'll belong to the Alcazar and to the Collective. You'll become soldiers of magic, soldiers working together, soldiers of peace. Soon, my children, we will be teachers and mentors for all those without the Quy. We can protect those without the power with our gift. The Quy sets us apart. We will be the elite in the years to come, revered for our power. We must lead those less blessed for they are slightly blinded.

"The word is being spread among other kingdoms. Magic's time of rest has ended. We now begin the era of the Collective!"

Cheers roared through the assembly. Lazo scanned the crowd. He didn't recognize any faces. Only the people outside the walls were loyal to Ren, and they couldn't fight an army of magic. What commoner would oppose a four hundred year old sorceress?

"So, my children," Ista said. "I'll train you and together we'll become the defenders of the Alcazar and soldiers of the Quy. We won't belong to one Land but to all the Lands!"

A chant formed and soon all the people were joining in. Lazo felt his insides quake as the multifarious voices rang out in one great thunderous blast.

"The Quy sets us above! The Collective gives us strength! With both we are one! With both we rule! With both we make peace!"

Valor stepped forward to stand beside Ista. "Friends, we have begun to rebuild the Alcazar. The new Calvet stands before you, a willing guide to the future of the Collective."

The crowd roared. Ista bowed her head in humility, a small smile touching her lips.

"We're living in perilous times," Valor said. "Magic has brought greed and eradication in other kingdoms. The Collective may have to be called on sooner rather than later to annihilate these threats to the Lands. Bostic of Ketes has closed his borders. The messengers we have sent in peace haven't returned. We assume them dead."

"They have violated the Collective's call for peace, my lord," someone yelled from the crowd. "Let us name a new king!"

Impetuous shouts of agreement echoed one after the other. Foot stomping and angry exclamations escalated with the rising voices.

Ista stilled the crowd with her look. "I fear we may have to do just that. The Collective will have to react to this outrage as soon as possible. We must make haste to learn the Quy.

"If this was the only infringement of freedom, we could crush it swiftly, but Bostic isn't the only threat. Ramie of Yor, the supreme ruler of Oldan, has closed Yor's borders. He has also ordered Oldan citizens to cease their pilgrimage to Zier. Reports of people being killed at the Newlan border have come to my attention."

A multitude of angry shouts reverberated in the marble hall. A few of the men shouted that Ramie needed to be stripped of power.

"My children, we will have to right these wrongs. New kings will need to be appointed." Ista stopped, her vehement green eyes scanning the spell-struck crowd.

"As I have said, the Collective will promote goodness to all the Lands. How better to do so than to appoint from within?"

The crowd went mad. Ista bowed deeply. Her eyes found Lazo's and her hand motioned to the guards before she turned and walked off the balcony to the study beyond.

The chant rekindled. "The Quy sets us above! The Collective gives us strength! With both we are one! With both we rule! With both we make peace!"

The guards led them through the mob as Valor began to speak of his plans, but Lazo didn't hear him. The twins whispered frantically but he shoved them out as well. He didn't see how Ren could win the battle before him. There were too many of the Collective.

But Ren was the Chosen, Lazo reminded himself. There was a chance, no matter how slim it was.

Ista would dominate the Lands as Barracus had tried to do. Although Barracus ruled by force, Ista ruled by subtleties. Lazo didn't know whom to fear more. At least in conquest you had a clear definition of your enemy. With Ista's cry for peace the enemy was vague and Ren would have a more difficult time proving his just intentions.

Lazo knew the Zier people still believed in Ren. Ista indicated Bostic of Ketes did as well, and if Ramie was committed to counter Ista, they had a chance.

When they stopped at the entrance to Ista's study Lazo refocused on the twins, offered his encouragement and included a soft warning for them to be prepared. One of the guards rapped on the thick wooden door. A muffled voice came from within.

One of the guards shoved Lazo inside. Ista's glare met him, along with the savory scents of meats and sauces, fruits and breads, desserts and wine. Despite his effort to keep his eyes on Ista, Lazo's gaze flickered to the multiple trays lining the far side of the room. Roasted chicken was piled high on a silver platter, along with large bowls of delectable sauces, medleys of fruits, a fresh loaf of bread, and rich pastries. His mouth watered as his stomach released a low rumble. Forcing his eyes from the food, he met Ista's gaze.

She stood before the Red Eye. He could see the desire in her eyes, and he knew her thoughts. If only they had the power she would have a weapon of force. Twins and triplets fed off one another and were stronger mentally because of it. The learning of the Quy would be no exception. Lazo already sensed the power doubling, even tripling inside him, and hoped for the thousandth time Ista wouldn't discover their deception.

Ista slowly drifted past the trays of food. She took a piece of chicken and dipped it in a bowl. Lazo stiffened as Ista walked closer. The fragrance of spices hung in the air as Ista took a slow, deliberate bite.

"I would offer to have you sit with me and partake of the table before you but I fear I cannot tolerate those loyal to the enemy of the Lands." Ista put her hand on Lazo's arm. Lazo had already pulled into his other side where his power would be undetectable.

Ista turned to Jasta. "I'm sure Lazo has conveyed my desire to awaken the Red Eye. Lazo has been, shall I say, helpful?" Ista paused and raised a sarcastic eyebrow. "The problem is," Ista continued, walking past Jasta to look at Justin. "Lazo claims the Red Eye doesn't speak in ways he understands. I don't believe him."

Ista turned and caressed the Red Eye with seared fingers. Dipping her hand in a washbasin, she wiped her brow. Her eyes flickered back to them. "I'm sure he's told you the Red Eye's memories are alive. I'm sure he's also told you he's sent children to their deaths. I doubt he would be so rash if one of you attended the ritual."

Lazo's mouth went dry. Beside him, Jasta and Justin stiffened.

Ista chortled deep in her throat as she dipped her hand into the washbasin once more. After dousing her brow, she turned back to Lazo. "The Mar is the worst horror one of your kind could experience."

At the mention of the Mar, Jasta and Justin's inner whispers started. Ista saw their fear and brushed Jasta's cheek with her palm. Lazo held his breath, praying to the Maker Jasta had reached her other side. When Ista's hand dropped, Lazo exhaled.

"Yes, the Mar." Her eyes flickered between them as she stroked the Eye. "A triplet can leave the others in small doses but a twin can never be confined apart from his or her sibling without the Mar's effects. Two of you will be in the ritual, the third will not. If the ritual isn't over within heartbeats, the third will die of the Mar."

"Who remains behind?" Lazo whispered.

"Not you, Lazo. That way you'll make haste, no?"

- - -

Korin stood outside Davis's door.

The blow had come after his ride with Marianne. His deceit was known. He was out of time. Brice had ordered him to kill Davis. Ista knew of his deception, and if Davis wasn't found dead in the morning Korin would die as well. Then he wouldn't be able to help Mari.

Davis's deep laughter wafted to him. Korin turned and quickly walked down the hall.

There was only one solution.

He would tell Lorlier everything.

Korin closed the door to his room and heaved a sigh. Books, notes, sketches, formulas and styluses were strewn over the floor. He had been poring over the books ever since he had returned from his ride with Mari, trying to find anything Ista could have done to her. Now his efforts were futile.

As if on cue, a sharp, stabbing pain seared his mind. Ista was calling, her insistence evident from the fire she sent inside him.

He clawed for the crystal he kept in a side pouch. Ista's deformed features were sneering with pleasure inside the hazy blue ball.

"Worried about Marianne are we, Korin? You should be. She'll die if you don't slow the infection."

"How?" he managed, knees buckling from the pain.

Ista lost her smile. "My child, surely you don't think I'll tell you? I've given you an assignment. You need to carry it through. Once you've proven your loyalty to me I'll give you what you need to save the one you love. You see how love weakens you, Korin? You see why I lectured so long on hate? Now you're more vulnerable than ever. Do your duty and Marianne can live."

"Why not just kill me, Ista?"

Ista sneered. "Oh, Korin, don't you see? Lorlier loves you like a son. Davis will be dead. You'll save Marianne from death's clutches. How do you think Lorlier will reward you?"

"You don't need me, Ista. You have the Collective."

"But I do need you. Do you think I've been blind? Do you think I didn't know your heart?

"You're special, Korin, that's why I've allowed you to live. You're much stronger than anyone else I've raised. You'll be a vessel for me. Soon you'll never resist me again, for you'll house another."

Korin shuttered as he thought about how Ista would soon use the Red Eye.

Ista's brow furrowed. "How are you not one of the Collective? How have you evaded me all these years?"

The fire flamed hotter. Korin's vision blurred as he fought with all his strength to keep breathing. "I don't know. I swear I don't know."

"How?"

Sweat broke out on his brow. Ista's deformed features laughed at his agony.

As quickly as the pain had come, it was gone. He gasped for air. The crystal dropped from his fingers and rolled across the floor.

"Korin!"

Alise knelt beside him, laying a concerned hand on his shoulder. Her eyes flickered to the crystal and then back to him.

"I'll get it for you."

"No!"

Alise's jumped at his abrupt tone. He put a hand on her arm. "I'm sorry, Alise. I just don't want you touching that vile thing."

Korin managed to stumble across the floor and retrieve the crystal. When it was securely in his pouch, he turned back to Alise. He had grown fond of her over the past few days. Alise came to him every sun's click, begging him to teach her a little magic. Her openness and zest for knowledge was invigorating.

Korin almost broke down in tears as he looked at her. Her family was in danger because of him.

"What is it you need, Alise?" he asked, trying to mask his worry. "Do you come to learn a little magic?"

Alise's eyes lit with excitement, all former tenseness forgotten. She grabbed his hands. "Teach me something, Korin! Please!"

Korin smiled. Alise's energy was contagious. He would think about Ista only after he taught Alise a fraction of his knowledge. He was irrational now. He had to divert his thoughts.

"I'll teach you how to find the Quy, but then I must return to my studies. Your father has put a lot of trust in me."

"Oh, Korin!" she said, spinning around. "Thank you!"

Korin repressed a smile. "I'll only teach you if you promise not to try anything else until you're supervised."

"Fine, yes, I promise."

Alise and Marianne were more opposite than Korin had realized. Korin had been in many wagers with the men about which was more attractive. Each was uniquely alluring. Marianne had long, wavy brown hair and big brown eyes. She was tall and thin, without much shape, but Korin considered it regal.

Alise had straight brown hair and sharp hazel eyes, taking after her father. She was extremely shapely and much less shy than

Marianne. Some considered Alise one of the guys, with benefits, and Marianne an untouchable snob. When Alise smiled her entire face lit with an enthusiasm rarely seen. Alise knew how to live for the day and never considered the consequences.

Korin motioned for Alise to sit. He looked down into eyes that outshone all the candles in the keep. "First rule, Alise, is what?" Her thin eyebrows furrowed. Korin repressed another smile. "Never try more than the teacher tells you. Repeat it."

Alise grinned and repeated it.

"Now close your eyes and clear your mind. Don't think about anything, not even magic. Relax your limbs and melt into yourself. Good, that's it," Korin said as he watched Alise's features relax. "I want you to become aware of something inside you. It's always been there. You've been aware of it yet you know nothing about it. You'll find it in your core. It rises inside silently yet forcefully. Do you feel it?"

Alise gave a slight nod.

Korin smiled. He knew Alise would find the Quy with little difficulty. "Call to it, Alise. Think of the Quy as air inside a room. You're looking at it through a windowpane. I want you to open the window. Let the air free."

Alise gasped, eyes open wide.

Korin grabbed her hands. "Hold it. Before you can use it you must sense it. Feel it flooding through every vein. It's fire and ice together. Just when you think it will burn you through it becomes elation."

"It's beautiful," Alise said as her eyes fluttered to him and widened even further.

"Yes, it's beautiful," Korin smiled. "The Quy is everywhere inside you, churning just below the surface, waiting for your command. But until you try to use it, you must learn how to master your emotions. That will be my first objective when I begin training."

Alise blinked, the Quy's light still lingering in her eyes, and smiled her thanks.

"You're strong, Alise. Tomorrow you'll be able to find the Quy even more easily."

"Really?" Alise's hazel eyes lit with fervor.

"Yes, really," he said, wishing he could be the one to teach her.

Alise put her hands on her hips and raised an eyebrow. "How do you know so much already?"

Korin forced a cocky grin. "You forget I've been learning for days."

Alise nodded in satisfaction and then broke into a smile, already thinking of another subject. "I wish Mari had the power. You know, I thought she did. When magic was reborn I thought I saw the pain in her eyes, but I must have imagined it."

"You must have." Korin sat at his small desk and opened one of the books, insinuating he needed to be left alone.

"But it was strange. As soon as my pain was gone she fell backward against the wall, saying her heart hurt, almost cramping."

Korin spun. "What?"

"After the power was born," Alise repeated, "Mari said her heart hurt."

"Holy Maker," Korin said. Why hadn't he though of it before? He should have thought of it before. Ista hadn't infected Marianne, but Ista would know the cure.

He ran to his closet and grabbed the silver dust he kept concealed on the top shelf. He heard Alise's questions but didn't bother to respond. There was no time for explanations. Korin dismissed Alise with a glance and ran down the hall toward the royal suites.

He heard Alise's footsteps behind him but didn't slow. He prayed he wasn't too late. If it had spread through Mari's bloodstream she didn't have a chance.

When he reached the royal hallway he turned down the corridors leading to Mari's private chambers. He knew the path by heart. He had passed through the suites many times just for a glimpse of her.

As always, guards stood outside her door. He didn't pause. He sprinted between them, crashed through the door, and slid to a halt inside chambers he had always dreamed of entering. The guards grabbed him by the arms and tried to pull him out. Marianne sat on her bed in her nightdress, hair spilling down her back. Korin's heart went to his chest. The terror he now felt was unprecedented by anything Ista had ever done. If Mari died nothing would matter.

Marianne dropped the book she was reading as her eyes flickered over the guards. She quickly pulled a blanket over her shoulders to conceal her nightdress. Alise came to a sudden halt beside Korin, ordering the guards to release him at once. Korin had yet to take his eyes off Mari, and when the guards released their hold he almost fell, unaware of how hard he had been straining to reach her.

Candles were lit around the room. Their flames were reflected in Mari's eyes and cast a soft glow around her loose hair. Korin wished he could have been sitting with her, talking of books and dreams, of future plans and children. She was so gentle, why did this have to happen to her? That was why. She was gentle.

He fell to the floor and took her frightened face in his hands.

"Marianne, listen to me. I want you to concentrate and answer my questions as best you can. When the power was released Alise said you felt pain afterwards, is that correct?"

She nodded.

"In your heart?"

"Yes," she said, placing one of her hands on his outstretched arm. Her hand was cold. Korin fought back tears.

"Have you noticed any discoloring or bruises on your body?"

The door burst open as Lorlier pushed his way in, along with two guards Korin knew well. There was confusion in every eye, but also duty. Korin understood. He would have alerted Lorlier as well. He was an intruder in Mari's room. It didn't matter that he was a trusted soldier in Lorlier's guard.

Lorlier's sharp hazel eyes flashed with anger. "Korin, what's the meaning of this?"

Alise put her hand on Lorlier's arm and stopped him with her eyes. The scene would have been comical under other circumstances, Alise so small and Lorlier so large, but the king softened under Alise's worried gaze.

Korin turned back to Marianne. "Marianne, did you hear me? Do you have any discoloration?"

She looked at him with wide-eyed innocence. Korin bowed his head, knowing the answer before it was spoken. "Yes, my toes." She took her feet out from under her. Her toes were turning a bluish color and her toenails were brittle.

"Oh please, dear Maker," Korin whispered.

"What is it, Korin?" Lorlier asked.

Korin tried to conceal his inner terror. "The backlash."

"What's the backlash?" Alise asked.

Korin turned to Marianne. Her brown eyes were full of apprehension, and something else – love.

He didn't deserve her love. He was an impostor in her home. He had to tell Lorlier everything. Mari and Davis were out of time. Together he and Lorlier would find a solution. Davis would live, but Ista must think him dead or Mari would die. He brushed Mari's cheek in affection, knowing it would be the last time he would ever see her. When Lorlier heard his history he would be banned from Fest.

He squeezed Mari's hands, trying to convey all the love he felt inside. "Mari, you had the power but you didn't accept it. You pushed it away because it frightened you. It forced its way in anyway, except it did so in a different fashion. The power has now turned into a disease called the backlash. Because you didn't let magic take hold, it's taking what it can from you."

Korin looked up at Lorlier. "My lord, it's slowly eating her alive. She'll die if we don't find a cure."

- - -

Korin was exhausted. He didn't know how many more questions he could take. He had answered everything at least twice. He was sick at his own revelations.

Lorlier barked another question. Korin answered it. He rubbed his hands as if he could wipe off the stains only he could see.

He recalled the look of horror crossing Marianne's features when he had first revealed the truth. She looked at him as if the words he had spoken in the stone enclave had been a lie. Nothing, no amount of pain, no anguish Ista could send, no rejection he would live, would ever be as tormenting as the look in Marianne's eyes.

If only he could hold her one last time, assure her of his love, he would make her see how special she was, how beautiful. But that day would never come. He would never speak to Marianne again. He would never have a chance at life. He had just sentenced himself to death.

At least he had made the last play of his life against Ista. That gave him a small pittance of pride.

They had long since left Marianne's room and now it was just Lorlier and himself, along with the two guards flanking him.

He would give anything for Marianne's life, even his own salvation. He had cast a magical weave over her with silver dust. Although it would slow the infection, it may not be enough to stop the disease until he found what he needed to cure her.

The backlash was something he had read about in Lorlier's books. The books said the only cure for the backlash was "a blanket of power" to draw out the contaminated force residing in the victim.

He didn't know what that meant.

Lorlier cleared his throat and Korin wearily raised his head. His king's hazel eyes glared at him. It was a dagger through Korin's heart.

"Give me one good reason why I shouldn't put you and Brice to death immediately," Lorlier said.

Korin didn't hesitate. "Because I'm expendable and expendable people are sometimes sent on hopeless journeys."

Lorlier raised his eyebrows, indicating for Korin to continue.

"My lord, Davis' life is in danger. Ista believes I'll kill him by sunup. Marianne will die if a cure isn't found. Ista knows the cure. If she believes Davis lives she won't hesitate to kill me, and Marianne will die. If she believes Davis is dead I'll live and be able to help Mari. Please, my lord, let me help her. I give you my word I'll come back and then you can run your sword through me. I deserve life less than the disease living in your eldest daughter. Please, Lorlier, I beseech you, trust me one last time."

"Trust you!" Lorlier rose from his seat, eyes filled with rage. "How could I ever trust you after what you've revealed!"

Korin flinched. "You can't, my lord, but I'm Mari's only chance."

Lorlier bowed his head. "My Mari, my first born, how I love her."

Korin turned away. He was unworthy to witness Lorlier's sorrow. He was formed in the pits of the lower plains and would reside there for all eternity.

Korin heaved an unsteady breath, desperate to make Lorlier understand. "Ista doesn't care if Marianne lives or dies, my lord. She only holds it over my head to force me to do her bidding." Korin swallowed and looked to the floor, unable to take the look of betrayal in Lorlier's eyes. "Ista thinks if I find a cure, and if your only son is dead, you'll allow me to wed Marianne."

"I would never!"

"I know," Korin said softly, "but that's what Ista believes. She'll give me the cure because she says I'm strong in the Quy. She wants me despite my deception. I'll be a vessel for someone else. She means to send a spirit of a wizard inside me. She'll be able to control me still, even with a spirit inside."

Lorlier took a deep breath and sat back down, face softening. Korin thought he saw compassion on his king's features but quickly disregarded it. How could Lorlier have compassion for one of the demon spawn?

"What will become of you if a spirit enters you?"

"I'll be no more. Spirits of the ancient wizards will overpower all remembrance I have. I'll no longer exist. But if we work together, my king, we can deceive her."

Lorlier was silent, so Korin continued. "She told me she would give me the cure. I'll have to travel to Stardom to retrieve it. When I do, she'll send a spirit inside me. She'll send me back here to save Mari. As soon as I save Mari, kill me."

Lorlier was silent. Korin lifted his head. The king's expression was unreadable. Korin waited.

"I'll let you go," Lorlier said quietly, "but if you don't return you better be dead or I'll hunt you down and kill you with my bare hands."

Korin nodded with doleful relief. "I can't tell you what to do about Brice, but if you kill him Ista will be suspicious and she'll turn on me. If I'm dead I can't help you. But that's for you to decide. You need to announce Davis' death by morning so Brice can authenticate it. If I were you, I'd send your son far, far away from here."

"I'll send him to Ramie," Lorlier said, thinking aloud. "Davis can inform the king of Yor we'll join him in mounting an offensive against Ista. Ista will die for her crimes." Looking back at Korin, Lorlier's eyes hardened. "Make sure you're well away from her when I attack." Korin had never felt so small, so undeserving. The king thought Mari would die, and he still let him go, let him live.

Korin walked to the door, saddened that Lorlier had no idea how much he had come to love him and how much he truly loved his daughter.

"My lord," Korin said, staring at the worn door in front of him. "I know you can't believe what I say, but please hear me with your heart. All I've ever wanted my entire life was freedom, salvation. When I came here I found something far better. I found love. I didn't mean to fall in love with your family but I have, knowing all the while I was unworthy of your trust. But know this. I would have stopped anything from hurting you. My life is yours, not Ista's. That's why I tell you what I know. That's why I want you to take my life when I return. I want to die at the hand of someone who knew me as the man I wanted to become. And please, my lord, tell Mari . . . "

Korin couldn't finish the sentence. He opened the door and walked out.

Chapter 21

Lazo and Jasta sat before the Red Eye. Jasta crushed Lazo's his hand in her own. Although her grip hurt, he didn't pull away. Jasta needed him more than she had ever needed him before.

Justin stood behind a glass window that filtered in light from the afternoon's sun. He appeared calm, but inside his thoughts were chaotic. He and Jasta were murmuring with quick, constant force, as if they could store up their contact while the ritual was taking place. Lazo refrained from joining their murmurings. The twins' relationship was special and Jasta and Justin needed every breath remaining to immerse in their incessant world of chatter. Lazo forced himself to remain content just hearing their familiar tonality even though he desperately wanted to speak to Justin one last time. He knew he would never see his brother again.

Jasta knew it too, and she was frantic.

Justin would only survive if they came back quickly, but Lazo didn't know how long it would take for the Red Eye to reveal its secret. No twin had survived an alienation past two days, but most died within a sun's click after the separation.

Because of Lazo, Jasta would survive, but Justin would succumb to the killing Mar within heartbeats, and if Jasta wasn't back soon thereafter Justin would be forever out of reach. He would die from the Mar even if Jasta was by his side. Once the connection was severed it was severed for eternity.

Lazo squeezed Jasta's hand. There was no hurrying the Red Eye's apparitions. The amount of time it took depended upon the aura the Eye brought forth from his timbering drone.

Lazo sat naked, as did Jasta. Nothing but flesh and the object in question could enter the ritual. Thankfully, that included their chains.

When he started to hum the rite Ista had taught him the Red Eye began to glow around the edges. A circumambient luminescence slowly emitted from the Eye, growing outward until it encompassed them in one large orb.

The murmurs of Jasta and Justin were abruptly silenced. Beside him, Jasta began to weep. Lazo tenderly drew her into his lap, opening his own mind as wide as he could. She clung to him both physically and mentally.

The orb of light surrounded them in a haze of muted red. The outside was no longer visible. Lazo continued to hum, frantically urging the Eye's memories to be quick. The haze soon began to move in a torrent of shapes, mixing vermilion waves with rosy hues. It was a dizzying effect, and this time Lazo didn't force his eyes away. Jasta appeared almost hypnotized by the frenzied swirls of color.

Black soon began to mix with the sanguine images, forming shapes of people and buildings. Shouts and screams reverberated around them as men fell to their knees in terror. Visages of women killing their children and specters of men raping and eviscerating their wives rose over and over as the shrieking escalated. Blood and bone and entrails littered the floor.

The scene wavered and shifted until the people were gone. A lone man stood peering over the Eye, brown hair in disarray, eyes frantic. He held another Eye in his hand. Lazo knew of the Silver Eye. It was kept at the Alcazar as a symbol of magic's strength. The man bellowed a curse and from out of nowhere a hideous, blackened creature with eyes a murky white tore past him, shrieking a soulless cry. Its jawline took up half its face, its eyes the other half. Two tattered ears protruded from its black skin and eight arms drug the ground as it ran, bouncing as if they were merely trinkets it donned. Its legs were squat and it ran hunched over. Two pinchers opened and closed at its chest.

The creature came to an abrupt stop and focused its large, murky white eyes on Jasta. Lazo scooted backward, pulling Jasta's quivering form with him, but came to a sudden halt when his back hit the outer edge of the muted orb. The jaw of the creature dropped open, revealing fangs as long as Lazo's hand. Inky saliva inched down the white protrusions. It sprung straight for Jasta.

Lazo quickly changed the inflection of his hum and the creature disappeared. The whirls stirred again. Jasta released a moan of terror as Lazo whispered assurances in his mind, acutely aware he could have saved the children the same way if he had seen the apparitions attacking them.

The memories continued. A building with large columns began to form. People stood in line outside the door, waiting for entrance. Occasionally someone came out and another ventured in. The etching on the edifice was in an ancient tongue but the meaning was clear. It read: *"Truth Above All."* Just as quickly as the scene came, it disappeared.

A bone-chilling scream descended on them. Lazo looked up and cowered as a black wyvern flew from the heavens, crashing to the ground in a torrent of dust. The two-legged dragon screamed in warning as a beautiful woman rose from beside the Red Eye, dark hair billowing from her body. She reached for the Eye but the wyvern was too quick. The beast toppled her, pawing her with its talons before grabbing the Eye and taking to the sky.

The grizzled pulp of flesh lying before them was unrecognizable, but the woman was still alive, thrashing on the ground in pain.

The swirls escalated again, taking the woman with them. The image of the building reappeared. A silver dragon rose from its steps. One of the dragon's talons was bloodied. A regal woman dressed in white bent over the wound and whispered a blessing. The talon was immediately mended and the silver creature groaned in appreciation. Another woman, wearing scant cover, walked forward and caressed the creature with a slender hand. From the way her lips moved Lazo realized she was whispering her thanks.

The regal woman stepped back, holding a gleaming ball above her head. She nodded and the dragon spewed fire over her form. Lazo could only stare in mute shock. It was as if the woman had welcomed the fire. His senses reeled, but before he could form a question in his mind the fire abated and the woman, without burns or blemish, lowered a glowing red ball in her hands.

It was the Red Eye.

Lazo drew in a sharp breath. The Red Eye had been brought to life by silver dragon's fire. If silver dragon's fire had formed it, it could awaken it. The silver fiend in the prophecy was the silver dragon, and because Ren hadn't destroyed it Ista had a chance to release the Red Eye's power through silver dragon's fire.

Lazo quit humming. The visions disappeared and they were back to reality. Jasta jumped to her feet and ran toward the corridor leading to the outside, where Justin barely clung to life.

Lazo felt profound relief that his brother was still alive, but when his eyes found the Red Eye he sunk once again into despair. Jasta would reveal all she knew to reach Justin, to try to save him from the clutches of the Mar.

"I'm sorry, Ren," Lazo whispered, knowing the silver dragon would soon become Ista's captive. He couldn't bear the thought, but there was no escaping it.

Lazo walked to the table in the far corner of the room and pulled his advisor's robe over his head, finding small comfort in the way the familiar black fabric cleaved to his body.

Run!

The intensity of Jasta's message caused Lazo to fall to the floor. No thought from the twins had ever hurt him before, but this time Jasta's words were fire.

She touched me Lazo. I wasn't in my other side! She knows! Leave us!

Lazo pushed himself up as he heard his brother's scream echo down the corridors. Lazo spun, unsure of what to do. He couldn't leave his siblings. Although a triplet wasn't joined as deeply as the others, they would die without him. He was the strongest.

Run, Lazo! Jasta's command left no room for doubt.

Triplets with the power could wipe out nations. He would help cause that destruction. He remembered Jasta's rare smile and Justin's frequent laugh. Neither would want that fate. If he separated from them he would cause their strength to be broken. If he severed he would stop the Quy from growing any more puissant inside them. If he didn't sever Ista would find him and he would be used as a weapon of force, against Ren, against righteousness, and against honor.

Lazo started toward the door. No guards were present. Jasta had rushed out, revealing all she had seen, stalling the onslaught of guards. He could escape if he kept his wits about him.

Lazo stumbled forward, the intensity of Jasta and Justin's screams making him lose all sense of reality. They were far worse than the blackened creature he had seen in the Eye's memories. They were anguish made voice, terror made noise. They were his own soul tearing from him.

I'll come for you. I'll get you out!

No, Lazo. She's asking me where you are. I can't hold out much longer. . . Separate, Lazo! Hurry!

Lazo separated, crashing to the ground as he felt the last of the twins leave him. Lazo had never separated so completely.

Lazo forced himself up and turned toward the library where the secret passage was hidden. The twins' screams followed him down the corridor.

Jasta and Justin, his life, his family, would die.

He might die.

Terror and panic built inside him. Soon the Mar would set in, and in the Mar there was only a vast expanse of nothingness. No twin had ever survived it; no triplet had ever tried.

- - -

"I can't thank you enough," Chris whispered.

Carter smiled. He didn't know how to feel. Part of him wanted to laugh in elation at Manda's escape. She had been gone since high moons and an alarm had yet to sound. Giving his life for Manda's was something he couldn't describe. It was a gift no one could take from him. But that gift also spurred fear. At times during the night he had almost been delirious from apprehension. At other times he had wanted to run.

During those times Carter turned to Chris and let the third emotion claim him – savagery.

He wanted to kill. What Alezza had done to the man before him was unforgivable.

Off and on in the night Alezza would call to Chris. Sometimes it was a sharp pain, other times a long passionate thrill. When the pain came, Chris curled up into a fetal position and tried to control the spasms. When it was passion Chris body reacted with lewd elation, but his face was a mask of loathing. Carter wondered how long the prince would live. Chris already had deep lines in his face from lack of sleep. Only Manda had kept Chris sane, and now Manda was gone.

Carter had stayed in the same position all night, ensuring to the best of his ability the passing guards would think he was Manda. He had draped what was left of her clothes around him and stayed in the corner shadows. He was a small man. He would fool the guards until dawn.

It was almost dawn.

He hadn't spoken of his fate during the night. He had only whispered stories of his childhood, wanting to try to take Chris' mind off his inner torture.

Chris' whispered thanks was all the prince had uttered since Manda's escape.

The first rays of light sliced through the tent's partition and touched his face. A flood of emotions surged inside Carter: exuberance, regret, fear, hopelessness and anger. When those emotions subsided only dignity remained.

He was Lieutenant Carter Donovan Meal of his crown prince's guard seeing an order to completion. He was Carter Meal, born of Sethavian Meal, and his father had taught him to put others before himself. He was Carter, a man who loved his prince, his land, and his honor. He was a man who was angry, for the man beside him, chained and tortured, and the girl he now gave his life to free.

He winked at Chris. Chris smiled.

Carter tightened the grip on his sword. He would take out as many solders as he could, not for himself, but for Ren, for Chris, and for Manda.

An alarm sounded. Muffled curses wafted to them. Carter exchanged a confused glance with Chris. No one had entered their tent.   The alarm hadn't sounded because of Manda's escape. Thundering footfalls ran past.

Chris' brow furrowed as he looked at the tent's partition. The sunlight made his green eyes glow with emerald fire. Disgusted oaths and foul curses became prominent as they listened to the story unfold.

Bort was dead. He had been found tied to the poles of his tent, choking on his own private parts. The meaning was clear: if he had lived he would have never raped another.

Chris chuckled. Despite the imminent danger, Carter joined him. Manda had taken her revenge.

But then the chaos stilled and the air filled with an oppressive silence.

Chris screamed.

Carter leapt to his feet and made an arc with the sword, ready for the soldiers sure to come.

And come they did, one right after another.

- - -

"We must hurry, she's losing strength," Aaron said, face twisting into a mask of fortitude as he spurred his horse into a gallop.

It was the Avenger talking, not Aaron. The Avenger had found the betrayed with his feelings, and she was dying.

The sparks of the Avenger's impetus were moving violently around his body. Fraul could see their glow even through Aaron's dark clothes. Fraul hadn't slept the past few nights. Aaron was a fascination to watch in the dark. He glowed like a seraph come to life under the stars.

Now Aaron glowed brighter than ever. The particles of power moved so quickly Aaron appeared to be a living sun, shaded by a black garment in the bright of day.

Fraul wondered how much of the day's heat came from Aaron, for it was exceptionally hot for the season, and although it was a warm day Fraul doubted the actual temperature near Aaron was the same as everywhere else.

Perspiration rained from Fraul as if he rode through the high heat of the Sesanie desert. Fraul had been in that wasteland lying between Ketes and Byn only once in his life, and what he felt now matched if not surpassed its intensity. It felt as if the heat were being sucked from him only to be replaced with more fervor. It was draining from the beginning and exhausting in the end.

The Avenger's cape slashed the air, sending more of the oppressing heat in Fraul's direction. The landscape was a blur as they rode into the unknown. Fraul felt the excitement building inside him. This was the Avenger's purpose. This was his duty. This was what Aaron had been born to do.

But would this time be different? This time would the Avenger live?

Fraul's jaw set with grim determination. Aaron would live this time. Somehow Fraul would help Aaron remain in this world.

A lone rider crested a distant hill. Fraul turned to Aaron. From the anguish written in the contours of Aaron's face Fraul knew the rider was the betrayed. Aaron spurred his horse faster, his glow intensifying to an even greater illumination.

Aaron's black stallion closed the distance within heartbeats. The rider had collapsed on the back of her mount. Aaron jumped off his steed and stopped the approaching horse. It reared. The girl's head tilted as if coming out of a daze, but she was never in danger of being thrown. She was one with the horse.

Fraul cringed as Aaron pulled the beaten girl to the ground. She was thin, her jaw broken, and if the bruises on her neck and face were any indication of the condition of the rest of her, Fraul knew she was near death.

Her reddish-blonde hair was wet with sweat and clung to her skin, but it wasn't from the heat. She was burning with fever. When she looked up into Aaron's face she began to shriek. The terror in her dull green eyes told more of her story than Fraul wanted to hear. She had been beaten and raped. From the look of her, Fraul knew it had been more than once.

Her hand slid to her waist, reaching for the dagger in her belt.

The Avenger stopped her hand. His black gloves shimmered with the avenging power. The Avenger's eyes glowed a metallic gold as he looked down at the broken figure in his arms. The Avenger brushed the girl's hair from her face. "My child, what's happened to you?"

Aaron's voice was filled with an incomprehensible love. Fraul took a step back, feeling inadequate next to someone who felt so much. The stories the Avenger had told him came back in a maddening rush.

One question stood out in Fraul's mind. Was love worth the pain?

The betrayed's torpid eyes widened and she tentatively reached up to touch Aaron's cheek. All people had heard the story of the Avenger. Everyone knew his look and his compassion. The betrayed's eyes filled with tears, endowing them with a vitality previously absent. The edges of her mouth rose into a semblance of a smile. It came close to breaking Fraul's heart.

The girl began to relay the story. Ren was mentioned. Fear for both Ren and her brother was evident in her broken voice. Fraul slowly became aware of who lay before him: Manda of Crape.

As Manda's tale started to unfold, Aaron became almost blinding to look upon. Sparks circulated outside his clothing as if they were too multifarious to remain confined.

When Manda finished speaking, Aaron hugged her close.

"I want to watch you do it," she said. "Let me come with you. I want to see him die."

Aaron pulled back. "No, my child, you must wait for me here. I'll be back, and then we'll find your brother."

Aaron lifted Manda and put her in Fraul's arms before jumping on his black stallion and turning in the direction of Stardom. Although Valor would be dethroned, Fraul felt no joy. The girl in his arms drained all elation from him. Fraul gritted his teeth. If Manda's fever didn't break soon she would die of malnutrition. He would kill Alezza for this.

Fraul glanced up and watched in amazement as the Avenger's stallion left the ground and galloped paces above the terrain, almost too fast for the eye to see.

- - -

The horse took to the air upon the Avenger's command, galloping on air particles that had formed a bridge over the castle wall. As he landed on solid ground the guards sounded the alarm, but when they recognized him they fell back, stumbling as they went. He was used to the sight. He had lived it for centuries.

His name was whispered among the onlookers like a plague. Some faces drained of color. Other mouths gapped open in awe.

The Avenger spurred his mount forward, barely taking notice of the people. He had witnessed the scene a thousand times before. Those backing away were those who had betrayed friends and loved ones. The others, the ones transfixed by the sight of him, were pure. Not many were pure.

Now that the final avenging power surged inside him he saw all the betrayals of those he passed. A guard to his left hung his head in shame for claiming it was his arrow that hit the mark, not his friend's, which advanced him into the king's guard. Another had betrayed a lover, insisting it was she who seduced him into fornication. Another had denounced a prominent man in an accusation of molestation. Yet they weren't the ones Aaron came for. He only avenged betrayals that could cause death.

His horse's hooves were the only sound ringing across the courtyard, but no one moved to stop him. To try and destroy him was sure death. One spark of his pain was too much for any mortal to bear.

He concentrated on the road ahead, feeling his anger building until it reached a zenith. Then love welled in his soul for the girl he had held in his arms, caressing the anger. When the love reached the point of hurting, the pain built even higher. And so it continued: the anger, the love, and the pain. He was like a rod electrified with the three internal elements. Just as the anger reached a high, the love overwhelmed. Just as the love culminated the hate, the pain surged into a profusion of anguish.

All the while Manda was at the foremost of his mind. Something was special about her, something almost sacred. She had been in unspeakable pain, but not for herself. Her only concern was her brother. It was the mark of true beauty: caring for another so much you were oblivious to your own pain.

Valor had betrayed both his children.

Anger rose inside Aaron like a torrent of darkness. It almost blinded him.

Stardom's main entrance was open. The guards beside it had run for their lives.

He dismounted, letting some of his power remain around his horse. The black stallion sizzled with sparks, protecting it from any who may try to stop him, though he knew none would.

Aaron drew his golden sword in the silence that had descended upon the castle and lifted his head to the balcony where he felt the betrayer's heartbeat. A breeze swooped down from the north, causing his cape to billow behind him like wings of death.

His eyes locked on Ista's deformed face. Her gaze displayed no concern. She knew he didn't seek her. She hadn't betrayed anyone for she had never loved anyone, and she had never insinuated otherwise. But she was black with deaths, and her soul was condemned hundreds of times over.

Then he saw the betrayer backing into the shadows. The Avenger shifted his gaze, watching the betrayer watch him. The betrayer's heartbeat quickened in the Avenger's ears. The king of Crape, ruler of Newlan, turned this way and that, seeking escape.

The betrayal sword began to sing a song of blood. It hungered for it. The Avenger turned and strode into the now deserted hallway.

The betrayer's heartbeat continued to sound in his temples. Valor's murmurs echoed like screams in the Avenger's mind. The Avenger thought of Manda again, her lost innocence, her broken body, and her tears. He wanted to make this betrayer suffer a long time.

He continued onward, drawn by the betrayer's blood. The guards he passed fell back. Some cowered like wounded animals. The Avenger walked on, his footfalls tolling like knells of death.

As he entered a long-domed hallway, Aaron recalled the stories Fraul had told him about Ren. He could judge enough about people through others to realize this Ren was someone he would be proud to know. In a strange way he felt like he was avenging Ren as well. It was the betrayer who had taken over the crown prince's kingdom.

As he walked up the black marble stairs leading to the upper reaches of the castle his vision narrowed into one path, directly to the betrayer. A doorway to the left was where the pathway stopped. The Avenger marched on. With each step his blood pumped with a greater drive toward vengeance. With each step he breathed in more of the betrayed's pain.

The Avenger reached the landing and turned toward the door. He clutched the golden sword tighter. Its hunger for the betrayer's blood escalated in intensity. When he opened the door the betrayer looked at him with the same green eyes as the betrayed. The ruler of Newlan fell against the stone balcony, begging for forgiveness, weeping in fear.

The golden betrayal sword now sung with a deafening pitch, shrieking its hunger for the blood of the betrayer. The Avenger licked his lips in anticipation, yearning to feel the sword's tip find the betrayer's heart and drink the blood of a man who didn't deserve to live.

The Avenger raised his sword and put its tip over the betrayer's heart, pinning him to the balcony. The betrayer murmured to the Maker, but the Maker had already turned his back on the scene. The Avenger was the Maker's righteous judgment. When Aaron was born the betrayer had lost all chance of salvation. Slowly, the Avenger sunk the golden tip of the sword into the betrayer. The power surged through the Avenger like a deluge, flowing through the sword and inside the betrayer. The Avenger began reliving all the pain of those before Manda. Their pain rose inside him, seeping into his sword and out the tip into the betrayer's heart.

The betrayer screamed in agony as the sword's magic began to work. Both the physical and the mental pain churned inside him, condemning the betrayer to the fates of every betrayal Aaron had ever avenged. Valor was burned, drowned, raped, beaten, starved, cut, and skinned.

Aaron felt it all as well, surging inside him, sending all the pain with white-hot fury into the betrayer. But the Avenger was used to the pain, the betrayer was not. As Aaron relived every sin of every betrayer and felt the pain of each betrayed Valor died as the horrors of each betrayal happened to him, was condemned as all of the betrayers' sins weighed on his shoulders, and through it all Valor felt no remorse.

Then Manda's own pain surfaced: the cry for her father as she realized the horror of his betrayal, her rape, her beating and her suffering for Chris. All came in a torrent of force. Valor released an agonizing cry as Manda's pain tore through him. The Avenger stood in judgment, watching as his own hand took the life of another. Although he hungered for the betrayer's blood there was no joy in the act, only profound sorrow that he had to stand in judgment at all.

Valor's punishment was unmatched by any other before, just as the last Aaron's sword had pierced was unmatched by his precursor. With each additional betrayal there was that much more pain. The Avenger watched Valor's body slowly begin to incinerate as the love and pain of the betrayed damned his soul.

After Valor collapsed in death, the Avenger turned to look at the woman crouched in the corner. Ista's eyes were wide, but they held no fear. She only cowered to avoid the sparks from his body. He could see her trying to determine how she could capture him, use his power, as she had done, and would continue to do to many others.

Aaron stepped closer, feeling as if he were wading through diablerie as he did. Despite the repellent sensation he leaned down until he was only a hair's breath from Ista's face.

"You want me, Ista?"

She remained quiet, but her eyes flashed with hunger. Aaron breathed in his power, letting a few sparks fall dormant to the ground. "Make this sword turn gold again, Ista. You can have all of me then. I promise you that."

Ista's eyes flickered to where the betrayal sword had turned its true silver, satisfied with the betrayer's blood.

Aaron waited until Ista's eyes refocused. When he spoke his voice was low, grating. "May choice evade you, may chance turn from you, and may the Maker's fates condemn your soul." It was an ancient curse, one he had never spoken before.

Turning, he strode back the way he had come. No one stopped him. No one dared. The Avenger walked with righteous judgment, and all knew they were deserving of his sword.

- - -

When Lazo left the tunnels the Mar had yet to claim him, but he could feel it swelling inside him like an underground stream. Soon the stream would overflow and he would be drowned.

Lazo was tired. His back ached from the weight of his emotional burden and the blazing sun left him parched. His bare feet already had blisters from the rugged terrain and it was just after midday.

Ever since he was born he had been in schools and palaces, obtaining knowledge and training to become an advisor. The extent of his travels had been from one school to another, and during those travels he was either reading in a private room on board a ship or being read to as he rode across country.

What was he to do about food? He knew all about animals and vegetation, weapons and strategies, but nothing about making a trap or carving an arrow. If he lived he would entreat the Advisor's Convent to teach its pupils how to survive without castles and servants.

Lazo was so engrossed in his thoughts he didn't hear the pounding hooves until it was too late. He began to run with all his might but his lungs were on fire and his feet stung with each step. Then the horse was beside him. Lazo fell to his knees, knowing escape was futile.

"Running from Stardom?"

Lazo looked up into golden eyes. Small pinpricks of power surged over a muscular body.

Lazo nodded, unable to find his voice.

"Ally of Ren." It wasn't an inquiry. It was a declaration.

Lazo nodded again.

The Avenger studied him, dark hair billowing in the wind. The Avenger looked into Lazo's soul, stripping him of all sin, dissecting each action and each step his life had taken. The Avenger extended his gloved hand. Lazo took it and swung up behind him. Profound relief flooded through him as the horse began to move faster than the wind. He turned to watch Zier become only a small dot on the horizon.

It was the end of his life as he knew it. He would never hear Jasta or Justin's quiet murmurings. He would never share with them a silent inner smile. He would never again be part of something as wonderful as their siblinghood.

Lazo collapsed on the back of the horse. The grief he hadn't allowed himself to feel stole over him like a thief. The stream rose higher. A silent trickle of despair leaked free.

He fought to damn the water. He couldn't give into the Mar. It was too soon. The water stilled. The trickle abated.

When gentle hands lifted him from the horse, Lazo opened his eyes. The Avenger still glowed with a soft light but it had lessened. A gray-haired man looked up from where he knelt by a fire. Something tugged at Lazo's memory. It was Fraul, Ramie's captain. Lazo noted the concern in Fraul's gray eyes as he looked down at the girl bundled in blankets beside the fire.

"I've broken her fever, Aaron, but she won't stop shivering."

Lazo was shocked. How had Fraul met the Avenger? It seemed they were close. Lazo questioned his former conclusion. Maybe he had been mistaken?

No. The man glowed with power. The man's horse rode the wind. There could be no mistaking the man's identity.

The Avenger walked over and knelt beside the girl, whispering words in a foreign tongue. Lazo stepped forward, feeling out of place but somehow drawn to the bundled form by the fire. His eyes fell on the mound of red hair.

"Manda!"

Aaron turned. "You know her?"

Lazo nodded, leaning down to take Manda's hand. Her face was severely battered, her jaw broken. Fates! What had happened to his Manda!

When Manda had first visited Stardom they had grown close. She followed him everywhere, fascinated by his contrasting eyes. He tried to coax her to play with other children, but she always replied he was the only friend she needed. It had touched him deeply.

Every year thereafter when she visited Stardom they spent countless days together. Manda told him it was her mission in life to see him smile. And smile he did. Manda's cheerfulness and winsome charm could bring a smile to any man's face. The older she became, the closer they grew. They would sit for days and discuss books and history. She was voracious for knowledge, soaking up every morsel of information he could give. He loved to teach and she loved to learn.

Manda was the only person besides Ren who saw him not as a triplet, but as an individual. He was twenty years her senior but he carried a love for her that was a mixture of romantic and fatherly love.

Now, he almost didn't recognize her. A slow understanding crept over him. He turned to the Avenger.

"Valor?"

Aaron nodded. "She needs you, my friend. She needs you to talk to her, bring her out of this. She isn't sick in a physical sense; she's sick at heart. She's afraid to awake, afraid the world will bring her more pain. I can't help her for I am pain."

Lazo nodded, sensing the truth in Aaron's statement, and moved closer to Manda. Fraul and Aaron walked away, talking softly. Lazo lifted Manda's head and placed it gently in his lap. He took the towel Fraul had been using to cool her brow and dotted her forehead. Inside, the stream calmed, for his fears lay forgotten. Lazo began speaking to Manda, telling her how much her laughter meant to him.

Chapter 22

They had entered a region of Crape where rolling hills ceded to dense forests. The abundant hickory and spruce allowed brush and vines to grow freely, sometimes impeding passage and daunting swiftness. Ren much preferred the large redwoods of Zier that kept undergrowth to a minimum, but he had to admit the way the sunlight filtered through the branches of the hickories and skipped over the flowering vines gave this particular region of Crape a special enchantment.

The path they rode was well traveled and the new growth did little to hinder their passage. The sun's rays were stifling without the shade of overhanging branches but the light was welcome. The past few days had been filled with erratic downpours, putting everyone except Neki in a gloomy mood.

With each day they moved closer to the ruins of the Alcazar, but Ren was growing restless. As if he could see the stars in the bright of the day, Ren squinted up at the sky. The previous night the foggy haze Grauss had given the cognomen of "The One" had moved closer, but Ren didn't know if he was approaching the One or if the One was approaching him.

Ren clicked the reins, urging his mount faster. The mare broke into full gallop. Ren gave her free rein, welcoming the hurried pace. With each day that dawned he felt more urgency to find the One.

His mount seemed eager for the ride. She moved so quickly Ren thought he heard the wind scream his name. The trees moved inward with daunting swiftness. Occasional rocks and rubble blocked the trail, but Michel had the mare well trained. She took the obstructions with little difficulty.

The mare skidded to a sudden halt and reared. Ren was unprepared. He landed on his back with a heavy thud. The horse bellowed a warning and cantered back toward the others. Ren rolled to his side and gasped for air. When it came, he swallowed greedily. Nothing was broken, but his back would be sore for days.

He stood in a slight clearing where the path broke in two directions. He saw no sign of danger.

From the distance he heard Markum scream his name. When he turned to answer his call the words he was about to voice froze on his lips. The sphinx stood before him, heralding an invitation to the Oracle. Ren blinked in awe as the majestic stone figure came to life.

Its beauty was something he could never put to words. A woman's face gazed at him from the white stone, but instead of appearing hard her face was delicate and sensuously curved. Her hair tumbled halfway down her lioness body, accentuating taunt muscles and subtle curves.

As if sensing his thoughts, the sphinx smiled. "Answer my riddle and you shall pass. Miss it and you shall die." Although her voice rumbled with a rich, amiable tone, there was a warning as sharp as a sword's edge slicing through its warmth.

This was his last chance to retreat. If he refused the riddle he could walk away, but he would never again have the chance to enter the Oracle. Ren swallowed back his fear and nodded.

"No!"

Markum's scream echoed in the clearing, but Ren barely heard. He remained transfixed by the stone eyes before him. Markum's hands tugged at his tunic, but Ren didn't turn. Galvin's voice drifted to him from some distant place: "It's too late, Markum." The hands left him.

The sphinx straightened and focused her arresting gaze not on him but through him, as if delivering a herald of death. "I'm not something you acquire," she said, "but you must work for me each day: intangible and invisible, through fields of fire I am made. I am stronger than your fear and more powerful than your blade. I can damn you or I can raise you, be your curse or be your stave."

Ren stood as still as the sphinx: something that could damn him or raise him, be his curse or his support.

"Time is running out," the sphinx purred. Ren thought he may have detected a hint of compassion in her tone, but when he looked into her eyes he saw no resonance of that emotion.

The sphinx had said 'fields of fire.' That could only mean hardship. What was something he would he have to work for constantly, something intangible and invisible, something that could see him through hard times?

Ren smiled. "Faith."

Not even the leaves stirred in the breeze. It seemed the very air had gathering to wrap him in the folds of silent suffocation. He heaved for breath. The air was heavy, solid; but just as quickly as the air coagulated it dissipated into a refreshing breeze. The sphinx smiled and stepped aside.

"Clever," he whispered as he passed her. The sphinx purred in reply.

As he brushed by her he thought he heard her murmur, "Go with the Maker."

Ren slowed his step. The sphinx moved back into place as some of his men tried to follow. Ren looked around him in silent awe. He walked where few had ever been and where even fewer returned. He was about to meet the guardians of the Oracle.

Turning back to the sphinx Ren opened his mouth to ask where the ancient temple resided, but his voice waned when he saw he stood alone. The sphinx, the clearing, and his friends had disappeared. In their place was a long, serpentine trail, reaching farther than the eye could see.

Ren followed the trail in front of him, expecting the temple to appear around the next bend, but the dense forest seemed to have no end. He had always thought the Oracle would be visible right past the sphinx. He was wrong. Ren trudged on, watching the sun dance across the sky until he knew he had traveled for at least half a day. A twinge of frustration surfaced but he quickly brushed it aside. He couldn't question the Oracle's idiosyncrasies.

His mind wandered until his own footfalls lulled him into placid contemplation of the surrounding woods. After a time he began to wonder if he was supposed to turn in a different direction or walk through the dense brush to either side in search of the ancient temple. Almost as soon as the thought was out he caught sight of vegetation he hadn't seen before. Trees, gnarled in a silvery gray, dotted the woods, and when he peered farther into the distance they became more prevalent.

With quick calculation he concluded more than ten men would have to encircle the trees' trunks from fingertip to fingertip to encase their monstrous diameter. Fur-lined vines drooped from their branches, enwrapping the trunks in an affable embrace. Ferns with triangular leaves and exquisite white blossoms grew around the their bases, emitting a balmy fragrance.

There was no dampness in the air, but the entire forest appeared vivid and verdant. Ren stopped and drew in a breath, sensing the crystalline air could sustain his body better than any food. It was as if he were feasting on tender meat, tasting a delectable pastry, and drinking wine all with each breath.

The air was life itself.

The sun filtered through the branches, enchanting the trees with sentiment. A few lone fur-covered vines swung down the path, leading him on.

The trees became denser with each step and soon he walked through vines that barely cleared his head. A few moved toward him, touching his arm or shoulder in welcome. He brushed past them, careful not to break their soft leaves. Just when he thought he must have taken a wrong turn, he walked into a clearing.

The building rose before him, bathed in the glory of the sun. Its white stone had silver striations twisting through its surface. Ren knew the silver wasn't part of the stone, but magic, caressing the stone in soft, shivering waves.

The temple was immense. Stairs rolled out from the piazza like a long, luxurious carpet. The piazza, lined with six colossal columns, supported a huge edifice that crowned the pillars with regal simplicity. The columns were plain, as was the building, but the Oracle needed no decoration. It sparkled with austere beauty.

Ren squinted up at the precipitous height, shielding his eyes from the sun. He was about to meet the Maker's messengers. As he approached the shadow of the sanctum he noticed it wasn't completely unadorned as he first thought. On the smooth crown above the columns three words were written in ancient script. There could be no doubt what those words said: *Truth Above All*. Ren glanced down at his sword. The same words were written repeatedly on the blunt of the silver.

There was a finality to each word, a toll of warning. The elation he had felt leaving the sphinx was gone. All that remained was his naked soul standing before the Oracle.

As he mounted the steps, his footfalls didn't make a sound. In fact there was no sound, not even his soft breath. All was still. It was as if the Oracle's magic soaked up all evidence of blasphemy, even those things intending no harm.

When he reached the piazza he felt even more exposed. Ren stood below the culmination, dwarfed by the immensity of the columns. They were far larger than the trees he had passed and their shadows left a foreboding of the most sinister degree.

But the guardians were good. They were sent by the Maker to aid those who sought their guidance. He had to keep that at the foremost of his mind.

His sword quivered when he reached the entrance. The inscriptions on the hilt – the arrows, the astragali, and the spiral – were all glowing with a brilliant light, making them take on a three-dimensional effect. The sword bore the emblems of Choice, Chance, and Fate and most assuredly knew it neared its namesakes.

Ren walked to the massive door and traced its grain. It was made from the silver wood of the surrounding trees. Three words were written at eye level: *Truth Above All.*

This time the phrase caused a slight chill to pass through him. When he walked through the door he may very well find a truth he didn't care to know. The inscription was the Oracle's way of warning those who entered to take its teachings to heart. But as Ren continued to study the words a peace settled over him, a surety that once he left the Oracle the truth he learned would guide him down the correct path.

Ren pushed open the door and walked inside.

The door closed with a soft click, but the sound resonated throughout the nave with finality. Ren's eyes fell on the three thrones at the front of the chamber.

They were empty, but Ren put one fist to his forehead and then to his heart. "Truth above all," he whispered. The guardians deserved every respect he could give them. He whispered a silent thanks to the Maker for granting him entrance.

The stone thrones remained empty. He wondered how long he would have to wait before the guardians appeared.

His sword pulsed with life. He placed a hand on its hilt and looked around the chamber. The nave extended to a vast height. Its hollow pinnacle allowed the gentle rays of the sun to flicker in, carpeting the white floor with glorious light. To each side six columns marched down the nave's length, framing the Oracle's treasures.

Dark slabs of stone were propped between every other column to the right. They stood in stark contrast to the white stone of the Oracle. To the left, paintings were hung. Ren could make out a few details from where he stood. Most contained images of people, perhaps the people who built the Oracle.

As he stepped forward his boots made a hollow, heavy sound. The stone beneath him was engraved. It read:

You are entering the Oracle
Make sure our words are understood
Everything happens for a reason
And in that reason there is divine good.

Ren thought about all the times he had prayed to the Maker, asking for guidance. He had always thought the Maker hadn't heard him, that he wasn't good enough in the Maker's eyes to be heeded. Perhaps that wasn't it at all. Perhaps the Maker answered in a way he didn't expect. Perhaps the Maker could use suffering and darkness to produce goodness and light.

Ren whispered for understanding as he stepped around the engraving and walked to the first stone slab. If the guardians hadn't appeared they may want him to study the Oracle's treasures. Both may inform him of how he needed to act when speaking with Choice, Chance, and Fate.

The first dark gray stone contained a diagram of the three external elements in a depiction he had never seen before. It was in the form of an equilateral triangle. The three end points depicted the external elements.

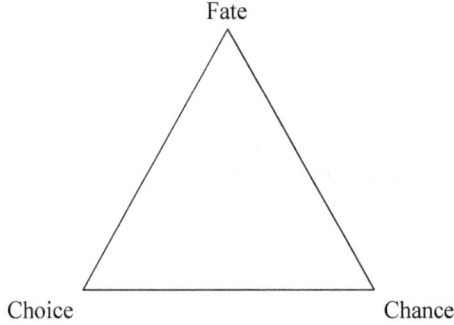

Ren read the inscription below the diagram:

Why things occur has been one of the most talked about subjects since the beginning of time. Some believe it's a mix of one, others of two, others of three, and still others believe only they influence their lives:

Some believe it's fate, a destiny you find,
A road carved for you, carved before your time,
Even if that road will cause your soul to cry.
Others believe it's chance, just a circumstance in life,
That bends events in ways and determines what you find,
Even if that chance leaves emptiness inside.
Some believe it's choice, an intelligence per say,
You make a choice at the time and in that bed you lie,
Even if that choice will haunt you to the grave.
Others believe in naught, there's nothing in their eyes,
Their souls are full of poison, their bodies full of lies
Still they continue, as if their fate was theirs to find.

What do you believe in, Dragon Tamer? Why have you been chosen? How will you conquer the darkness threatening to destroy us all?

Ren blinked in surprise at his cognomen. The Oracle must adjust its lessons for each person who entered. The Maker had sent the Oracle as a guide to man. The Oracle was teaching him what he needed to know to walk the path the Maker wanted him to walk.

Ren read the words again, ingraining them in his mind. What did he believe in? He believed all three influenced life but he also believed the Maker guided those elements and could bend them to His plan. Ren glanced back at the inscription on the floor – everything had a divine purpose.

Turning, Ren walked to the first painting in the opposite hall. There, painted with exquisite detail, were two full-length images of him, just like Markum's dream.

The first image was as he was, but with a haunted, terrified gaze. Black blood oozed from a wound near his heart. The second image was covered with snakes and the left half of his face wasn't his own. Ren studied it as a sense of foreboding crept up his spine. He knew the other face from paintings he had seen of the Wizard War. It was Barracus' face.

His eyes slid up the length of the two images. The one with Barracus' image stared at him with an animosity he couldn't describe. Just looking at his left eye repulsed him. It was vile, wicked and so black it shone with a greenish hue. Although Barracus' hair was slightly longer, his jawline stronger, his nose wider, the image formed to his own so well the difference was almost undetectable.

His face wasn't all that had changed. His entire left side wasn't his own. The change was subtle but unmistakable. Barracus' neck was wider, his shoulder less defined, his waist more barrel-shaped, and his thighs thicker. Ren read the inscription below the painting.

Take heed our warning. Both you will be. One you will become. Which one depends on thee.

Both you will be. Ren gritted his teeth as he looked back at the paintings. The deformed image made his skin crawl, but the haunted look in the other's eyes terrified him. They were without hope, hollow, and empty.

A surge of anger stole over him as his mind fought to deny the Oracle's claim. He should have never come. He knew all who returned from the Oracle changed in ways no one could understand. People came for answers but what they learned . . .

Was the truth.

The thought hit him with full force: *Truth Above All.*

Ren turned from the paintings. If this was the truth he didn't want to know it. He felt Barracus' eyes on him. His anger melted. This was the truth. He had come for answers and now he knew. He would have to choose between those two figures. He would have to be one of those men. The Oracle wasn't trying to torment him but to prepare him. He needed to remember: sometimes the truth could be painful.

He looked across the nave to the second stone slab before glancing at the thrones again. They remained empty. Choice, Chance, and Fate wouldn't come until he saw every inscription and image they had displayed for him.

Ren walked to the second stone slab. The diagram it portrayed was in the same pattern as the first, except instead of labeling the external elements of choice, chance, and fate it labeled the internal elements of love, pain, and hate.

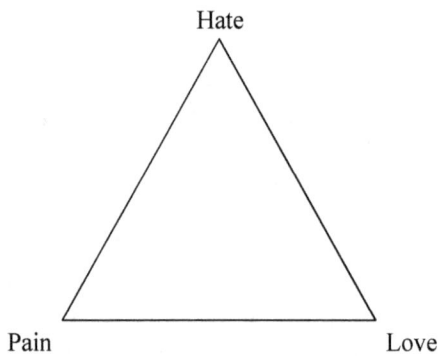

His eyes flickered down to the inscription below the diagram.

The internal elements assist the external elements, driving them backwards or forwards. All internal elements are found in the equilateral figure shown above. Without love, hate is ubiquitous; without hate, love is undefined; but without pain, love is unreal:

Hate is strong, but not as strong as love.

Love is stronger, but not as strong as the pain love brings.
Beware if hate is in your soul without love,
For then the darkness takes control.
But know where there is love there is also pain.

Dragon Mate, are you strong enough to stand the pain? Are you strong enough to choose love over hate? For hate is easier felt than love.

Was he strong enough to stand the pain? Dragon Mate preceded the question. Could the Oracle be referring to Aidan? Aidan had related their connection to marriage. Ren felt hot emotions well within him. It could only refer to Aidan. The Oracle associated her with pain. A sick feeling rose in his stomach.

Ren glanced to the thrones resting atop the small rise at the front of the nave. They remained empty.

He walked to the second painting. It depicted three scenes of his life. One was labeled "choice;" the other "chance;" the third "fate."

The first scene depicted him and Aidan in the dungeon. She was touching his cheek and he had his eyes closed, welcoming the feelings she bought. That was choice.

In the second scene he stared into the eyes of the silver dragon when it had broken free of its chains. That was chance.

In the third scene, the Quy knighted him with the sword that now glowed hot in its scabbard. That was fate.

At the bottom of the pictures it read:

The Chosen's choice will drive his pain;
The Chosen's chance will end in love;
The Chosen's fate will spur his hate.
But which one makes his soul?
And which will he choose?
To guide him in his role?

Ren read it again. Aidan had already brought him pain. He had just found her only to lose her again. Now it was his mission to release her from the dragon. But did the Oracle refer to more pain or the pain he already felt without her?

The silver dragon would drive his love. Was the Oracle saying he would be able to release Aidan or that he wouldn't? Ren looked back at the first scene. Aidan would drive his pain, but the silver dragon would end in love.

The Quy would spur his hate. The Quy had knighted him as her defender, charging him with this quest. Could it mean the quest would ignite his hate? His eyes flickered to the painting of him joined with Barracus. If the quest would spur his hate he had a better chance of becoming corrupt than remaining whole.

He looked at Aidan once again. The feelings she invoked rose to the surface, haunting him. She had changed him forever. He feared living without her, yet he also feared living with her. If she ever discovered his true feelings how would she respond? He traced the lines of her face, murmuring what was in his heart before ambling toward the final gray slab. In his peripheral vision the thrones loomed above him with terminal resolution. He felt the air stir. The guardians would soon appear.

He forced his mind to focus on the stone slab. Its diagram showed the two triangles merging into one. Hate joined with fate. Choice merged with pain. Chance absorbed love.

The inscription read:

Choice, Chance, and Fate
Merged with pain, love, and hate
Can embrace the light,
Can embrace the dark,
Heed us well Our Chosen.

The sword grew hot in Ren's hand. He looked down at the weapon, trying to remember when he had unsheathed it. The blade flickered with power. Sparks of silver light bounded down its length with unimaginable speed. The sword wasn't just a weapon. It was also filled with the Quy. He felt the power filter through him as he tightened his grip on the hilt.

The Quy had told him many would try to use her for evil, transforming her world into darkness. He recalled his horror at her words and how much he wanted to make her world light. He read the inscription again, taking the warning to heart. He finally understood what the Quy and the Oracle wanted him to know.

All were vulnerable, no matter how good or true the heart, to the darkness. The Oracle's talk of pain wasn't a warning. It was a statement of truth. Pain came to those who sought the light, who fought for righteousness. The very definition of love held pain. If you chose love you would hurt when a child cried, a friend bled, or a loved one breathed their last. If you lived only with hate, pain didn't exist.

If hate was the dominant emotion, the pain of love would be consumed, swallowed alive, and never sensed.

If he chose to fight for truth, pain would be felt daily. Some pains he wouldn't understand, others he would fight to deny, but they would be real. If he ever gave in to the pain, doubting the light, he would turn to the darkness.

They were warning him not to succumb to the darkness, to the hate that would drive the pain away.

Slowly the quest before him began to take shape. He had to overcome the pain in his own soul to triumph over the darkness or he would give in to the darkness. If he refused, the Quy would be drowned, the world would be drowned, and everything would be consumed by hate.

Although he felt dwarfed by the monstrosity of the task, he also felt empowered. He gripped the sword tighter, letting the tingle of the Quy bounce off his fingertips.

The air stirred again. The thrones remained empty, but Ren sensed the guardians' presence as he strode to the last painting.

When his eyes fell on the scene, he immediately took a step back. It was a picture of the silver dragon, wallowing in its own blood, but that wasn't what had caused his retreat. He stood on the dragon's back, holding a bloodied sword. There was no mistaking the weapon the Quy had given him. It glowed with power. The twin dragons on its hilt laughed in mockery at their fallen colleague.

Then he saw something that tore a silent scream from his lips. The dragon's eyes were violet.

Ren fell to his knees as the sword dropped from his hand and hit the stone floor. The ringing of the metal echoed in the temple with cold resolve. His chest welled with both repugnance and anguish. Slowly, he raised his head, hoping against hope the expression on his face portrayed his horror. When he saw the truth a groan escaped his lips. His expression was wicked, cruel. Then he noticed the chains. The dragon hadn't even had a chance to fight. It was chained to the ground, defenseless. He had slaughtered the creature with intense hate.

May the Maker have mercy. He would never do such a thing.

And if he can't destroy the silver form the darkness will begin.

"No," he whispered. The pain poured out and encased him in a torrent of waves. It wouldn't happen. This was not the truth. He would never! Rage surged through him.

He reached for the sword, justified in his anger, and lunged forward, shredding the canvass with the tip of his blade. He would never do such a thing!

Ren spun to face the thrones.

The guardians stared blankly ahead, formed from the white stone of the Oracle, as cold and dead as the thrones beneath them.

But Ren felt their power and knew they were as alive as he. He glared at austere and unwelcoming faces. Their lifeless eyes were filled with righteous judgment; their shoulders were stiff with regality; their entire presence warned of caution.

Ren let caution fly. "I will never do it!" he shouted. "You lecture on keeping my emotions between love and pain and yet you portray me slaying a dear friend with hatred on my face!"

He glanced back at the torn picture. It looked even more gruesome hanging in ruin. He quickly turned away. Choice, Chance, and Fate stared at him with expressionless eyes.

He marched up the steps. He wanted answers and he wanted them immediately. As soon as he had taken the top step a glow came from the stone floor, lighting words in aureole warning.

As he read them, his anger became even more defined.

The Rules of the Oracle:
You must wake each of us or you will die.
You must not talk or question or you will die.
You must never tell another what we say or you will die.
You must believe us or you will fail.
You must heed us or you will fail.
Have strength, have restraint, take heart.

Have strength? Take heart? How could he? The Rules talked about death, told him to be silent, and demanded he do as they say!

They were telling him he had to choose between a haunted man and a vile man. They indicated pain would be the dominant element in his future. They told him to slay the silver dragon.

How dare they!

And now they had ordered him not to ask any questions – the one thing he had come to do! Have restraint, they said. Restraint? He didn't like their demands. In fact, he abhorred them.

He turned and marched down the steps. As soon as he reached the first column, a gust of air hurled him back. He spun to face the thrones. Now they were threatening him!

"How can I take heart? How can I believe you when you tell me I will slay the silver dragon, damning all hope of saving Aidan?" He brandished his sword at the shredded painting. The guardians remained motionless, impassive. Ren's eyes fell on the third stone slab.

Choice, Chance and Fate
Merged with pain, love and hate
Can embrace the light,
Can embrace the dark,
Heed us well Our Chosen.

Ren's world crashed down. He sank to the floor, ashamed. It had already begun. He was already rejecting the pain. He wanted to flee from it, tear it from his soul, but if he did the darkness would claim him.

Truth above all.

His eyes flickered to the painting. There were some things he would never understand, some things he would never fully accept, but he couldn't give into hate. The guardians didn't want to cause him pain. They were the gift of the Maker to the world of the living. Pain was the last thing they wanted to bestow.

He had no answers. He could only believe that somehow, some way, he would overcome the end the Oracle portrayed. Prophecy clouded the truth. The Oracle's paintings could cloud the truth also. He knew they were true, but they may not be true in a literal sense. It may not be as bad as it appeared.

Ren stood, shoving his feelings of animosity down to drown in his pain. When his hate had dissipated he raised his eyes once again to the figures on the thrones. They still stared blankly ahead, but this time he saw something he hadn't seen before: righteousness, integrity, honesty and, yes – love.

He ascended the steps and read the glowing slab once more. Instead of feeling anger, he only felt a profound disappointment that he would be unable to ask his questions.

He thought of the third painting. Surly the guardians wouldn't ask him to do such a thing. He was being senseless. Choice, Chance, and Fate were righteous. Ren drew a deep breath, allowing the honeyed air to give him a small amount of comfort.

Ren turned to the first statue on his left. Choice sat with a quiver of arrows propped against his chair and a bow in his left hand. A flowing paludamentum covered his broad form. A triangular clasp secured it to his left shoulder. His wavy hair and beard were cut with a majestic air and his brows were furrowed in a look of deep concentration.

Ren's heart quickened. Not even the Watcher's gaze could come close to the severity of Choice.

And Ren had to wake him. But how?

A short stone table stood beside Choice. Three arrows rested on it, forming Choice's symbol, the same symbol etched on Ren's sword. The sword tingled in his hand as if the thought had brought it to life. He heard a soft, distant humming – the voice of the Quy.

May Choice, Chance and Fate be with you for all three play a part. Always choose the right, and when you roll the dice let life's kiss prove your heart.

Choose the right, the Quy had said. Ren glanced back at the table. One arrow pointed away from him, another pointed down and to the right, and the third pointed down and to the left, just like his sword. Ren touched the arrow pointing down and to the right.

Choice opened his eyes and turned his cold gaze to Ren. Ren retreated as the statue's white stone came alive like flesh. Choice's gaze seared through him, shaming his soul for his accusations and filling his heart with white-hot fear. When Choice rose from his throne, he towered over Ren. Choice's brow drew together in disappointment. Ren fell to his knees and bowed his head, desperate to escape Choice's eyes.

"Have you read the rules, Chosen?" Choice's voice rose in the nave, so deep and poignant Ren felt his insides vibrating. He nodded, humbled in front of Choice. When Choice remained silent Ren forced his eyes to flicker up the length of Choice's torso, back into his eyes.

They froze him where he knelt. No smile appeared on Choice's harsh face, no absolution.

"You will have a choice in time, a choice to allow one's death. I will tell you whom you must choose, whom you must betray. Heed my warning, Chosen. Heed it well or you will fail. Choose your mother, Renee. Choose her immediately."

Choice's eye's closed as his flesh turned into a lifeless mass once again. Ren continued to stare. Had he heard him correctly?

Betray his mother?

He tried to rationalize Choice's words. Renee would somehow be under Ista's command, unsalvageable. Renee would have a horrid disease and he would be forced to command her death. She would be in pain and he would choose to let her die. The thoughts poured from him. But he knew in his heart, in his soul, none were real.

Renee would be whole and he would choose her death.

How could that be the Maker's wish?

He couldn't send his mother to her death. Somehow he would avoid it. He would escape the choice, escape the betrayal in her eyes.

Ren forced his thoughts to still. He stood and walked to Chance.

Most spoke of Chance with a smile. If someone ever wished another luck, they wished for Chance to be with him. She was the most loved and the most talked about of the three guardians. All loved her winsomeness and allure. Women wanted to be compared to her, men wanted to court her, but Chance was the one guardian Ren always found mysterious and inaccessible.

Most men spoke of Chance with sexual innuendoes. Ren had always thought uttering lewd references to Chance was scandalous. Seeing her now he understood why sexual connotations always followed Chance's name. Chance was scantily dressed, with a loose-fitting cloth tossed around her breasts and looped over one shoulder. The long skirt she donned hung from her hips, just below her navel. A provocative chain clung to her dainty waist, drawing the eye. Chance herself was draped over her throne, legs dangling over one side, one arm wrapped around the back and the other placed teasingly at her side. A crooked grin dominated her face and her long hair cascaded down her bare midriff to tickle the chain.

Roll the dice, the Quy had said. The table below Chance's dangling feet held a variety of dice. Ren perused each pair. There were no astragali. Some of the dice were large, some oblong, but none were astragali.

He thought about the astragali on his sword. They had double sixes showing: the sonnez or luck roll. He looked again at the dice. One pair had a sonnez showing. Although they weren't astragali they were elongated, with four sides. Just as Ren reached to pick them up a wave of apprehension stole through him. Something wasn't right.

He glanced at Chance. Her grin had widened. In her second hand, now propped on one knee, were a pair of astragali, each with a sonnez showing. Ren wiped his brow, remembering the stories of Chance's jests.

He didn't find this one very humorous.

He took the dice from the cold stone that formed Chance's hand and threw them on the floor.

A thin slit of stone slid up from Chance's eyes. She peered at him with mild amusement. Tilting her head, she glanced to the ground.

"The sonnez roll, Dragon Lord. Maybe luck is smiling on you today." Chance's grin broadened. Ren wanted to believe her words, but he knew she toyed with him. There was no luck today. He had to betray his mother.

"The news hasn't been kind, I see," Chance said. Her voice oscillated in the air like a harp being plucked by a skilled minstrel. "I don't know if you'll like what chance will send your way either, Dragon Mate."

Ren tightened his grip on the sword, daring Chance with his eyes to order him to kill the silver dragon. He would never harm it, and he would never harm Aidan.

Chance tittered with alluring charm. The hollow echo of her laughter sounded odd in the stone chamber. "You have a spark, Dragon Mate. I see why you're the Chosen. The Maker chooses well, though I would have made you a little less," Chance paused and put a finger to her lips, "gracious. More severity would attract more fear, more attention, and perhaps more caution."

Chance's stone eyes turned harsh and her thin lips wilted into a frown. If Ren had thought Choice looked threatening, Chance looked sinister.

"Heed my voice and heed it well, Dragon Mate. Chance will come again. The silver fiend will land. Though you aren't required to kill it physically, as the picture shows, you must kill its heart so it will never be the same. You must face it with malice, look at it with loathing, and wound it with your words. When it comes, hide your feelings, bury them deep inside. Tell her you denounce your union. You must deny your heart, Dragon Mate. You must deny it completely."

Ren staggered backwards as Chance transformed into lifeless stone. The truth he so desperately wanted to deny was upon him. He sat on the steps and buried his face in his hands.

If he did as Chance commanded Aidan would give up on life. She would begin to merge with the dragon.

"Aidan," he whispered, "please have faith in me."

Now he knew what the prophecy meant. It didn't mean killing the beast, it mean destroying Aidan. Buy why? Why would denying his feelings for Aidan help destroy the darkness?

"No," he said. "Please let this not be true."

He began to pray he was living an illusion. Over and over he prayed, again and again, until the cold floor below him warmed.

When he looked back at Chance she was watching him with cold, stone eyes.

Ren rose to his feet. His legs were lead as he climbed to the landing for the third time.

Most feared Fate more than Choice and Chance. Choice, no matter how bad the options, still embodied different paths from which to choose. Chance was associated with luck, and luck was what everyone wanted. Fate was feared. You had no control over your destiny, and you could never stop the sands of time. Once you were in the spiral there was only one way to go: to your fate, to your end.

Fate didn't sit on her throne like the others. She stood holding a sundial in one hand and an hourglass in the other, indicating it was only a matter of time before your fate would come. A glacial cold shivered through Ren as he looked into Fate's stone eyes. She was older than Chance, with wrinkles just beginning to appear around her lips and eyes, but she was elegant. Her gown clung to her, showing every curve yet revealing nothing. Her hair was piled high on her head while one thick strand made its way around her crown and fell halfway down her back.

No table stood beside her. There was nothing but the throne, the hourglass, and the sundial. *Let life's kiss prove your heart*, the Quy had said.

Ren stopped paces from her. He didn't want to know the fates, not if choice and chance were what they were.

He turned from Fate and sat on the steps. He fought to understand the messages in the pictures. He fought to change what Choice and Chance had told him. He couldn't. The Oracle never lied, and those who disobeyed the Oracle's commands suffered ten times more than if they had obeyed. If he didn't heed them he would fail.

Ren drew in a breath and looked back at Fate. He had no choice. He had to finish what he started. He walked to Fate, kissed her cheek and stepped back.

Her stone eyes opened and she smiled. The smile warmed his heart. He thought how ironic the expression, "May Fate smile upon you." That idiom hadn't held its true meaning until then. Fate was beautiful, more alluring to him than even Chance. In a small way Fate reminded him of his mother, regally distant yet somehow holding a compassion that radiated from her soul.

"Your heart is true. Believe it. Your soul is good. Believe it," her sweet, yet powerful voice commanded.

What she did next startled him. Fate bowed, tresses falling around her shoulder. He stood, wondering what he should do. He should bow to her, not she to him. She rose and touched his cheek with her hand. It was surprisingly warm to the touch, and soft, although it still looked as hard as the stone that formed her.

When she took her hand away a profound sorrow crossed her features. "Ren, Chosen, Dragon Lord, Dragon Tamer, Dragon Mate, I will ask you a question. Do you know of fate?"

His lips parted. She quickly put her finger to them, stopping him before he replied. Remembering the rules, he just stared at her. How was he to convey what he wanted? He thought he knew: the spiral, the end. But he wanted to hear what she had to say.

Her lips lifted into a small smile as she nodded in understanding. "What I do is unorthodox, but you have proven your compassion and I see your pain. I want to tell you a truth I feel you must know, but what I do risks much, for if the weapon that is to slay a beast is dulled, the beast will live."

Ren nodded, knowing he was the weapon to which she referred.

"Fate is a spiral," Fate said as she twirled her hand. Where her fingers touched, the air glowed with a white light, leaving a perfect image of a spiral hanging between them. "Some believe one can't escape the spiral." Fate paused and took a bead from a pin in her hair. She placed the bead on the hovering glow. It rolled to the tip and disappeared.

"This is a false prophecy."

Ren's mind worked furiously to follow her words. He had always thought fate was unavoidable, that every choice you made, every chance that happened, couldn't change your ultimate fate. It was as if choice and chance were confined in the spiral and no matter where you were or where you went your destiny still resided at the end of that spiral.

"Every choice and every chance can lead you to a different fate," Fate said. "Don't misunderstand, fate is real, but it is multifarious. At each breath you have one fate and one fate only. But the next breath, within your next choice, your fate may change. Fate is what it is, but it is more like this." Fate dropped the hourglass. It shattered on the floor. The dust it contained stormed around them and quickly formed multiple spirals: below him, beside him, above him, hundreds upon hundreds of spirals of all different sizes and shapes.

"If you didn't have free will you would have only one spiral. You would have only one fate. But that isn't so. The Maker allows you to make your own decisions. You may first start with one fate, a choice leads you away, a chance still further, until you are on a different spiral, a different end." With Fate's every word the bead leaped from one spiral to another, weaving its way in a frenzied fashion.

"You can deny Choice today, you can deny Chance today, you can even deny your fate, but the truth is this . . ." Fate moved closer, her face fraught with concern. "There is only one way you should go. There is only one fate you should seek. There is only one spiral you should be on.

"Ren, in every choice there is a right one. In every chance there is an opportunity. If you deny the truth you will deny your fate, and that fate has a divine purpose. I pray you don't stray from the path placed before you."

Fate bowed her head. All of the spirals dissipated except for the one she had first drawn: his fate, the one true fate he was supposed to seek.

When Fate lifted her head, she had lost her compassion. Her face became as the others: cold, unfeeling, and commanding. She pointed to the lone spiral beside her.

"Follow your fate. Follow your destiny. Your belief will damn you or raise you. Heed my words and heed them with everything you have. You must destroy your soul."

Ren watched as Fate walked back to her throne. She turned and looked at him one last time before she closed her eyes. As soon as her eyes shut the building began to shake. Fate crumbled until she was only a heap of white stone. Stones and pillars crashed around him. As Ren turned and ran three voices echoed through the destruction: *You must believe us or you will fail. You must heed us or you will fail. Have strength, have restraint, take heart.*

End of Book One

Ren's adventure continues with Book Two of The Oracle Series.
Faith of the Dragon Tamer
More information at www.colepain.com

www.ingramcontent.com/pod-product-compliance
Lightning Source LLC
Chambersburg PA
CBHW051415170626
46809CB00006B/2166